DARK KNIGHT

J.L. BECK

AUTHOR'S NOTE

Dearest Reader,

I'm so excited for you to read Dark Knight and cannot wait for you to dive in. However given the subject matter in this book I feel it's needed to share the list of triggers with you. Please use diligence when choosing to read this book as some scenes, and situations may be disturbing to you.

Triggers included in this book are: rape, violence, loss of pregnancy, stalking, murder, domestic violence, child-abuse, self-harm, depression, anxiety, and sexual content.

CHAPTER 1

TATUM

Ten Years Ago

I blink my eyes open, a smile splitting my face because today is the first day of: *summer vacation*.

After nine months of school, it's finally summer break. Excitement would be an understatement to describe how I'm feeling. Knowing I won't have to do a single sheet of homework, that I won't have to go to bed early, and that I can wake up whenever I want, at least for the next three months.

Freedom, it's so pungent I can almost taste it. I already can't wait to spend the whole summer out by the pool soaking up every last bit of sun. I'm hoping to be a lovely tan shade come the fall once school starts up again, and not this ghostly pale white that I am now.

The reminder that Bianca, my best friend, will be here in a bit sends me over the edge. Her dad doesn't usually let her do sleepovers unless it's a birthday party or something else special. Bianca says he's strict and likes to know what she's doing and who she's hanging out with. I'm sure it must suck having an overbearing dad. My dad always wants to know those things, too, but he still lets me visit with my friends and go shopping. Not alone, of course.

When I go out, I always have to take one of my father's men with me, since he's usually too busy to take me to activities or drive me to the movies. Maybe that's why Mr. Cole doesn't like letting Bianca come over...I mean, my Dad is here, but he's usually working in his office, so we have the whole house to ourselves. The only people to keep an eye on us are the guys my dad pays for security, and honestly, there's not much they can do—so long as I'm not, like choking to death or drowning or something. Most of the time, they look the other way.

With Mr. Cole being a detective and all, he knows how messed up life can be. That's what Bianca tells me, anyway. The excitement of Bianca's impending arrival is what gets me out of bed and into the shower, even though I could have slept another hour or two.

I didn't know kids had chores, not until I got to know Bianca better. I'm not stupid. Not everyone has staff hanging around the house to cook and clean for them. I figured parents took care of that stuff, but for Bianca, it's different. She's constantly cleaning the house, doing her own laundry, and even doing some of the cooking since it's just her and her dad. Like me, she doesn't have a mom in her life. Although, in her case, she can visit her mom in the cemetery.

I don't know where my mom is most of the time.

Seeing how Bianca's good and pure, she's really rubbed off on me. It made me realize that I could at least make my bed and clean my bathroom. So after I'm done in the shower, I tidy up my bedroom. Once I move my things to the unused wing of the house, like Dad promised I could once I start high school, I'll have more responsibility.

It's one of his rules: *If you want more from me, you have to show me you're responsible enough to have it.*

I might as well get in the habit of showing him I'm serious about wanting to take care of myself. I want to prove to him that I'm not a little girl anymore. I'm getting older, and I want him to see that.

Once I'm finished, I have the rest of my day to look forward to. It's already almost eight-thirty, and Mr. Cole needs to be at work by nine, so Bianca will be here any minute. I grab a green one-piece suit that matches my eyes—Dad won't let me wear a two-piece yet, no matter how many times I beg him.

"*I'm paying for it, so you're going to wear what I think is appropriate.*" It's during those times I wish I had a mom willing to step in and take my side, yet I can't even get her to answer the phone when I call, much less defend me against Dad. I'm pretty much on my own most of the time.

I can feel the sticky misery and sadness that clings to me when thinking about my mom, so I squeeze my eyes shut and push the thoughts away.

I pull on the suit and add a pair of cutoffs before pulling my blonde curls into a bun on my head. *Perfection.* I give myself a once-over in the mirror. I'm tall, and thankfully, my body is finally filling out more. I was worried for a little while that my arms would always be longer than my body. But luckily, I grew into them. My skin is pale and sickly looking, and since Dad hardly ever lets me wear makeup – which will change this year – I always look this way. A *Casper The Friendly Ghost* look-alike.

Whatever, with all the sun I'm going to get this summer, it won't matter. I'm halfway down the stairs when I hear my father's voice.

Yay! I might be able to say good morning to him before he locks himself inside his office for the remainder of the day. *I wonder if I can get him to go swimming with me sometime. He can't work all the time, can he?* It seems unfair that grown-ups don't get summer vacation the way kids do. Maybe I need to remind him that there are other things in life besides work.

Right away, I find myself smiling since he's not usually around. Maybe we can have breakfast together. Or if he's busy and on his way to the office down the hall, I can bring him some food. I want to spend some time together this summer before starting high school. I know I will be super busy with activities and studying once the semester begins, and I miss just sitting and talking to him. We used to be closer, but with each year passing, it feels like more space grows between us.

"I'll have keys made for you," my father says, his voice getting louder the closer he comes to where I'm standing while the dress shoes he almost always wears during the day snap against the wood floor. "You can come and go as you please, though it would be better if you stay on the grounds as much as possible. If you need anything, let me know and I'll arrange it. It's important that you lay low for a while."

"I understand."

I'm at the bottom of the stairs when I hear that second voice. *It's deep.* I don't think I've ever heard it before. Whoever it belongs to is going to have keys to the house? *A new guard?* The idea makes me roll my eyes. There's enough of them wandering around this place.

Confused, I'm still standing on the bottom step when Dad walks out of the unused east wing. His eyes widen with surprise when they land on me. "Good morning," he says before looking over his shoulder at the man behind him.

"Good morning, Daddy. I wanted to catch you before you went into your office. Can you come swimming with me and Bianca today?"

He steps aside, and I get my first look at the man he had been talking to.

I really wish Dad would let me wear a two-piece suit. I also wish I was wearing something nicer than cutoffs right at this moment. I peer up at the man, who must be the most gorgeous man I've ever seen. Even cuter than Johnny Townsend.

The mysterious guy is around Dad's height, six-two or three, with thick, black hair and dark blue eyes that scream *leave me alone*. They look like they could burn a hole through anything he stares at, and all I can think at that moment is how captivated I am by his presence.

Unfortunately, he doesn't stare back at me. Rather, he looks at the floor, walls, and ceiling like he's pissed at them. His full lips are pulled up into a sneer. I've never met anybody who looked at objects so angrily just because they exist. My gaze lingers down his body, stopping on his hands. They're huge, and I watch as he runs one through his dark hair—which could use a cut, not to mention a wash—before he jams it into the pocket of his black jeans.

He was a dark knight if I ever saw one in real life. That's who this man is. Rugged, dark, and mysterious. Butterflies take flight in my belly, and heat creeps up my neck and into my cheeks. I stare intently at the stranger, trying to figure out who he is and what makes him tick, but all I can seem to observe is anger.

Dad clears his throat, dragging my attention back to him. "Romero, this is my daughter, Tatum. Tatum, this is Romero. He's going to be staying with us for a while."

"What? Not in there, I hope?" I nod toward the open doorway they just walked through. "You said I would get to move my stuff into that wing once I start high school in the fall."

"I said *maybe*," he sighs, narrowing his eyes. I know that look. It means whatever patience he had has suddenly vanished. "I know you wanted to move your stuff in there but that's hardly the most important thing right now. Romero needs a place to stay, and rather than give him a room near yours, I think he would do better to have his own separate wing. Eventually, I might move him out to one of the cottages on the property."

My chest aches, my heart tightening in my chest. Forget the mysterious knight, the jerk just ruined everything! Yes I know it's just a room, and I shouldn't feel this let down over something so small but I was really looking forward to it. Another step in the direction of maturity and responsibility.

My father is a businessman in every aspect of his life and once he's made a decision, that's it. Since I don't want to look like a spoiled baby in front of a cute boy, even if I'm disappointed, I grit my teeth and choose to swallow it down. Does it really matter that I was looking forward to having all that extra space, plus the added privacy? I guess not. I'll eventually get over it, just like I get over everything.

"Okay," I mutter, digging my nails into my palm instead of lashing out like I want to.

"I see you're dressed for swimming," Dad points out like he didn't hear me inviting him to join in the fun.

"Yeah, Bianca's coming over, remember? That's why I asked if you wanted to go swimming with us."

"Oh. That's nice sweetie, maybe next time. I have a bunch of work to get done." His attention drifts and he turns back to Romero. Suddenly it's like I was never here to begin with. "In this house what is mine is yours. Anything you want, you only have to ask. We have a cook who comes six days a week. She takes off Saturday nights and all day Sunday, but always makes sure the kitchen is stocked."

They pass me on their way out to the kitchen and all I can do is stand there and stare at them. It's not like I expect to have a say in anything, because I never do. Not really, but I can't deny the anger that blooms inside my chest at his clear dismissal. Obviously, whatever Romero's story is, Dad wants to help him and that's cool, but at the expense of brushing me off like I'm nothing. I reach the kitchen in time to hear Dad introduce Romero to Sheryl, our cook, and she's as kind to him as she's always been to me.

"Can I fix you something for breakfast?"

"No, thanks," he mumbles his gaze on the floor, his voice thick and raspy. "I'm not really hungry."

"That's fine, but you be sure to stop back whenever you want." She notices me hanging around and gives me one of her bright, kind smiles. "Good morning, Miss Middle School Graduate. I fixed your favorite: French toast and bacon, plus fresh orange juice."

"Oh. Thank you." And now Romero knows I just graduated middle school, which means he knows how old I am. Cue the embarrassment. I have to open the refrigerator door to abate the way my cheeks heat up.

Behind me, Dad speaks up. "You should really eat something."

I'm almost jealous of the concerned tone he gives him. Yes my father loves and cares about me, but he never seems concerned, not like this. It's more like he's especially interested in Romero, like he cares if he eats.

Why? Who is he? And what about him would make my father care so much?

"I've made plenty," Sheryl adds. "It's only a matter of pulling an extra plate from the cabinet."

Great. He gets the wing I was supposed to move into, and now Sheryl is making him a plate of my special breakfast. I have to bite my tongue as I pour orange juice into a glass without asking if Romero wants any. He can get his own since he obviously lives here now.

"I'm really not hungry." The edge in his voice becomes sharp, angry. *Why is he mad? Because people are being kind to him?* That seems ridiculous.

"Fair enough," Dad murmurs in that gentle, caring way. "So long as you know everything you need is here. You don't have to be shy. Why don't I show you around the grounds, and then you can get settled into your room?"

Nothing hurts worse than to see the hand he places on this strange, rude kid's shoulder as they walk out of the room. If I thought he'd give me the whole story, I'd think to ask Dad later why Romero is here and how long he'll be staying, but I know my father. He'll tell me to go hang out with Bianca or go swimming, or shopping. Whatever it takes to keep me out of his way.

Especially now that he has the son he always wanted.

I don't know where that thought comes from, but it takes away my appetite until I have to finish the rest of my food. Sheryl went through all the trouble, and I don't want to insult her like Romero did. Not that she seems to mind—she's busy humming to herself as she pulls produce from shopping bags and washes it in the sink.

"Tatum?" My spirits lift immediately when I hear Bianca's voice echoing through the entry hall.

"In the kitchen!" I call out. A few seconds later, she hurries in, all flushed and wide-eyed.

"Who is that boy outside with your dad?" She flashes an embarrassed little grin at Sheryl, who just laughs.

I give her a look that means we'll talk about this privately while getting up from the table and leaving the dish next to the sink. "Do you want anything?" Sheryl asks Bianca, who politely declines before I pull her by the arm outside onto the back patio. It's already hot and sticky for this time of the day, and I can practically feel my curls frizzing thanks to the humidity.

"What's going on?" Bianca's carrying a backpack over one shoulder and a beach towel in the other arm, both of which she sets down while I pace the ground in front of her.

I'm not mad. I'm... bothered, actually annoyed.

"First of all, that boy is moving into the empty wing," I whisper before grinding my teeth. "I don't even know him, but somehow he's so important my father gives him the bedroom that he promised me."

"Ugh, that's crappy." She sits down, shaking her head. "I know you were looking forward to moving all your stuff into that room."

"I was. And it's just ... I don't know. The guy showed up five minutes ago, yet it already feels like I don't exist anymore." I have to laugh at myself. "Not like I did before this morning, but still, it's less now."

"That's not true. Your dad was just as happy as any other dad at graduation, and he took us out to dinner and everything." She makes a sour face. "Sorry, my dad was so weird about trying to pay."

I wave it off because men are generally weird, and I was surprised he even wanted to go to dinner with us in the first place. I've always gotten the vibe he doesn't like my dad, though he's always been nice to me. "It's okay, men are weird, but that's the thing. Last night, Dad cared about me. He actually paid attention to me. This morning? It's all about Romero. No explanation. No anything. Just like, hey, here's this guy who will live with us now. Have a nice day by the pool."

Bianca shrugs. "It could be worse. The guy could be gross and ugly looking."

She's not wrong about that. Even though he's kind of a jerk, I already can't wait to see him again. "He's older than us—maybe sixteen or seventeen. I don't know, Dad didn't tell me, of course. So for the whole five minutes I met him he stared at the floor like he was pissed off. I doubt he'd talk to me anyway, that's if I even wanted to talk to him."

"Besides," she adds with a giggle, "it's not like your dad would let you hang out with an older guy."

"Ugh, also true." To think, I was in such a good mood when I first woke up. "Happy first day of summer vacation, I guess."

"It's all going to be okay. Don't let this get you down." She hops up from her chair and removes the sundress she wore over her white suit. "Come on, let's enjoy the pool and try not to think about them. We'll play some music and relax."

She's right. I know she is. I don't have to pay any attention to Romero. He can be another one of my father's guards or whatever it is he pays them to do to keep us safe. I'm not supposed to know about any of that.

I do know one thing, though: The first chance I get, I'm buying myself a two-piece suit. If Dad's going to ignore me for this guy, whoever he is, I'm going to start doing what I want.

CHAPTER 2

TATUM

Ten Years Later

If I didn't know better, I would think Bianca was trying to break my ribs with how tightly she wrapped her arms around me in the courtyard in front of the house the morning after she married my father. Yes, it's complicated, and I don't want to discuss it. She's my stepmother now, and I still can't get over it.

"Please, be safe," she whispers before giving me one last squeeze. "And keep me posted, okay? I'm going to go crazy not knowing where you are or what you're doing."

"I will. Who else am I going to talk to?"

We both glance at Romero, who's having a last-minute talk with Dad. Their voices are hushed whispers. The two of them might as well be planning D-Day or something. I know it's not easy for my father to let me go, even if he knows it's for the best. I need space, time, and freedom.

Part of me knows I'm lucky he's letting me go and not locking me up somewhere. I wouldn't put it past him to do that, and it's not like he hasn't threatened it. We both know that a mental hospital wouldn't help me any more than living in that big ass house did. Thus, the choice to leave arose. Only, of course, he wouldn't be my father if he made things easy for me. There was one stipulation: I can't go alone without a guardian always watching over me. Why would I ever want to take a breath without somebody hovering over my shoulder?

And why, of all the guards my father employs, would he not choose the one who lives to piss me off every single day of my life.

"Not him," I mutter with a soft sigh.

Sure, he's been a little nicer this past summer, but it's only because he felt sorry for me once he discovered everything I had been through. Not because we've ever gotten along. He might as well be a robot for all the personality and feelings he shows.

"You don't have to go." My chest aches when she bites her lip and her eyes well up with tears. I could be bitchy and call it pregnancy hormones and pretend she doesn't really care about me, but that wouldn't be true. I've been low enough recently that I told myself that more than once. She doesn't care. They don't care. They have each other now, and a new baby on the way. There's no room for my trauma and drama and bullshit. But I'd be lying if I ever tried to force myself to believe that.

"I do, and we both know it, so please don't try and talk me out of it. There's nothing here for me anymore." All my answer does is give her more pain, and I'm sorry for that. She doesn't deserve it. She's only ever been my friend, my best friend. Now, she's my stepmother. She's pregnant with my sibling—no, I haven't been able to wrap my head around that yet, but I'm happy for her, and my father.

Still, underneath everything, she's Bianca. I don't want to hurt her. That's why it's better for me to go because if I stay, I might end up doing just that. It wouldn't even be her fault. I'm too fucked up right now to be the person I used to be, which would only make her life harder.

"Once everything is settled, you'll come home. Right?"

"We'll see. Maybe, maybe not." It's the only answer I can give her because I don't want to give her false hope. I doubt there will ever be a time when we don't have to worry about Dad's enemies hurting us. If it's not Jack Moroni kidnapping us and murdering my mother, or Jefferson Knight blaming me for his asshole son's disappearance, it will be somebody else. Do I want to come back to that? Or should I start a new life of my own and put the past behind me?

I take a step back and let my gaze linger over the sprawling house one more time. Yesterday, it was the site of a small, intimate wedding ceremony, but that's the only recent happy memory I have here. Before that, I'd have to go back months and months to find a time when I wasn't scared. Hiding. Empty, so empty. This house has been my refuge and my prison combined. I can feel tears at the back of my eyes but blink them away. I've cried so much over the last couple of months, and for what? Those tears have done nothing to soothe the ache.

The truth is I can't spend the rest of my life hiding behind these walls, hoping things will get better. I need to get away, to start fresh —though how I'll manage to do that with Romero gatekeeping my every move, I don't know. I'll figure it out. I have to, especially since the only alternative is slowly dying.

Dad steps away from Romero, and when he opens his arms to me, I step into his embrace again. "Listen to him."

He can't see the way I roll my eyes. "I'll try."

"Don't make me regret letting you go. It's bad enough that I won't be there if you need me."

"I'll be on my best behavior." I pull back, smirking up at him. "Come on. If I promised without giving you any shit, you would know I was lying."

"That's true." He takes my face in his hands and stares down at me, concern etched into every line on his face. I don't think he's slept yet, and not because it was his wedding night. The dark circles under his eyes and the stubble on his cheeks add five to ten years to his age. I hate worrying about him, except what can I do? I need to get away from this place, and while I know he is definitely worried about his only daughter going somewhere even though he won't be able to visit, this is what I need.

"Don't forget you can come back whenever you want," he whispers before pressing his lips to my forehead. "We'll be waiting for you."

A sudden rush of emotion tries to choke me, but I push it back like I have for months and force a smile. "Take care of your wife and that baby. I'll be fine."

"I will." He looks over the top of my head, his expression hardening, and I know he's looking at Romero. I can't think of a time I felt sorry for him, but this could be the first. If things go wrong somehow, I wouldn't want to be in his shoes.

"We better get going," Romero announces behind me. Dad bought him a new car for the occasion, an SUV big enough to fit everything I'm bringing, plus the few bags he's packed for himself. I don't know why he has to live like a hermit, but I can't complain—more space for me and my things.

I should feel something right now, shouldn't I? There should be more emotion as I walk away from the only home I've ever known. Even during college, I lived here. Bianca's the only person I would have wanted to be roommates with, and she was living with her useless boyfriend at the time.

Even the tears standing in Bianca's eyes as Dad puts an arm around her waist aren't enough to break through the numbness clouding my mind. I'm sorry she is sad, but I can't help thinking she'll be better off without me. *They both will.* I'm too messed up now, and the girl I used to be might as well have never existed. That's the person they love; that's who they miss. Not me, not the person I am now. Old Tatum died back in France.

My mother's dark blue urn is waiting on the front passenger seat, and I pick it up, holding it carefully as I climb in and close the door. I notice how Romero eyes the urn through the window—and he'd better think twice about sharing his opinion, considering I genuinely don't give a shit. This is all I have left of her, and I'm not packing her up in a box. She might have spent the majority of my life ignoring me, but I can still care for what she left behind.

Good thing I didn't expect a speech from him once he joined me in the car, seeing as I didn't get one. Settling into the driver's seat, he starts the engine and raises a hand to Dad before shifting the car into drive. I don't bother looking back. I can't look back. It feels like nothing and everything at the same time.

The silence buzzes all around me, and I hate it. It makes the thoughts and memories inside my head louder. To elevate it, I do the only thing possible. I talk to my robot bodyguard.

"Is there a reason we had to leave at the ass crack of dawn?" I grumble, noticing the first rays of sunlight creeping over the horizon by the time we turn onto the road, running past the front gate.

"Yes. One, you should always experience a sunrise, and two, I want to beat the traffic."

"Traffic? Where the hell are we going?"

That was the other stipulation. Romero got to choose the location. At this moment, I'm half tempted to jump out of the moving car door to avoid living with this man for God knows how long. If only the reminder of Jefferson and his threats didn't pop up in my mind at that very instant.

"You'll find out when we get there."

What a surprise, he doesn't want to tell me. "Don't you think I deserve to know? I know my father said you got to decide where we were going, but it'd be nice to know if I'll be able to order anything from Amazon and have it delivered this year or if I'll have to send messenger doves to contact Bianca."

"Where do you think I'm taking you?" He pauses and shakes his head. "Better yet, don't answer that. You'll know where we're going when we arrive. It doesn't make a difference anyway."

He wouldn't understand. For ten years, he hasn't seen what difference it makes if I know things. If I'm treated like I matter. I remember over the first few weeks of his time in my house, he went from being moody and resentful to basically shutting down, and that's how he's been ever since. Except when he's treating me like a worthless, spoiled brat. He seems to take pleasure in that.

"You know, you're the one who offered to do this with me. You don't have to act like somebody put a gun to your head and forced you to be here."

"I didn't say that. Just sit back and relax. Here I was, thinking you'd be too tired to talk after yesterday."

I grit my teeth, my jaw aching from the pressure. "I know you don't think I'm capable of much, but I can attend a small wedding and still have the energy to speak the next day."

"Stop putting words in my mouth. I was trying to give you credit, for what it's worth. You put the whole wedding together in no time, and it made them happy. I thought you'd be exhausted."

The thing is, I am. I'm exhausted, drained, worn out. Now that it's over and I don't have adrenaline keeping me moving, I'm basically a husk—not that I've been that much better than a husk lately.

It's nice to know they were happy, making all my work worth it. At least I know I left them with a good memory. I've already given both of them plenty of spectacle.

"So, the place where we're going. Is it, you know, in a city? Please, tell me you're not taking me out to the middle of nowhere."

Looking at him from the corner of my eye, I catch the way his firm, freshly shaved jaw tightens. But that's all that happens. He doesn't say a word. I might as well have never spoken. Heat stirs in my chest, and I'm suddenly more convinced than ever that this is not going to work. This was my stupidest idea yet. We'll be lucky if we don't kill each other in the first few days.

What's the alternative, Tatum? No surprise, my thoughts mock me. There is no alternative except to hang around the house while receiving increasingly threatening messages from my ex-boyfriend's father. Even thinking about him makes my skin crawl.

In the end, that's all I could do regarding Kristoff. Brace for impact. It's been months since I packed my things and pretty much fled in the wake of our last disastrous trip together, and I haven't seen him or heard his voice since, but I know that's not a good enough excuse for his father. Not when Kristoff has essentially fallen off the face of the earth since then. His father wants answers I can't give him, and if Jefferson Knight doesn't know where I am, he can't get to me. I need to keep telling myself that.

"I'm sure your dad will find a way to shut Jefferson up for good," Romero offers, almost like he's reading my mind.

You mean the way you shut Kristoff up for good? No, I don't know that for sure, but I don't need it spelled out, either. I knew once I confessed what Kristoff did to me during that awful trip to Europe that I was jeopardizing his life. Still, the other option was to keep everything bottled up inside, and that wasn't helping any more than the stupid anxiety meds. Which only dulled the pain yet didn't take it away. I was falling apart—I still am.

And I can't exactly tell Jefferson how my dad probably killed his son due to him being an abusive asshole, leaving me with no choice except to get out of town until things cool down. Plus, I need the space.

When I don't offer any rebel, he continues, "And then, you can get back to your life. Put all this shit behind you."

He probably thinks it would be that easy, too. If I had it in me, I would laugh.

"You can, you know, maybe see about getting that internship back. Starting a career."

"No offense, but I have to ask why you seem to care," I blurt out. "I'm not a child. You don't have to offer me ice cream and a pony as long as I behave."

Slowly, I turn my head to find him staring straight ahead while his jaw works like he's grinding his teeth. Five minutes in, and I'm already tired of him. "If I want to get a job and move on with my life, I will. I don't need you to encourage me. I will pass on the pep talks since you suck at them anyway."

His lips press into a firm line. That seems to have shut him up. There's not much I hate more than being patronized, which is precisely what he's doing with all this fake positivity shit.

"You have to do something with your life," he declares because, of course, he has to have the last word.

"By all means, let me take advice from *you*," I snarkily reply while staring out the window to my right. "Maybe one day I, too, can be a glorified babysitter." Finally, I have to close my eyes. At least he'll stop talking to me if he thinks I'm asleep, so that's a bonus.

The babysitter. That's what he is, too. And I'm the baby, as always. I mean, I know I haven't really taken good care of myself lately. However, having people assume I need a caretaker is insulting. It amazes me that it took so long to figure out what my father does for a living. For years I was naive to the darkness that surrounded me, instead telling myself he was in business and made a lot of money and that money was what put us at risk. Hence the guards and the extra security. I told myself you can't build an empire without making enemies. I'm sure that's true, but it was a convenient excuse I used to comfort myself while ignoring the brutal truth.

That brutal truth is staring me right in the face now. It wasn't enough that my boyfriend hurt me—badly, repeatedly, when I was thousands of miles away from home. I had to be kidnapped by one of my father's enemies. I had to lose my absentee mother in the process. I know it was her fault for working with an evil man so she could get back at Dad, but that doesn't erase the pain of knowing I will never get to tell her all the things she needed to hear. There's no such thing as closure. There's no moving on. The weight of it all rests heavily on my shoulders.

She never even had a funeral. Her murder had to be a secret. She was cremated and delivered to the house in a little box. Until now, I didn't understand that funerals are for the survivors, not for the people who died. I didn't get to say goodbye. I blink-squeeze my eyes closed and will back the forming tears away. And Bianca wants to know when I'm coming back? It would be better if I didn't. I don't know if I could stand to lose anything else, all because my father is an arms dealer with layers and layers of blood on his hands. I'm sure he never imagined blood splashing back on me the way it did.

I must drift off for a while because a sharp right turn startles me awake. A look at the clock on the dash tells me an hour has passed, and as I peer around at my surroundings, I discover we're no longer on the interstate. I can't say I'm impressed with what I see around me now: tiny homes sitting behind chain link fences, scrubby front lawns covered in kids' toys, and rusted swing sets. Looming in the distance is what looks like a factory or a steel mill, something industrial like that. The morning has gone cloudy, adding to the gloomy sense of foreboding that plagues me.

"When I said I wanted to get away, I was thinking of something a little… less like an episode of *Dateline*," I murmur, noticing a pair of scrawny kids smoking on the corner. Their shifty eyes make me nervous. Where the hell did he bring me?

"Sorry, Princess." We turn onto a narrow street where the houses look at least slightly nicer. Not bigger, but better cared for. The siding is clean, and the windows are intact. "If you think what you're seeing now is bad, you would've lost your mind if you saw this place years ago."

I turn in my seat, staring intently at him. "Wait… you're familiar with this neighborhood?"

"Sure am—or rather, I was."

Holy hell. "Okay, where are we, exactly?"

"Just across the state line."

He pulls the SUV into a shallow driveway beside a neat-looking two-story house that's in better condition than anything I've seen thus far on the block. The light blue siding is newly updated, and the windows are clean. There's not so much as a single weed coming up from the sidewalk, and the front porch is free of the leaves that have started to fall now that autumn is here. From where we're seated, I can make out what appears to be a small garage ahead of us.

I mean, this isn't what I had in mind when we discussed my leaving, although it could be worse. Now, the only thing I can think about is the million and one questions rushing through my brain.

"What is this place?" I pause. "Is this another safe house? Who does it belong to? Does Dad know about it?" I don't mean to bombard him with all the questions, but I need to know an answer, at least something.

At first, he only sits in silence, staring straight ahead. I can't read his expression—is he pissed, frustrated, or just full of dread? It might be a mix of all three and then some. Knowing him, he's probably regretting he ever agreed to do this.

All his silence does is intensify my curiosity. "Can't you tell me anything? You expect me to live here, but I'm not allowed to know what made you choose this place?"

He releases a long sigh before speaking—and when he does, I can barely make out his words thanks to how he's clenching his jaw. "I chose this place because it's mine. I grew up here; it belongs to me."

CHAPTER 3

ROMERO

I haven't even gotten out of the car yet, and already I know bringing her here was a bad idea.

Here come the questions.

"Your house? You own this place?" Her head swings back and forth as she takes in everything around us for the first time. She doesn't have to say a word—I can hear her thoughts ringing loud and clear. She's spent her entire life living like royalty, with household staff to take care of her needs and an entire wing of the mansion to herself for the better part of the ten years since I came to live with them. This place is dirt compared to where she comes from. This entire house could fit in that wing. More than once.

She's been through some awful shit recently, but that doesn't erase the fact that she's lived her entire life on easy mode. While I have no problem giving her a dose of reality and have wished countless times for the opportunity, she's already giving me a headache with all the questions.

Confusion is evident in her face, while her green eyes narrow. "I don't understand. Have you been visiting all this time or something? I mean, it looks... nice."

"Did you think I grew up in a cave?"

"That's not what I meant," she snaps. Funny, but when she's

pissed at me, it's the only time she shows life anymore. The fire that used to leave me cursing her in my head returns, and she's almost her old self. *Almost.* "I meant, like, taken care of. Not abandoned for ten years."

"It's not abandoned. I have someone come out every couple of weeks to do maintenance on the place. Mow the lawn, and make sure the doors and windows are intact."

"Sounds like a really great place. So, I guess it used to belong to your parents?"

And look at that, I'm already tired of this conversation. "It's mine now, and that's all that matters. Fortunately for you, no one else knows about it. You'll be safe here. There's no way Jeff will come knocking on this door."

The way she winces at the mention of his name makes me feel like a dickhead and wish that I hadn't said it at all, but then there's no point in tiptoeing around the obvious. She's here because she's running away—not that I can blame her. We're sort of between a rock and a hard place when it comes to the Knight family. We can't strictly come out and say that I had that bastard picked up the second he stepped off the jet upon returning to the States. Or that we held him in a warehouse until I had the pleasure of slitting his throat and watching him bleed out.

He deserved it. I wouldn't take it back if I could. After what he did to her, he deserved much worse. Even in the end, when he was looking death right in the eyes, he had the nerve to blame her for the abuse he doled out. That was the final straw. I went deaf to everything except the rush of blood in my ears and sliced him from ear to ear. I wish it had been slower, more drawn out. I'd acted purely on impulse, letting my emotions rule me. It was why I tried my best to remain calloused, and *robotic,* as Tatum called it. I didn't like the person I was when I let my emotions overcome me.

Because of all of that, we're dealing with a worried father. A worried father with money, and resources, that he could use to dig around. Not to mention the shitty attitude he clearly passed on to his son. Rather than find out the sort of person Kristoff really was, he's seeking to blame Tatum for something she didn't do. Father like son, I suppose.

"Well... thanks, I guess," she manages, even if she looks pained. "This is a good idea."

"Hold everything. Did I just hear you say thank you?"

Crimson floods her cheeks. There it is again. It's like the real Tatum peered through the curtain for a split second before disappearing behind it again. "Don't make me regret it."

Staring back at the house, I take in that it is the first time I'll walk through that door since the night I left. *Ten years.* I hardly remember the kid I was back then.

"You know, I never did discover why you ended up working for my father." I can feel her watching me as I round the shiny new SUV, opening one of the rear doors.

A box immediately tries to fall out, and I use my shoulder to stop it. Jesus Christ. "Did you bring everything you own?" I groan at the chore ahead of me. "It's going to take all day to unload this shit."

"Way to avoid answering the question."

"You didn't ask a question." I hand her a tote bag before digging out a wheeled suitcase and dropping it on the ground.

"Watch it, Mister! You break it, you buy it."

"What's that mean?"

"It means if you break my suitcase, you'll have to buy me a new one."

I'll never admit it out loud, but the way she looks at me, with her nose turned up, her eyes narrowed, and that sassy mouth spitting out words left and right in a vain attempt to cut through my icy exterior... It's the hottest thing I've ever seen, and the funniest, because I know she thinks she's better than me. And, in many ways, she is. But here in this house, on my turf, we're the same.

"I will not be *told* to buy you anything. On the off chance that I felt guilty for breaking your precious luggage, I would replace it."

"Somehow, I doubt you could afford it." If I wasn't fully aware of her past, and her father wasn't my boss, her ass would be bent over my knee, and I'd spank her until she apologized, but unfortunately, none of those things will happen.

"I don't work for free, you know. I have all the money I need and then some."

"And I'm sure my father never charged you rent." She makes it a point to add that dig in at the end. Her tone always comes across as resentful or jealous. No surprise there. I've always felt her resentment, even if I didn't know where it originated.

"He never charged you, either." I give her a tight, nasty smile to match hers before it's time for the inevitable. My stomach tightens into a ball of anxious knots. I have to go inside sometime. Rationally, I know there's nothing in there that can touch me. It's only a set of walls, with a floor and roof. There isn't even a piece of furniture from the old days inside. I double-checked.

Nothing in this house can hurt me, but somehow, I'm still that little boy, reliving all those days in this house. After my mother died, I never intended to come back here.

"How old is this place? How come you've never been back? Did you at least check to ensure the utilities were turned on before we arrived? I can't handle being in the middle of nowhere with no electricity or running water."

I can't be bothered to answer. She'll figure out soon enough that everything's turned on and working fine. Does she really think I'm that stupid? I didn't spend ten years at her father's side without learning a thing or two about covering my bases. If she only knew the sort of shit I've juggled for him, the last thing she would be worried about is the electricity and water being on.

Once I've slid the key into the lock, she finally voices the singular question I knew was coming. "Are your parents deceased?"

The creaking of the swinging door is the only response she receives. Rather than stand here and allow a flood of memories to slam into me, I step aside to give her room to enter before setting down the box in my arms.

"Feel free to look around while I bring in the bags and boxes.

You can take the big bedroom facing the street. It has the biggest closet." I jerk my chin toward the stairs up ahead and to the right.

We're standing in the living room, while beyond that is the eat-in kitchen, visible thanks to the half-wall separating the two large rooms. Upstairs are the master bedroom and a pair of smaller rooms with a bathroom between them.

"This is where you grew up, isn't it?" I can't tell what's behind the question when she stops dead in the center of the living room and turns in a slow circle, scanning it. The new furniture, the bare, freshly-painted walls.

"Yes, this is where I grew up, Princess. This is where I became the person I am today, although it looked wildly different back then."

The look she gives me could rival that of a serial killer right before he kills his first victim. "Shut up. How is it different?" Color me surprised that she's interested in learning something about me, but even worse, why?

"You're standing in it, for one thing." She mutters unintelligibly behind me as I step onto the porch and return to the car.

This isn't fifty questions where we try to get to know each other. I'm not sure where she ever got the idea that I might be in the mood to answer questions about my life before I knew her. I was being a smartass with the cave joke, but now I have to wonder if she ever gave me any thought before now. It was like I didn't exist before the morning we met—the most challenging morning of my life.

Sixteen years old and in an entirely different world than anything I'd ever imagined. A mansion behind a stone wall, accessed through a wrought iron gate. Guards posted out front. Ceilings that towered high over my head and so much space—stepping back into my childhood home is a stark reminder of how vastly different we are.

"*You don't have anything to worry about.*" Callum's voice was strong, clear, and precisely what I needed. I could hold onto it. He seemed like a man who had the whole world by the balls. Somebody I could trust and believe. "*You'll be safe with us.*"

I was safe... mostly. Thanks to the world Callum exists in, there have been dangerous situations, but I've never regretted a minute of it. Until now, that is. I told myself I'd never come back here.

There's one silver lining in all of this. After ten years, I highly doubt anyone will recognize me. A decade makes a big difference. Everyone I grew up with has moved on by now, and those who haven't would've forgotten I ever existed. Which works out perfectly for me since the last thing I need is someone recognizing me.

Once I return to the house, I find Tatum in the kitchen, opening cabinets and looking through the fridge. On the outside, she's the same girl she always has been: blonde, petite, with a body I've wished more than once belonged to a different girl. Anybody but the daughter of Callum Torrio. From looking at her, nobody would guess that she's gone through months of mental and physical anguish. There's no hiding it. There are no physical wounds to the naked eye, but I see the deeper scars every time she flinches or the faraway look she gets in her eyes sometimes when she appears lost in thought. It's in her thin frame—thinner than she's been since she was the gawky kid I first met. Her body is lost in the oversized sweats she wears now, a far cry from the too-tight, too-short skirts and dresses she used to don. It's in her drawn face, the eyes that seem to be constantly moving. Like she's waiting for the next surprise, the next terror.

It's in the fucking urn now sitting on the mantle over an unused fireplace. As if I need the constant reminder of Amanda Torrio, absentee mother and all-around venomous bitch. If anybody ever got what they deserved, it's her, but now her daughter carries the weight on her already weakened shoulders.

"I'm kind of shocked right now. You even had somebody bring food in?" Tatum eyes me over the top of the refrigerator door before bending again, sliding things around on the shelves.

"The basics and then some. Believe it or not, I know what I'm doing. You're safe here."

"Easy for you to say," she mumbles under her breath, probably thinking I can't hear.

"That's the whole reason you're here, remember?" I set the bags down before heading for the door again. I let out an exaggerated sigh. "This would go a lot faster if you'd help."

Placing a hand on her hip, she says, "You told me to look around. Make up your mind."

"Listen up." Something about how I say it grabs her attention, and she closes the refrigerator before folding her arms across her chest, her foot tapping against the wood floor impatiently. There's the brat I know. If anything, it's easier to deal with her when she's like this. I know what to expect. "I think it's time we set a few rules."

Her sickeningly sweet smile leaves a bad taste in my mouth. "I agree."

"No, I don't think you understand. I'm setting them, and you're following them."

Her arched eyebrow does something to me, the way it always has. My pride rears up, and all I want is to put her in her place. Nothing matters more.

"I know you aren't used to following rules or listening to anyone of authority, but while you're here, you'll do as I say." Okay, maybe that came out a little more authoritative than necessary, but apparently it does the job, because her mouth pops open before she releases a breathless laugh that causes me to raise my voice. "Tatum, you know damn well what your father expects you to do. He trusts my judgment, and I need you to do the same. Screwing up is not an option."

"And I need a month in the Maldives and a hundred million bucks in my bank account and, oh yeah, a man who doesn't boss me around and expect me to fall in line just because that's what he wants."

I grit my teeth to the point of pain. This woman knows every button possible to push. "You're here for a reason. This isn't a game or joke."

"I'm sorry." Touching her hand to her chest, she flutters her lashes. "Did I give you the impression I thought any of this was a joke? Have you not been paying attention?"

"Then maybe drop the smart-ass quips and get real. You're here because you want to drop off the radar for a while and keep yourself out of Jeff's crosshairs. Fair enough. But that means playing it safe, which is all I'm concerned with. I know it's coded in your DNA to go against me—"

"That's not true."

"No? We've been here for a few minutes, and you're already starting shit. On little things, fine. If it makes you feel better, treat me like the enemy. Although, try not to lose sight of the fact that I'm here with you, opening my home for your safety and peace of mind. The least you can do is take some precautions, but you'd rather dig your heels in like a spoiled brat who refuses to hear the word *no*."

When her jaw juts out, it means she wants nothing more than to unleash it like a snake and swallow me whole. I won't pretend there haven't been times I've deliberately pushed her to that point—a man like me doesn't have many diversions, not when work has taken up most of my waking hours ever since Callum started giving me responsibilities. What can I say, pissing Tatum off is my favorite pastime.

"For example, if you go out, I go out with you. No exceptions."

"That's bullshit."

"No, that's the *rule*, and that's how things are going to be."

"I'm not in active danger, Romero. You said so yourself. Nobody knows about this place. Nobody's going to find me here."

"Doesn't matter. Consider me your permanent shadow."

"It's not going to happen."

"Yes. It is. Unless you want to take chances and have your ex's dad find you."

Pain pinches her features, and a flash of regret makes me wish I never said it. Then again, this is what she needs to hear. There are real stakes involved. "You think he will be okay with you ignoring him forever?" I growl, watching her lose a little more of her nerve with every second. "I'd be surprised if he doesn't already have somebody out there looking for you, since he's got it in his head that you're the reason Kristoff never came home from that stupid fucking vacation you took. The longer you're silent, the more convinced he'll become and the crazier he'll get."

"So you're saying I should have done or said something differently? Are you saying this is my fault?" Her voice shakes and I doubt it's anger alone that causes it.

"I didn't say that. I just think it's better for you to stay quiet. It might have been one of the first smart things you've done."

"I hope you don't expect me to thank you for that insult."

"I would never expect that from you," I mutter. "Eventually, he'll grow desperate. That's all I'm saying. The smart move is to lay low and take it seriously."

"You mean to tell me I can't even go for a walk by myself?"

Does she think I didn't notice the way she looked at the neighborhood? As if she was already imagining the casket she wanted to be buried in after she was murdered on the street. Why would she want to take a walk alone? "I don't trust you to go for a walk by yourself. There's no telling where you'll end up or who you'll end up with."

Before she can go on a rant, I add, "Or did you forget where I found you a little over a week ago?"

Her head snaps back, color rising in her cheeks. She had to know the people she was with were bad news– mainly since she stuck out like a sore thumb, cosplaying somebody much tougher and less pampered than she's been all her life. Whatever she needs, she thought she could find it in some dingy underground club. Lucky for her, I followed her there after noticing the way she'd been sneaking out.

Even luckier, I never told Callum. If I had, she'd be tied up somewhere, under twenty-four-hour surveillance.

She averts her gaze, chewing her bottom lip. "I'm allowed to have a life of my own. To make choices for myself."

"You were in some skeevy, underground club. It was barely eight o'clock, and already half the people there were wasted out of their minds. Did you even know any of those losers?"

"Yeah, actually. I was getting to know them. We were becoming friends until you decided to act like a goddamn caveman and drag me out of there."

"What was the alternative? To leave you there? I don't think so. Do you realize what your father would have done to me if he found out I let you hang around with those losers?"

Callum would've murdered me on the spot.

"Right. My father. Your boss. Always do what he says and ask how high when he tells you to jump."

"You aren't going to lure me into a fight and distract me from what we're talking about. Your judgment has been shit lately, and you're here because you're hiding from an asshole who probably thinks you killed his son. Now is the time to stop being stubborn and get real."

"Yeah, and the way to get me to go along with you is to act like a dictator instead of trying to compromise." Her sarcasm always hits the spot.

"This is not a situation where compromise is an option."

"Says you."

"That's right. Says me. In case you forgot, I'm the guy who's here to protect you."

She couldn't look me up and down with more contempt than she is at this very moment. "You're my bodyguard, not my boss. I'm going to do what I want."

Turning toward the door, I call out, "Within reason."

Her voice is barely audible when I reach the porch. "Yeah, we'll see about that."

She's right. We will. She's going to be gravely disappointed when she finds out I only got as close as I have to her father because I'm willing to do whatever it takes to get shit done.

This means not even she will get in the way of me doing my job, no matter how determined she is to destroy herself.

CHAPTER 4

TATUM

Stupid, spoiled little bitch. You're only good for one thing, anyway.

My eyes snap open at the sound of a gunshot. My ears ring as if the gun was shot right beside me. Darkness surrounds me. Suffocating me. I'm frozen, every cell in my body clenched in terror so profound it's wound around my limbs like steel bands squeezing the life out of me. No matter how I fight to suck air into my lungs, I can't breathe.

I'm going to die here, in the dark, all alone. This is it. This is how it ends.

Light splashes across the ceiling, coming through the windows to my right. A car driving past with the headlights shining. Because I'm on a street, in a neighborhood. This isn't an apartment in Paris or a hotel room in Venice. Kristoff is nowhere near me now. He can't ever say those ugly things to me again, and I'm no longer in that warehouse.

I'm in Romero's house. It was just a dream.

And all at once, my muscles unlock, and my lungs fill with air.

It's okay.

I'm safe.

I'm not being held somewhere against my will, and Kristoff isn't going to hurt me. He's not going to hurt me anymore.

Breathe. In, out. I take my time, making each breath slow and deliberate. I'm fine. Everything is fine. I'm safe. There's no one with a gun, nobody throwing me into a car. I'm in bed in my new room. It's not a bad room, and the bed is pretty comfortable. From the feel of it, it's also brand new. Like practically everything else in this house.

That's what I need to think about. Anything else, so long as I can distract myself until the nightmare loses its power and fades to nothing the way most of them eventually do. I can think about how strange it is that Romero owns this house yet never visited. How strange it is to smell the lingering fumes of fresh paint hanging in the air. Did he have all of this done for me?

I run my hands over the satin duvet cover and focus on how it feels to ground myself in the present. It's one of the many things I learned in my online therapy sessions. Soon, the uncomfortable sensation of being covered in cold sweat makes me wrinkle my nose, so I sit up, tugging at my T-shirt to pull it away from my damp skin. I'm too sweaty to get comfortable. There's no way I can lay back down, not with everything damp and disgusting.

What's the point in trying to go back to sleep, anyway? My nerves are frayed. Another car drives past, and the sound of it makes me jump. I freeze again, holding my breath, afraid they'll stop in front of the house. As if they're coming for me, as if Jeff sent somebody to grab me—or worse, to pay me back for whatever he thinks I did to his precious little boy. The dread and fear gnaw at my insides.

I can't live like this. I don't know how much more I can take before I crack. There's a storm in my head, lightning flashing, thunder rumbling. I can't take the pressure. I can't stand hearing Kristoff's voice in my mind. And when it's not him, it's the men Jack Moroni sent to kidnap Bianca and me.

I wasn't even supposed to be there—they were only supposed to take her, hoping to use her to get money from Dad. Her and the baby she's carrying.

"*What is she doing here? She's not supposed to be here.*"

I squeeze my eyes shut, but it's no use. There's no blocking out the memory of my mother's sharp and clear voice when she realized there was a mistake. It's sick, but there have been times in the weeks since that terrible night that I have thought to myself at least she cared enough to say that. She started raising hell before they knocked me out, and I didn't hear what happened after that. I'm glad I didn't, because whatever it was killed her.

All these emotions, pain and sadness, are locked inside me. I carry them with me wherever I go. No wonder my feet are heavy when I stand and cross the room full of furniture nobody had ever used before I arrived three days ago. Three of the longest, most boring days of my life. It's not like I did much this summer, locked in my room most of the time, but that was my choice. And yeah, it was my choice to leave home, but that's the last choice that's been really mine ever since. I'm right back where I was before, at the mercy of people who think they know what I need better than I do.

Then again, I still need to figure out what I need. It seems like no matter what I try, nothing changes. For example, I'm creeping barefoot down the stairs right now, wincing when my foot lands on a creaky board. As if he's going to fling the door open all at once because he's always listening, always watching. No matter how I try to avoid him, his attention is always on me. It's enough to make my skin crawl.

I freeze, listening hard, but there's no sound from the middle bedroom Romero claimed as his own. I'm guessing it was his bedroom when he was a kid, but God forbid he admit it. It might mean admitting he's human, and he wouldn't want to do that.

Eventually, the silence surrounding me is enough reassurance, and I keep moving, rounding the banister and heading for the kitchen. Even in the dark, I can't help but notice how sparse everything is. There's a sofa, a pair of armchairs, and lamps on the end tables. A large flat-screen TV is mounted on the chimney, above the mantle where I placed Mom's ashes when we first arrived.

In other words, the room has everything you would expect but never lived in. It's like when you stage your house before you sell it, and I guess that's exactly what it is. I bet until now, this place sat empty. Cared for, but probably full of whatever furniture was here before... *Before what?* I don't have the first clue, and I can't pretend I'm not interested in learning more, but I might as well bang my head against a wall because that's what it's like trying to get anything out of him.

The kitchen floor is cold beneath my bare feet, but I welcome the sensation once I cross the room and flip on the light under the range hood. I wonder how many meals Romero's mom cooked here, if she cooked at all. I wonder what she was like. What kind of woman raises a son who turns out like him? Clearly, some serious shit must have gone down for him to be the way he is: closed-off, able to bottle up his feelings, totally detached most of the time. I can count on one hand the number of times he's shown any actual, genuine emotion.

One of those times wasn't all that long ago. When I first woke up in the hospital with a raging headache, I found him sitting by my bed. He was leaning in, hardly breathing, when he asked if I could hear him. If I knew who he was. I remember the long, shuddering breath he released when I asked where I was and why he was in my face. There was a second when he seemed... *real.* Human. Then, like turning off a light, he went cold again, standing and leaving my room to find Dad and bring him to me.

Even then, Dad was happy to see me awake but distracted by his worry for Bianca and the baby. Even then, I couldn't take the top spot on his list of priorities.

I shake my head, hoping the movement will dislodge all the thoughts and make them disappear. Thinking about this shit isn't helping. I fling open the cabinet doors, scanning what's inside. I need something to calm me down, the way Sheryl's tea always does.

What I wouldn't give for a pot of that fragrant chamomile she always has waiting for me.

Ugh. I could scream I'm so frustrated right now. There isn't a single tea bag in the kitchen. Not even the bland, basic crap on sale at any corner store. It's just tea. It shouldn't bother me so much. Yet all I can do is stand here staring into a cabinet that doesn't hold what I need while the pressure builds in my chest and behind my eyes.

Get it together. Don't be a baby.

I can't help it. This is the straw that broke the camel's back. All I want is a cup of tea so I can maybe calm down enough to get back to sleep. *Silly, stupid bitch Tatum can't even have that.* I couldn't mourn my mom when she died. I couldn't defend myself against Kristoff. I was never important enough for my dad to pay attention to me for more than a few minutes before returning to what mattered. And now, I can't make a single fucking cup of tea to soothe myself.

No. I will not do this. I will not stand here and weep like a scared child because I can't have a cup of tea. I'm not going to fall apart. This is the problem with remembering things. Eventually, all the pain returns, so much pain I don't know what to do with it. The sort of pain that wants to tear me to pieces, wants to shred me.

I can't handle it. It's going to kill me.

My breath comes fast and short, no matter how I try to calm myself down. I can no longer recall the breathing techniques or the ways to ground yourself. My heart pounds, loud and heavy. The sound deafens me, filling my head with the steady beat of a drum.

Stop, stop, this has to stop, but I don't know how to stop it. My teeth sink into my lip to hold back a hysterical cry threatening to rip through me while my gaze darts over the shadow-filled room. I need something, anything, to make it stop. I need it to go away. I need the pressure inside my head to disappear, the voices, the pain. I need to release it.

I don't know what draws my attention to the knife block on the counter. It makes me think of a girl I knew in high school who wore long sleeves even on hot days and always turned down invites to come over and swim. Eventually, one of the administrators caught on, and she ended up... *somewhere*. I feel bad now, thinking back on how disgusted I was when I heard she was cutting herself. Her best friend told me she did it because it made her anxiety and stress disappear for a while. I didn't understand that at the time. Why would anybody want to hurt themselves?

Now? I'm so fucking desperate; I would try anything. My chest is going to explode if my head doesn't explode first from all the pressure building in it. I don't have the conscious thought to reach out and run my fingers over one of the plastic handles. Before I know it, the idea of using one of these knives to make the pain go away is too much to resist.

Nothing serious, nothing permanent. Just a little cut. Enough to take the edge off.

When the overhead light suddenly flips on and floods the room with bright, glaring light, I'm too disoriented to understand what happened. I drop the knife back into the block and whirl around to face Romero, who's standing with his hand still touching the light switch. He's staring at me like he's never seen me before.

I still can't breathe, yet there's a different reason now. It's one thing to see him out of a suit lately— strange enough. However, seeing him in nothing except a pair of low-hanging gray sweatpants steals my breath from my lungs and makes my mouth dry.

That's not the weirdest part. There's a flutter in my belly, something familiar but totally unexpected because this is Romero. So what if his abs make it look like he spends his life in a gym? So what if it's not a knife I want to reach for anymore, but his waistband? I want to see what's underneath, hinted at by the sharp V of muscle leading down to…

"I hope this isn't what it looked like when I first walked in."

Just like that, the fluttering ends. All it took was the sound of his voice, especially that deep note of disapproval resounding through it.

"And what did it look like?" I want him to say it; I want him to look me in the eye and say it out loud.

He makes a big deal of looking around, finally landing on the empty butcher block counter. "I don't see anything you'd have a reason to cut. Why would you need a knife?"

"That's my business, not yours."

"I hope you don't think that would solve anything. Hurting yourself." He folds his arms over his chest, and I have to force myself not to stare at his pecs or how his biceps bulge. I knew his physique was amazing thanks to the way his suits have always hugged his broad, muscular frame, but seeing it without layers of fabric is a whole other story.

"My body. My business.."

"I don't care if it's your body. I won't allow you to do that to yourself, not on my watch. Understood? It'll never be enough anyway, and it won't take away your pain. It might give you some sort of satisfaction, but it will never solve the real issue."

I'm not sure it's the right thing to do, but my surprise emits laughter. "Are you speaking from personal experience, or?"

"Maybe?" He lowers his brow, his icy glare piercing me in the chest. It's either ice cold indifference or raging disapproval. Like a penny, heads or tails, you always know you'll get one or the other. "You're not the first person I ever met who went through some serious shit. The kind of shit that makes you believe there's no end in sight."

"Did they get through it?"

He snorts, then lifts a muscular shoulder. "I don't know. I hope they did. But life took me in a different direction."

My heart skips a beat when he comes closer, placing himself between me and the knife block. I have to back away—being this close to him is the last thing I need when he looks the way he does, like a GQ magazine had a baby with Ryan Reynolds, and smells so good, clean, like soap and musk, cinnamon and sleep. "You don't need to do that. There are much better alternatives."

"Ha, you mean like going back on medication that makes me feel like a zombie, so all I want to do is sleep all day? Or maybe I should go back to therapy and dredge up all this shit over and over and only feel worse when I leave. Maybe you don't remember, but I already tried that. I won't do it again."

"Those aren't the only options available, but I can promise you, your solution isn't at the end of that blade."

This is different. I'm not sure how to feel. It's like we're having an actual conversation. If I didn't know better, I would think he really cares what happens to me. Everything about him, from his posture to the stern expression he's giving me, paints the picture of somebody who genuinely gives a damn.

I hate to admit it, being that Romero is a pain in the ass, but for the first time in months, I don't feel so alone. Bianca tried. I love her for it, but it still felt like she was on the other side of a deep, vast body of water, and all we could do was shout to each other from opposite banks. This is different. This feels genuine. He sees me the way I am now, not the way he wishes I could be again.

"I'm here to protect you." There's a ghost of a smirk fading in and out at the corners of his generous mouth. "Even if that means protecting you from yourself."

I'm glad he said it. I am. Otherwise, I might have forgotten what a cold, heartless prick he is. "Of course," I whisper. "I almost forgot, you can't risk disappointing your boss, right? Wouldn't want to report bad news."

"No surprise there. Of course that's the conclusion you'd jump to. Forgive me for assuming we were having a real conversation." He lets out an annoyed sigh. Just like that, the bubble of attraction has popped.

"Like you said, this is your job." I reach out and give his arm a soft smack, grimacing. "Good thing you made it down here when you did, or you might not have anything good to tell him when he calls to check in."

The last thing I see before turning and leaving the room is a glimpse of his stony face. As always, everything's shoved down deep. I bet he even believes he needs to be the way he is if he wants to do a good job. Remote. Removed.

It's a shame he sucks at hiding the hatred burning behind his eyes. He can harden his jaw and go still as a statue, but he can't cool the fire. It's that blazing light I'm thinking of when I crawl back into bed feeling much better than before. No pressure. No pounding heart.

And when I fall asleep again, the nightmare doesn't follow me. Maybe the solution to all my problems lies in the one man I consider to be an enemy, the one man who maybe isn't my enemy at all.

CHAPTER 5

ROMERO

"You've been bitching and moaning for days over how you can't stand sitting around here with nothing to do." I grab my leather jacket from a hook near the front door. "Now, I ask you to go for a walk with me, and you can't be bothered."

"You didn't *ask* me to do anything." She lifts her gaze from the book she's reading. From the looks of the dark cover, it's a thriller. It's probably the last thing she needs to be reading when you consider what she's been through, but what do I know? It might help her process things.

"Didn't I? I told you, 'Tatum, we're going for a walk.'"

"And what part of that involves a question or a request? You *told* me we're going for a walk." She purses her lips and turns to the next page. "I declined. I'm reading my book."

"Your book will be here when we get back. There's something I want to show you."

"Will that something still be there when I'm finished reading?"

Forget running away from Jefferson. I'll be the one who ends her worthless, stupid life if she doesn't quit it with this bullshit. I understand how frustrated she is—God knows I understand. I'm walking around the house like a caged animal with nothing to do but the tasks I can accomplish remotely, and even then, I have to wait for them to be assigned instead of taking the reins myself. Not being able to call out to the boss from my desk or cross the hall to ask a question is driving me out of my skull.

It never occurred to me until now how busy I always was. Sure, I knew I had a ton of pans on the fire at all times and more when shit was going down—new deals, broken deals, research on potential partners. That was the easy stuff, the everyday tasks I could perform without thinking much about them. Writing up contracts and sending emails.

Then, there was the reason I always carried a gun. Still do. It's a hard habit to break, especially since I'm only here to keep this stubborn, vindictive little brat safe. It's a good idea to keep myself armed in case things go south.

Tatum must remember it would take no effort for me to put a gun to her head. I'm not the type of man who she wants to push too far. All that's stopping me right now from scaring her out of her mind is the thought of her father and how he knows this house exists and would blow my brains out after flaying the skin from my flesh if I so much as moved a hair out of place on her body.

"And here I was, thinking you wanted to know more about how I grew up, and all the other gory details."

Her nostrils flare and her eyes stop moving. She's either staring at the same sentence, or she doesn't see the words anymore. I doubt she's read a single word since I came downstairs after my post-workout shower. All she cares about is whether or not it looks like she gives a shit that I'm breathing.

"How long is this walk going to be?"

"Do you have somewhere you need to be, Princess? I wasn't aware you were on a tight schedule." I'd swear my dick twitches a little at the kitten-like growl she lets out. "Not long. A few blocks, maybe." She looks back from her book to me, like she's contemplating. Jesus, does she always have to be temperamental? "Don't act like you aren't interested, or I might just make you stay inside the house the entire time we're here."

I wouldn't do that. It's the last thing she needs. I brought her here to heal. She did more than fall apart back at the mansion. She shattered. This place is supposed to help her grow. Even if ten years ago I wouldn't have considered this to be the place where growth would ever exist.

"Don't threaten me, Romero. If I remember correctly, you volunteered to bring me here and stay, so whatever misery you experience is yours." She sets the book aside, then reaches for the sneakers sitting under the coffee table. "Now, thank you for asking. I'd love to go for a walk. I could use the fresh air, anyway. I sort of gave up on the idea of leaving the house like a normal person when you were all freaked out over me going for a walk on my own."

"You missed the most important part. *Alone.* I said you couldn't go for a walk alone." I didn't bring enough painkillers to take care of my constant headaches since we arrived. "Hurry your ass up. I already wish I hadn't bothered."

"Do you go out of your way to be a grumpy asshole, or does it come naturally?" She stands, then stretches with her arms over her head. My gaze drifts to the little bit of skin that shows, and I grit my teeth. Tatum is a temptation I cannot afford to fuck up. I desperately need to get laid if a brief glimpse of creamy midriff is enough to make my mouth water.

"What can I say, certain people have a habit of bringing it out in me." Staring at her would be bad enough without the added trauma she's still suffering. The last thing she wants or needs is a man putting his hands on her, and I'd love to do that, but in more of a "let me wrap your hair around my fist while I brutalize your pussy until all you can feel every time you move is me" sort of way, but that'll never happen.

Tatum rolls her eyes before bending to tighten her laces. *God help me, I'm only human.* There are only so many of my natural instincts I can ignore. Those black leggings she's wearing don't do anything to hide her plump round ass. Now, there's no imagining it. My cock hardens to steel. It was easy enough to ignore her beauty in that giant ass house, but here, there's no escaping her.

I have to turn around and look out the storm door while she pulls on her jacket. A few houses on the block are empty, or at least they appear to be. It's an occupational hazard to observe my surroundings and make connections based on what I see. I could be wrong, but the block appears to be clearing out. I don't know whether it's a fluke or if there's something else going on.

I could be making this up in my head as a result of boredom. *Fuck.* I have to have something to think about beyond the next meal and the weather and how fucked it is for me to be in this house. I look around now and see it the way it is with the new paint, furniture, and even new flooring, but the old images from my memory exist alongside what I'm seeing.

I half expect to hear heavy boots pounding the upstairs floorboards any minute. As a little boy, I hated that sound. *Dreaded it.* There was never any way of knowing which version of him would stomp down those stairs. He was a tornado barreling down on you without a warning. He stomped when he was in a shitty mood and when he was feeling chipper. It took almost a year of living at Callum's before the sound of approaching footsteps didn't have me bursting at the seams with nervous energy.

A quick nudge against my arm makes me turn to find Tatum staring up at me. Something in my expression must have confused or surprised her since she fell back a step, wearing a puzzled look. "What?" It comes out like a bark from an angry dog. It took me a long time to learn that not all dogs bark that way when angry. Sometimes, it's because they're confused or threatened.

Her shoulders hunch protectively. "You, like, zoned out for a minute there. I was asking if you were ready to go or not." I immediately notice the slight tremble of her body. *Fuck me.* I shouldn't snap at her like that, not with the history she's experienced.

All I can think of in that instance is how often Kristoff did that to her? I would never hit a woman—not for any reason, not even this woman who's made it her life's mission to piss me off—but there doesn't have to be a fist involved for someone to get hurt.

"Yeah, I'm ready. I'm sorry for yelling, you just startled me."

She's still wary, almost tiptoeing her way around me before stepping onto the porch. It's unseasonably chilly, enough to make her shove her hands into her pockets and shiver as I lock the front door. "I wonder if we're going to get a bad winter if it's this cold in early October."

"The worst winter I ever experienced, I was wearing shorts right up until Halloween. I think I was maybe eleven or twelve." I slide the keys into my pocket and follow her down the steps. "The first snowfall came before Thanksgiving, and it felt like it didn't stop until March."

"I think I remember that winter, now that you mention it. We got a lot of snow days that year."

"Which we only had to make up at the end of the year and cut into summer vacation."

"That's right! Oh, that was so annoying." Still, though, she's wearing a funny sort of smile. "See, we actually have shared experiences. Who would have thought?"

She has a good point. Neither of us knew the other existed. I doubt we were aware there was such a world as the world the others lived in, but some experiences are universal.

"So, where are we going? What's the first stop on the Romero tour?" Even though I bristle at her sarcasm, I know it's a good sign. If she's being sarcastic, she's not stuck in that jail cell also called her head.

"No place in particular, and don't treat this like a documentary, whatever you do. This could easily turn into the world's shortest walk."

"And after all the bitching you did to get me to come out." She clicks her tongue in mock sympathy, making me dismiss a sarcastic comment. The self-control I've shown since we got here should earn me sainthood. Considering the amount of unsaintly shit I've done—both for Callum and otherwise—that's saying something.

We reach the end of the block, and I turn left, then point to a playground up ahead on the other side of the street. "I can't make up the shit that we used to do on that playground," I muse, snorting as the memories return. "That was where all the kids in the neighborhood got together. We'd ride our bikes and play ball, and eventually it was where we went to drink and smoke. Half the time, we could do that at somebody's house when their parents were at work."

"For some reason, it's not easy to picture you as that kid, though I can definitely believe you were a bad boy."

"I wouldn't call myself a bad boy."

"Then what would you call yourself?"

Loaded question. *What would I call myself?* A boy who wanted to be anywhere but at home, for starters. "I was a kid from the neighborhood, like all the other kids. We sort of did what everybody else did. What you see around you right now isn't close to the way it was back then. See how clean the playground is? The new equipment?"

She nods as we walk. "Yeah, it looks nice. Clean."

"Maybe one day, you'll stop sounding surprised when you say that." That comment earns me an eye roll, and I snort again. "Anyway, it was nothing like this back then. The swings were always breaking and the slide was metal and rusty. The first time I got drunk, I threw up all over the old sliding board."

She wrinkles her button nose. "Charming."

"It was practically a rite of passage." My lips turn up at the sides, and I can't believe I'm grinning at the memory. "Since the vomiting wasn't your thing, maybe telling you I got my first hand job on the swings is better?"

"Is that when you broke the swings?"

"That was one of the times." We exchange a grin that's foreign yet not unpleasant. It's nice to see her smile.

"It's a shame they had to wait until you were gone to make improvements."

"It's just the way things were. Nobody thought about it. It was all we knew. The only thing that mattered was that we had someplace to go and get into trouble. Many of the kids who lived in this neighborhood wanted to be anywhere but at home."

"What about you? Were you one of those kids? Did you want to be home, or were you trying to escape?"

No, we are not doing that. Every nibble of truth I give her will only lead her to asking more questions, and I'm not ready to share anything else.

"Take a look around," I say, instead of giving her the information she so obviously wants. "It's pretty bleak. Small homes, old cars, most of the people around here rent—at least, they did when I was a kid. My mom was so proud we owned that house. It's probably why she wanted me to have it." Damn it. Already, I'm telling her more than I intended.

"It's a little... dreary, now that you mention it."

For once, she's being diplomatic. "It was a lot worse then. For one thing, back when the factories were open and people were working, there was always smoke in the air. There would be soot on every surface. You couldn't open your windows on breezy days if you didn't want the house filled with that shit. Nonetheless, it got worse when they started to close down, when the companies started moving. Then, people were out of work. *Dreary?* That would have been a vacation. It was bleak, sad, and depressing. Families started leaving to look for work elsewhere, so more and more houses were left empty. Those houses got boarded up at best or squatted in otherwise. It sort of snowballed."

"Wow." For once, she doesn't have a snarky comeback. A glimpse of her troubled face reveals how serious she's taking this. I guess I never expected her to take anything I say seriously, not when she's lived the life she always has, with every single want and desire within reach.

She turns, using a hand to shade her eyes from the midday sun. "Everything still looks closed down over there," she points, gazing at the factory and refinery, among other buildings less than a mile away. When I was a kid, I used to think there was a castle out there. *What did I know?*

"That's because it is closed."

"But things have gotten better around here—so it seems from what you've described."

"Well, a lot of money has been pumped into the area." I raise an arm, pointing to a long, brick building on the other side of the playground we've passed. "Like that rec center. That was built maybe two years ago so kids would have somewhere to go and something to do besides cause trouble."

It surprises me how she falls silent, and I welcome the silence after days of questioning. It's not until we've walked another block and come to a stop in roughly the middle of a line of row homes that she turns to me. "I don't get it."

"Don't get what?"

"How did you know that about the rec center? If you haven't been back in all these years. Do you keep in touch with people around here?"

If there's one thing I've always known about her, it's that she's not stupid. She might make incredibly shitty decisions, but then again, most people do no matter how intelligent they are, but under those blonde curls is a very sharp mind. She gets that from her father. "I haven't kept in touch, although your father has."

Her head snaps back like she's been struck. "Pardon me?"

"Your father's kept in touch with people around here. Rather, he's reached out to figure out what the community needs, and he's put money into a lot of projects. That industrial complex back there? It will be redeveloped into housing and shopping and whatever else the developers can come up with."

"Okay, wait. I don't get it. Why would he do that?"

Slowly, I turn to look at one of the houses. There's nothing more than a small patch of grass in front of it, next to a short set of concrete steps leading to the front door. "These houses here? They were all built for the workers at the mill, the factory, and the refinery. That's what this town was. Everybody worked in the same places, and the bosses got the bigger homes closer to the businesses." I nodded toward the house we were standing in front of. "And that is the house your father grew up in."

I can count on one hand the number of times I've watched someone's mouth fall open in legitimate shock. Count that number five. Tatum's green eyes widen with surprise, and she stares at the house like she's finally seeing it rather than waiting for us to move on.

I give her a minute to absorb her surprise before continuing. "You've always wanted to know how I ended up with your family. Now you know. Our parents grew up together. I never met your father until the night he came and took me from this place, but my mom remembered him. I guess they stayed in touch once he left."

"I had no idea. Absolutely no idea." She blinks rapidly, sputtering. "I knew he didn't grow up rich, but… it's so tiny."

"And it was in worse shape when he lived here—hell, it was in worse shape than when I did, but he put money into improving the block. It might've been the first block he focused on. The money he poured in meant jobs for contractors, too."

"I didn't… I mean, I never…" She blows out a frustrated sigh. "I didn't think he ever did good things with his money."

"Now you know. He's never been showy about it. He doesn't want anybody to know, but this is one of his side projects, I guess you could say, and he let me oversee some of the funding and sort of manage the projects on our end."

The look on her face leaves me wanting to reach out and take hold of her. I can't tell if she's going to laugh, cry, or scream. I had no idea so many emotions could simultaneously wash over a single face. Before I can ask if she's alright, she laughs. "There's one more thing to add to the list."

"What list?"

"The list of things I don't know about my father. Things he never thought I was worthy of knowing."

"I wouldn't put it that way."

"I would," she fires back. "You're an insider, while I've always been on the outside." She folds her arms across her chest, tucking her chin in. "I didn't know how far outside I was until now."

"I think…" This is tough. I can't make my mouth form the words at first. It's out of character for me to go out of my way to comfort her, but she's already been through so much. And I don't need her carrying this resentment. It will only fester until there's yet another reason why we can't coexist. I have to push through my resistance to get the words out. "I think there's a lot he wants to shield you from, and it's not always easy to tell the difference between someone trying to protect you or shut you out. I've gotten to know him pretty well over the years, and I can tell you he doesn't mean to shut you out."

"I know he loves me," she sighs, still staring at the house like she's expecting him to walk out the front door at any second. Her body's practically vibrating with anticipation. "It's like you said, I can't tell the difference between him keeping me away and his attempt at keeping me safe."

Suddenly, the curtains in the window of the house next door shift. We've got onlookers. I take that as a hint that it's time to move on. "Let's go. People don't like seeing strangers hanging around near their house." It's clear she's reluctant to follow me, but eventually, she falls into step beside me. I have to slow my pace to keep from leaving her behind.

"So your mom and my dad were friends?" she murmurs, staring ahead.

"It would appear that way."

"Did you ever meet Dad before you came to live with us?"

"No, he was just a friend Mom talked about sometimes. You know, hometown boy makes good and all that. I think she wanted me to be like him, to study hard and go into business."

"Business?" She slides a sly glance my way. "I'm guessing she didn't know what he really does."

"A lot of his business is legit."

"Yes, but that's not how he made his money in the first place."

"You're not wrong," I have to admit. He would hate knowing we're talking like this, but I get the feeling she needs to have this conversation. For once, somebody's being honest with her. She can speak freely after holding so many things back.

There's still tension between us, unspoken questions that I know are on the tip of her tongue. They would be on the tip of my tongue if our roles were reversed. Hell, I can remember the many questions racing through my head when I first met Callum Torrio and in the days immediately after. For the first time in my life, there was a man who actually gave a shit about me. He asked me questions and listened to my answers. He was calm, friendly, and paternal, unlike the deadbeat piece of shit whose presence in my house left me wanting to be anywhere else.

I even tried to convince myself Callum was my father for a little while. To me, it made sense. A rich guy shows up out of nowhere and takes me away to an entirely different world where there's space and light, and the furniture isn't broken because some drunken asshole decided to throw things around to ease the pain of his shitty existence. To me, it was something out of a fairytale. I had to devise a reason why he'd go to those lengths to bring me into the fold; if it meant having another man as my father, that would be a bonus.

I'm lost in memories when she speaks again, chuckling a little before releasing a heavy sigh. "Sometimes, I think I'll never know all the secrets my father has kept from me. Both of you, always keeping secrets."

She has no idea. It's better to keep that to myself, so I only shrug while turning toward home—or what used to be home before my mother placed that pivotal, late-night phone call to the man who changed my life, inevitably tangling my existence with the blonde haired girl who drives me absolutely insane.

CHAPTER 6

TATUM

"You're going to what?"

Never in my life have I wanted so desperately to slap the expression off somebody's face. The way he's smirking, you'd think I told him I'm going to run a marathon tomorrow. Or maybe climb Mount Everest or something else ridiculous and unattainable. It takes a deep breath and a reminder that I'm stuck with him to keep from giving him the tantrum he wants. I can tell. He's practically holding his breath, waiting for it.

"I'm going to cook dinner."

He lowers his brow. "You."

Thanks to how I keep grinding them together, all of my teeth will be broken by the time this is over. "What is so unbelievable about that? Do you think I'm completely clueless? That I can't use a stove?"

"I don't think you really want an answer to that question."

All I can do is shake my head. It's that, or I might lurch across the room and strangle him. "What does it feel like, being so high up on your horse all the time?"

"It's not so bad."

Yes, his face is begging for a slap. So much so that my hand twitches, and I have to shove it into the pocket of my hoodie or else risk making a mistake that will feel really good at the moment but that I might regret later. "What's the point of having a fully stocked pantry if we don't plan to cook anything? I swear, if you force-feed me another French fry, I'm going to scream." To make my point, I go to the trashcan and pull out the latest paper bag from today's fast food meal.

"Okay, you don't have to keep arguing." He holds his hands up, scowling like he does when he's not smirking like a smartass. "I swear, you don't know when enough is enough."

All that does is make me laugh. "Well, first, it's never enough. I'll always have something to say, so either cover your ears or walk away if you don't want to hear it." He follows me into the kitchen, and I am really going to need a mouthguard before long if he doesn't get off my back. I fling open the cabinets, scanning the contents. I don't know what I expected – it's not like anything will be different. It's the same stuff I've been looking at for days. "Hmmm, I can make spaghetti." Since that's easy enough and, since I really don't know how to make very many things. It seems like the simplest and least dangerous option.

"Are you sure you can handle making that?"

The slam of the cabinet door makes him flinch. It's enough to make me want to open it again just to slam it a second time. "Is there ever going to be a point where you're tired of insulting me? Please, let me know so that I can prepare."

All he does is snicker and fold his arms across his chest, and even his charcoal gray T-shirt isn't enough to make me forget what he's hiding beneath the cotton. I haven't been able to shake the image of his muscular bare chest from my mind for days, no matter how much I try. I don't need to be thinking of him that way. Things are messy enough as is. Besides, what would I do if he noticed me staring and decided to do something about it? As it is, I flinch when he passes close enough to give me a whiff of his cologne. Even when I know he has no intention of hurting or touching me, his nearness makes me freeze.

Yet another thing that bastard took. Being too close to a man is enough to make my heart seize in my chest.

Once he pulls a bottle of water from the fridge, he heads out to the front porch. "I have a phone call I need to make." Not that I asked what he was doing, but it allows me to catch my breath and relax a little. Being in such close quarters sometimes makes me feel like an animal in a zoo. It doesn't help that he always seems to be watching. Waiting for me to crack.

It's my fault I'm stuck with him, too, which makes everything worse. Of all people to go to when it became too much, keeping the secret that somebody I stupidly believed would one day be my father-in-law had been harassing me. I didn't want to go to Romero–anybody but him–but he was the only other person besides Dad who might've been able to do anything about it. I figured he could at least give me a little advice on how to respond since I knew without being told that he must have witnessed whatever Dad did to Kristoff.

I might even have hoped he would confess. Give me a little closure so I can finally stop assuming what happened. I should've known better–he's the human equivalent of Fort Knox, locked up tight. I tried as long as I could, as hard as I could, to keep it to myself. Everything Kristoff did to me, all the terrible things he said, the way he made me feel. Small, useless, like a stupid slut. I'm still ashamed, even if I don't know why. I didn't do anything wrong. It was Kristoff who was wrong. It was Kristoff who hurt me. It was Kristoff who made it impossible for anybody to get too close to me without my body seizing up in panic.

Like that night at the hotel. Maybe it was dumb, running away with Bianca. I was pissy, finding out Dad went behind my back and offered to arrange a marriage with that dickhead Dominic Moroni. He wasn't serious about it. He told me so afterward, and I believed him, but that didn't mean I was happy about being used as a pawn, even if it was all pretend. I was hurt and upset and used it as an excuse to run away. I'm not proud of myself. But I wasn't thinking very clearly then, either. I was worse than I am now, which is saying something, considering I can't stand having men touch me.

But back then? Then, I figured I would try and see if I could get over it somehow. Like maybe I could get it out of my system. It's easy to look back now and wonder what the hell I was thinking. You don't just magically get over something like being abused and raped because you want to, no matter how much you will yourself to move on. And I did. Did I ever.

So it made sense to take an interested guy back to the room after we had a little too much to drink down in the bar. I was even eager to get up there. I wanted to prove to myself that Kristoff hadn't ruined me. That I was still in control of my life, my body.

That illusion flew straight out the window the second the poor guy, whose name I don't remember, joined me in the bedroom and placed his hand on me. Something snapped in my head. I started to scream and cry and beat him back with my fists until he ran off. It's not like I wanted to. I honestly couldn't control myself.

That was the night I finally confessed to Dad. I had to. And I knew at the time I was probably signing Kristoff's death certificate, only it didn't matter when I was falling apart and there was no hiding it anymore. I couldn't bear pretending that I was okay when I wasn't. A secret like that eats at you. It breaks you down bit by bit until you don't recognize yourself anymore, especially seeing as you've put all your energy into keeping it buried inside.

Now, Jeff wants to know what happened to his son. I can't tell him because even I don't know, but I do know he got what he deserved.

It irks me that Romero knows all of it. Like I'm exposed. It's as if he knows what a weak, pitiful person I am for letting somebody hurt me. For thinking if I only worked harder, things would be okay. Whenever he looks at me, I wonder if he's asking himself how I could've been that stupid. I guess it's part of being my father's daughter. I've spent my whole life trying to be strong, the kind of daughter he would want since he never had the son I'm sure he would've preferred. Then again, he got that son, didn't he? The day Romero came along.

My teeth are on edge by the time the water starts boiling. Romero's probably talking to Dad right now out on the front porch, sharing their little secrets I was never allowed to know about. I know what Dad would say, too, if I complained. He didn't want me to be part of his world. Surprise, surprise, I got dragged into his bullshit anyway. He could only shelter me for so long.

Cooking dinner gives me something to do, at least. Maybe I should hone my technique or whatever while we're here. It's better than sitting around doing nothing. I could come out of this with a new skill. I could learn to bake, even. However, I don't know where that would get me. Just like I don't see where a degree in Public Relations and Marketing will get me when my skin goes clammy the moment I have to talk to strangers. It's so pathetic and the opposite of who I used to be. I want to be her again. Bubbly, carefree. I just don't know how.

At first, I dismiss the soft laughter coming from Romero—but it's not him. It's coming from the back of the house, not the front. Besides, who the hell am I kidding? Romero doesn't laugh. I've literally never heard him laugh in the ten years he's practically lived at my father's side.

The hair on the back of my neck rises and I freeze, a box of pasta hovering over the boiling water until the steam from the pot burns the tips of my fingers, startling me. I place the box on the counter with a trembling hand before the creak of old, weathered wood tells me there's somebody at the back door—somebody who's laughing.

"What, you think you can lock me out? Do you think that's going to change anything? You've got some fucking nerve, parading around like a slut and then pretending you don't know what you did. You think I want everyone in Marseille to know I'm dating a slut? Huh? How do you think that makes me look?"

I wince, expecting the door to come flying open the way it did that night. My heartbeat thunders in my ears. Every muscle in my body is poised to run. But the door's too close; I won't be able to get away.

What am I supposed to do? I have to stop him. I can't let him hurt me.

The knife block is close to my right hand, and I reach for it without thinking–I can't function with all the screaming in my head. My fingers close around the handle, and I slide it out of the block.

The heavy knock on the door makes me tighten my grip as I raise the knife into the air. It's like having tunnel vision–everything but the back door goes dark, out of focus. All I see is the top of a man's head—his short, dark hair.

I'll cut his fucking heart out.

The sudden presence of a hand wrapping around my wrist forces the pressure in my chest out of my throat and into a scream cut off by another hand clamped firmly over my mouth. "Tatum. Look at me."

At first, It would appear I'm blind. I can't see him. He's a dark blur pinning me against the counter with his body. A firm body with a hand like steel that presses into my cheeks and another that grips my wrist like he wants to break it.

"Tatum. You don't need this." Romero works my fingers from around the knife handle. "Remember, you're safe. Nobody's going to hurt you. I want you to breathe. Slowly."

Romero. It's Romero. And it's Romero who smells incredible, whose touch is so warm and almost caring. He's touching me, and I'm not freaking out–no, actually, I feel better. My heart isn't pounding out of control anymore. He lifts the hand from my mouth, and I'm able to whisper.

"There's somebody at the door."

Like the stranger heard me, the man on the other side knocks again. "Yo, Pierce! It's freezing out here!"

His eyes close for a brief moment. "It's just a couple of old friends of mine. They're not here to hurt anybody."

"Romer-o!" a second voice calls out. "Where you at?"

"Two old friends," Romero mutters before sighing and raising his voice. "Give me a goddamn minute, assholes." The knowing laughter on the other side of the door tells me they don't take his response personally.

"You have friends?"

He tips his head to the side. "You're feeling better if you can be a smartass. Now, listen to me." His blue eyes narrow to slits. "We don't talk about what I do for work. Understood? Not a single word. I don't even want them to know your last name."

"You called them your friends. Why wouldn't they know what you do for work?"

"Friends is a very loose word. I haven't seen them in ten years. I don't know anything about the people they are now." He side-eyes the door when the guys call out again–teasing, taunting, maybe even a little bit drunk.

A lot can change in ten years. The brooding kid who showed up at my house somehow turned into a full-grown man full of secrets and suspicious of everybody around him. A man who smells like leather and coffee and something that does things to me it shouldn't. My insides get all hot and jumpy, and I wish he would touch me again because his touch makes my breath come fast, but not out of fear.

"Just for once, keep your mouth shut," he warns. "And maybe try not being a rich brat for a few minutes."

Like magic, my insides go cold. I wipe the back of my hand over my mouth like that could erase his touch. "I can't wait to ask your friends if you were always a heartless asshole."

And just like a heartless asshole, all he does is snicker on his way to the door, which he opens to allow a pair of guys his age inside. They practically tumble into the kitchen like two big, goofy dogs who throw their arms around Romero for a split second before punching his shoulders while shoving him around.

Typical men. They don't know what to do with their feelings, so they'll beat the hell out of each other.

Their questions overlap. Where's he been? When did he get back? Why didn't he reach out? "We heard you were walking around this afternoon," the taller of the two says. He's the one I saw in the window–his friend's hair is sandy blond and long enough to brush the back of his neck. "I didn't believe it. I figured somebody put you out of your misery years ago."

"Or you got yourself locked up," the blond chuckles, elbowing Romero while wearing a smirk. He has a scar running down his cheek, and I don't think it came from shaving.

Only now do they notice me standing by the stove, and it's then that they both go silent. "Uh..." the dark-haired one grunts, while the blond clears his throat.

Romero's clearly at a loss, too, which would make this maybe the first time I've ever seen him that way. I could get used to it. He's almost... *human*. "Tatum, this is Dex." The blond gives me a jerk of the chin. "And Austin." The dark-haired one gives me a little wave.

"I was just about to start dinner," I announce, and no meal anywhere in the world could be as delicious as the discomfort that twists Romero's features at that announcement. It doesn't even matter that they're strangers, and I don't know what to expect from them–besides, he could take both of them out with one arm tied behind his back. "I could make extra if you'd like to stay for dinner?"

The way their eyes gleam doesn't mean half as much as the way Romero's darken. As soon as his icy gaze lands on mine, I feel myself growing warmer. Who does he think he is? If he thinks I'm going to pass up this opportunity to discover all of his dirty secrets, he's out of his damn mind.

CHAPTER 7

ROMERO

ord, please give me the strength I need not to murder her. Why does she have to be this way? It's times like this I wish her father wasn't who he is. I might be able to get away with leaving her on her own, washing my hands of the whole damn thing. Why did this ever seem like a good idea? It's not enough that I have to deal with her. Now, I have the past staring me right in the face. *Literally.*

"I could eat." Dex exchanges a look with Austin, who nods eagerly. At least one thing hasn't changed: neither could ever pass up a free meal. Although, back in the day, it was more because they couldn't count on a meal at home. They couldn't depend on much of anything at home. It was something we all had in common.

How much could we possibly have in common now? I'm not really in the mood to find out. That probably makes me a shitty person, but I never claimed to be a saint. A lot of water has passed under the proverbial bridge since the night I left this house for what I figured would be the last time. They can't know about a lot of shit, and I've got this unpredictable, spoiled brat in the mix. What happened to being afraid of them? Now she's inviting them to stay for dinner.

I realize they are looking at me, waiting for... what? Permission? "If you want to pull up a chair, go ahead," I offer with a shrug.

Dex smirks, clapping me on the back with a chapped hand that looks like it's been put to hard use. "Shit, don't be so warm and welcoming. I might burst out crying."

Austin, meanwhile, nods slowly as he looks me up and down with the same shrewd, steel-gray eyes my mother used to call *haunted*. He grew up seeing things no kid should have ever seen, back when this town was at its worst and his mom did what she needed to do to get by.

"You look good. A hell of a lot better than I figured you would after all this time.."

"Got a lot of time to lift, bro?" Dex flexes his bicep while staring at my arm. "Shit. I need to follow whatever regime you're doing."

"I don't know what you're talking about. You both look good." Better than the scrawny kids they were back in the day, that's for sure. Their jeans and heavy-soled boots have seen better days. Still, they're in good shape. I have to stop myself once I realize I'm sizing them up the way I size up all newcomers. What can I say, once a work habit, always a work habit.

Tatum offers a snide laugh as she stirs pasta in the boiling water. "Please, don't inflate his head any more than it is."

"Are you sure you guys want to stay for dinner?" I counter. "I know it's only boiling pasta and heating up sauce, but you might be taking your life into your own hands." I feel her eyes burning into the side of my head as I take the guys' fleece-lined denim jackets. She wants to be a snide little bitch? Be my guest, but I won't stand here and take it just because we have company.

"So, for real. Where have you been all this time? You just… disappeared."

Dex straddles a chair at the round table, folding his arms over the back. Are we really the same age? Or do I look ten years older than I think I do? The difference between the face I see in the mirror every day and the one looking up at me now is startling. The lamp over the table shines on the sharp angles in his slightly sunken cheeks. Stress lines are in the space between his eyebrows and the corners of his eyes. They don't smooth out when he smiles. He works outside, I surmise, in the wind and sun. I've lived a soft life compared to both of them.

Of all the things I tried to prepare for prior to making this trip, I didn't think to prepare for this. I was kidding myself, thinking nobody would remember me, that nobody would be around after all this time. That I wouldn't have to face the way my life diverged from theirs or consider where I could've ended up.

Rather than come up with an answer, I jerk a thumb toward the fridge. "Want anything to drink? I have some beer in there."

"I'll take one." Austin takes a seat, sitting back with his arms folded. It's obvious he hasn't slowed down with the partying he was infamous for when we were kids–his face is puffy the way a drinker's tends to be, for one thing. And at some point, he was on the losing end of a knife that left a scar zig-zagging across his cheek. It seems we've all lived complicated lives. I was already grateful for everything Callum did for me, yet that gratitude has grown in the last few minutes since these two showed up.

"I ended up going to work for a family," I explain with my head in the fridge. "Sort of an internship."

The looks of utter confusion — and possibly disbelief — when I emerge with beers in hand don't surprise me. "An internship?" Dex asks. "Since when were you trying to get an internship anywhere?" At least Tatum keeps her mouth shut, too busy trying to find a saucepan to add her two cents.

"I don't truly know the specifics, and I didn't ask. It's something my mom put together."

"Oh, yeah, she always wanted to get you out of here."

Austin's offhand remark makes my hackles rise. I know Tatum's listening hard over there, and I would appreciate her not knowing things she has no business knowing.

"What about you guys?" I counter. Anything so long as they're not asking for details on me.

"Same." Dex can't keep a straight face, breaking out in one of his familiar laughs before he lifts his bottle in my direction. "Welcome home. We missed you."

"Is it for good?" Austin asks before taking a long swig from his bottle.

I settle for shrugging. "What are you guys doing? For a living, I mean."

Dex flexes one of his chapped hands. "We both work in construction. It's been good lately, the past couple of years. Lots of new buildings, plus rehabbing the old houses."

Shit. Even Tatum glances over her shoulder, arching an eyebrow when her eyes meet mine. She knows what I'm thinking. Her father inadvertently scored jobs for my old friends. I wonder what they'd think if I told them.

"I've noticed a lot of improvements around here," I murmur, shooting her another look. *Keep your mouth shut.* They're practically strangers, both of them, and they don't need to know where my life has taken me. There would be too many questions I have no way of answering.

"Sure, and there's a lot more in the pipeline. We're looking at steady work for at least the next couple of years, if not more."

"Sorry to interrupt," Tatum interjects, turning away from the stove with a wooden spoon in hand. "Could I get some help with setting the table?"

I can see through the question. "Sure." Once at the counter, reaching into the cabinet, I lean into her ear and whisper, "Not. A. Word."

"I wasn't going to say anything. Jesus." Raising her voice, she asks, "Do you guys want salad? I think we have some lettuce and veggies in the fridge." Look at her, the little hostess. If she wasn't doing this to get a rise out of me, I might take it as a sign that she's progressing.

As it turns out, the lettuce that's been here since before we arrived isn't looking edible. "We need to get out to the store," I point out with a sigh. "Sorry, guys."

"Whatever. I hate vegetables, anyway. I just wasn't trying to be rude." When Tatum grins over her shoulder at Austin, he grins back, then focuses on her when she turns back to the stove.

Anybody could read the meaning behind his stare from a mile away.

There goes my blood pressure. "I don't see any rings on your hands," I point out while setting out plates. Time to start gathering info if these two think they're going to hang around here and stare at her ass all night.

Dex manages to stop choking on his beer before answering. "Rings? Right. Seeing as I had such a great example of a wonderful marriage growing up."

"Your ring finger is empty, too, man." Austin nods toward Tatum's back, full of questions. I lower my brow, snickering, and instantly regret it since his eyes light up like I gave him the go-ahead. *Fuck.* She is the last woman he or anybody else needs to get involved with.

"I don't have time for that," I tell them, and it's the truth. I don't have time for much of anything except the work I do for Callum, and that's enough. It always has been. That's not exactly something I can explain even if I wanted to, so I leave it there while Tatum drains the pasta. I didn't have high hopes, but at least she appears to be handling that much without scalding herself.

"So you guys were friends when you were kids, I guess?" she asks.

To my surprise, Austin scowls. "Not good enough friends that we got the heads up this one was leaving."

"I didn't know it was so sudden," she muses.

The sudden rush of rage that almost knocks me on my ass and leaves me gritting my teeth to keep from lashing out is intense enough to stun me. She can't leave it alone. She has to know more.

"Everything happened fast," I explain. When Dex opens his mouth like he's about to make a smart-ass comment, something inside me snaps. His mouth closes, and he sits up straighter. It's apparent there was something on my face that convinced him to shut up.

"It's not much..." Tatum sets a big bowl of pasta in the center of the table, then adds a smaller bowl with the rest of the sauce. "Maybe I can fix something a little nicer for you guys next time."

Next time? She is bound and determined to unravel what little is left of my control. It takes everything I have not to glare at her as we take our seats.

I need to keep the conversation away from the topic of me and what I've done with my life. Why I left so suddenly—that's the last thing we need to be discussing. "Are there a lot of people still hanging around? The ones we used to know?"

"Sure, practically everybody except for a few of the guys who… went away for a little while." Austin slides a guilty look at Tatum.

A look she doesn't notice since she's too busy plating her spaghetti. "Away?"

"I think he means they went to prison," I mutter, taking the bowl from her when she offers it. Instead of serving myself, I pass it along out of habit. I don't even realize I'm doing it until it's done. *"Did you work to pay for this food? Then you wait until the people who did have taken what they want."* After so many years of blocking it out, I can still hear his voice in my head. I have to wonder how much shit is rattling around in my head without me knowing about it.

Tatum's cheeks turn roughly the color of the sauce she spoons over her pasta. "Oh. Sorry. That was stupid of me."

"It's cool. So what do you do, Tatum?" Instead of picking up his fork and digging in, Austin smiles at her. I remember him being pretty charming in the day—the girls couldn't get enough of him. Was I ever so young that it used to bother me?

Stop kidding yourself. It's bothering you now.

But the charm's not working since his question unlocks what she's been working so damn hard to suppress. The light leaves her eyes as she withdraws. "I graduated college back in May." She stares down at her plate, pushing food around. "I've been looking for work."

"What kind of work?"

"PR. That sort of thing." She swallows hard, and red flags start waving in the back of my head.

"Probably not much opportunity for that out here," I offer. "Ya never know. Plenty of work can be done remotely."

"And why are you out here?" Dex asks. Innocent questions, the sort of things you ask a stranger if you're trying to make conversation over dinner. Questions she can't answer.

I make a point of nudging her to grab her attention. "I've got to say, this isn't half bad."

And it works, popping the bubble of tension that was starting to swell around her. "I know how to boil noodles," she mutters.

"But you didn't over- or under-boil them. Bravo."

"How were you ever friends with him?" she asks the guys, both of whom laugh and wipe away any lingering discomfort.

I wish this didn't feel so much like tiptoeing through a minefield. I wish I could relax and enjoy seeing people who used to be a big part of my life. There were times when they were all I had, when Mom was either too depressed or sick to be more than a ghost, that I'd have to remind her to get off the sofa and wash her hair. Even then, I knew it wasn't her fault—she wasn't to blame.

They were my refuge, being that neither of them had it any better than I did. We could depend on each other. Yet I forgot them so easily, didn't I?

"Excuse me." She pushes her chair back from the table and stands. "I'll be right back." Her footsteps ring out on the stairs a moment later, and the creaky bathroom door closes.

I would swear they were waiting for just this opportunity. "What's the story?" Austin asks, leaning in.

"Are you fucking?" Dex whispers.

"Oh, Jesus Christ."

He rolls his eyes. "I'm sorry. I guess that *internship* you went away for made you too good to use the f-word. My bad."

"It's complicated." When all they do is stare at me like they're waiting for more, I take a deep breath and release it slowly. "The work I do, where I came from before coming back here, I don't talk much. Sharing stuff. I don't mean to come off rude or shitty. It really is good to see you guys, even if I'm not acting like it."

Another thing about them that hasn't changed is that they're both quick to forgive and shake things off. Dex finishes his beer before asking, "How long do you think you'll be around? Straight up. You know plenty of people would like to see you, hang out."

Christ. Because I need that in my life. "I don't know for sure." I leave it there when Tatum starts down the stairs. Once she sits, I notice the damp hair at her temples. She was splashing her face. Probably trying to get herself together. She doesn't need this in her life, either.

Or so I want to tell myself before she clears her throat. "Do you guys know of any jobs in the area? Doesn't matter what. I need something to do."

"Are you sure about that?" I don't care that the guys look at me like I'm nuts for asking. She's the one who's out of her fucking mind if she thinks this will fly with either me or her father.

Her sunny smile tells me all I need to know about why she's doing this—anything, so long as she can get to me. "Yeah, I'm sure. I could use something to do while looking for a permanent job."

"There are a few places down on Main Street with *Help Wanted* signs in the window," Austin offers. "And if you want, we could take you around and introduce you." Yeah, I'm sure he would love that. So helpful. It has nothing to do with the way he can't stop staring at her.

"I could take her around," I announce.

"What if nobody in town remembers you?" she counters. "You're just another stranger to them."

What the hell kind of game is this? "I could stand to reacquaint myself with the town and the people." I can't think of much I want to do less, but I'm not letting her go gallivanting around alone. And not only because her father would strangle me... for starters, before the actual violence began.

The relief I feel when they push their chairs away from the table is indescribable. "We're supposed to meet up with a couple of the guys over at O'Neal's—you want to come? No way you'd be paying for a drink tonight." Austin winks at Tatum. "Same with you."

For once, she's smart enough to do the right thing. "I'll have to take a rain check, but maybe next time." She gets up and gathers the plates, taking them to the sink.

"Same here," I tell them with a shrug. "I have some work I need to take care of." They obviously want me to elaborate, but it won't happen. *Fuck me.* I can just imagine the conversation that's going to take place at the bar now that I've been so secretive.

At least they leave well enough alone, shrugging it off while taking their jackets from pegs by the back door. "We'll see you soon. Thanks for dinner." Tatum nods to both of them, smiling, while I show them out the door.

"Do me a favor?" I venture once we're on the back stoop. "Don't make a big deal about me being back. I'm not trying to broadcast it."

"Whatever you say, dude." They share a laugh, shaking their heads as they cut through the backyard, hopping the fence like I watched them do countless times over the years. They haven't changed much, but then they never left. They didn't have any reason to change.

I barely have time to close the door before turning to her. What a relief not having to perform anymore. "What the fuck was that about? Are you suddenly interested in bagging groceries? Or maybe you could sweep up hair at the beauty parlor."

"They're called salons."

"Maybe where you grew up, Princess, but not here. I'd love to know what goes through your fucking head when you say some of the things you do?"

She slams her hands against the edge of the sink hard enough that I know it has to hurt, but she gives no sign of pain. "Do you know what's about to go through your head? Maybe we'll start with a beer bottle."

"That's not the kind of work you need to be doing, and we both know it."

With a snide laugh, she turns my way. "And just what the hell is that supposed to mean?"

"Come on. Let's be real. You were ready to slice both of them open because they simply knocked at the back door. That's not normal, and you know it."

She turns back to the sink, gripping the edge with both hands. "I don't need you to tell me what to do or how to feel."

"Somebody has to. If you're not going to help yourself, fine. But I won't stand by and let you make a mistake."

"All of a sudden it's a mistake to want a job?"

"It's a mistake to do it just to piss me off."

"Oh, is that what I was doing? Thanks for letting me know. There I was, thinking I wanted to be useful."

"Try being useful to yourself, damn it. I can't spend the rest of my life making sure all the knives are present and accounted for."

"Do me a favor and stop acting like you give a shit about me healing or whatever it is you've taken an interest in me for. We both know you're just my father's lap dog, and you're here just following orders."

Her father's dog. The words shouldn't cut me the way they do—they're just words flung at me by an angry, scared, spoiled little nobody. I can't ignore their sting any more than I can ignore the steady *plink, plink, plink* of water dripping from the faucet. It's the only sound in the room besides our breathing for what feels like an eternity.

Long enough for me to imagine walking away. I don't need this. I have more than enough money saved to start a new life anywhere I want. She can fend for herself—we'll see how far she gets. It's a nice fantasy, but that's all it is.

Callum wouldn't stop until he tracked me down like the dog his daughter thinks I am. She'd go back to him, and he would support her rather than let her flounder the way she deserves. She doesn't have the first clue what it means to fight for survival. To come home to a war-torn battlefield every day, to hold her breath when she hears footsteps overhead, to put herself in front of a flying fist for someone else's protection.

She does, however, flinch when her phone buzzes. It's been

sitting on the counter all this time, face-up, and from where I'm standing, I can easily read the message in capital letters.

Jefferson: WHAT ARE YOU HIDING?? I'M GOING TO FIND YOU AND MAKE YOU WISH YOU HAD TOLD ME THE TRUTH A LONG TIME AGO!!!

"Why the hell didn't you block his number yet?" I growl, reaching for the phone. However, she grabs it first and clutches it tight in her shaking hand.

"I don't know." I can barely hear her, she's whispering so softly. I'm reminded instantly of what she's fought against and that she has ghosts of her own she still battles. I'm not the only one in this house who knows the feeling of holding their breath for fear of what's coming next.

"Do it now." I cover her hand with one of mine, trying my best to soothe the ache I know she's feeling. "There's no need to put yourself through his torment. Let his screams and threats fall into the void."

"You're right." She swipes at the tears that have begun to fall with her free and then goes through the motions of blocking that asshole's number. Part of me wonders then that if she knew the truth, if she knew that I slit that bastard's throat for her sake, would she still think of me as the heartless asshole?

CHAPTER 8

TATUM

I take it back—all of it. I thought life was boring back at the mansion. Sitting in my room, watching TV, drifting in and out of sleep. That was my choice, though. It was how I needed to live. I didn't have it in me to put on a happy face and pretend everything was okay. Not only that, but I felt dirty, used, and ashamed.

I thought that if I was feeling this way, everyone else could see it, too. I was trying to hide from the world. I wanted solitude, silence. I couldn't handle the emotional exhaustion of being who I used to be, no matter how much I wanted to be her. I still do, even though I'm pretty sure that part of me died.

After wasting the last few months on my depression, anxiety, and fear, the last thing I want to do is spend the rest of however long we're going to be here hiding in the house. Romero wants me to heal? That's not going to happen. Not within these four walls, especially since I can barely do anything in this house without running into him.

I've been thinking about it ever since Austin and Dex came over a few nights ago. No, it's not like I meant it when I said I wanted to get a job. I was just trying to get under Romero's skin, to shake him up a little bit. I'm sick to death of his calm, cool, untouchable attitude. It's like nails running down a chalkboard, but a million times worse. My entire soul cringes at how self-assured and closed off he is.

I smile, thinking back at the icy glare he threw my way. I definitely got to him, crawled right under his skin and took a shit. I also know him well enough to recognize it's not enough to threaten him. I need to follow through, or else he's never going to take me seriously, and I want him to take me seriously.

I want him to see the real me, the broken, cracked, beyond-repair pieces; because through it all, Romero has never looked at me with pity. He's never tried to make me feel like what happened was something I'd just forget. He's the only one that seems to understand, and while his understanding is great, it's also annoying as fuck. But do I really want some low-level, low-paying job? I'm a college graduate. That should count for something. Then again, many people are leaving college with no job prospects. I'm not completely out of touch, no matter what certain people think about me.

I think back to how he said he didn't want me going around town by myself. *Fine.* Then he can come with me, like he said he would. I'm not going to spend another full day in this god-forsaken house. I need to get outside, socialize, smell a flower, and touch the grass.

He's upstairs, having just finished a workout in the basement. There's no equipment down there besides a heavy bag and a few free weights, and I lost track of how long he was punching that damn thing this morning. I only know it's amazing that he can use his hands afterward. You'd think repeatedly hitting that bag for fifteen or twenty minutes would be a problem.

Hell, you would think it would improve his mood a little. Then again, maybe it does. Perhaps the version of Romero I can barely coexist with is the nice version. *The friendlier version.* I shudder to think how much worse he could get—a monster lurking just beneath the surface.

I don't know what I'm thinking. Maybe I'm not thinking, and that's the problem. Perhaps I'm too busy already fighting with him in my head to take a second and catch up with what my body is doing. I trot up the stairs, ready to battle it out the way we always do, before coming to a stop at the partially open bathroom door. The steam drifting out tells me he's taking a shower, but for some reason that doesn't compute in my brain fast enough to stop me, and I march right up to the door. I'm about to push it open the rest of the way and demand he come out with me... when a noise fills my ears.

At first, what I'm hearing doesn't register in my mind. I'm listening to it, but I can't figure out what I'm actually hearing. His soft pants make me think he's stretching or doing squats or something, and I want to tell him to give it a rest already. Like, I get it. You are devoted to physical fitness, but that's not what this is.

From this angle, I can catch his reflection in the mirror over the sink. It reflects the shower, or rather what's going on behind the partially frosted vinyl curtain. I can't make out the details of him or his body, but I can see enough to realize he's jerking off.

My gasp is barely muffled by the hand I clamp over my mouth. *Idiot.* I don't even know why I'm gasping. He's a human male with sexual urges, even if he likes to act like he's some untouchable robot. Still, there's something shocking and confusing about standing here, staring at the mirror, secretly hoping it doesn't fog up. His soft grunts grow louder and make my heart skip a beat. A warm flush awakens my senses as my skin starts to feel warm.

I need to stop. This is an invasion of privacy and wrong on so many levels, but my feet have grown roots. There's not much in the world that could drag me away from this spot.

His head falls back and he grunts again. Even when I stand on my tiptoes, I can't see much of him below his midsection. I would have to push the door open further and poke my head inside the door to get a better view and no way would end well. All I can do is let my imagination run free. His hand wrapped around his shaft, pumping up and down, going faster and faster. The way I'm sure his jaw tightens and his nostrils flare while his blue eyes close as pleasure takes over. I wonder if he looks as pissed off when he comes as he does when he's talking to someone?

"Fuck..." The word is a broken whisper, and it's that deep, gravelly tone that has the effect of tightening my nipples and spreading heat through my core. Suddenly, my insides are molten, swirling and seething, and I want. *I want.* For the first time in months, desire is bubbling up inside me. Not because I feel like there should be or because I feel like I need to try like I did with the guy in the hotel. No, this is different. My body is reacting on its own so strongly that I think I might be broken. I guess that's not really a shock at this point.

Romero's breathing becomes harsh. *Faster.* He's getting close. I need to walk away, to stop watching, and I should absolutely not be listening. There's no coming back from something like this—I'll never be able to look at him the same way again, but there's no walking away either. My body is literally requiring me to finish this through.

"Oh... oh... fuck...!" His heavy, ragged breaths and soft groans steal the air from my lungs and the thudding of my own heartbeat swooshes in my ears. It's so loud I can barely hear him anymore. *What is wrong with me?* I can't believe I'm still standing here, watching, listening. *I'm supposed to hate this man, despise him, and yet...*

My core tightens, the warmth in my center pulsing with newfound life. I haven't been aroused in months or even considered touching myself or trying to reach an orgasm, but I can feel the desire pooling in my stomach.

The center of my panties feels damp, my pussy clinging to the cotton. I can't believe how aroused I am. Shit, I need to get out here. Clearly there is something wrong with me. I need fresh air to clear my head. There must be some kind of gas leak in the house because that's the only excuse I can think of for what I just did.

First, there's the matter of tiptoeing away from the bathroom door. The shower is still running, so I doubt he could hear me, but I'm going to be as careful as I can anyway. With my luck, I'll step on a creaky floorboard and announce my presence. I'm so disappointed in myself. Not because what I did was wrong or anything like that—I mean, it wasn't right, but that's not why I sort of want to sit in the shower with my clothes on and bleach my brain.

The biggest problem is, I need help understanding what it means. After all this time, I get all hot and bothered because of him? It has to be because he's the only decent-looking guy for miles. Even I can admit he's handsome. His friends aren't ugly, either. Although, compared to Romero, they might as well walk around with paper bags over their heads.

But this is Romero. *Romero!* Someone who has never wasted an opportunity to make me feel small, spoiled, and stupid. He has never once held back for the sake of sparing my feelings, and somehow I'm dripping wet over him. It's pathetic. Just the thought of how he'd react if he knew makes me want to crawl into a hole and never come out.

Once I'm down the stairs, I head straight outside to the front porch, where a cool breeze touches my overheated skin and makes me sigh in relief. I pull in as much air as my lungs can hold and then let it out all at once, almost like I can blow away everything I'm feeling inside. That shouldn't have happened. Now, it will always be in the back of my mind. I'll forever know what it sounds like when Romero comes.

As usual during the day, the street is quiet. Most of the people on the block are at work on a weekday afternoon. Even when they're home, though, there isn't usually any disturbance other than some shitty kids who like to shout back and forth while riding their bikes. Maybe they aren't shitty. Maybe they're just kids. It's been so long since I was one of them, I forget what it was like.

I'm becoming old and bitchy before my time. Sour. Reclusive. Goodness, now I hang around partly open doors and spy while someone I can't stand jerks off. I need help. I need something to occupy my mind. I'm so wrapped up in hating myself that I'm startled by the sound of a woman's voice.

"Excuse me! Can you help me?"

This is the first time I've seen the old woman who lives next door up close. I've noticed her once or twice—sweeping her porch, sprinkling breadcrumbs in her backyard for the birds. She appears sweet. Though, I'm basing my opinion on watching her from the window. She could be a murderer for all I know. Right now, she's struggling with a paper bag of groceries that looks like it's ready to explode.

"I just know I'm going to drop these eggs!" she calls out. Knowing I'll feel bad if I witness her struggling any longer, I hustle down the steps and over to her, where I grab the overloaded bag without thinking. She's got to be pushing seventy. Her wrinkled face is kind and she offers me a gentle smile. "Thank you so much. Sometimes, I go a little overboard at the market and forget I have to carry the bag home by myself."

"No problem. I'm glad I was able to help." She runs a gnarled hand over her salt-and-pepper hair, neatly pulled back in a low ponytail. "My name is Millie Cooper. What's yours?"

"I'm Tatum."

Her face lights up for some reason and her faded blue eyes sparkle. "Tatum! What a pretty name. You don't hear that one too often. It's nice to meet you. And it's nice to have that house in use again. It was empty for so long."

Now I'm tingling again, but curiosity makes my pulse flutter this time. "Have you lived here long?"

"My late husband and I bought this house... oh, forty years ago. No, forty-five." She chuckles, shrugging before she starts going through her oversized leather purse. It's seen better days, scarred and scratched. "It's easy to lose track of time when you're as old as me."

"I guess you've seen a lot of changes around here."

"Oh, yes. Ups and downs. I considered selling the house a handful of times. Things do seem to be picking up again."

She looks at the house next door, keys in hand. It seems like she forgot she meant to use them. "I've seen him. Romero. I was happy to find he came back. I always wondered about him. He always seemed like a nice boy."

Yeah, we'll have to agree to disagree on that one, lady. "Did you know him well?"

She doesn't get the chance to answer before the door to his house opens and he pokes his head out. His eyes narrow when he spots me one house over, and I can practically feel the waves of boiling rage from here. "What are you doing?"

"Getting to know our neighbor." Let him be a dick now in front of a witness.

"Hello, Romero!" Millie calls, waving. "I've been hoping to get a chance to tell you how nice it is to see you back."

His features shift from indignant anger to… plain old anger. It's almost like it's such an imposition, having to talk to a human who seems glad to see him for some reason. Personally, I can't imagine it. "Mrs. Cooper. Hello. It's good to see you as well." Even those few words seem like they bring him pain. God forbid he has to be friendly or social.

"Thank you, Tatum. It was nice to meet you, but I can handle it from here." I hand the bag over, and she leans in, whispering. "You come by anytime you want, sweetheart. I miss having someone to bake for. What a shame you weren't here over the summer—I had a million tomatoes to give away."

"I'm sure we'll see each other again soon." I'm not in a hurry to get back, but I can't avoid it forever. He's glaring at me like I… well, like I listened in on him pleasuring himself in the shower. Evidently, he has no knowledge of that, but it feels like he does.

My feet are cinder blocks even as I force myself to keep a quick pace, like there's nothing wrong in the world. Once I'm at the foot of the front steps, he whispers to me, "What the fuck do you think you're doing? Making friends?"

"What if I was? I mean, please don't get me wrong, you're such great company." All he does is lift an eyebrow, so I do the same. "What? I came out here to get a little bit of fresh air, and Mrs. Cooper was having problems with her groceries. What gives?"

"I don't need the whole neighborhood knowing our business."

"You sound crazy right now. Do you realize that? You sound unhinged. Our business?" I make air quotes around the term. "I was helping an old lady carry her groceries before they landed all over the ground. That doesn't have anything to do with "our business." Plus, she seems like a nice lady, and I could use a little friendly conversation in my life."

His scowl tells me he disagrees, which comes as no surprise. "She's a busybody and always has been."

"Do me a favor and lighten up at some point." I fold my arms, bracing myself, trying my best to forget the sound of his groans as they intensify in my memory. "I want to go into town and do a little job searching, and you need to come with me. If I don't do it today, I'm going to go crazy. Maybe I'll burn the house down? That sounds like fun."

"Is this supposed to convince me that you're mature? Threatening to burn the house down?"

"I would happily go by myself, if it would make you feel better."

"You know damn well it wouldn't, and I also know damn well you have no intention of getting a job."

"That's not true. Maybe I'd like to earn a little money of my own and make a few friends along the way."

He snorts softly but manages to keep from laughing out loud. "I can't believe this… you're serious? Are you really this determined to make an ass out of yourself?"

My spine stiffens, and I lift my chin, staring at him with determination. "Fuck off, asshole. I'm doing this either way. Your options are to either come with me, or I'm going alone. Please, let me go alone. I'd probably have a better chance of obtaining employment without you scaring people with that face of yours." I do my best attempt at scowling the way he does.

For one silent moment, we play chicken, staring at each other, waiting to see who blinks first. "Fine," he grunts, nodding. "We'll do it your way, but only because I wouldn't miss the opportunity to see you make a fool out of yourself."

The thoughts of what he sounds like as he's about to explode disappear from my memory, and all I want to do now is punch him in his stupidly handsome face.

How is it possible that winning the fight feels so much like losing?

CHAPTER 9

ROMERO

"What? What are you snickering at?" Tatum's demanding tone is like an ice pick piercing my eardrum, reminding me of why I came to resent the shit out of her in the first place. She's acting like a whiny, petulant brat who never learned how to leave well enough alone, and I'm about to take her over my knee and show her a lesson.

"I didn't snicker."

"Yeah, you did. In fact, you've been snickering at me ever since I changed my clothes. What's so funny?"

"Nothing." I walk the last block before reaching Main Street with my hands jammed in the pockets of my jacket and my short nails digging into my palms. Not because I'm sick to death of hearing her voice, but because it's not doing me any good to react. Sometimes, the best response you can give is no reason at all.

"Bullshit. Why are you laughing at me?"

"I'm not doing any such thing. You're being delirious." That was a poor choice of words, and I immediately regret them. If she is out of her mind, she's got plenty of reason to be. "Stop being so touchy and defensive," I mumble as an afterthought.

"Is there something wrong with the way I'm dressed?" She looks down, examining herself and the designer clothes she's wearing. "What's wrong with jeans and boots?"

"Nothing." Except the people around here are going to see those clothes, including her suede jacket that matches her brown ankle boots, and they'll know she's not from around here. They're going to ask themselves why a girl in clothes more expensive than their whole wardrobe combined is looking for a job in a little town like this. No matter how she tries, she sticks out like a rose in a field of weeds.

There's also the fact that she insisted on printing out her resume at the office supply store five miles outside of town. I drove her out there but returned the SUV to the driveway so we could walk. It's one thing for her to stick out. I don't need the added attention. It's bad enough I'm sure the boys told everybody at O'Neal's about my return.

"I swear, I'm not nervous enough."

This time, I do smirk. "You're nervous?"

"Yes, those of us who feel real human feelings go through things like this. I know it must be difficult for you to relate to." From the corner of my eye, I find her looking me up and down as we walk side by side. "Maybe some of your components get rusty occasionally or your central system gets overloaded. That's probably as close as a robot ever comes to feeling things."

"You really should drop that shit." All it does is bring the memory of killing Kristoff Knight into sharper detail. Never in my twenty-six years had I experienced the sort of soul-deep satisfaction I did as I drew the blade across his flesh. I couldn't tear my eyes away from the sight of him opening and closing his mouth like a dying fish while his life force poured over his chest.

The blinding rage that drove me to it? That, I'd felt before. *Only once.*

"Then maybe you should drop the whole laughing at me thing," she retorts like the child she is.

"Then maybe you should stop doing stuff that makes me laugh." I can't help it. The enjoyment I get from the way she growls and huffs is too good to pass up.

She tosses her blond curls over her shoulders with a frustrated sigh, and the gentle breeze carries the scent of her floral shampoo directly into my nose. I wish it didn't make me want to bury my nose in her hair. "In case you forgot, you didn't have to come along."

"Yes, I did, and we both know I did. So shut up about it. You're wasting your breath."

Slapping a palm to her forehead, she groans. "Of course. You wouldn't want to tell your boss that you let me walk around alone in a town where nobody knows I'm staying, God forbid."

I do not have enough patience to deal with this woman, and yet somehow I refuse to let her lure me into a fight. The satisfaction of reacting to her stupid remark. That's all she wants. It's the only thing she has to keep her mind occupied, fucking with me. I should be happy she wants a job, even if I know she never will get one. She has no intention of actually working. Maybe I should encourage this, come to think of it. The less time we spend together, the less chance I have of murdering her.

But if I want her to stop kidding herself, I need to stop doing the same. I would have to tell Callum, and he would never go for her being on her own for hours every day.

It's like she can read my mind. "Are you afraid of what Dad will say?"

"He is my employer, and my job is to—"

"Enough. I don't need to hear it. I know what your job is. I don't need to be reminded." She stares straight ahead, her heels clicking loudly against the sidewalk before she steps off the curb... and almost gets her ass run down by a speeding car.

"What the hell is your problem?" I pull her back by the arm, half a second before the car would have mowed her down like she was nothing but tall grass. The sound of a blaring horn fills the air and mixes with the insults the driver screams out their window.

Her green eyes have gone from flashing with anger to widening in shock. "I... I wasn't thinking..." she whispers while the color drains from her cheeks.

"No shit, you weren't thinking. Jesus Christ. Do I need to teach you how to safely cross the street? What about tying your shoes? Think you can handle that?"

She shakes herself free of me, her lip curling with disgust. "I don't need lectures from you. It could happen to anybody."

"If you pay a little less attention to insulting me, you could pay more attention to what's happening around you."

"I'll be sure to keep that in mind." Let her sigh and mutter and snarl all she wants. She's shaken up the way anybody with half a mind would be after a close call. Even I'm a little jumpy as we cross the street and come to the west end of what passes for a downtown district around here.

Main Street has mostly stayed the same, not that I expected it to be totally different. A few of the brick façade buildings have different names now. There's fresh paint, and the weeds that used to choke the cracks in the sidewalk are nowhere to be seen. The trees that were only saplings a few years ago when Callum had them planted are thriving, their leaves beginning to turn orange and red.

Aside from those things, it's like stepping back in time. Lori's Deli still sits on the corner with the same faded Coca-Cola sign in the window. Another ten years of sunlight have turned the red background to a faint pink. Olde English Pizza Parlor sits on the other side of the street—we've ordered from there twice already, and I'm glad their quality hasn't suffered. Next to that is the real estate agency. The beauty parlor, barber shop, and pet store bring back enough memories to rock me back on my heels. While seeing the big, neon O'Neal's sign at the other end of the block is almost enough to sicken me. How many times did I heave my guts up in the alley behind the building after being served beer when I was way too young?

"It's not much," I admit, watching her from the corner of my eye as she looks up and down the block.

Instead of wrinkling her nose or scoffing, her lips quirk in what can pass for a smile. "It's quaint. Cute."

Says the girl who took a nearly two-month European vacation for her college graduation present. "I know what that's code for. It's sad and boring."

"You don't know half as much about me as you think you do."

That is entirely wrong. I know her better than she knows herself. I've had plenty of time to observe her, and it was my job to keep an eye on her for a while. I can read her like a book. "Well, it looks like they want help at the pet store. Would you like to apply?" I point to the help wanted sign showing in the window.

"Sure." So far, she's committed to the bit, determined to make it look like she intends on working.

When I move to follow her through the door, though, she scowls back at me. "I can go in alone. In fact, I would rather go in alone."

"Not going to happen, Princess."

"For fuck's sake." With a stomp of her booted heel, she whirls on me. Teeth clenched, and her eyes narrowed to slits. Damn it, why does her rage turn me on so much? Of course, my cock twitches at that very moment. "I'm not bringing a babysitter in with me. What do you think is going to happen? I'm going to sneak out through the back door?"

I tilt my head, pretending to think. "Now that you've brought it up, I wouldn't put that past you."

"You can see just fine through the window," she mutters, jerking a thumb toward the glass that makes up most of the front wall. "Watch from the sidewalk. Don't embarrass me."

"Okay, okay." I put my hands up in surrender. "You win. Good luck."

"It's amazing how you can say one thing, but it sounds like you mean something entirely different."

I'm content to stand back and watch as she approaches the woman behind the counter. The dazzling smile she wears almost makes me feel sorry for her. She's trying so damn hard—whether she's doing it to prove a point doesn't matter.

There are tan and white puppies in the front window with ears that flop when they climb over each other to get close to the glass. I can't help smiling as the runt of the litter climbs over his brothers and sisters to get a spot closest to where I'm standing. I always wanted a dog when I was a kid—one of many things I wasn't allowed to experience.

I'm surprised when the door opens less than a minute after she went in. Her eyes shimmer with tears, and her cheeks are red. And, for one stunned moment, I have to wonder what the hell the woman said to her to make her cry. The possessive need to protect her against anyone and anything creeps up on me. It's unexpected and different, being that she does not need physical protection but mental.

"What did she do?" I demand, looking through the window.

Shaking her head, she mutters. "Allergies. Something in there decided it wants to kill me." She then sneezes hard enough to make the puppies bark wildly. "So that will be a no."

"Okay…" I scan the opposite side of the street, then point. "What about the beauty parlor? It doesn't say what kind of help they want, but if you're looking for a job…"

"Yeah. Might as well try." I have to appreciate the way she rolls her shoulders back and lifts her chin like she's ready for the next challenge. This time, I don't bother trying to go in, instead taking a seat on the wooden bench between the parlor and the music store beside it. I can't remember how much music I stole from that place over the years, sliding CDs into the big front pouch of my hoodie. It didn't occur to me until years into my shoplifting career that the kids working there knew what I was doing and didn't give a shit. Why should they? They were barely making minimum wage and were probably pocketing CDs themselves.

She's in there for longer than I expected but still comes out shaking her head. "They want somebody who knows how to cut hair. They already have somebody to answer the phones and wash the towels and stuff."

The sour note in her voice surprises me. "You're serious about this, aren't you? This isn't another way of pissing me off."

"I know it's shocking, but not everything is about you." When I continue staring at her, she rolls her eyes and folds her arms over her chest. "Fine. It started that way. But when talking with Mrs. Cooper earlier, I realized how much I miss being around people. Just having conversations, asking how they're doing. Socializing. I miss feeling like somebody wants to talk to me."

"Oh. I didn't think about it that way." I'm not much company. I was never supposed to be. I guess it's a good sign that she wants to get back out in the world rather than stewing in a bed without changing her clothes or showering for days on end.

"Yeah, well, why would you?" she asks before opening her shoulder bag and pulling out yet another copy of her resume. "You hardly ever talk. You would probably rather be left alone for the rest of your life."

I can't bring myself to be annoyed by her sarcasm. "That actually sounds blissful." Something about her stubbornness warms the heart she thinks I don't own. I can't blame her. There have been times when I was unsure whether it existed.

The only other business with a Help Wanted sign posted in the window is the gas station that sits diagonally from O'Neal's. There's a handful of cars parked in front of the building—it's expanded since I left, with what looks like a mini grocery store inside instead of a few racks of candy and a single cooler. "Go ahead, but grab me a bag of corn chips and a pack of M&M's."

She blurts out a laugh when she begins walking away. "So much for healthy food. It's like being back home brings out another side of you." I don't bother replying, seeing as she's never been inside my cottage when I'm on the grounds of her father's compound. There are plenty of snacks stashed in the pantry. I rarely go home except to sleep, though, so I don't eat much of it. I've been putting in extra time with the heavy bag and the weights down in the basement to counteract my current eating habits.

She's opening the door to go inside when my phone rings.

Timing is everything. One thing I know for sure: I'm not about to tell Callum what she's doing. It's probably not worth mentioning, since it's not like she's going to work at a gas station. Not Tatum. She'll do plenty of things to fuck with me, but she has limits.

"Boss?" I murmur upon answering, one eye on the store. She's waiting in line behind a couple of teenagers buying sodas, while a man in a dark suit and an expensive haircut stands behind her. He must be the owner of the Porsche—not exactly a car one sees much up around here.

"Any updates?"

Your daughter is currently handing in her resume at a gas station. "Nothing since she blocked Jeff's number a few nights back. Things have been pretty quiet."

"That's good to hear. I knew you would call if anything happened, but…"

"I get it." He's not exactly big on patience, especially concerning things he cares about. There isn't much in this world he cares about more than his daughter besides Bianca and the baby she's carrying.

"Actually," I continue, still watching her, "I've been doing a lot of thinking, and I might have the beginning of an idea of how we can get rid of him. I need a little time to pull it together, but I think we can manage it."

"By all means."

"Let me do a little digging, and I'll update you in a day or two."

"Otherwise, is she okay?"

"She's fine. Stopped at the gas station during a walk, and she went in to grab a snack."

"Does Vinnie still own the place?"

"His name's on the sign, but I don't see him around."

"Christ, I thought he was an old man when I was a kid. He must be in his eighties by now. I guess not much has changed."

"Except for what you've changed. It looks nice around here. More like a tiny little town, and less like a town you put your foot to the gas pedal as you pass through."

"That was the idea."

She starts to walk toward the door with a plastic shopping bag in hand. "I'd better let you go. Like I said, we'll touch base, but everything here is fine."

"Tell her we're thinking about her, and Bianca said she'll call her later."

"I'll let her know." I end the call, surprised when she stops with the door halfway open and looks over her shoulder like someone caught her attention. It's the guy in the suit, and he's standing much too close to her for my liking. I'm on my way before I know it, crossing the paved lot in seconds, almost throwing the door open.

I'm in time to hear him say, "Give it some thought. I could use a pretty face in the office. People like to see a girl like you when they first walk in."

"What's going on?" I ask, standing close to her while I glare at him.

His overly bright, hard smile doesn't do much to soothe my suspicions, and I can't help noticing the hardening of his dark eyes. Like he can tone down the charm now that I'm here. "Hi, there. Chaz Drummond. I'm handling a few projects in the area and could use some administrative help. I overheard your girlfriend asking about a job."

I don't bother correcting him, wrapping an arm around her waist and pulling her close. It's better if he thinks she's taken. "Come on, babe. We better get going." She nods, looking overwhelmed with her pale face and eyes as wide as saucers. *He got too close to her.* Only now do I notice her trembling body against me.

"Here, take my card." He holds it out, and she snatches it away before tucking it in her pocket without a word. It doesn't seem like he's put off by her behavior or that he even notices. I steer her out of the store and wait until we're outside to speak.

"It's okay."

"He was, like, on top of me all of a sudden. I almost hit him."

"I know. I'm sorry I didn't get to you sooner."

"No." She's breathing hard, her face twisted into a mask of rage that only intensifies with every step. "No, damn it. I refuse to spend the rest of my life afraid to go out in public or be around people. I need to get over this, and that's only going to happen by exposing myself to people. Right?"

I want so much to tell her she's wrong, but that would be unfair. And I am the one who told her she needs to start healing. "Right. You're right. And you handled it well."

"Well? I almost peed my pants."

"I couldn't tell." She releases something close to a giggle, and it's only once we're halfway down the block that I realize I still have my arm wrapped around her. As soon as I realized it I let her go, but there's reluctance in my muscles. This is what she needs. She needs to remember how strong she is, and that's not going to happen if I baby her.

"What are you going to do with the card?" I ask once we're a few houses down from mine. By now, the late afternoon sun paints everything in shades of amber and gold. Leaves blow past our feet, and it smells like someone's burning them somewhere in the neighborhood. It's damn near idyllic.

"I don't know. I'll think about his offer for a little while. Mull it over in my mind."

I hate the defensive way my words come out. "What's there to think about? The guy was a total sleaze."

"You don't know that. Maybe he's just straightforward."

"Yes, I do. It was written across his forehead with a permanent marker."

"Well, he wouldn't be the first sleaze bag I ever dealt with." And because I know the more I fight, the harder she'll dig her heels in, I have no choice but to let the conversation go.

Besides, the less we talk about it, the easier it will be for her to forget about this crazy job idea.

CHAPTER 10

TATUM

I'm not sure what sparked me to believe it would be easy to find a job, or even something to do in this damn town. *I really don't.* False hope, maybe? Or maybe I was thinking God would give me a break from Romero to spare his life, but even that was too good to be true. Don't get me wrong – it's not like I wanted to get a job. It was more to give myself something to do, but it's been a letdown every step of the way.

That's not entirely true. There is the offer from that Chaz Drummond guy, but something tells me Romero's right about him. Now that I've had a few days to reflect on our interaction, I can see it. The guy should've been wearing a name tag that said **Asshole.** There was no reason for him to stand close to me—but at least he backed up when Romero inserted himself like the typical caveman he is. I'm thankful he stepped in, even if I am a bit annoyed. He won't always be there, and I'll need to learn to handle situations like that on my own.

Which leads me to wonder if I could handle that guy hanging over me all the time.

Somehow, I need to overcome this paralyzing fear of being around people. It is incredible how much he broke me, not just Kristoff. Getting kidnapped and thrown into a van in the garage of

Bianca's office building didn't help things, nor did waking up in a hospital bed afterward.

Still, life isn't always roses, and I need to learn to deal with the pain and trauma that occurred so I can move on with my life.

My days have started to fall into a pattern. I force myself out of bed right away before the temptation to pull the covers over my head and pretend I don't exist wins out. I go to the windows and open the blinds to find dark clouds in the sky, waiting to be released. It rained at some point overnight, and it's probably going to rain again. It would be one thing if a rainy day meant an excuse to curl up with a book or watch a movie or two, but when that's all your life has consisted of for a while, it isn't a treat anymore.

The fact that the tub is wet before I enter the shower tells me Romero's already up, even if his bedroom door is closed. That's no way to determine anything since it's always closed, even when he's awake.

He's been weirder than usual. I hope he doesn't think we're going to be friends or something just because I sort of broke down a little after that Chaz guy overwhelmed me. I know it's stupid, and I'm probably hurting myself in the end. Plus, I hate feeling like he knows so much about me when I know so little about him. It seems unfair. It's childish, but I want to balance the scale somehow. I'm not sure how I can do that when there's hardly anything around here that was here when he was a kid except for whatever he locks in his bedroom.

He's got to be hiding something. Otherwise, why go to the trouble? Somewhere along the line, he got the idea that he was some dark, mysterious figure. Like a spy or something.

He's not that important.

Still, I want to know about him. I hate feeling like there's a power imbalance here.

Bianca wasn't much help when I asked if she knew anything. I mean, she's close with Dad. He has to let something slip, right? "Callum's never really talked about him," she finally confessed. "You probably know more about him than I do, being where he grew up and everything." I stopped short of asking if she could find something out for me, because we're not kids anymore and this isn't middle school and I'm not desperate to find out more about a boy I'm crushing on.

He's in the third bedroom, the room at the back of the house that faces the yard. I hear him muttering on the other side of the door and would rather believe he's on the phone than imagine he's talking to himself. I've already gotten myself into enough trouble lingering close to a door while he's unaware, so instead of lurking and trying to overhear something, I head downstairs for breakfast.

It's not like he has a clue I listened to him jerking off. If he does, he hasn't shown any hints of knowing. I doubt he would let something like that go without making a snide comment or scolding me like I'm a child. I know what I did, and I can't forget it. I also can't help but hope it happens again, if only because my body showed the first signs of life below the waist in ages.

That might not be the honest answer but it's the one I'm going with. Otherwise, I'll have to admit that the sound of Romero getting off turned me on, and that is unacceptable. No fucking way.

My jacket hangs by the front door, catching my eye as I round the banister for the kitchen. I left Chaz's card in the front pocket. *Should I call him?* Romero will lose his shit if I do, which isn't exactly enough to convince me to forget it. It's sort of the principle of the thing. I did say I want a job, and I do need something to do besides sit around and wait until it's time to go back to bed. But I just don't know. Getting used to being around people is one thing, but being forced to talk to multiple people over the course of a day might be more than I can handle. It's like learning to be a person all over again, going back to square one.

A smile touches my lips as my eyes land on the coffee pot. At least he made coffee, though I do miss the espresso machine back home. Regular coffee doesn't scratch the itch the way a cappuccino or a latte does. Maybe I can convince Romero to buy one?

What am I thinking? I'm just going to order one. I don't need his permission.

To think, I graduated college five months ago. I figured I'd be living it up right about now, eating expensive dinners with new friends I met at the agency. I would surely have landed a full-time position, meeting interesting new clients and having an apartment of my own. Obviously, I would hire someone to come in and clean for me once a week because I would be way too busy to worry about things like tile grout in the bathroom.

It's so funny I could almost laugh through emptying the dishwasher and mopping the kitchen floor. How glamorous. But I was different back then, before graduation and Europe. Somehow, I was caught up in this idea that I could make my relationship work if I just changed myself enough to make Kristoff happy. I may as well have aged a couple of decades in less than half a year, and I wish so much I could go back and give that girl a hug and tell her she doesn't need him. That she's better off without him. That there is bound to be a better life, and a much better boyfriend out there for her. I would have also told her to stay home instead of flying to another country with a man. That's life. It's always easy to look back at what we should have done.

Once there's nothing left to clean in the kitchen and I'm finished with my coffee, I'm sort of at a loss. I'd love to go out and take a nice, long walk—the rain has held off, and when I open the window looking over the tiny backyard, a rush of cool air makes me smile. This is the kind of day when you want to drink a lot of hot chocolate and maybe eat a bowl of soup, something cozy and comforting. I don't have either of those things. There's very little comfort in my life when it still feels like my insides are cold. Icy.

"Goddamn it. Little bastards."

My ears perk up at the voice coming from out back. Rather than find something to watch or search for a new book on my tablet, I go to the back door and open it quietly, like I'm trying to sneak out. Which is ridiculous, being that I'm not trapped here. I peer outside and find Mrs. Cooper, and from the way she keeps throwing her hands into the air, she appears to be pretty distraught. When her chin starts to quiver, I have no choice except to go outside and figure out what the hell is going on, especially since I can't stand the idea of watching a sweet old lady like her break down and cry.

"Mrs. Cooper?" I call out from the back steps. "Are you okay?"

Her head snaps up, like I've startled her. Her wrinkled cheeks are red with emotion. "Oh, Tatum. Hello."

"What's wrong? I'm sorry, I'm not trying to be nosy, but I heard you out here when I was in the kitchen."

"These little bastards." She shakes her head with a hopeless little sigh that goes straight to my heart. "Look what they did. Hopping the fence so they can cut through my yard."

Her mums were a beautiful yellow, orange, and purple yesterday. I was admiring them and wanted to compliment her on them the next time we ran into each other. I even considered asking Romero if we could get some for the front porch—I'm not trying to go so far as to plant them in the ground, since I don't know the first thing about planting, but a few pots might be a nice start.

It hurts to see what was so beautiful yesterday trampled and broken up this morning. "Oh, goodness. I'm sorry!" I cry out, approaching the fence to get a better look at the wreckage.

"I don't mind them cutting through. It's a shortcut, I understand. But why do they have to trample on my flowers?" She draws her thick cardigan tighter around her trembling shoulders, and I gently pat her arm over the chain link fence.

"Do you want some help cleaning them up? I was thinking about finding a lawn and garden store around here to get some flowers for myself. I'd be happy to—"

"No, no, not at all, dear. I can head out and do that."

"At least let me help you clean up a little. Please?"

"Well, I'm a bit overwhelmed, and the cool, damp weather doesn't do my joints any favors," she admits with a soft laugh. Romero could easily look out the window and see me on the other side of the fence. I don't know why it matters that I'm visiting with the old neighbor. She's as innocent as can be, so why does he appear to be so bent out of shape every time he sees us together? What he thinks or wants doesn't matter. I walk through the gate that connects the two yards.

"Here's a pair of gloves. We don't want to ruin those pretty hands of yours." She smiles, and I gratefully slide my hands inside. With gloves protecting my delicate hands, I gather the broken blooms. "I'm going to go inside and grab the broom so I can clean this up." I give her a nod. I don't know how successful she'll be if everything is wet, but I don't say that.

"Do many of the kids around here behave like this?" I ask when she joins me again. "I noticed a group of them riding their bikes around a lot. They're always yelling and cursing at each other. They seem kind of...I don't know...rough?" I shrug for lack of anything better to say. These kids are nothing like the kids I grew up with.

"Oh yes! They prowl around this neighborhood looking for trouble, I swear. In fact there was a rash of tire slashings just last spring. Up and down the block. Everyone had a tire slashed."

All I can do is shake my head. "Those little fuckers!" She lets out a startled laugh. "Sorry, but seriously, fuck them kids. Someone should teach them a lesson."

"Oh, I agree, sweetie, but that's how kids are. Harry and I weren't blessed with any of our own children, but I helped raise my younger siblings. If I've learned anything, it's that children don't understand the value of things."

"I didn't understand the value of much when I was a kid, but I would never slash people's tires for the hell of it."

She raises a brow in question, "I'm sure you were always a nice girl, just the way you are right now, huh?"

I snort. "I had my moments." We share a smile that makes me feel warm all over. Now that I'm thinking about it, she sort of reminds me of Sheryl. Kind, gentle, but willing to cuss you out if you deserve it. She never had to do that to me, but I overheard her snapping at more than one of Dad's guards over the years when they made the mistake of making themselves a little too comfortable in her kitchen.

"Let me guess, was Romero one of those kids when he was

younger?" I ask. Now that I have picked up the broken blossoms, I dump them into a paper bag she left near my feet.

"Romero?" She wrinkles her nose, her expression clouding with guilt. "Like you, he also had his moments. Not that he had a very easy upbringing. I can't really blame him for some of his behaviors."

The back of my neck tingles, and I have to keep myself calm in the face of a possible clue about his past. "What do you mean? He's never told me much about how he grew up."

"Oh, there were troubles. But then there are troubles in a lot of families. It's not for me to judge." Though the very firm set of her mouth tells me she's got plenty of opinions, just the same. I wonder what it would take to get her to spill some of those opinions. Why is he the way he is? What makes him tick? And why the hell did he come to live with us in the first place?

"Tatum? Is that you out there?"

I look up at the second floor of the house to find Romero looking down at me. Big surprise, he's not happy. "I was just helping Mrs. Cooper. Some kids made a mess back here."

"She's very helpful and sweet," Mrs. Cooper tells him, waving. "I made a couple of loaves of banana bread. Would you like one?"

Even at a distance, his tight-jawed discomfort is obvious to me. "That would be nice," he decides, lifting a hand before backing away from the window. At least he tried to act like a regular human being.

"He's busy working on something," I whisper, rolling my eyes, because I still feel the need to make excuses for him. "He might as well be in another world."

"I'll go in and get the bread for you." When I try to protest, she waves me off. "Nonsense. When you were so helpful? It's the least I can do. And like I said, I have extra." I pull off the gloves and brush dirt off my knees, and by the time I finish, she emerges from her kitchen with an aluminum pan covered in foil. I peek underneath the foil, and my mouth waters at the aroma of bananas and cinnamon that wafts from the warm loaf.

"Thank you so much. I can't wait to try it. And I meant it when I told you I'd be happy to pick up some new mums for you if we go to the store. I'll let you know." By now, Romero is at the back door, peering through the glass cut-outs toward the top. I take my time entering the gate and wandering down the concrete path that splits the yard in two. Some garden beds would be nice back here, come to think of it, though it's probably the wrong time of year to start something like that. And we won't be here by spring. I can't handle the thought.

"What did I tell you about her?" he mutters as soon as I'm in the house.

"Could you please shut the kitchen window before you act like an asshole?" I whisper back, closing the window before turning and glaring at him. "She is a nice lady, and I felt sorry for her. She was crying and everything."

"That's her problem."

"How can you be such a dick? She's an old lady, and I wanted to help her. God, I need to do something around here! I can only wash the kitchen floor so many times in a week."

"I told you, she's a busybody."

"Afraid I might find out you're human?" I ask, smirking. "Because I can't imagine another reason why you would be so against me talking to her."

Seeing him baring his teeth in a snarl makes me shrink back—no matter how strong I want to be, I can't control my reaction. "Just leave her alone," he growls before going downstairs. He's not even in his workout clothes, but it's only another moment or two before I hear him punching the heavy bag. He's doing that so he won't punch me, I realize, and the thought makes the banana bread look a little bit less appetizing. Maybe I'll try it later, when I'm not imagining him losing his shit on me.

One thing is for sure: I need to get out of here. I'm going to go out of my skull if there isn't something fun to do. People to talk to, some laughs, maybe a drink or two. Life, in other words. There must be something around here I can do, some way to get out without him knowing. Because if I'm not even allowed to talk to the next-door neighbor, I might as well shrivel up and die.

He can't tell me what to do. He doesn't own me.

* * *

It's been an hour since Romero closed his bedroom door, which means it's been two hours since I came upstairs pretending I was getting ready for bed. I even brushed my teeth and washed my face to keep up the act.

Then, I retreated to the bedroom, locked the door, and got myself ready to go out.

It's a risk, and I know it, but I can get an Uber and he never needs to know I was gone. He always leaves his house key in the dish by the front door. It'll be back in the dish long before he gets out of bed.

Just a few hours, that's all I want—a few hours out in the real world, around people besides him. I just want to feel normal again for a little while, but anonymously. I don't need to ever see any of these people again.

It feels like I can leave safely now. There hasn't been a sound down the hall in at least half an hour. I'm sure he's asleep by now. I take one last look at myself in the mirror on the back of the bedroom door—it's been ages since I dressed up like this, wearing the tank top and a short, leather skirt, knee-high boots, and a thin cardigan on top since it's not exactly warm outside. My smokey eye makeup almost reminds me of the person I used to be, the girl who used to have so much fun going out and dancing for hours on end.

I'm going to be her tonight. I have to try.

I turn out the light, then slowly open the door. There's no light coming from under Romero's door, and I take that as a good sign before tiptoeing silently down the hall and down the stairs. Once I reach the darkened living room, I pull out my phone. My heart's racing, my blood pumping as I open the Uber app and prepare to request a ride. I've been checking throughout the night, and it seems like a decent number of drivers are in the area. Thankful, the club is only a few miles away so this should be easy.

"Going somewhere?"

My phone hits the floor while I shriek at the sudden sound of Romero's voice. He flips on the lamp next to the sofa, where he's sitting with his arms folded across his firm chest. He's looking at me like my dad used to when I came home late at night. Son of a bitch. He's still dressed and everything.

"What the fuck is your problem?" I snap, bending to pick up the phone. "You're lucky I didn't break this, or you'd owe me a new one."

"Because any of this is my fault. Not the fact that I caught you trying to sneak out."

"What am I, sixteen? Trying to sneak out past curfew, Dad? Newsflash: You are not my father, and you don't get to treat me like you are. I'm a grown woman, damn it!"

"Then why don't you act like a grown woman instead of tiptoeing around like a sneaky little kid?" He looks me up and down, then rolls his eyes. "Where do you think you're going dressed like that?"

"I'm going to pick out a casket for you, you prick. What the hell do you care?"

"I care because you're not going anywhere without me."

"Fine. You want to pick out your own casket? Go right ahead."

"Drop the bullshit." He springs up from the sofa and my heart stutters when he advances on me in short, menacing steps. "You're not going anywhere by yourself, especially not to a bar or a club. Do you know the kind of trouble you could get in?"

"I've been going out by myself for a long time." My back hits the wall at the foot of the stairs, and he stops just short of pinning me in place. Oh, God, why does he have to smell so good? Why does he have to stand so close? Again, I can't help but notice how his nearness doesn't freak me out. No, he makes me want to lean in, to leave no space between us at all. I want to bury my face in his neck and inhale his cologne—I swear, there's some kind of addictive chemical in it, because it's driving me crazy and making me think things only a crazy person would.

"If you're going out, I'm going with you."

I manage to push aside the bizarre rush of lust. "No, you are not."

"Yes, I am. Either that or you're not going anywhere." He folds his arms, biceps bulging, and I recall the night he caught me in the kitchen and how good he looked without a shirt on.

This is Romero. Dad's little lapdog. He is not a man to lust after. Look what happened the last time I lost it over somebody who made my hair stand on end and my blood pump and my adrenaline race. I wound up... well, I wound up the way I am now. It's not worth it. He's not worth it.

"Well? Make up your mind, Princess. Either we go out together, or you wasted a lot of time sneaking around up there, thinking you were being quiet."

A smirk passes over his full lips. "What's it going to be?"

CHAPTER 11

ROMERO

"You are so full of shit." She can't give up, can she? She has to keep up this act. So sassy, sarcastic, tough as nails. The defiant princess.

It's as if I haven't seen her at her lowest. Like I don't know what she's battling with. That's probably part of the reason she hates me so much. Because I see what she only wishes she could hide.

"Keep stalling, Princess." I throw a pointed look at the clock on the wall over the TV. "The night is passing, and you already wasted enough time waiting for me to go to sleep before you tiptoed down here. This club you want to go to won't be open forever."

"You honestly think I want to go anywhere with you?"

"Who asked whether or not you want to? What you want does not play a factor in this."

Anger washes over her features before they harden. "What a surprise. Since when does what I want matter?" There I was, hoping the spoiled princess act would wear thin once she got a glimpse of how I grew up. I thought maybe she'd give up the *woe is me, I'm so sheltered* bullshit.

She looks me up and down, folding her arms like that will hide the way she trembles. Is it fear or resentment, or both? Probably both. "We can hardly stand being in the same house together. What makes you think we could handle a night out?"

"Once again, you're missing the point. I'm beginning to think it's deliberate." I take a second to savor her indignation. "This isn't about us going out to have fun together. I'll be going along to keep an eye on you."

"You can't possibly imagine how humiliating and insulting it is to hear you say that. I am not a child."

"You made a pretty good impression of it tonight. Did you think I didn't know something was up? Do you not realize how creaky that bedroom floor is to somebody downstairs?" She wouldn't, of course, since I don't go in that room. On the other hand, I can't count how many times my stomach went icy at the first creak of those floorboards while I crouched down here.

"You sat down here in the dark, waiting for me? That's weird. Don't you know how weird that is?"

"Don't change the subject. You thought you were being slick, and you found out you weren't, and now you're pissed."

"I'm pissed because I had to sneak around in the first place."

"You absolutely did not have to sneak around. You could have approached this like an adult and said 'hey, I want to go out'."

"Right." She lifts her chin, defiant as always. "Because you have been so accepting and willing to go along with things up until now. It's, like, your nature. You're just an easygoing sort of guy."

I'm not going to pretend she's wrong. I would have shot down the idea before it finished tumbling from those pouty lips. Lips that keep catching my eye, thanks to the glossy red color she painted them—ripe, juicy cherries begging to be tasted.

Finally, I find my voice. "I compromised on the job search, didn't I?" Her mouth opens like she's ready to fight, but she soon realizes she doesn't have a leg to stand on because I'm right. "Why do you default to being sneaky?"

"Why do you default to being weird and secretive and telling me I'm not allowed to talk to the neighbors? Can you blame me for assuming you'd have a problem with this?"

"Can you blame me for assuming you'll have a problem with it? Or have you already forgotten what happened at the gas station?"

If her shoulders don't stop lifting defensively, they'll cover her ears. "You know I haven't. But you're the one who keeps telling me to heal, right?"

"There's a big difference between healing and throwing yourself into a situation that's bound to hurt you."

"Do me a favor and let me decide what will hurt me, okay?"

Everything about her challenges me, but never as much as it does now. I haven't seen her dressed up like this in a long time—not since dinner with the now-dead Moronis. That might as well have been a lifetime ago. Even then, she was dressed for an evening at dinner with her father and his associate, not for a night out at a club. She wasn't showing so much skin, like the creamy expanse of cleavage revealed by a low-cut tank top. The smooth, lean legs encased in supple leather boots. A leather skirt so tight it's like a second skin.

The dark makeup around her eyes makes them appear emerald green as they flash and burn. Damn it, she wouldn't be such a smart ass with my cock shoved down her throat, would she?

The force of the desire behind that thought is staggering. What in the fuck am I thinking? Even if she wasn't as fragile as she is now —and she is, she can't hide it—I would never make a move like that. Not if I wanted to live to see tomorrow. Anybody but Callum Torrio's daughter.

I need to get laid, and soon. This train of thought is dangerous for both of us.

"How about we frame it this way?" I suggest. "I'll come along with you and stick around, but I'll give you space. I'll be there if shit goes south or you can't handle it. Otherwise, I'll leave you to yourself."

Her lips twitch and damn it, I want a taste. "You mean it, don't you?"

"I do."

"So you're going to go to a club? Romero Pierce, hanging out with a bunch of people, dealing with the music, bodies, and sloppy drunks?"

"You should be a writer. You know how to paint a picture with words."

She giggles before she can help herself, and now there's no holding back a knowing grin that lights up her face. "You are going to hate it."

"That's my problem to deal with, isn't it?" The more I think about it, the more I have to agree with her. The thought of being surrounded by a bunch of drunk, sweaty strangers sends bile rushing to my throat, but I'm not backing down now. Not when we've already gone back and forth like this. It would be too much like letting her win, which she cannot do. If I give her an inch, she'll want a mile.

"Okay. This might actually be more fun than I originally thought." She stands up straighter, brushing back her blonde curls. "Let's roll."

I hope we don't both end up regretting this.

* * *

"So, how are we doing this?"

"What do you mean? Doing what?" I wouldn't say I like the looks of this place. The façade's painted black, there's no sign, there's not even a light over the front door. Someone thought they were being particularly edgy when they came up with this idea. It comes off lazy, not to mention that somebody has an overinflated sense of how cool they are.

"Hey." She snaps her fingers close to my face and I swat her hand away.

"Do that again, and I'll break your fingers."

"Sorry, sorry. Maybe if you'd pay attention when I ask you a question instead of scoping the place out like Secret Service or whatever..."

Do not engage.

It's getting harder and harder every day to take the high road. She would love nothing more than for us to get in a fight out here and for me to walk away, leaving her alone to do whatever she wants. It's not happening.

"What were you saying?" I ask with what probably looks more like a grimace than a smile.

"How are we doing this? Are we hanging out together? Are you hanging back at the bar? Do we pretend we don't know each other?"

"If only it was that easy." I don't like the looks of the guys walking in right now. Seven in all, young, looking like they shared a copy of the *How To Look Like A Douchebag* manual: tight shirts, gold chains, cologne strong enough to choke me at a distance. None of them can help looking her up and down, though she's too busy glaring at me to notice.

"You could have stayed home."

"So you say."

She shivers in her thin cardigan, rocking back and forth on her heels. "Let's go in, yeah? I'm freezing out here."

"If you didn't insist on being half naked..."

"Not your decision," she reminds me through gritted teeth. "Not my father."

I have to bite my tongue while paying the cover charge for the both of us. She's not a stupid girl, far from it. Why does she have to be so hardheaded? What seems like common sense to me is mystifying to her. I've never known anyone so hell bent on having their way even if it hurts them, and I'm not sure as we enter the dark, sort of seedy club what bothers me most: her defiance or my inability to help her.

I hate EDM, but that seems to be the music of choice around here. The vibration from the heavy bass travels up my legs and makes my head pound. I know better than to complain because she'll only set down roots and refuse to leave until the lights come up and we're all kicked out. Even if she's miserable, she would do it to spite me.

That's why I put on the most neutral expression I can. "You know, it's been a long time since I've gone out. Thank you."

"Fuck off!" she shouts back. "Don't even pretend you're enjoying this."

"We just got here. I'm trying to keep an open mind. I especially love how sticky the floor is." Spread out before us is a sunken dance floor two steps down from the outer perimeter of the room. In that perimeter there are chairs, tables, and a few booths in the back, with a railing separating drunken spectators from drunken dancers. I guess there would be more than a few accidents if there was nothing keeping people from tumbling down those steps. To my left, spanning the entire wall, is a well-stocked bar currently two or three customers deep from end to end. She picked a popular place. I guess there's no accounting for taste.

"Want a drink?" I shout close to her ear. It's a struggle, pretending the floral perfume she wears doesn't make hunger pool in my gut, hot and needy. *Get it together. This is a job. Callum would castrate you.*

She nods and turns toward the bar, weaving her way through the crowd like she was born to do it. She's much more practiced at this than I am, obviously, but it does impress me that she seems to be handling her surroundings well. She's in control, I realize. She's not at the mercy of groping hands... yet. Judging from some of the grinding on the dance floor, it can only be a matter of time.

It's strange, the things that go through a person's mind at the oddest times. I can see my mother's face in front of me and almost hear her voice—disappointed but patient. *"One day, you'll understand when you have kids of your own. It feels like watching them make mistakes and knowing there's nothing you can do to stop them. Some things you have to figure out on your own."*

And that's what this is tonight. She has to figure it out on her own. She has to go out in the world and see what she can handle. When I look at it that way, I can almost admire her bravery—though I'd rather cut out my own tongue with a hot knife than admit it. She would never let me live it down.

She asks for a vodka tonic, and I order one along with a soda for me. "You're not going to at least have one drink?"

"I don't drink, really."

"Why not?"

"I thought we weren't supposed to know each other."

Even in the dim light, there's no missing the way she rolls her eyes. "I'm trying to make conversation, you douche. Could you lighten up for once?"

"One of us has to keep a clear head."

"God forbid you not be superior just once!" She shakes her head, turning her back on the bar to scan the dance floor. I stay still, watching her from the corner of my eye. I don't want her to know I'm watching, since that would make her self-conscious.

She's worried. Her brow is furrowed, and her teeth are sunk so deep into her bottom lip it won't be long before she draws blood. "Here," I shout, thrusting the drink her way.

"Thanks." She wastes no time emptying the glass before giving me a defiant look that I choose to ignore. For all I know, she wants to start a fight, so we'll go home. I won't let her do that. She wants to push her limits? She can be my guest.

"Go ahead," I urge, nodding toward the dance floor with its blue and purple lights swinging in all directions from overhead. "Have fun. I'm not stopping you."

"Fine. I will." She is every inch an empress looking over her court as she strides away from the bar before getting caught up in the crowd, expertly working her way to the dance floor without getting caught up in the flow of moving bodies.

Fuck me. I didn't consider this. What it would mean to watch her dance. She's not far from where I'm standing near the railing, but she doesn't so much as glance my way before she swings her hips to the pounding rhythm. Her eyes close, and after a few minutes, she loosens up and her movements start to flow. She's not thinking about what she's doing now. She's in her body, letting the music guide her. There's no self-consciousness, no worries.

With my free hand, I grip the brass rail until my knuckles ache.

How easy would it be to meet her down there, to step up from behind and take her by the hips. To pull her close so she could grind against my dick, so I could bury my face in her neck and inhale her. The smell would intensify the hotter she gets, and soon it would mix with sweat that would bead at her hairline and roll down her neck.

I truly need to get laid. But I'm not sure even that would help at this point, considering it's more than just physical shit with her. I want to break her down. I want her on her knees, begging for me. For my touch, my kiss, my cock.

But I'm here, and she's there, and that's the way it's supposed to be. That's the way it has to be if I want to walk out of this with my life.

It's no surprise when she finally catches the attention of a tall, blonde guy in a tight T-shirt. He's on the other side of the floor, but I catch him watching her, following her every movement with eyes that bring the word *hunter* to mind. He has spotted his prey, and now he begins crossing the floor, turning sideways to work his way between writhing bodies. I don't know what's louder: the music or my heart pounding. I have to restrain myself rather than go out there and get in his way. This is how she wants it? This is how it has to be.

Her eyes are closed still, and she's too deep into the trance she's fallen into. I want to call out, to warn her, but I know she wouldn't hear me. There's nothing to do but brace myself and hope she can handle it.

Her eyes fly open and she stops moving when he leans in and says something that makes her head snap back. She doesn't flip out, nodding and offering an overly bright smile. A group of girls pushes their way past her from behind and she stumbles, but rights herself before she falls against him. My eyes are glued, and I realize I'm holding my breath. *Don't you touch her. Don't you dare fucking touch her.*

He says something else and she shakes her head, shrugging, and I can taste my relief when she begins moving away toward where I'm waiting. He calls out, but she shakes her head, waving her hands.

And that's when he makes his mistake. That's when his arm shoots out, his hand circling her forearm. He's even smiling. Mr. Nice Guy wanting nothing more than to buy her a drink.

He's not smiling once she pivots on her heel and drives a fist into his chest.

I can't hear him, but it's easy to read his lips. "What the fuck?" He leans down, his head tipped to the side. "What is your fucking problem?"

He's too close. I know it, and that's what gets me moving, seeing the way he leans over her, the way she shrinks back, the way she shoves him with both hands until he stumbles backward so she can flee, her blonde curls bouncing as she fights her way through the crowd and out the front door.

I should follow her, but instead I go to him, taking him by the shoulder and spinning him in place. He doesn't have time to register what's happening before I pull back my fist and drive it into his nose. There are gasps and shouts all around us, all of which we ignore in favor of shoving him to the floor before charging out after her.

I knew it. I knew this was going to happen. Why the hell can't she ever listen to reason? When will it be enough? And she wanted to come here alone?

How am I supposed to help her?

I didn't realize how warm I was until the cool air hit me in the face on emerging into the night. My head swings right and left, but there's no sign of her. She couldn't have gotten far. There are clusters of people around the entrance, vaping, smoking, and laughing. "Did a blond girl run past here?" I ask, but all I get are shrugs.

Fucking useless. Useless like I am. Unable to help her, like I've been all along. Like that night at the hotel, listening as she confirmed all of my suspicions about that bastard she was dating. I always knew he was no good, unworthy of her, bad news. It wasn't anything I could put my finger on; besides, it wasn't my place to voice my opinions. There was always something sly about him, something secretive. He was the sort of person who couldn't be trusted—I knew it instinctively, having grown up with a lot of people I wouldn't have trusted if my life depended on it.

And all I could do was stand there, listen, absorb her agony, and know there was nothing I could do to take it away. It was the same with the hospital, when she was lying there unconscious, trapped in a nightmare I couldn't wake her from—the helplessness, this sense that I had let her down somehow. I'm right back in that place, only I'm no longer sitting by a bedside. I'm searching the street, scanning the area, knowing she couldn't have gotten far in those heels but unable to find her, just the same.

Until I hear a woman crying up ahead in an alley between two darkened buildings. She made it two doors down before she gave up and retreated to the shadows where she could crouch against a brick wall and bury her face in her hands. She reminds me of a beaten puppy, trembling, her high-pitched sobs echoing in the narrow space until they're almost as deafening as the music in the club.

"Tatum." I lower myself to one knee in front of her, careful not to crowd her too much. "You're alright. You're safe."

All she does is unleash a fresh burst of anguished sobbing. I feel myself shutting down, pulling away, even turning my face toward the street because I can't stand watching this. Anything but this. I've never been good with tears, but there are only two people who've ever left me feeling this way. Helpless, useless, knowing there's nothing I can do or say to take it away and wanting more than anything to do just that. I'm not angry with her. I'm furious with myself for letting it go this far.

There's got to be a way to get her through this. I have to find it, whatever it is, because she cannot spend the rest of her life breaking down in alleyways. After all, a man grabbed her. "I'm proud of what you did," I murmur, still watching the cars passing mere feet from where we are hidden in the darkness.

Slowly, she quiets down, but she remains in that protective hunch with her face covered. "You were fierce," I offer. "He grabbed you, and you didn't hold back. That was a great punch."

She sniffles. "I'm sure he didn't feel it."

"His pride did, and sometimes that stings a hell of a lot worse."

"I couldn't handle it."

"This time. But you tried. That's worth something." I feel so fucking stupid, saying whatever comes to my head, what I would want to hear if I were in her shoes.

We stay like this for a while, until she steadies herself with a deep, shuddering breath and swipes her hands over her face. All the trouble she went to with her makeup, only to end up looking like a raccoon. "Let's go home."

"Okay. Here." I pull off my leather jacket and drape it over her shoulders, then walk with an arm around her shoulders until we reach the garage at the end of the block where I left the SUV. She doesn't say a word, and I won't force her to talk. What else is there to say?

Still, there's something unspoken hanging between us throughout the ride back to the house while she rests her head against the seat with her face turned away from me. I can't help wondering what's going through her head, just like I can't help wishing I was who she needs me to be now. She needs a friend, and I don't qualify.

I can't let it go, though. Something inside me won't allow her to go to bed without at least offering my support. I know it will drive me crazy throughout a long, sleepless night if I don't try. Once we're inside, she goes straight for the stairs but pauses when I speak. "We can talk tomorrow about what happened over there. Get some sleep, and you'll feel better about it in the morning."

"Is that your professional opinion?" she whispers, not bothering to look my way. Instead, she stares up into the dark hallway, one hand around the banister. "Don't worry about it. I'm used to dealing with shit alone. I don't need your pity, and I don't want your remorse."

I'm too stunned to respond, not that she gives me any time before she rolls her shoulders back and sends my jacket falling to the floor. She pays it no mind, marching up the stairs. The closing of the bedroom door punctuates her cold rage.

And only ignites mine.

CHAPTER 12

TATUM

"Get back here. Don't you walk away from me!"

My pounding heart startles me out of sleep and thrusts me into reality. Sunlight floods the room–this isn't the first time I've woken up this morning. I did the whole wake-up routine... up to a point. Once I was dressed and the bed was made, it occurred to me I'd have to face Romero next. Instead of dredging up the humiliation, I chose to hide by flopping back on the bed and brooding. I guess I fell asleep.

But I'm safe here. I know that. There's no Kristoff. He's not going to hurt me anymore.

It's my dream I'm not safe from.

And the rest of the world. My heart aches when I remember what happened only hours ago, the pain and humiliation and disappointment fresh. Ready to drown me in bitterness.

I don't know what I expected last night; I honestly don't. I hoped things would be different. I hoped I could get through it without losing my shit. And I might have, I really might have gotten through it and woken up this morning feeling good about myself and my future. I might've had *hope*. I might've been able to visualize a life where I don't have to brace in fear whenever somebody raises their voice.

Only I forgot one thing: you go to a club and dance alone, and you might as well be waving a red flag in front of a horny, drunken bull. I'm surprised it took that long for someone to approach me, and not because I have a high opinion of myself. I'm a woman. That's all it takes.

I lift my left arm and push back my sleeve to examine for any bruises in the cold light of morning. I'm not surprised to find my skin clear—the guy, whoever he was, didn't grab me that hard. Compared to how Kristoff used to grab me and yank me around like a rag doll, it was hardly anything. But it didn't have to be. All he had to do was put a hand on me after I told him I didn't want a drink, and something inside me snapped.

And *he* had to see it, didn't he? He had to be there. Watching. Witnessing my breakdown. Acting like my big, benevolent protector. He even wanted to talk things out today. What a joke. Like that would do anything. He wants to be my friend all of a sudden? The guy acts like he knows me so well yet doesn't have the first clue. The last thing I want is to feel *pitied*.

He pities me, and the idea makes searing hatred burn through me like acid. I felt it last night in the arm he draped over my shoulder. I never thought I'd crave sarcasm, but he left me wishing he'd call me spoiled or reminded me this was all my own fault. That, I can deal with. That, I can brush off the way I have so many times. It's sort of a skill I've had to master.

Kindness? No, thank you. He was only acting that way because he felt like he had to. It was pitiful.

He thinks I'm weak. Broken. It doesn't matter if that's how I feel sometimes. I don't want *him* to think it.

What am I supposed to do? How do I face him now?

Out of habit, I snatch my phone off the nightstand. There's one person I've always gone to for advice when I need it the most. But when I pull up my text history with Bianca, all I can do is hover my thumbs over the keyboard, frozen. I don't want to tell her about last night, either. Besides, it's too much to text, and I might get emotional if I have to describe it. I've done enough crying and questioning my sanity.

But as much as I love her, and as long a history as we have, what if she tells Dad? We're best friends, but he's her husband—God, it's still weird to think about it. Her loyalty to him might outweigh our loyalty. It's not like I did anything wrong, but he might be pissed if he finds out Romero let me go to a club. I wouldn't put it past him. And as much as I don't care if Romero gets in trouble, I don't need him being bitchy about it while I have no choice but to live with him.

I settle for texting something plain and low-stakes.

Me: How is everything going? I miss you.

I drop the phone on my chest, staring up at the ceiling. The silence around here is deafening. I don't hear him down the hall or downstairs, and it's way past his usual wake-up time. He's one of those people who likes to get up as early as possible for some bizarre reason. We're pretty much opposites in every way possible.

The phone almost buzzes its way off my chest—I wasn't expecting her to get back to me right away, but her quick response has made me smile for the first time since waking up.

Bianca: I miss you! Things are okay here. How are you?

It's not like I've never lied to my best friend, and it's for the best that I do now. She doesn't need to worry about me with the baby and everything. She's been through enough drama as it is. The poor kid will end up being born with PTSD.

Me: I'm okay. Bored out of my mind. Wishing we could have brunch or go shopping.

It makes me sad when I look back at all the missed opportunities to do those things. I pushed her away just like I pushed everyone away all summer. It was too exhausting trying to put on a happy face. And once she knew the truth after spotting my bruises, I couldn't shake the feeling that she imagined me being hurt whenever she looked at me. I know now, like I knew then, that she wasn't trying to make me feel bad, which is why I didn't lash out at her. No, I would lash out at Romero instead.

Bianca: Me, too. This will all be over soon. And then you can come home.

Will it be that easy? The thing is, it doesn't matter where I am. The memories are always there. I can't escape my own head.

I drop the phone on the bed, scrubbing my fists over my eyes. I really should get moving—I'm breaking my pattern and was starting to like having more structure in my days. But damn it, I will not let him look at me the way he did last night. I'd rather stay up here all day than shrink under the crushing weight of his pity.

Something tells me Mr. Abs of Steel will pull me out of this room kicking and screaming if I don't show my face at some point today. He'll tell me it's for the best, that he's only thinking of me, and whatever else he thinks I need to hear because he's being paid to say it.

I need to stop obsessing because every time I think back on crouching in that alley and sobbing until I couldn't breathe, I want to shrivel up and die. There's got to be a way to distract myself that doesn't involve showing my face downstairs.

Why, of all times, does the memory of Romero jerking off in the shower come up now? I guess my subconscious is trying to humanize him, reminding me he's just a man no matter how he pretends to be big and bad. I'm sure he's got his weaknesses, though he's damn good at hiding them. But if he wasn't so desperate to hide, he wouldn't be so against me being friends with Mrs. Cooper, right?

She's not who I want to think about right now, when the memory of Romero's moans makes my nipples peak. I brush my hand across them and suck in a surprised gasp at the intensity of the sensation that rolls through me. It's sweet and hot enough that I do it again and bite my lip to stifle a moan.

Holy shit. I'm on fire, and all because of a few soft touches.

My eyes drift closed, shutting out reality to sink into something better. Somewhere, there isn't any fear or pain or regret. A place where Romero walks in on me writhing on the bed, my hands rubbing my body over top of my sweater before that's not enough, and I have to dip underneath my clothes to touch my bare skin.

At first, he would only watch, shocked, until he could do nothing but let go for once. He would forget what he knows he's supposed to do and choose this instead. He would cross the room and crawl across the bed like a predator who'd spotted his prey.

"Touch yourself for me, Princess." Instead of infuriating me, the word would roll off his tongue in a heated whisper, making my skin tingle like it is now. *"I want to watch you come on your fingers. Can you do that for me?"*

"Yes," I whisper now, lifting my hips and yanking down the waistband of my leggings to give my hand room to find its way between my thighs. Oh, fuck, the first contact with my mound makes me gasp, even with cotton panties in the way. I jam my hand under them and note the wet patch on the crotch–but only vaguely, somewhere in the back of my mind because what's at the forefront is how incredible it feels. The delicious tension builds in my core with every brush of my fingers against my wet folds.

"Take what you want," Romero whispers in my head. I can almost feel his hot breath on my neck and I want so much for his lips to touch my skin. With my free hand, I stroke that spot and imagine it's him and it's enough to take my breath away. *"Touch your pussy. Fuck yourself with your fingers. Nice and deep."*

Now both hands are in my panties–one to massage my clit, the other to drive two fingers deep in my hot, wet pussy. My hips lift and I grind them in slow circles, panting the way he did in the shower. I can hear him now, like he's panting while he watches me, wishing he could take over. "That's right. Come for me. Let me hear how good you feel…"

"Romero!" It's a whisper, a breath, filling the room a second before everything explodes and I'm left writhing and moaning behind my clenched teeth. It doesn't end right away, either, the blissful tremors going on and on until I'm left floating in a river of warmth and sweetness. Complete blissful relief.

Only to realize once I open my eyes that this is the first orgasm I've had in months. Since before Europe and everything that happened there. I tried more than once over the summer to make myself feel good, to feel *anything*, but I could never get anywhere close to the finish. This time, the finish was inevitable.

And it was because of... him?

Every fiber of my being pushes that idea away even as I pull my hands free, and my insides still flutter with aftershocks. The evidence is pretty straightforward. Thinking of him, imagining his dirty talk and what I wished he would do to me, got me over the edge.

Or it was simply a matter of not coming in months and finally being able to relax into it. I mean, my body was bound to need release eventually. I'm young. I'm healthy. He was just a convenient fantasy. It doesn't have to mean more than that.

One thing is for sure: I can't lie here forever after coming all over my hands. I doubt he's upstairs, anyway, though if he is, he's probably in his office with the door shut. Shutting out the world because his work is so important.

I'm like a wannabe spy in a cheesy sitcom, opening the door a crack and peering into the dark hallway. The office door is open, except the room is empty. I crane my neck to find the same true of the bathroom. I dash on tiptoe down the hall and let out a sigh of relief on closing the door. *Congratulations. You made it to the bathroom, you dork.*

After washing my hands, I splash my face like that's going to wash away the weirdness of getting off on fantasizing about the man I'm hiding from. Like it's not enough I have to hide from Jeff.

My jaw juts out when I meet my gaze in the mirror. No more hiding. If he tries to broach last night, I'll shut him down. I don't need to talk about it. I know exactly what happened and why. Performing a post-mortem isn't going to change anything.

The first thing I hear when I venture into the hall is a noise behind the house. Probably Romero, but it sparks my curiosity. I'm not going to take the office as a sign that he trusts me—he probably doesn't leave anything he feels is vital in that room. Either way, my conscience doesn't bother me as I cross the room and go to the back window to scan the yard.

And the sight of a trio of kids in bulky hoodies clustered around the door to the garage makes my blood boil. They can't be older than twelve, maybe thirteen, and two keep a lookout while the third messes with the padlock on the door.

These little bastards! I raised my hand to bang on the window, but that's not enough. It would scare them away, but it wouldn't send the right message. Instead, I run full out down the stairs and to the kitchen, flinging the door open and relishing their open-mouthed surprise.

"Stay the fuck out of here!" I scream while they scramble away, two of them hopping the fence easily but the third getting his jeans caught on the twisted metal prongs running along the top of the chain link. I laugh at how he tumbles to the ground before scrambling to his feet. "We're installing a fucking camera! Think about that the next time you shitheads have nothing better to do!"

Okay, so I've become an old woman, screaming at neighborhood kids to stay off her lawn. But this is serious. They were trying to break into the garage. Granted, I have no idea what the hell is in there, but there has to be a reason there's a lock on the door.

The moment my heartbeat starts to slow, it occurs to me that Romero didn't come running when I screamed. There goes my Spidey Sense, tingling like crazy. It's when I hear his fists making contact with the heavy bag downstairs that I realize he probably works out with earbuds in. I wonder how loud he keeps the music if he can't hear what just happened.

I also see an opportunity.

Call it boredom. Call it curiosity—years of it, stretching all the way back to the morning after my middle school graduation, when I woke up to find him in the house. Whatever the reason, it makes me head for the key ring on the table near the front door. I'm probably not doing myself any favors by taking them, and he'll probably hide them from me from now on, though I will happily point out that would be a mistake. What if he was injured and couldn't tell me where to find the car keys? What if something happens and I need to get away fast while he stays behind?

I could ask myself *what if* until the cows come home. Instead, I go through the keys on my way out the back door and through the yard. The garage sits at the end of the driveway, beyond the fenced-in section, and I would guess it's big enough to drive a car into but as far as I know, Romero has never so much as opened the doors. At least, not since I've been here.

There's a small, silver key on the ring that fits the padlock—and when it turns easily and the lock pops open, I can't keep my hands from trembling. I'm an explorer who finally found what they were looking for, or at least came one step closer. With a quick look over my shoulder to make sure he's not watching, I open the door and step inside. The air is dry, stale, and there's a faint scent of old books and gasoline.

There's a switch to the left of the door and I flip it, lighting a bare bulb in the center of the ceiling and illuminating a surprisingly clean space. I wouldn't be surprised if he had it emptied out like he clearly did to the house before bringing in new furniture. Whatever used to be in here, he kept only what mattered most.

Either it didn't matter, or he wanted to forget it ever existed. Maybe I should thank those shitty kids for inspiring me to do this, since it gives me another clue–however fuzzy–about what makes Romero tick.

It makes me think back on what Mrs. Cooper said when I asked what kind of kid he was. *He had his moments.* I wonder if he was anything like those kids—getting into trouble, being mischievous. It doesn't take much thought. Something tells me he was, and it makes me smile to myself when I remember that sullen, moody kid I first met.

There's not all that much in here besides cardboard boxes stacked along the far wall, on the other side of a big, bulky shape covered in a giant tarp. I walk around it in favor of reaching the boxes, pulling one from the top of the stack and hoping there's something inside that would give me a little insight. Who is he? Where did he come from? Why did he ever leave, and of all places, why did he end up with us?

There are no such answers to be found when I lift the lid and peer inside. No letters describing a painful past or family secrets, no diary or anything that obvious. There are, however, photos. Envelopes of them. I vaguely remember a time when we would get pictures printed at a store, and they would come in envelopes like these. I grab one at random and open it before carefully lifting the top photo and holding it up so the light hits it.

There's a couple sitting on a couch with a big floral print. They're probably in their mid-teens, and he's got his arm around her while she's snuggled close to him. She's wearing a choker necklace and a spaghetti strap camisole, while he wears a dark red flannel. His black hair hangs down to his shoulders, while her short, brown hair is held back with tiny clips across the top of her head.

She looks happy. So does he.

And they both look like Romero. The guy's blue eyes and chiseled cheekbones, the girl's full lips. They have to be his parents. It's hard to believe two happy-looking people could create... him.

The happiness didn't last forever. Another of Mrs. Cooper's comments repeats in my head. *There were troubles.* She didn't have the chance to go any deeper than that.

I don't know how much more time I have before he finds me out here, so instead of looking through more photos, I replace them and then return the box to the stack. I can always come back out here another time, like right after he goes downstairs to work out. He's usually down there for half an hour or more, so that will give me plenty of time.

I should go, *now*. Only when I turn, prepared to slip out and lock up again, do I trip over the corner of the tarp and bump against whatever's underneath. I can make out the shape of handlebars under there somewhere. A bike? But much bigger than anything I ever rode as a kid.

What the hell? I lift the corner and peer underneath. My eyes widen when a little overhead light leaks in and gives me a glimpse of polished chrome.

"What are you doing in here?"

I let out a yelp before I can stop myself. "Fuck!" My heart's about to burst out of my chest—when I put a hand over it, I feel it pounding away under my palm.

He's standing there in the doorway, arms folded, with a sweaty patch on the front of his gray T-shirt. I can barely pry my eyes from it while my cheeks flush from embarrassment at being caught... and when I remember what I fantasized about earlier. I'm lucky if it isn't written all over my face. "You need to wear a bell or something!"

"How could I catch you sneaking around where you don't belong if I did that?"

"I wasn't doing anything. I was only looking around."

"Which means you are doing something. There's a reason this door is locked."

"Those asshole kids were trying to break in, and I figured I should at least know what's in here if I'm going to keep them from breaking the lock and taking what's inside."

He lowers his brow, studying me. Probably trying to decide if I'm telling the truth. I don't dare blink. I can't give him a reason not to believe me.

"They're lucky I didn't catch them," he decides. "Well, you're in here. You might as well take off the tarp."

It's not quite as much fun with his permission, but I doubt I'll ever get this chance again. "You're sure? You're not going to throw this in my face later?"

"The clock is ticking, and your window of opportunity is getting smaller."

"I'm just saying. Maybe I'll learn something about you, and I know how much you hate that."

"That's what this is all about, so don't even think you've got me fooled. I bet those kids were out here, but you can't stand not knowing about me."

I toss my head even though he's hit the bullseye. Why is he so damn perceptive? "Get over yourself. You're not that important."

"It's just that usually, people sit down and ask questions instead of going through personal property." For some reason, there's no edge to his voice like I would expect. It's not exactly soft or tender, but he doesn't seem angry. Resigned? Like he knew this was going to happen? He's an idiot if he didn't. There had to come a time when I would find something about him.

"And usually, when people are asked questions about themselves, they don't shut down and refuse to answer or get all pissy about it." He grumbles but offers no reply, while I decide to take him up on it before he changes his mind.

"Holy… shit." I can barely breathe once the tarp is off to the side, and a gorgeous motorcycle is revealed. I'll be the first person to admit I don't know a thing about motorcycles, but I know a beautiful piece of machinery when I see one. The Harley Davidson logo on top of sapphire blue paint stands out–that, I recognize. The chrome gleams like it was recently polished.

"Now you know my darkest secret." I glance away from the bike to find him smirking. "I own a motorcycle."

"It's yours?"

"No, it's Mrs. Cooper's."

I shouldn't laugh and encourage him to be a dick, I can't help it. "Can you imagine?" I whisper, laughing harder as I imagine her flying down the highway. "She's feisty enough."

"You're right. She is."

"How did a kid end up with a motorcycle like this?"

"It's a long story." Did he steal it? I don't know how to ask that question without getting told off, so I'll keep it to myself, for now.

Instead, I settle for studying him, lifting an eyebrow. "I don't see it."

"See what?"

"You on a motorcycle. I'm sorry!" I insist when he bursts out laughing. "I just don't. You're so…"

"What?" he challenges with a grin, jerking his chin like he's challenging me. He's always challenging me. "Say it."

"You know what I'm saying."

"Not until you use your words like a big girl."

"I was going to say *constipated*." This time, we both laugh, and I can almost forget what happened last night when he's relating to me as a person and not a mission to be accomplished.

"Alright, I asked for that," he admits, shaking his head. "But yeah, I used to ride around a lot on it. It didn't look so nice then, but I sent a little money over to have it fixed up while I was gone. Once I started making money, that is."

He joins me on the other side of the bike, placing a hand on the leather seat and looking over the machine with something close to love, softening his features. "In case I ever came back."

"It's beautiful. It really is."

"You want to go for a ride?"

"Shut up."

"What? I'm serious. It's been way too long since I've gone out on it. You should come with me. Aren't you the one always complaining you have nothing to do?"

It's one thing to admire a beautiful piece of machinery, but another thing to take a ride on something that could end up killing me. Goosebumps erupt all over my body, and my heart starts to race with apprehension... and maybe something else. Excitement? There is something thoroughly exciting about being scared. Only that seems a hell of a lot safer than what I'm considering now.

All at once, a question tumbles out of my mouth. "Do you think I'm weak?"

His eyebrows shoot up. "What?"

I don't know where it came from. I'm embarrassed that I asked. "Never mind. Forget I asked," I mumble, staring at the logo when I can't bear looking at him.

"All you're doing is stalling." I'm glad he chose to interpret it that way. "What do you say? Are you in, or are you out?"

"I..."

"Come on. Don't chicken out on me." Then, in a truly bizarre move, he makes a noise that sounds suspiciously like a chicken's cluck.

"This is embarrassing," I murmur. "I'm embarrassed for you right now."

"I'm going in for a quick shower." He backs away, holding my gaze. "Then, I'm hitting the road. If you feel like living a little, you'll come with me. Or you can stay home, clutch your pearls, and let me have fun alone."

Damn him. He knows I can't back down from a challenge. It's, like, in my DNA.

Looks like I'm going for my first motorcycle ride whether I want to or not.

CHAPTER 13

ROMERO

Weak? She wants to know if I think she's weak? That's what rings through my head over and over while I take a quick shower and throw on dark jeans and a long-sleeved Henley before shoving my feet into heavy boots. She thinks I see her as being weak.

I knew better than to ask what she meant when she tried to gloss over it. She'll shut down on me and probably make it impossible to talk to her for the next few days, if not longer. While I don't exactly mind the peace and quiet, it almost feels like we're starting to understand each other a little. At least she's not making my life as miserable as she used to at her father's house back in the day. Sometimes, I miss exchanging barbs, but then again, we still have that back-and-forth I came to appreciate. Perverse? Maybe, but also, no one has ever called me normal.

Why would she think that? Because of what happened last night? The last thing I'd call her is weak after she honestly tried to take a step in the right direction. The fact that she's still here and trying to build a life proves she is far from weak. That's how she sees herself, and I would bet everything in my bank account that being Callum's daughter has something to do with it. She holds herself to a higher standard because that's how he holds himself. He has to be tough, brutal, even ruthless. I know that through firsthand experience.

But there are different kinds of strength. Sometimes, it's not about how hard you can hit. How steadfast you are in the face of danger. Sometimes, strength can be a matter of getting out of bed and facing life. Fuck, I've seen that firsthand, too. More times than I could possibly count.

I know better than to try to change her attitude through talking —it's not like talking is my strong suit, anyway.

But I can show her. And I can do that starting now.

She's waiting for me in the garage, wearing her suede jacket over her thin sweater. It should be enough to keep her warm on the ride. She stands with her arms folded, chewing her lip, tapping her toe, and eyeing the Harley like she's waiting for it to attack. "Don't forget this," I tell her as I pull a black helmet from a box while pulling one out for me.

"Really?" Her nose wrinkles like she smells something rotten as she examines it.

"Listen. If you want to do this, you need to wear a helmet. I'm not going to negotiate."

"This was your idea, remember?"

"Don't pretend you're not into the idea. Riding with the wind in your hair and all that."

"It won't be in my hair if I'm wearing a helmet."

"Put the damn thing on." Because really, there's only so much I can stand before she pushes me to the end of my patience. "It's a shame you can't find a job being a pesky little brat. You'd make a fortune." She only grumbles behind me as I wheel the Harley out of the garage, locking the door behind me before continuing down the driveway.

Note to self: Invest in motion lights for nighttime. A security camera, too.

I'm not trying to play games with these little punks. How do I know they're punks? Because I was one.

"Okay." Once we're at the curb, I make sure her helmet is

strapped securely while ignoring the light, intoxicating scent of the perfume she's wearing. It makes me want to lean in and take a deep breath. "You're all set," I tell her, backing away before I do anything stupid.

"What should I do?"

"Just hold on to me. I'll take care of the rest."

"You make it sound so easy."

"It doesn't have to be difficult." I swing a leg over the saddle and settle in. It's been a long time since I've ridden the old girl, but everything comes back at once—memories included. A hell of a lot of memories.

She's still standing beside me, shifting her weight from one foot to the other. "Do you need to visit the bathroom before we go?" I ask.

My question has its intended effect, snapping her out of her indecisiveness. "Sue me for being nervous," she snaps. "What do I do now?"

"All you have to do is sit behind me. Arms around my waist." It takes a moment but she climbs on, then makes a big deal of wiggling around to make herself comfortable before linking her arms around me. I can't afford to think about the sensation of feeling her body so close to mine. Her tits as they press against my back, her quick little breaths hitting the back of my neck.

Get a hold of yourself.

"Try not breaking my ribs," I grunt when she decides to squeeze me like her life depends on it. "We won't get very far if I puncture a lung."

"Sorry, sorry."

It's not long before she squeals as the engine roars to life. "Oh... my goodness!" she adds with a laugh. "It's very rumbly!"

"Yeah, enjoy yourself," I advise with a laugh while adjusting my mirrors. "You ready?"

"No?" But she's laughing, which I'll take as a good sign.

Her arms tighten when we start off. I expected that and can handle it, so long as she doesn't squeeze the shit out of me for the entire ride. "Relax!" I call out, raising my voice so she can hear me over the engine growling beneath us. "Enjoy it."

Slowly, her grip loosens while I steer us off the block, past Main Street, and onto a rarely used road running along the outskirts of town. It borders the old industrial complex, meaning there's not much traffic running along it anymore. That could change once the new development is complete, but there's a lot of ground to cover before that happens.

I figured she'd feel better if we weren't surrounded by other vehicles, and my instincts were on point since she actually laughs. "You okay?" I call out.

"Yeah! This is so cool!" I don't think I've ever heard her so completely enthused over anything. At least, I can't recall the last time her voice was so light and bright, so free of the cynicism that's become her trademark over the years.

She thinks this is cool? She has no idea.

"Oh... oh, my God... *Romero!*" She ends on a shriek and my laughter carries on the wind now that we are flying down the road. I can't remember the last time I felt this free—and something tells me she feels the same, since she can't stop laughing and whooping with joy while the wind hits our faces and the world passes in a blur. Now I wish we were on a road trip, with days of this ahead of us.

Instead, muscle memory takes me to the one place I could be alone when I needed it most. My refuge. My escape from the hell my home could be, especially on mornings when I came downstairs to find the first floor littered with beer bottles and overflowing ashtrays. That was when I could count on ugliness on the horizon, which is when I would haul ass to the lake only fifteen minutes from the neighborhood. It might as well have existed in a different world during those difficult, often violent days. Back then, I didn't have the words to express what it meant to escape here, and I doubt I could bring myself to express it now. The reminder that somewhere not far away there existed peace. Serenity.

"It's beautiful!" There's a genuine wonder in her voice, ringing out loud and clear now that we've slowed down so I can navigate the trails winding through thick woods. The scent of pine needles and moist earth brings a flood of memories to the forefront of my mind. The foliage is turning red, orange, gold, and even I'm left breathless when we enter the clearing leading down to the shore of the lake. The trees lining the banks are a riot of color as far as the eye can see, highlighted by midafternoon sunlight. It's like something out of a postcard, something almost painfully perfect that leaves a lump in my throat. I was a different person the last time I came here.

"That was amazing! Oh, my God, how did you go so long without doing that?" As soon as I've put the kickstand in place, she practically jumps to the ground and yanks off her helmet. Her eyes sparkle like the water behind her, her cheeks flushing pink from the cool air and her excitement. She has never looked so exquisite.

"I guess I forgot how much I like it," I confess after removing my helmet. "It's a rush, isn't it?"

She bounces on the balls of her feet, sputtering like she's searching for the words to express herself. "I never imagined feeling… that… free! Once I got used to it, it was like flying. Can you teach me to ride?"

Red flags wave wildly in my head at the thought. "One thing at a time."

"Please, don't give me some sob story about how my dad would kill you if anything happened to me."

"You know damn well that's exactly what would happen." She's too happy to roll her eyes or make a smart-ass comment, so instead she walks to the water's edge and stands with her hands in her pockets, gazing out over the sparkling ripples until the rapid rise-and-fall of her thin shoulders slows down. I can't decide if she looks lonely, determined, or pensive. I don't know if she wants to be left alone the way I did back when I would come here. I wish there was a user manual when it comes to this girl. I wish it didn't always feel like I was making the wrong move.

I join her, yet give her space, and eventually begin walking away once I catch her attention. She follows, and I glance over my shoulder to find her picking up smooth, polished rocks and turning them over in her hands. "Isn't it amazing?" she murmurs, and at first, I'm not sure if she's talking to herself or to me. "The water seems so gentle. It does here, anyway. It's practically still. But these little stones and rocks get smoothed out over time."

"It takes a long time," I point out. "Probably longer than you or I have been alive."

"And I guess they'll be here when we're gone." She tosses one of the larger stones into the water, and we both watch the ripples that extend one after another until the surface goes still again, except for the occasional bubbling from a fish swimming beneath it.

It's easier to speak with my back to her. Before I know what I'm doing, I say, "The answer is no."

"Okay. And the goose flies at midnight," Tatum replies with a snort. "Are we speaking in riddles now?"

"You asked me a question earlier. The answer is no. I think you're the strongest person I know."

The touch of her hand on my shoulder makes me come to a stop. "Really?" she whispers.

I turn slowly, almost dreading what I'll find. For all I know, she's going to claw my eyes out or at least slap me for being insensitive or taunting her, which I'm sure is how she'll choose to take what I meant with all sincerity.

All I notice at first are the tears shimmering in her eyes, turning them to the purest emerald. I could drown in their depths just as surely as I could drown in that lake. "Knowing everything you've been through?" I murmur, shaking my head. "How could anybody call you weak? I hope that's not what you think about yourself because it's untrue."

Her chin trembles before her lips part to release a shaky breath. "I want..." She lowers her head to stare at the sandy soil beneath our feet.

"What do you want? You can tell me." Because I know what I want, and it can't be. My hands flex, aching to cup her cheeks. To draw her close, to kiss her. Hard. Deep. For long enough that her knees buckle and she clings to me for support. I've never known a desire this deep, this overwhelming. It sits so heavy on my chest that I can barely breathe. My hands tighten into fists, shaking from the fight to hold myself back when it would be so easy to give in.

A soft, broken whimper escapes her parted lips. "I want it to all go away—all the memories. I just want them gone. How do I do that? Is it possible?" Her voice breaks, and she shudders, turning her face toward the water like that will do anything to hide the anguish she's struggling with.

I would kill him again here and now if I hadn't already done it. There she was: beautiful, intelligent, bright, and energetic. A royal pain in the ass, yeah, but she had the whole fucking world laid out in front of her. She was poised to take anything she wanted. And he turned her into this, and there is no escaping the memories because God knows I've tried to escape my own. You can only push them down for so long before something happens to bring them up, like having to confront them in your childhood home.

"Tatum... I wish..." *That I could help you. Tell me how I can help you.* The heart I was so sure I didn't have calls out to her, yearning to hold and protect her from the world and all its demons, but I can't force the words out.

And before I can find a way, someone calls my name. "Yo, it's him! Romero!"

Motherfucker. I want to pretend I didn't hear it, but that's impossible. She heard it, and now she looks over my shoulder while swiping her hand under her eyes to catch the emotion that overflowed in the form of reluctant tears.

"Romero!" With a soft groan, I turn around, scanning the water's edge until I find Dex waving his arms over his head a few hundred yards from where we stand. "Hey, man! Come over!"

"Over to what?" I call back.

"We got a fire going and drinks and shit!"

"Who's we?" I mutter. It's incredible how quickly my walls come up, and my defenses go into overdrive.

"We can't ignore them," Tatum points out. "And really, how many people are there in the world who actually want to spend time with you?"

It's so easy to forget how broken she is inside when she gets smart with me. It could be for the best. It's easier to fight back the incomprehensible desire that keeps springing up when she's acting like a spoiled smartass.

"Yeah, sure," I call back before reluctantly continuing the walk. The wind shifts, and I can smell the fire Dex was talking about. It's a shame I didn't smell it before now. We could have gotten out of here before being spotted.

It's more than just a couple of people. Five big tents are arranged in a circle with a fire crackling away in the center. There are multiple chairs, a couple of coolers, and ten people milling around, drinking, laughing, and having a good time.

"Hey!" I barely recognize Andrew, another one of the kids we hung out with back in the day. He was always the smallest of the group, but he's grown more than a foot and put on a lot of muscle between then and now. Before I can register what he's doing, he throws his arms around me and even lifts my feet off the ground. Tatum's choked laughter is no help.

"Hey, man. It's good to see you." He sets me down and gives me a playful shove. "Where the fuck have you been? We thought you were dead!"

"No, I'm alive." And that's all I'm going to say because that's all anybody needs to know. Looking around, I recognize the many faces and can't help wondering if this is where I would have ended up: getting drunk at the lake, chain-smoking, fucking around with people I've known my entire life. Not that there's anything wrong with that, and they all seem cheerful and happy, but I know now that there's so much more in the world. This world seems so small in comparison.

One of the girls comes over and gives Tatum a little wave. She's a cute little redhead I vaguely remember–I'm sure she caught my eye when we were kids, but she couldn't have made much of an impression if I'm left searching for her name. "Hi. I'm Chloe," she announces after giving me an appraising look. Probably sizing me up the way I'm doing to her and trying to pair the past up with the present.

Tatum has no such thing to think about, instead offering a bright smile. "I'm Tatum."

"Do you want a beer?" She nods happily, and they head for one of the coolers. Well, it didn't take long for her to warm up. Chloe introduces her to Brian, who jerks his chin in greeting when our eyes meet across the campfire. We were never close, but he always hung around on the periphery. The way they look at each other tells me they're a couple.

"You want a drink?" Dex holds out a fresh bottle of beer, but I shake my head.

"Just water for me. I've got the bike out for the first time in forever, so I want to stay clear-headed."

"Hey! There you are!" Austin emerges from one of the tents and drapes an arm around Tatum's waist on approaching her from behind. I watch closely, pretending to listen to Dex talking about God only knows what. Torn between wanting to lunge in and protect her but hanging back because she needs to handle this herself.

She flinches, but no more than a person normally would when surprised. When she recognizes him, she smiles and leans in a little in a brief moment of friendly nearness, and he's smart enough to drop his arm when she pulls away.

"I had my first motorcycle ride today!" she tells him. A smile lights up her face until she's glowing brighter than the fire and, I swear to God, I would give anything to make her smile like that all the time. No self-consciousness, no fear, no ugly memories rearing up to slap her down and make her feel so low and small.

"I could take you for a ride sometime," he offers with a grin that can only mean trouble.

It's not until Dex nudges me and laughs that I realize I'm staring daggers across the fire. "You said it was complicated, right?" he asks, reminding me of our dinner and how reluctant I was to open up about her. Reluctant and, let's face it, unable.

I don't answer, instead asking, "You guys come here a lot?" I have to ignore it. This is none of my business. She doesn't belong to me and, hell, she's enjoying herself for once. I'd be an unforgivable prick if I got in the middle of it.

"We try to hang out a couple times a month. This is probably one of the last times it'll be warm enough to come out here and camp overnight, so we figured we would take advantage."

"Cool. It's good you're all still hanging out."

"You are more than welcome to join us anytime you want." I settle for nodding and giving him what I hope passes for a grin. All the while, I have one eye on her. She and Chloe giggle together like they've known each other forever, and if that was as far as things go, I would be glad for her.

If only it wasn't for Austin, who hands her a second beer once she drains her first. She takes it, smiling, and turns back to Chloe while he continues staring at her. Something bitter and dangerous churns in my gut, growing larger and more corrosive the longer I watch. This is her life. It's up to her what she decides to do. I have no business caring.

And this is Austin. He's harmless. Or he used to be—I don't know him very well anymore.

I can't remember the last time I got together with people and didn't analyze the shit out of everything they said and did. I don't have to think about it anymore. It just happens whether I want it to or not. What are the chances of him trying to get close to her? What are the chances of her being into it?

Brian raises his beer to me. "Hey, have you seen Becky?"

It's like a needle scratching a record, bringing everything else in my head to a stop. All eyes turn to me, even Tatum's, once she notices the change in the air.

"No," I mutter, shrugging. "Should I have?"

Dex barks out a laugh while Andrew whistles. "That's pretty cold."

Tatum arches an eyebrow but remains silent, sipping her beer instead. "I don't know what to tell you," I offer with a dry chuckle. "We haven't run into each other." Dex opens his mouth like he's going to say something but closes it when I give him a look that can't be misinterpreted. *No Becky talk.* Jesus, it's like every aspect of my past is coming back to haunt me all at once.

"They were pretty serious," Austin tells Tatum. She only nods, and when she raises the bottle to her lips again, I notice them twitching like she's trying to hide her glee. Terrific. Like I need her to have more ammunition to use against me. I think it's about time we get out of here.

Of all times for Austin to decide to make his move, he does so by snaking an arm around her waist again and pulling her in before leaning in closer. Laughing as he does. As if that's going to change the fact that he's going to kiss her, or try to. He closes in and her eyes widen at the last second. I can almost hear the breath catching in her throat.

And that's what does it. What makes everything around me go red. I drop the water bottle on my march around the fire, then take her by the arm and pull her away from him. She's wide-eyed, confused, sputtering. "It's time to go," I growl, glaring at Austin in a way that can't be misinterpreted.

"Wait... what...?" Her questions add to the general confusion, but I can barely hear them over the roaring in my head. The fucker is lucky I'm in control of my temper, or else I'd knock his ass flat.

"Why are you doing this? What is wrong? I had it under control!" Her feeble attempts at freeing herself mean nothing. I don't let go until we reach the bike, where I jam the helmet over her blonde curls before doing the same for myself.

"We're going home. That was a bad fucking idea."

"You can't just do this."

"Yes, I fucking well can. Or did you wanna go back there for that fucking slimeball to paw you? Is that what you want?"

"You don't have the first clue what I want!"

"Are you sure? Now come on, unless you feel like spending the night sleeping in the woods with those assholes." She chews her lip, her eyes darting back and forth between the bike and the campsite. Nobody followed us—I'm sure they know better. They'd better hope they do, anyway.

Once I start the engine, she knows she has no choice but to climb on behind me. "This is bullshit. You're not my father, damn it!"

"No, but I'm his proxy while we're here." All I hear is her derisive laughter in my ear as we pull away, winding down the trail leading to the road.

"His proxy? Is that what you're calling it? Man, you've got some big opinions of yourself, don't you?"

I need to get to the road so I can pick up speed and drown her the fuck out between the engine and the wind. This is why there's no getting along with her. She doesn't care if she walks straight into a shitty situation, so long as she calls the shots. She's taught me the meaning of cutting off your nose to spite your face. I'm surprised hers is still intact.

"You can't tell me what to do!" she screams, and her voice drills into my skull. "Aren't you embarrassed? You made a fucking fool of yourself back there in front of your friends. And you made a fool of me!"

Fuck this. I'm not going to spend the entire ride home being scolded. I pull over to the side of the road where the sun's angle makes the trees cast shadows over us. "Get the fuck off," I snap while removing my helmet and tossing it onto the shoulder of the road in impotent rage. "I'm not yelling over my shoulder."

For once, she does as she's told without arguing. "You can't do things like that!" she shouts, pulling off her helmet before stomping her foot. "That was humiliating!"

"I was trying to help you."

"How the hell was that supposed to help me? You dragged me out of there like some caveman and embarrassed the shit out of me! That's supposed to help?"

"That guy at the club did a hell of a lot less, and you hauled off and punched him. How was I supposed to know you wouldn't do the same thing to Austin?"

Her mouth snaps shut, her lashes fluttering like she's considering what I said. "I had it under control," she mutters, jamming her fists into her pockets. "It was no big deal."

"Were you going to let him kiss you?"

She snickers. "No. Not my type."

"You sure about that? Because you didn't push him away or anything."

"He took me by surprise!"

"You said earlier that you want to forget. You want all the memories to go away. Is that how you plan on doing it? Making out with some random guy you don't know?"

"I told you I wasn't going to!"

"Good, because you never know what will trigger you next. I've watched you freak out around men for weeks. And nobody could blame you, but Jesus Christ, you can't keep walking headfirst into situations that are going to set you off. Men trigger you."

She tosses her head. "Not you. You do not trigger me."

And in those few words, something shifts. Something deep. Something I couldn't explain if I tried. It's the sort of thing you can only feel. Like the sun breaking through clouds, only deep inside where everything's been dark for so long. Now, rays of light are shining, uncovering what's been hidden.

"The feeling is mutual." Reaching out, I take her by the waist and draw her close, making her gasp. "I'm only trying to help you. That's all I'm ever trying to do. You don't have to be a fucking brat about it."

"When I need your help, I'll ask for it. And if I didn't think I could handle things back there, I would have told you so."

But that's not enough, although she can't know that. She can *never* know. I don't care whether she could handle it, not really. At the heart of this, there's the burning jealousy still churning inside me when I remember him touching her. As if he has the right. As if he's anywhere good enough.

As if he could kiss her the way she needs to be kissed. The way I could kiss her.

When her eyes fly open, I realize I'm leaning in. Her body stiffens and I realize I've crossed a line. I didn't mean to do it. Since when am I not in control of myself?

"See?" I murmur, letting her go before she can feel my trembling. "See how you froze up? That's my point. You can't handle it." She looks at the ground, breathing hard. Is she buying it? She needs to. I can't have her knowing she has this hold on me.

I don't have to tell her to get back on the bike once I do after grabbing my helmet and brushing the dirt. At least she's no longer screaming as she links her arms around me. It's a silent ride back to the house.

As far as I'm concerned, it can't end soon enough. The less time she spends close to me, the better for both of us.

CHAPTER 14

TATUM

There was one good thing about living at my dad's: I had my own wing and could hide out for as long as I wanted with nobody bothering me. I'd creep out at night for food, when everybody was asleep and only one or two guards were on patrol. They knew better than to get in my way or engage me in conversation. That wasn't their job.

I could avoid people.

I can't avoid Romero much longer. Not in this tiny house. Not when I now know the floorboards in my room creak loudly enough for him to hear when he's downstairs. I might as well be a bug under a magnifying glass. I almost want to break out my old tap class moves from when I was little and dance my way across the room.

Instead, here I am, hanging out in bed and hoping I'll eventually fall asleep. I only tiptoed downstairs earlier today when I heard the basement door open and close through my own partially closed door. Pathetic? Yes. I'm wholly aware. But I'd rather be pathetic than face him.

He looked like he was about to kiss me. He really, truly did. Two days have passed—days I've spent holed up here mainly because I'm still furious with him—and I'm just as sure as I was that night. He was about to kiss me.

That's not the worst part. Not by a mile.

The worst part is, I wanted him to. I was surprised, sure, but I wasn't going to stop him. If he hadn't stopped himself, I would now know what his lips taste like and what sounds he makes kissing. How he groans and sighs. How he...

YEAH, I need to stop this right now, or else I will end up with my hands down my leggings again.

THE FACT IS, it's a waste of time to think about making out with that dickhead. To imagine what it would be like, locked in his arms, kissing him desperately. I'd rather kiss that nobody friend of his if that's what it came to, because Romero doesn't actually care about me. I'm just a job for him. I mean, he's certainly told me so enough times to remind me of how he sees this. Dad's faithful little dog. Obeying orders, telling me what to do, and pushing me around.

MY CHEEKS FLUSH with embarrassment even now when I think about the scene he made. I mean, I don't have to see any of them again. It's not like we have anything in common, really. But it didn't matter at the campsite.

Chloe is not the kind of girl I would ever have met before now, but she was nice. Instantly accepting. She has the sort of open, warm personality that makes you want to be friends with her. It's been a long time since I've met anybody like that—hell, Bianca might be the only one.

From the first day we met, I knew we'd be best friends, and I've never regretted that decision. It felt like we had known each other our whole lives. And when I think about it, Bianca was raised in a different world than mine, too—the daughter of a cop versus the daughter of a notorious arms dealer with a billion-dollar empire. Talk about your unlikely duos.

There was a moment, before Austin came in and ruined it, when I felt happier. More relaxed, and more present in the moment than I had in ages. Between that and the motorcycle ride, I was flying high.

But of course, just like back at the club and so many other times, a man came in and thought he had the right to demand something of me. The memory makes me grab a pillow off the bed and punch it the way I should've punched Austin. It was one thing to be flirty, overly touchy, but to lean in for a kiss? I did nothing to encourage that kind of thing. You let a guy hug you; he thinks he has the right to stick his tongue down your throat.

Still, nothing he did was bad enough for Romero to drag me out of there like a fucking caveman claiming his possession. I'm curious if he'll even bother apologizing to those guys for causing a scene in the middle of their party. I doubt it. Romero doesn't apologize. That might mean taking responsibility for the asshole things he does.

I'M ALREADY SO WORKED up that a sudden buzz from my phone makes me jump a mile. Instantly, my blood curdles, my stomach clenches, and my heart takes off at lightning speed. It takes a second to calm down once I remember I have Jeff's number blocked. The arrival of a text doesn't mean facing another nasty, threatening message.

HE HAS YET to go so far as to reach out from a different number. Maybe he's too stupid to figure that out.

BIANCA: How's it going? Are you doing okay?

ROMERO IS AN ASSHOLE. No, I can't type that. It's not like she doesn't already know what I think of him, but I can't give her anything to worry about. That would make Dad worry, making him call

Romero, and a whole bunch of bullshit would come out of that. I am not in the mood.

Me: Same old. Trying to pass the time.

Bianca: Did you read those books I gave you? I know that's not an exciting night, but I'm dying to talk about them with somebody.

The books are on the dresser, three thick hardcovers with bright, colorful, lush cover art. It's a historical romance series she first became obsessed with back at school, and the latest book came out over the summer. I eye them, unimpressed, but what the hell? I'm not doing anything else.

Me: I'm going to crack the first one open now.

Bianca: Awesome!!! You'll love them!

At least she's happy. One of us should be. And who knows? I might be able to sink into the story rather than obsess over what's happening in the real world.

After changing into a nightshirt, I grab the first in the series from the pile and settle in with pillows at my back. A cup of tea would be nice, but I don't want to take the chance. It's dumb, and I know it, but the idea of coming face-to-face with him is still too much to even consider. The longer I avoid him, the worse it will be

—I know that's true. When it comes to him, I guess I'm a coward. I don't know how to handle the weirdness between us whenever we spend more than a split second together.

I BARELY HAVE time to open the book to the first page when my phone buzzes again. I love her, but I have to roll my eyes. "Seriously, you could let me read," I whisper into the otherwise quiet bedroom before picking up my phone and checking Bianca's latest text.

BIANCA: Check your email. I just sent you something. I would have sent a physical copy, but I don't know your address.

SHE IS A NUT JOB SOMETIMES. Instead of losing myself in the story, I open the email app on my phone to find a link to download another book. In the message box, she typed, This is the first book in the spinoff series, so you can start it as soon as you finish the first three.

She has a lot of faith in how fast I can read, not to mention how much I will like these books. I guess she knows me pretty well and can assume. But I feel like I'm in school now. Will she expect a report once I'm finished? Like I'm doing anything else with my time.

BEFORE I CLOSE the app and try to get started again, another email catches my attention.

I lose my breath, staring at the subject. Re: Kristoff Knight

NO. No, not this. Not again. I can't take it. I need to pretend I never saw this. I need to take the phone to Romero and show him. He can handle it. I don't need this, and I don't want it. I don't want any of it. When will he stop? There's got to be something wrong with me, like deep down wrong. Why else would I tap the message to open it? Why would I subject myself to this?

TATUM — *you have wasted enough of my time. Attached, please find documents from my lawyer's office instructing you to contact them with any information you have about my son and his disappearance. You have ten business days to comply before this matter is handed over to the authorities. For both our sakes, you had better make the right decision before this gets ugly.*

THE WAY I throw the phone across the room, you'd think there's a spider on it. Hot, bitter tears fill my eyes. Damn him. When will this be over? Why can't it just be over? Why won't he leave me alone?

For one crazy second, I remember the knife block in the kitchen. Yes, that's what I need. I need some way to ease the pain ripping me apart inside. The pressure in my chest and my head is like a pressure cooker, ready to explode. I need to ease that stress, or else it's going to kill me. Maybe I should let it. Maybe I would be better off. God, what am I going to do? What am I supposed to do? I can't even see his ugly, filthy name without bile rushing into my throat and every little bit of strength I managed to gather around myself dissolving like cotton candy in the rain.

MY BODY HEAVES in one wracking sob after another. I need to take this to Romero, but I don't want him to see me like this. Even now, I can't stand the thought of him watching me fall apart. I won't let him. If I do, he'll never, ever leave me alone again.

Why is your instinct always to be sneaky? I can hear him in my head now, asking me that question, and all I can do is yank the pillow from behind my head, clutch it in both hands then scream until my voice breaks and my throat burns and I can't breathe. I scream until I'm too tired to scream anymore. Until the pillow is soaked with my tears, my voice a weak croak. Like a dying animal.

Maybe that's what I am. Maybe that's all I'll ever be again.

* * *

"Tatum!"

My eyes snap open at the sudden, sharp sound. My heart's in my throat, and somebody's shaking me hard, so hard I would swear my brain is rattling around.

"Tatum, wake up!"

My throat's so tight, I can't breathe. I can't speak. I can only try to smack at him with both hands so he'll get off me. I need to get him off me. I need him to stop hurting me. I need to get away, far away. He's too big, he's too strong, he's too –

"Tatum!"

It's that last shout close to my face that snaps me out of it all the way. I'm not trapped in that house with Kristoff, thousands of miles away from my family and friends. He can't hurt me now. Yet literally, the second that thought goes through my head, another thought follows. He can. He still is.

"Jesus fuck." Romero finally lets go of me, then turns away and lets his head fall into his hands as he sinks onto the bed. "You were screaming so loud, I thought somebody broke in. Shit."

I would tell him I'm sorry, but I still can't suck enough air into my lungs to make that happen. Slow, deep breaths. That's what I need. It was just a dream. A dream can't hurt me.

No, but the person who inspired that little nightmare could if he put his mind to it.

"What happened?"

He lifts his head and stares down at me, and I almost feel sorry when I see how worried he looks. It's almost like he's in pain with his scrunched-up face. Did I do that to him? Do I have that power? I guess I must. He's supposed to be taking care of me, and I woke him up screaming my head off.

"It was a nightmare."

"I figured."

He closes the book I left next to me—I never did pick it back up after I got that email, did I? Now I don't know if I ever want to pick it up again when all it's going to do is remind me of this night. "What brought it on, do you think? It's been a while since you've had one of those nightmares, hasn't it?"

I work my way up until I'm sitting with my back to the headboard, being that lying here while he looms over me is sort of awkward. Like I'm at his mercy. "Yeah, it had been a while."

"You don't have to worry about him anymore. You know that. He's miles away, has no idea where you are, and has stopped trying to reach out to you."

It must be the way I wince — I can't help it – that makes him narrow his eyes like he's suspicious. "What don't I know?"

Right away, I have to defend myself. "It happened tonight. I was going to tell you in the morning. I didn't think it would give me a nightmare like that." Just thinking about it makes me lose my breath again. I can almost feel Kristoff's hand around my neck like a steel cuff, the way it was in my memory-soaked nightmare. Tightening until I was sure his twisted snarl would be the last thing I ever saw.

"What happened tonight? Dammit, Tatum—"

I wave my hands before running them through my hair. They're shaking. I can't get them to stop. "Just don't, okay? I don't need to hear it."

He growls before taking a deep breath. "What happened?" he

asks in a quieter voice this time, which is basically a freaking miracle.

"I threw my phone." I feel pretty stupid about it now, but oh well. I point to the corner of the room, and he gets up and finds it on the floor. He brings it to me so I can unlock it and then opens the email.

It takes no time to look over the message before he barks out a laugh. "This? You're worried about this? He can't do shit to you."

"I'm glad you think so."

"I know so."

"You're a lawyer now?"

"Come on. You know I'd never lie to you."

"True," I admit with a snort. That's the last thing he'd ever do.

"This is a scare tactic. It's not even all that good. He can't hurt you. He can't force you to say anything. Between your dad and me, we will find a way to make this stop for good."

"He is never going to stop wanting to know what happened. Would you? If this was your son, wouldn't you want to know?"

. . .

"I wouldn't bully a girl over it. What, does he think you killed him out there?"

"Yeah," I whisper without hesitating, knowing that's exactly what he thinks. "He's expecting me to break down and confess if he hounds me long enough. Like we're in an episode of Columbo or something."

He doesn't see the humor. "This fucking prick. I swear to Christ, he's lucky I don't—"

"Enough, okay? I appreciate it and everything, but it's not worth it."

"It's like this guy forgot who he's dealing with. You're not just anyone."

"I guess that doesn't matter."

"No," he growls. "He's too fucking brainless to quit while he's ahead. But we've got it under control. It will be alright." He leaves the phone on the nightstand before awkwardly patting my shoulder. "You'll be fine."

"It's just… whenever I think I'm getting better and a day or even two passes without me thinking of him…"

This time, he squeezes my shoulder and doesn't let go. "Something like this happens and sets you off again."

"Exactly."

But now I'm back in reality, and the dream is fading with every breath I take. It wasn't real. He's not here.

Though, I still don't feel safe, and it has nothing to do with the nightmare. It concerns the man sitting next to me wearing nothing but a pair of loose pajama pants. It's not like I forgot about the body under his clothes. Who could? Seeing his bare skin, his defined muscles… It's different.

Flashes of my fantasy play like a movie in my memory, while I stare at him in the present. I was so afraid I'd never feel like this again. I thought Kristoff took it from me. Desire. Need. Feeling like I'm in charge of my body and my hunger.

But here I am, and I'm starving.

At first, I only put my hand on top of his. He quirks an eyebrow and snickers softly. "What are you doing?" he murmurs, staring like he's never seen me before.

I don't answer, at least not in words. I don't know what I would say, honestly. I don't think I could put my feelings into words without coming off pathetically tongue-tied, so why try? Besides, some things don't need words.

"Tatum..." he groans when I lean in and brush my lips against his bare shoulder. "You don't need to do this."

I can barely hear him over the thudding of my heart. His skin tastes clean, and it's warm. The muscle underneath it flexes when he tries to shrug me off. "You don't know what you're doing."

That's where he's wrong. "I know exactly what I'm doing," I whisper while cupping the back of his neck.

He groans like he's in pain and mutters something under his breath that sounds a lot like a helpless curse. I don't care about that. His sense of obligation to Dad, his feelings about me, none of it matters. Not when I want him the way I do. I never thought I'd want anybody again. I can't let this go.

"Touch me," I beg in the softest whisper. I barely recognize my own voice or the need in it. There's no pride now – what good has pride ever done me, anyway? "Please, Romero, touch me."

He releases a shuddering breath. "You know I shouldn't."

. . .

BUT WHEN OUR EYES MEET, there's a different truth. He's as hungry as I am. As much as I need his touch, he needs mine more. I can see it, feel it. It's right there in his flashing eyes. Let him pretend all he wants, but I know what I see.

"I KNOW YOU WANT TO," I whisper back, pulling him in until our lips are dangerously close. "Please. Kiss me. Touch me. Help me forget. Help me…"

A GROWL RUMBLES in his chest, making the hair rise on the back of my neck before he captures my mouth, and something inside me screams in relief. It's like he's set a match to a very short fuse, and it takes no time before I am burning out of control, moaning helplessly into his mouth when he sweeps his tongue over my lips and plunges inside. My body is singing, my pussy throbbing, my heart ready to explode.

HE BURIES a hand in my hair, holding my head still while his tongue works against mine. It feels so good I could cry. For the first time, I don't know how long I'm in control. This is what I want, and I'm going to take it. No fear, no shame, none of it. I'm doing this for me.

HE GROANS into my mouth when I start to pull him down until he's on top of me, braced on his palms. I lift my hips, fighting for more of him and more of this. It's been so long, too long, and now I'm a starving woman in front of a buffet, gorging herself on everything. Running my hands over his back, indulging in the feel of his muscles, raking them through his thick hair and moaning, moaning with happiness and want and joy. I'm not dead inside, like I've been afraid of for so long. I didn't know how scared I was until now.

. . .

My nails drag across his shoulders and down his back until they reach his waistband. Instinct makes me tug at it, working it over his hips.

And everything crashes around me when he closes a hand over my wrist. "No."

He lifts his head, panting, and that hungry look is still in his eyes. It's stronger than ever, as if he's ready to devour me. And that's all I want. For him to take me hard, to make me forget everything but him. This. Us.

Except when I lift my head, straining for his lips, he pulls back further. "What is it?" I whisper in confusion, breathless and aching.

"We're not doing this," he grits out through clenched teeth a second before that lustful gaze hardens into something I recognize all too well. Regret.

Before I can hold him still, he breaks free, pushing up and off the bed, stopping once he's standing next to it. His cock is hard as steel, jutting out in front of him. Then, for one crazy second, I think about reaching out and touching it – maybe he sees that written on my face, because he takes another backward step, his chest heaving.

"What?" I breathe, sitting up. "We both want this. I need this. I need you to touch me. Make me feel good."

. . .

"We both know this can't happen," he grunts, straightening out his pants and tucking his dick into his waistband. "It's wrong. I can't do this with you."

He's back to being the old Romero, the one I know and hate. The one with all the walls around him, the one who doesn't feel anything, who doesn't care about anything. Like I only imagined what just happened. As if the version of him I saw, kissed, and touched was just as imaginary as my nightmares.

The ache throbbing between my thighs with every heartbeat reminds me of how much I want him. Finally, for the first time in forever, desire instead of fear has me in its grip. The one person who had the power to make me forget my fear doesn't want me. Not enough to go against what he only thinks is right. I'm not enough. I never have been. It shouldn't come as a surprise — if anything, it's my fault for forgetting the way things are.

"What's the problem?" I ask, folding my arms. "You're not interested in damaged goods?"

"What?" he almost barks. "You know that's not —"

"I guess I shouldn't be surprised," I snarl. "Nobody wants something somebody else broke. I can't blame you."

"You know that's not it. Don't turn this into something it isn't."

. . .

"Get out!" I shriek, pointing to the door he left open when he thought he was rescuing me. "Get out! I don't want to look at you!"

He's smart enough not to say a word, only turning on his heel and leaving the room, closing the door softly behind him. Once he's gone, my body goes limp. I don't have the strength to hold myself up anymore, so I fall onto my side and hold a pillow close, desperate for the comfort that was almost mine.

But I don't deserve that. I'm not worth it.
And for the second time tonight, I end up crying myself to sleep.

CHAPTER 15

ROMERO

The most recent message from my Italian contacts brings a brief smile to my face for the first time today. We're ready to proceed. Finally, something's going right. There might be a light at the end of this long, dark tunnel. And it means having good news for the boss.

And for her. This needs to end. Now. Last night was a glaring example of why we have to get the hell out of here. It's why I barely slept after returning to my room. Why I've spent the day working my ass off to lay the groundwork for our plans to shut Jeff up for good.

My work has kept me from thinking, too. Brooding over her. Over the disaster I should've stopped before it went as far as it did. I don't know what I was thinking – I wasn't thinking, is the problem. I should know better. Why do I let her do that to me? I came so close. Dangerously close. I don't know where I found the strength to push myself away from her, but I owe my life to whatever impulse took over for my weak body.

I know precisely what Callum would do if he knew how easy it is for her to tempt me. I'm so fucking weak for her, it's pathetic.

This is why I am the way I am. It's better, easier, for everybody if I keep my shit to myself. Until last night, I believed I had control over this situation, the way I've controlled myself all these years. There's no room to let it go, to lose control. I know all too well what happens when I do. Once, only once, I unleashed myself. I came to the point where there was no hope of holding back anymore.

And where did I end up? In a position where Callum saved my life. If it hadn't been for him... I don't even want to think about how my life could've turned out. I wouldn't have been spending weekends camping with the guys or working at some garage. That would've been a best-case scenario after years spent in juvenile detention, and only then if everything lined up just right and I was tried as a juvenile.

Here I am, so close to betraying him after everything he's done for me. Guilt has made me put off the phone call I know I need to make today, but there's no putting it off any longer now that I know we're ready to move. The research I've done into Jeff and how to get rid of him is one thing, but it doesn't do much good if we never act.

Now, all I need is the go-ahead. Something tells me I'll get it.

Considering what almost happened last night, I don't have a minute to lose.

Now, it's a matter of sacking up and calling Callum. I'm paranoid as fuck that he'll somehow know what happened. He'll hear it in my voice. Of all times for my conscience to decide it wants to wake up and make itself known. I figured it was long gone by now —I sure as hell haven't heard from it in years.

There are more important things at stake. If this plan works the way we need it to, I won't be here much longer. I'll be able to take her back where she belongs, and then...

Then what? We go back to the way things were before? As much as I want that, I wonder if it will be possible. Now that I know the feeling of her body writhing under me, grinding against my dick, pulling at my clothes... I'm supposed to pretend like none of it happened? Is it possible to forget something like that?

Get your shit together. I sit up straighter and shake my head at myself before reaching for my phone. I need to get it done. It's not like he'll be able to tell from my voice that I came damn close to fucking his little girl last night. He doesn't have to know she hates me worse than ever because of it.

When you've spent years working closely with someone, you pick up on their habits, their ups and downs. You might not mean to do it. I know I didn't start out wanting to know everything there was to know about Callum's personality any more than I wanted him to know everything about mine. Ten years can do a lot.

Which is why he picks up on my twisted mental state right away. "Why do you sound like shit?" he demands once he hears my voice. "Are you sick?"

"Just tired." Because I had a sleepless night after I almost fucked your daughter, and now I've gone out of my way to avoid her all day because my life depends on it. Sure, that would go very well. He would be in the car on his way here before he ended the call.

"Everything okay over there? Is there anything I need to know about?"

"No. Sometimes…" I hate saying this, but it's better to lie a little than to end up with my ass in a sling. "There's a lot of shit I spent a long time trying not to think about. There are moments when it comes back, whether I feel like dealing with it or not. I'm surrounded by it."

"I wondered if that would happen," he murmurs. "I know it was a risk, sending you out there. However, it was the only location nobody but the two of us knew about." I wonder if he's reminding me or himself.

"You don't have any reason to worry," I insist, clenching my fist hard enough to hurt. I owe him everything, yet I was ready to throw it all away. It's enough to make me wonder who I am. Whether I'm the man I thought I was all this time.

"You don't have to tell me that," he insists with a gentle laugh, and the sound is a white-hot knife in my chest. I am betraying him with every filthy fantasy. Every time I look at her for longer than I should. When I imagine the sort of shit I don't need to think about while I have him on the phone. I can't seem to control my thoughts anymore. What is happening to me?

155

There's a reason I called him, isn't there? Fuck, I need sleep. "I'm sending you the plans I drew up. Next steps. I think we start ramping up and move ahead with the arrangements we discussed."

"Absolutely. You have everything secured?"

"I've been working with my contacts. They've always come through for me. It might take a little time—there's some red tape issues, and the local government out there can take a little more time to work around, but things should move along once I give them the go-ahead."

"And how is she?"

She had to come up eventually. "She's ready to come home." At least that's not a lie. "Tired of my company, that much is for sure."

"What, my daughter doesn't like being told what to do? I'm shocked. Where is she? Trying to get her on the phone is like trying to get an audience with the Pope."

I gaze out the window overlooking the backyard. Mrs. Cooper is out there tending her new mums. "She is next door, with the neighbor lady. Helping with her garden." It's a lie, but the alternative would mean telling him I haven't spoken to Tatum today. I'm sure she's in the house – I've heard her opening and closing cabinet doors in the kitchen. It's a change from the way she's hidden herself the past couple of days. I thought after last night, she would be more determined than before not to see me unless one of her limbs was hanging off.

But this is different. I didn't just piss her off last night. I rejected her. So what if it took literally every last scrap of my self-control? All she cares about is not getting what she wanted, when she wanted it. She wants to turn it into something it's not. To accuse me of thinking she's weak and broken and unworthy.

Because he needs to know, I add, "Jeff emailed her yesterday. Empty threats, obviously. That's why I'm doubling down now."

"That spineless motherfucker," he growls. "And he's avoiding my calls, the bastard. It's easier to bully a young girl."

"That's exactly it."

"Make sure she knows she has nothing to worry about."

"I'm doing my best." My best isn't good enough. It never was, it never will be.

"And as for those old ghosts," he adds, and his voice is even tighter than before. "Turn your back on them. Let them go. They have no place in your life now."

"I know, you're right."

"Does she know about any of it?"

"What kind of question is that? Of course, she doesn't. She doesn't know the first thing."

"For all I know, the two of you sat up talking one night, and you told her everything."

"Talking isn't something I do much of, and she doesn't care to listen."

"I should've known better. I'll review the plan you sent and get back to you, but you know you have all my confidence."

He couldn't have picked a worse way to end the conversation. I need to let go of this guilt. It's going to eat me alive if I don't.

Rather than head downstairs to work out, I settle for push-ups on my office floor until my arms are jelly. I can exhaust my body and forget the excitement of wanting and being wanted. How long can a man deny himself what he wants most? How long before he cracks? It doesn't matter. There's got to be a way to get through the rest of our time together without totally fucking everything up.

Eventually I lose count, finally collapsing in a puddle of sweat that's dripped from my chin once my muscles are past the point of exhaustion. There's something about a hard workout, the sense of wiping the slate clean, clearing my head. At least, that's how it usually works.

Now? Even though I'm lying here, dripping sweat, breathing hard, arms like jelly, I can't wipe away the memory of her moans. Her tight body moving against mine, stirring up every dark, dangerous impulse imaginable. There has to be somebody around here I can fuck to get the need out of my system. I'm not feeling particularly picky – I have no room to be when so much is riding on my ability to control myself. Any wet hole will do at this point.

Right away, I see how pointless it is to consider it. What do I do, leave her here at home? Right. Why don't I call Callum and tell him what type of casket I want. That's not going to work. I'm stuck fucking my fist until we're out of here and I return to some semblance of a normal life.

Fucking my fist while remembering the way she begged me to touch her. All the need in her voice, the desperation. She would've crawled over broken glass if it meant getting her lips around my cock.

I'm only human. How am I supposed to forget that? How do I pretend she never offered herself to me like that?

Her pleas echo in my memory as I walk down the hall and retreat to the bathroom. The TV is on downstairs—a laugh track echoes up the stairs. How much longer can either of us live like this? What I wouldn't give to go back and do all of it differently. This was never going to work. Not for either of us.

Especially not if even the first sting of icy water isn't enough to soothe my need. I force myself to endure it for a count of ten before it's obvious my hard-on isn't going anywhere, so I turn up the heat before leaning against the tile wall with my eyes closed.

It's not only about claiming her. I need to break her down. I need her on her knees, looking up at me with those big, green eyes full of fear and desire. I need to know there's nothing she craves more in this world than the feeling of my cock inside her.

I'm hard as steel and practically dripping by the time I give in and take myself in my fist, seeing her in front of me. "Touch me, Romero." A groan stirs in my chest and my strokes pick up speed. I've been pushing aside dark, dirty thoughts and memories all day, and it takes no time for my pent-up desire to become a raging inferno blazing in my core and working its way through my extremities until there's nothing but sensation. Sweet, all-encompassing sensation while I imagine doing all the things I could never attempt in reality. Not the way she is, how broken she feels.

There are no such limits in my imagination. I can hold Tatum in place with a hand around her throat while I pound her pussy until tears leak from her eyes. I can fuck her face while she gags on me. She's not such a mouthy brat with my cock down her throat, is she?

Release comes over me all at once, and I empty my balls on the shower curtain, panting and groaning and wishing there was some other way to have what I crave. This needs to end before jerking off isn't enough anymore. I'm already dangerously close to that point now that I know the taste of her lips and the electricity of her touch.

It doesn't take long to clean up after myself, then wash off. Steam billows into the hall when I open the door, wearing a towel around my waist. I look toward her room, but the door still stands open the way it did earlier. What is she up to? Why do I care so damn much?

Once I'm dressed and on my way downstairs, I remember exactly why it's important to care. She's sitting on the sofa, arms folded, legs crossed, and the top leg swings dangerously fast. The girl is cooking something up. She doesn't bother hiding it.

"It's about time you came down today—rather, tonight." She hurls it like an insult, as if that's a crime. I'm reminded of somebody else who used to sit like that. Waiting. Silent accusations which wouldn't be silent for long hanging in the air.

"Says the girl who spent two straight days in her room." I cross my arms the way she does. "Some of us still have to work. What's this about? I don't have all night." My stomach growls as if on cue, and I realize I haven't eaten since early this morning once I gave up on trying to sleep.

"I've made a decision."

"Congratulations."

"I'm going out again."

"The fuck you are."

"Does it seem like I'm looking for your approval?" She didn't sound so snide last night when she begged for my touch. The reminder is ready to drop off the tip of my tongue before I get hold of myself.

"You're out of your goddamn mind, then. Have you forgotten what happened last time? Do you need me to remind you?"

"My memory's just fine, thank you."

"Then what gives? Why would you do that to yourself?"

"Because I have to try. I have to. Don't you get it?"

All I can do is roll my eyes at her ignorance. "No way. You're not going anywhere."

"I'm not asking permission."

"Why are you so goddamn determined to hurt yourself? Can you at least tell me that?"

"Why don't you try answering a question for me instead? Why are you so determined to hold me back?"

"Oh, so protecting you is holding you back now? I guess you've forgotten the way you sobbed in that fucking alley."

Damn me to hell for the satisfaction that rushes through me like wildfire when she flinches. I'm tired, dammit, exhausted after trying like hell to help somebody who can't be bothered to help herself. "I'm not letting you put yourself through that again."

"I need this. I need to keep trying. And I'm going whether or not you want me to — so you can either come with me like you did before, or you can leave me on my own."

What is it going to take? Clearly, nothing I say makes a damn bit of difference. And that's what makes my blood boil. What makes me want to cross the room and haul her to her feet by her hair. I want to shake her until she understands. Whatever it takes. Somehow, I've got to get through to her.

"I have a better idea." I cross the room, savoring how she stiffens her spine and sticks her chin out like she isn't afraid as my shadow falls across her face. She'd better be afraid. "How about I tie you up and spank your ass for being a disobedient little brat? How does that sound?"

Fuck me. It's out of my mouth and there's no taking it back before it hits me. For all I know, that's precisely the kind of shit Kristoff did to her. What the hell is wrong with me, threatening something like that when just last night I woke up with my heart in my throat thanks to her screams?

My jaw clenches against the wave of regret that threatens to drown me. "I'm—"

Before I can get it out, she shrugs. "Don't bother making threats we both know you're unable to keep."

"Excuse me? You're making a lot of assumptions."

"And so are you. You're assuming I care about your empty threats – and don't pretend they're not empty because we both know they are."

"You might be surprised."

"Somehow, I doubt it. Remember, I'm damaged goods you can't bring yourself to touch. Have you forgotten already?"

"I never said that. Stop putting words in my mouth."

"Save your breath," she retorts with a shrug. This snide little bitch. I might as well talk to a wall. "I don't care if you don't want me. I'm sure there's a man somewhere who does. It's just a matter of finding him."

No, this is all wrong. She's drawing me into her game, testing me like the spoiled brat she's always been. Whenever I forget her true nature, she finds a way to remind me. I ought to thank her for bringing me back to my senses.

"What's it gonna be?" she asks, arching an eyebrow. "I'm going whether you want me to or not. You can't keep me in prison here. And something tells me if I called my father, he would agree with me."

"Now you're deluding yourself."

"I don't think so." Her chin quivers a second before her bottom lip juts out. "Daddy, all I want to do is get out in the world and try to get used to being around people again. I even told him to come with me so I feel safe. But he won't do it."

"That would be low even for you."

"Ask me if I care about your opinion of me."

I hate her for this. Pinning me in place, smirking at me the way she is now. What I wouldn't give to wipe that smirk off her face. To watch understanding dawn on that pretty face when she figures out she fucked with the wrong person. The girl has no idea what I'm capable of. She might as well be tap dancing in a minefield.

"Fine."

She narrows her eyes, and for one brief instant, I might as well be looking at Amanda. That's the look the woman whose ashes sit on the mantle would get on her face whenever she knew she was in dangerous territory with Callum but didn't want to give an inch.

"Really?" Her head tips to the side.

"Yeah, really. What, are you scared now that you're getting what you want?"

"I'm not afraid, especially not of you." It would be cruel to remind her just how terrified she was last night, so I won't.

"Then you better go get ready while I grab something to eat. I don't feel like waiting around all night for you."

She's still wary as she rises from the couch, giving me a wide berth like I would give to a snake I came close to. She has nothing to worry about, at least not from me. I'm not going to hurt her – she's too busy trying to hurt herself.

And I'm too busy imagining killing some dumb bastard tonight for the crime of touching her when she belongs to me.

CHAPTER 16

TATUM

I can't believe I convinced him to do this. But we're actually here, in a club two towns away, where there's no chance of running into anybody he knows. Neither of us needs that tonight. The energy between us throughout the ride is tense, electric. I'm surprised my hair isn't standing on end by the time he parks across the street from a club larger than the one I visited before.

I didn't choose this place at random. I wanted somewhere bigger, somewhere darker. Somewhere I could melt into the shadows and lose myself. That's what I need more than anything tonight. To lose my inhibitions and let the chips fall where they fall.

I know better than to try to talk to him as we keep a quick pace while crossing the street. It's like he's in a hurry to get this over with, marching with his fists clenched in the pockets of his leather jacket. I can't help but wonder in the back of my head what this means for him. What he expects to happen tonight. I only know there's something different in the air. Something between us. After what happened last night, it's not a surprise. We know each other differently.

And I'm going to make him regret rejecting me. Let's see how he likes being reminded of how many men wouldn't do that if they were in his place.

Because here's the thing: he can't pretend now. I know what's going on in his head. Whatever reason he had for stopping what was happening, it was against his will. For once, I have power over him. And I am going to take advantage of it.

There's something almost feral in the air once we step inside. A primal energy that pulses through me with every beat of the music that drowns out everything. I like it. I like how it rumbles through me. It touches some deep, dark part of me. I would like to get to know it better; the side of me now lit up, warm, and glowing.

"Dirty martini," I call out before he asks if I want a drink, while running my hands down the front of my short, tight, black dress. Nothing special, nothing to make me stand out. I could be anyone right now.

My heart's racing as I scan the crowd pressing in from all sides, the air thick with perfume and cologne and the sweat from countless bodies. Everybody's looking for the same thing, whether they know it or not. We all want to forget. It's just a matter of what needs to be overlooked. A shitty job, an empty bed, whatever. Tonight, in the dark, with the deafening music, all of that will be forgotten. If only for a little while. Tonight, we can be whoever we want to be.

And right now, I want to be drunk. I want to feel free. I want to take part of myself back for once and for all.

Romero thrusts the martini glass my way, and I take it without more than a glance at his stony, disapproving face. He's not drinking—big surprise there. Wouldn't want to let loose. He might have to admit he's a human with human weaknesses. He might lose the thrill of holding himself above mere mortals like me and everybody else here tonight.

The crisp, cold vodka helps give me the courage I need to hand him the empty glass and leave him behind without saying a word. I can do this on my own, and I will. I don't need him. But by the time tonight is over, he's going to wish I did. He'll wish he hadn't turned me down when I needed him more than I've ever needed anyone.

I have to fight my way onto the floor, sliding between dancers, jostling around before I find a pocket of space I can move in. There's just enough light to see by, but not so much that any illusions will be broken. Everybody's in it for escape, and you can't escape in bright light.

I like it. The darkness feels dangerous, but nothing beats the sizzle of breathless, toe-curling danger of finding Romero watching me from his spot near the bar. There are girls gathered on both sides of him, but they don't exist. Only I do. His eyes seem to glow, burning a hole through me until I flush at the intensity of his stare.

He wants me; I know he does. Last night wasn't a fluke. It wasn't a one-time thing. And it's not the kind of thing you just forget and brush aside.

The heavy thumping of the music forces me to move to the beat. I don't care who sees, so long as he does. He wants to play this game? I can play, too.

I raise my arms and cross them behind my head, grinding my hips. I don't have to be me now. I can be anybody. It doesn't matter how many people are around — they brush against me and move on. I even feel a hand on my hip more than once, but they may as well not exist. Because now that I'm out here and he's watching, only one thing matters: making him regret rejecting me. Making him forget everything he thinks he should do in favor of doing what he wants. Nobody looks at me the way he is now if they aren't fighting like hell against what their body's telling them to do.

Come on. What are you going to do about it? I run my hands down my sides, lost in the beat. Lost in the thrill of being completely, totally present in my body. Fuck, it's such a rush. Being in control. Feeling like me.

And I don't know if that's because he's watching and knows me. He knows who I am. He knows most of the worst things about me and still wants me. Maybe that's why I dare to do this — that, and the vodka running through my system on an empty stomach.

I freeze at the sudden touch of a firm chest against my back. Before I know it, there are large hands at my waist, holding me lightly yet firmly. "Hey! Are you here alone?" the guy shouts into my ear. I can barely hear him over the music and the overwhelming pounding of my heart.

Run, run, I have to run. My body goes ice cold all at once while a wave of nausea rolls over me. I have to get away. He'll hurt me if I don't get away.

This time, I'm able to think before reacting. I will not run. There's nothing to be afraid of – I've got a hold on this. Whoever he is, he just wants a little fun, and I'm safe with Romero watching.

I'm safe, but this guy is not. What started as something dark, brooding, and dangerous hardens into plain old rage — I've seen it on his face before, usually while the two of us fight. He wants to tear someone apart, doesn't he? Poor baby. I bite my lip, trying to hide the glee that bubbles in my chest, letting the stranger grind against me. What are you going to do about it? Come on. Do something, tough guy.

At first, he stays still as a statue. The only sign he's alive is the glow in his eyes that intensifies when I let the stranger wrap an arm around my waist and pull me closer.

That does it. I can practically hear Romero's resolve break.

My heart skips a beat when he begins pushing his way through the crowd. "Thanks for the dance," I call over my shoulder, prying the guy's arm from my waist. "I think you better go." I don't even know what he looks like, and I don't care. He did what I needed him to do. That doesn't mean I want him to get his ass kicked for it.

Lucky for him, he takes the hint and disappears again into the sea of writhing bodies while Romero moves toward me like a lion stalking his prey.

I'm not going to make it that easy. I back away, eyes locked on his, drawing him deeper into the crowd. It's easier for him to push his way through, as big as he is, and my breath comes in quick gasps as he closes in. He's looking at me like he wants to devour me in one bite. And I can't decide whether I want him to or not.

Turns out it's not easy to back my way across a crowded dance floor. I end up stumbling against a tight cluster of sloppy drunk girls and come damn close to ending up on my ass before Romero's arms shoot out to take hold of me.

Oh, no. It feels too good. Too right. Being touched even like this, when my body was already buzzing off alcohol and dancing and freedom.

His lips brush against my ear and send a shiver running through me. "You're playing a game you will never win," he tells me, his voice low. But he's wrong. I did win, because I got him out here with me. I proved to him and myself that he can't handle seeing another man touching me. He needs me for himself.

The arm that snakes around my back forces the air from my lungs all at once. I want to melt against him, to give myself to him like I tried to before—but no, I can't make it that easy. Not again. Even though his touch makes me weak.

My legs shake, but he holds me up, backing me away from the thickest cluster of dancers and into the deeper shadows near the walls. Yes, this is it, this is what I want, I won. Beyond that is the screaming of my body, my nipples hardening, and my pussy growing wet as my back hits the wall and he cages me in with his arms.

He's breathing hard, the heat fanning across my face. "You don't know what you're playing at," he grits, his teeth clenched, his chest heaving. "You don't have the first fucking clue what you're doing to me."

"Don't I?"

I can't help whimpering when he runs a hand over my hair, the side of my face and my neck. He cups my jaw in his hand before his caress becomes more assertive, demanding. The hand he closes around my throat threatens to cut off my air but doesn't. He leaves me hanging in limbo, waiting to see what comes next.

"Don't you get it?" He rolls his hips, grinding his dick against me. It's just as hard as it was last night, and he sucks in a short breath at the contact while my pussy throbs. "Don't you know how much I want to fuck you? Do you feel how fucking hard I am for you?"

Yes! Yes, I knew it! He wants me. Anything else is an act.

"But you deserve better," he growls, touching his forehead to mine. He sounds like a man hanging onto the last threads of his self-control – or his sanity. "You deserve everything."

"But I want *you*."

"You don't."

"Stop telling me what I'm thinking and what I want."

He lifts his head and stares deep into my soul. I have nothing to hide now. There's no reason to lie. "Touch me," I beg him again. "Please, touch me. Show me what you're hiding under that mask you wear."

He groans, letting go of my throat so he can run his hand over my chest, cupping my breasts before moving on, over my stomach — the muscles jumping and fluttering—then against my hip. His fingers press into my flesh. Possessive. Demanding.

Then he slides it around, caressing the curve of my ass and setting me on fire. I can't deny the way every part of me craves him. Body and soul, I am his at this moment. Surrounded by people, we're alone in the dark. Only we exist. Nobody else. Nothing else.

"More," I beg between gasps for air. "Romero, please. Make me feel good."

"Are you really sure this is what you want, Princess?"

Am I sure? I've never been more positive in my life. "Yes!"

"Then you look at me," he growls while digging his fingernails into my ass cheek. It's then I realize he's slowly inching the dress over my thighs until his fingertips brush against bare skin. He chuckles when I gasp and strain against his unyielding body. "Look me in the eyes so I know you're here with me. Right here."

"Yes." My voice is a helpless moan. I could be signing over my soul, and I would gladly do it because this is what I need more than air. I need him. His touch.

I'm left confused when he pulls his hand away just as I start to burn with need. I'm seconds away from screaming when he brushes the rough pad of his thumb over my mouth. I part my lips on a sigh, and he takes the opportunity to sink two fingers deep inside. "Suck."

Staring into his eyes, I do as I'm told, sucking his fingers greedily while imagining it's his dick instead. Hollowing out my cheeks, I run my tongue over them. The pleasure zings through me. Can anybody see us? Do I even care? Part of me hopes they can, that they're watching us. The insides of my thighs grow slick at the thought while Romero pumps his thick digits in and out of my mouth, his breath quickening until finally, he withdraws them with a groan. "Good girl." My body glows under his praise.

His trembling hand returns to my ass. His body is now shaking against mine while he works his way under my dress. He's almost as overwrought as I am — why? He's not a blushing virgin. He's probably been with lots of other women.

There's nothing shy about the way he chuckles when he realizes I'm not wearing panties. "You came prepared. I guess I shouldn't be surprised," he mutters, chuckling again when I whimper at his electric touch against my aching flesh. His fingers slip easily through my wet folds, and I moan but force myself to keep my eyes open rather than close them. I want him to see what this is doing to me. I want to be his good girl.

"What do you need?" He's breathing like a wild animal, ready to pounce. "Tell me. What does your pussy need?"

Doesn't he know? Can he tell? I bear down on his fingers, but he pulls them back, shaking his head. "Use your words. What should I do?"

His fingers trace my quivering entrance until I want to scream. "Touch me. Fuck me. Please, now!"

Fire flashes in those dangerously blue depths before he gives in and thrusts them inside me. I arch against him, my cries smothered by the music. My God, it's so good. How did I live this long without being consumed by the fire now spreading through me?

"How does that feel?" he asks, taking his time, even smirking at me when I jerk my hips to meet his strokes like an impatient teenager. "Easy, now. Don't rush it. I want you to feel this."

I do feel it, and I want to tell him, but can't put it into words. I don't even know if he could hear me. All I can do is ride his fingers, chasing the high. Being this close to him, entirely at his mercy, without an ounce of fear or regret.

"So fucking tight," he mutters, his breath hot on my skin. "So fucking perfect, Tatum."

And I believe him. I feel the truth behind his heated whispers, just like I can feel his fingers moving inside me, driving me wild. "Does it make me selfish that I wish it was my cock inside you right now? That I wish you were gripping me, milking me dry. Fuck, you drive me crazy..."

Not as crazy as you make me. Everything's coming together at once: the tension, the friction, the sense that this is so, so wrong – and that nothing has ever felt more right. Finally, it feels right. I feel right. And it's all because of him, because of this, because... because...

It hits me all at once, like an atomic bomb exploding in my core. The shock waves radiate in all directions, stopping my heart, and forcing the breath from my lungs. I can't take it; it's going to kill me. It's too much, it's all too much. But it won't stop. It rolls through me again, until I am laughing and crying. And finally, finally, I can put it all behind me. I'm not broken. I just needed time. And I needed him.

And he knows what I need now. I need to pant against him so my tears will soak into his T-shirt while I shudder and cling to him. I feel split open, exposed. I want to hide, knowing he'll keep me safe like always. He pulls the pieces together and holds them in his arms, keeping me close enough that I feel his heartbeat against my cheek.

Just like that, it's over. I fall back against the wall when he lets me go and steps away, straightening his shirt, wiping his fingers on his jeans and looking anywhere except at me. My legs are still weak, and I'm dizzy and out of breath. Nonetheless, he's gone. I feel it. He was with me, and now he's not. We're back where we started, with his walls in place.

And something in me cries brokenly. Just when I felt whole, he took it away. Again.

"You good?" I don't hear it, but I read his lips. "Can we go now?"

We might as well be strangers.

That's all we'll ever be, because I will never not be too dirty and used for him to really want me for more than a few crazy moments. Give him a moment to think, and he realizes he's made a mistake.

I'll only ever be a mistake.

CHAPTER 17

ROMERO

I've never been any good at the "morning after" shit.

There's a reason I've never stuck around after fucking a woman. Not in the past ten years, anyway. Get it done. Get the hell out as quickly as possible. I'm never a dick about it. Not that I deserve a medal or anything.

Before that, it was different. With Becky. We were kids who didn't know any better. I thought I was in love, though you would've had to set my hair on fire to get me to admit it. Even then, I doubt I would have. Only pussies talked about stuff like that.

She was the first—and last, until now—I ever felt anything once my dick went soft and real life came back into the equation. No more lust, no more hunger. Years later, I understand more than I ever could back then. She was light. She was a refuge. She was a break from this house's constant bleak, colorless world. I guess I figured we'd end up married one day, even if the idea never quite crystalized in my mind. Around here, kids sort of fall into situations like that. It was what you did. You found somebody, you started fucking around. Maybe she'd get pregnant and you'd end up an old man before your time.

Like my old man did. Damned if he didn't make me pay for it just about every goddamn day after that.

A creak from upstairs startles me out of what was so deep it was almost meditation. I've stared out the front window long enough for my coffee to go cold, one memory after another leading me through the dark, twisted map of my past. Just as twisted as my guts at that sound from overhead. We've been here for weeks and I still can't shake that instant, icy, sick reaction.

The sun has risen in the time I've spent staring out the window without seeing much of anything but what's played across my memory. The distant past, the recent past. As recent as last night, in that club. I still smell her on me. I can almost feel her tight pussy clenched around my fingers. Her soft curls under my chin as she trembled and cried against my chest.

As massive a fuck-up as that was, I almost made it worse. I almost held her too long. I almost buried my face in her hair. Almost kissed her. Almost promised to make everything alright, always, for as long as I live. I almost called her mine.

And hours of thinking and cursing myself haven't made what's in front of me now any easier to stomach. I made this fucking mess. Now comes the time to clean it up.

I'm already no good at talking, sharing feelings, all that shit. Add in a night spent with my fingers up the wrong girl's cunt, and you've got a recipe for discomfort – if not disaster.

Usually, I'm gone before the woman in question can ask me to stay. This is different.

I can't leave, but that doesn't mean shit. We have to talk, whether I want to or not.

You weak, pathetic piece of shit. Not the first time I've called myself that since last night. Not even close. She hadn't even finished coming when I knew it was wrong and wished I could take it back. If I live to be a hundred, I'll never be able to wipe my memory clean of her disappointed, confused, almost childlike expression as she leaned against the wall and fought to catch her breath. I hope I never forget because I don't deserve to.

The kitchen smells like fresh coffee and bacon by the time her footsteps ring out on the stairs. The sound stiffens my spine and tightens my jaw. It has to be this way. Every fucking time I let my guard down around her, something unforgivable happens. It stops now.

The hair on the back of my neck lifts when I sense her entering the room. Something shifts in the air. I don't have to see her to know she's watching me.

"I hope you're hungry." She doesn't answer right away, so I glance toward her and my stomach clenches at the side of her in nothing but a thin T-shirt that barely covers her ass and a skimpy pair of black, lacy panties. Her hair is tangled and wild on top of her head, and the faint aroma of the perfume she wore last night still clings to her when she walks past me without a word, reaching for the coffee.

"You should get changed." I keep my eyes on my work as I divide scrambled eggs and bacon between two plates. "Hurry, before the food gets cold."

She picks up a plate from the counter and waits until I look at her to deliver her answer in a single word. "No."

Just like that. No. Like I'm nobody. No explanation, no reasoning. Just... No.

Right away, the blood starts pounding in my ears. If this keeps up, I'll have a stroke. Fine. Some things aren't worth fighting about. I force myself to take a slow, deep breath before turning toward the table with my own plate in hand.

She plops down on one of the chairs with a leg tucked under her and picks up a piece of bacon, munching without saying a word or looking my way. It's probably better that she does not speak. I need to get this out without her bullshit arguments and childish reasoning.

"We need to talk — or, I need to talk to you." She lifts a shoulder, using her fork to scoop eggs onto a piece of toast. At least she's eating. Just how she can do that, I don't know, since my insides are churning like I'm sitting in a boat in the middle of a stormy sea.

"Last night." Her chewing slows but doesn't stop. "That can't happen again. We can't go back and change the past, but we can't keep doing this."

To all of that, she offers a single, flat word. "Sure."

"That's it. That's all you have to say?"

Still, she won't look up from her plate. She only chews before taking another bite of bacon.

Not this time. I will not let her get to me this time. She's hurt, that's all. I'm not going to make her feel any better if I lose my temper.

"I'm sorry," I offer. The words stick in my throat, but I force them out.

She takes another bite of her food and chews slowly before washing it down with some coffee. "What do you have to be sorry for?"

"You know."

"No, I don't."

"Tatum, you do."

She sets down her cup before drawing the leg not tucked beneath her close to her chest, propping her heel on the edge of her seat. I can't see what's happening under the table, but I can imagine it clear enough: her lace-covered pussy on display. She's determined to exploit every single one of my weaknesses. "Maybe I need to hear it from you. Maybe I need to know what you're sorry for. Maybe you don't get off that easily."

It was pretty easy to get you off, wasn't it? I won't get anywhere by throwing that in her face, even if the impulse is so tempting. Almost as tempting as she was last night.

No. It was more profound than that. She's tempted me before and I was able to resist. Last night was something different. Deeper. Primal. I was already standing on the razor's edge, watching her body writhe while another man touched her... I didn't stand a chance. There was no hope of resisting. The animal inside of me had no choice but to claim her. She's mine.

She isn't. She can't be.

"Listen. Straight up." I push my plate away, unsure why I bothered to cook for myself in the first place. "You have to know I want you to get through your shit. I want you to heal and move on."

Finally her gaze lifts to reveal hard, wounded eyes. She can put on whatever act she wants with everyone else, but she can't hide the pain she feels, not from me, not once I see it in those emerald orbs. "Because it's your job," she taunts softly. "And you're a good, faithful boy."

"Because you don't deserve to feel the way you do." Though when she puts me through shit like this, I have my doubts.

She snorts softly. "I'm so glad you think so."

"Could you not turn this into a fight? You know I'm right."

"Do us both a favor and stop telling me what I know, okay? Because you don't have the first clue."

"That's not true."

"If you say so."

"This doesn't have anything to do with what he did to you."

She flinches but recovers quickly—or pretends to, which is probably closer to the truth. "Who?"

"You really want me to say his name? I'm trying to do you a favor here."

"Do us both a favor and drop it. I don't need you to do me any favors. I don't need you, period." Chair legs scrape across the floor when she shoves away from the table.

"I can't be the reason you get over him." She only scoffs on her way to the sink with her plate. Do not look at her ass. I might as well tell myself not to breathe. "And it's not because of what he did to you. I need to know you understand that. I'm not going to let it go until you tell me you understand."

When all she does is loudly scrape what's left on the plate into the sink, it takes a slow count of five to keep from blowing up. In times like this, I wonder if she really is dense or just likes to see how far she can push me before I snap.

"It was pretty obvious how much I wanted you last night and the night before. All right? You've got me. I wanted you, and you have a way of making me react before I can stop myself. I can admit that."

"That must be so hard for you. Admitting you're human."

"I never said I wasn't. You're the one who insists on insulting me and turning me into someone I'm not."

"You're somebody who only cares about the job you're doing for my father."

"Since when is that a crime?"

"It's not." She turns to me, folding her arms, and the morning sunlight streaming in through the window at her back turns her blonde curls into a halo. What a contradiction with the hatred etched across her red face. She's so angry, so hurt. It started long before me, but I'm not helping. I never could. "Unless you hide behind it. You use it as an excuse to stop yourself from doing what you want. From acting like a normal, regular person. And don't pretend you don't hold yourself above other people who feel things and want things. You do. You shut yourself down, and you keep other people out, but you're just as weak and vulnerable as anybody else. So you hide. And that's pathetic." Every word is like acid burning my skin, burrowing its way deep into my chest and through my skull.

I can't show it. That would mean giving her what she wants, and I can't. I refuse. "If telling yourself that makes you feel better, then fine. It doesn't change anything."

All she does is scoff and toss her golden head, staring at the wall behind me.

"It doesn't. This cannot be. It shouldn't be. It would never work out, and you would only end up hurting worse than you are now."

"Do me a favor and stop pretending you actually care about how I feel. What you care about is what my father thinks of you. How it would look if you failed him. That's what matters. You want me to be honest and face a few hard truths? Why don't you try doing the same thing for once."

"You want to hear some truth?" She raises her brows, expectant. In the time it takes my heart to beat, I know this is it. This is when I tell her everything. Why there's no way we could ever work, even if we wanted to. How, when the chips were down, I couldn't protect the person who needed me most. How I failed time and again, until one night…

I've been weak before, but I will not give in to weakness now. That's what it would be: weakness. Unburdening myself in some immature, pointless effort to one-up her. To make sure she knows who she shares this house with, so she knows what I'm capable of, why shouldn't push me too far.

"Well? I'm waiting. Illuminate me."

I stand slowly, staring her down. I'm not the only one who pretends. She's pretending now, acting like she isn't terrified of what's coming next. Like she's not fighting to keep her body from trembling. "I'm not the man for you and never will be. Which is why this ends here and now. No more games. No more screwing around."

You don't need a man like me after everything you've been through. Why can't I say it? Why?

"It makes sense, especially if all you care about is your job. You're, like, obsessed with work. With my family. Probably with the life my father makes possible for you."

Her gaze bounces around the room while she snorts. "I mean, who could blame you after growing up here? Listen. I get it. You found a good thing, and you're holding on tight to it. Hell, I might respect you more if you'd come out and admit it instead of giving me this silly crap about not being the right man for me."

The contempt radiating from her is enough to suck the air from the room. I can't believe how deeply, how desperately I need to break her down. To show her the truth and shut her nasty little mouth for good. She can't conceive of the shit I've seen. What I've done.

What I did for her.

"Nothing I say will change your mind, Tatum. You can think whatever you want.."

"I will, because it's the truth!" She begins storming across the room, prepared to escape with the last word, but it's not that simple. She's not running away, not until we get one thing straight.

My hand encircles her bicep and I haul her close, hard enough that she almost bounces off my chest. Her face is a mask of pale fear and her mouth pops open with shock. Something dark and twisted rears up inside me. Yes. This is how I need her. Quiet. Fearful. I need her to know there's a line she shouldn't cross unless she's prepared for the consequences.

"You do not know the first thing about me, Tatum Torrio," I growl, torn between tearing her to pieces and kissing her until we both run out of air. I'm tempted to throw her to the floor and drive my cock into her until she can't do anything but scream my name. I want her so bad I can almost taste it, but the temptation is too much. "So be careful with the things you say. You never know what's going to set me off."

"You don't scare me," she whispers. The tears welling in her eyes tell a different story.

"And you're full of shit." I release her with a sneer. "Now go ahead, run up to your room and pout like the child you are. It won't change anything. What happened last night isn't going to happen again." I have to turn away from the blank despair creeping over her, leaving my stuff in the sink and heading straight down to the basement before she can come up with a nasty reply. She has the power to set me off, the power to make me the person I've been fighting to never become again.

By the time I'm finished taking out my rage on the heavy bag, it's smeared with my blood.

CHAPTER 18

TATUM

"On your right."

I'd swear the guy is a ninja. How does he manage to sneak into a room and startle the shit out of me when I'm only fixing a cup of tea? Not only that, but he's been working in his office all day, which means he walked down the stairs without me noticing.

Maybe it has more to do with how distracted I am. By what? Ironically enough, by him. I was too busy thinking about him to hear him. Go figure.

How many times do you have to hit something to bruise your knuckles the way he bruised his? It's been four days since we fought here in the kitchen, and his hand is still purple and swollen when he slides past me to open the cabinet above the stove. I only watch from the corner of my eye – I don't know why, but I don't want him to know I care. It's not like I really care, anyway. I'm more curious than anything else. I mean, I won't make him an ice pack or something like that. He'd have to admit he needs help first, and he would rather cut out his own tongue than ever act like a normal human.

At the edge of my curiosity is a slight sizzle of fear. His knuckles prove he is nowhere near as controlled and disciplined as he pretends to be. I know there's something a lot darker inside him.

Something so powerful it could flatten everything in a mile radius when it explodes.

"I'm gonna be busy the rest of the day. Work stuff." He pulls a box of bran flakes from the cabinet and a bowl from the one next to it. It's early afternoon, and he's eating breakfast. As far as I know, this is the first time he's emerged from his office since he holed himself up there before dawn.

"That's not unusual," I point out, because it isn't. He's busy all the time. What's the big difference? As far as I'm concerned, it's another day ending in the letter Y, though the schedule seems a little long. I'd ask what my dad is putting him through, but I know better than to think I'd get an answer.

"I'm just letting you know we're getting close to shutting Jeff and his supposed attorneys up for good."

"You're going to kill them?"

His head falls back so he can stare at the ceiling. "Why would you immediately jump to that?"

"Hmmm, I can't imagine."

"You're wrong." He looks past me toward the bright, sunny afternoon beyond the kitchen window. "I want you to stay inside today."

Also, it's not unusual, but he doesn't usually come out and announce it like that, either. It's sort of one of those unspoken things. I know he doesn't want me to go out. He doesn't need to say it. But obviously, all that does is make me itch in anticipation of getting out of the house.

"Why?'

His nostrils flare as he pours milk into the bowl, then slams the drawer shut after pulling out a spoon. "Does it make a difference? I'm telling you, do not go outside."

"Is there some big event that I don't know about today? An alien invasion? Are all the birds going to suddenly drop dead and start falling out of the sky? Wait, is it going to start raining pancakes?"

Irritation fills his dark features, "Why is it not enough for me to ask you to do something? Why do you always need an explanation?"

"Perhaps I only want an explanation when it seems ridiculous what you're asking of me. What if I want to sit out on the porch?"

"I'm telling you to stay inside. End of story." The cabinet door bangs hard enough to make me flinch before he takes his bowl, his feet landing heavily on the floor as he marches off. "I have enough on my mind. The least you can do is give me one less thing to worry about, okay? For fuck's sake."

Once he's gone, I can breathe again. He sucks all the air out of the room. He sucks every rational, clear thought out of my head, too. My life has devolved into doing everything possible to avoid him while cleaning this house like it's my sole mission. What else is there? Too much time has passed since Chaz's offer for me to call him and accept the job offer—and I don't want to, anyway. I get the feeling I'd spend most of my time pretending not to notice him hitting on me.

It's easier if we see each other as little as possible. All it took was a few moments in the kitchen for us to start bickering. I don't have the first clue what to think about him anymore. I should be disgusted by him after he was so threatening and almost violent. But no, my screwed-up self can't help wanting to get close to him because, damn it, I felt more alive when he threatened me. Even more than when I had at the club.

In other words, he makes me feel alive again, and I don't know what to do about it.

I take my tea to the living room, where my gaze falls upon the urn on the mantle. It's stupid. I would never tell anybody about this, not even Bianca, and she pretty much knows everything there is to know about me. But I would never admit even to her that I have this habit now of talking to Mom's urn.

Now that she's dead, I can talk to her whenever I want. Access was the one thing she never gave me when she was alive. Over the years, I got used to it, but when I was a kid? All these years later, I still shiver when I remember the nights I cried myself to sleep. Like my senior prom. High school graduation. Dance recitals, birthdays, Christmas. Sometimes, I would get a call, though most of the time,

I'd sit up and wait until my eyes burned and my head nodded. No matter how hard I fought to stay awake.

Now, I look back and wish she had never called, since she only gave me hope that she would call again. It's pitiful, but I was just a little girl who wanted her mom. I wanted what other kids had. That's probably why I grew so close to Bianca. She didn't have a mom, either. She knew without me having to say the words what it felt like to be the kid in class who didn't have anybody to make a Mother's Day card for.

I mean, I could have, but it hurt when she never came around to collect the card. Most of the time, she wasn't even in town. I stopped around fourth grade. That doesn't mean I stopped caring and wishing for more.

The sapphire blue vessel won't talk back, but that's all right. At least it's something to talk to rather than a vague mental image that only got weaker as time went on without a visit from her. Eventually, she was more of an idea that I knew looked a lot like me.

I'm careful as I lift it from the mantle, holding my breath and listening for a sound from upstairs. All I need is for him to come down and see me with the urn and call Dad and tell him I'm having a breakdown.

He wouldn't understand. I can't shake the sense that he's haunted by this house, but God forbid he would admit it even to himself. He'd need to break down and admit weakness to relate to me.

There's a soft, warm throw blanket folded in one corner of the sofa. I wrap it around myself and get tucked in with the urn in my lap. It's nice here, by the window, where I can look out and at least watch the world, even if I can't be part of it. I'm turning into an old recluse. Maybe one day soon, they'll have videos of me on the internet, waving to school kids when they get off the bus. I am twenty-two years old, and this is all I can do with my time.

"I don't know what to do," I whisper, looking down at the urn. "What do I do about him? I can't decide how I feel. One minute, I want to kill him. The next minute, I want to kill him because he doesn't want me. I'm starting to think that's always been the problem. I want him, but he doesn't want me back. Or he only says he doesn't, and somehow, that's even worse. I don't need that in my life. I don't need him in my life. I've got enough shit to deal with. But for some reason..."

My chest aches, and there's a sudden stinging sensation behind my eyes. "For some reason, he makes me feel better. He makes me feel like myself again. And it's sort of like when I was a kid, and I would just get used to not hearing from you before you would call all of a sudden, or take me shopping, or you would send me a present. And I would get all caught up in you again. All I could think was, this time would be different. This time, it means something. I think it would've been easier if you had forgotten me, and I had forgotten you. I really do."

A tear rolls down my cheek before I can catch it. "And now, I know what it's like to feel better. He makes me remember how it was before Kristoff. He reminds me of who I was and want to be again. And then he takes it away." I snap my fingers with a sinking heart. "And I'm back to square one. My whole life, I've been going through this endless cycle. I don't know how to make it stop or even if it's possible to make it stop. I don't know anything."

What would a mother — a loving, caring mother — say at a time like this? God, I wish I knew. I wish I had the first clue. Ultimately, I'm still the motherless girl, wandering around, wishing somebody would love her. Not because they have to, but because they want to.

Fuck, I'm a mess.

What would I want my mother to say to me now, if she was alive, if she cared? What would I need to hear? That I am lovable. That I'm worth loving, even when I'm bitchy and needy. Even when I'm at my lowest point. I would want her to tell me everything is going to be okay. Kristoff is gone, he's never coming back, and the big bad wolf can't get me because people are protecting me. Romero hinted at that. Whatever he's doing now, it's to get rid of Jeff. I have to believe it will work.

I would want her to remind me that I was safe at the club. Before all the craziness with Romero, I was really safe. The guy touched me, but he didn't hurt me. He didn't want to, either. We danced like I danced with so many guys before him, just a casual thing with no meaning behind it. And I lived through it. There is hope.

Thanks to Romero. Why does it always keep coming back to him? I actually shoot a dirty look at the urn like it's the urn's fault and not my tangled subconscious, throwing thoughts and ideas at me. I felt safe because he was there, watching. I felt safe because I knew he would kill anybody who put their hands on me. That might be a euphemism for some people, but I know better. He would literally have destroyed anyone in his path.

So the way it looks right now, I'll be fine so long as he's always with me. The man who punched a heavy bag until his hands bled, all because we had a fight. No big deal.

I might as well wish for a unicorn for my next birthday.

The sight of a girl walking down the sidewalk across the street catches my attention. I'm so bored; anything makes me sit up and take notice. What stands out most about her is how pretty she is — long, black hair with killer cheekbones that look like they could cut glass even from a distance. She wears the general neighborhood uniform of torn jeans, sneakers, and an oversized hoodie.

And she's looking at this house like she's waiting for it to burst into flames.

I'm off the sofa by the time she crosses the street, placing the urn on the coffee table and watching from the window. She's not actually coming over here, is she? I don't recognize her from that night at the lake or any other time I've been out around here. She tucks a strand of hair behind one ear, chews her bottom lip like she's questioning herself… then walks up the steps and crosses the porch.

And here I am with my heart in my throat, all because of some strange girl. It's almost depressing. By the time she knocks on the door, I shake off my flash of fear — but that doesn't mean I fling the door open, either. With the chain in place, I open it just enough for us to come face-to-face. The surprise in her large, dark eyes says she wasn't expecting to see me.

"Can I help you?" I murmur.

She blinks rapidly, her smooth forehead creasing in confusion. "Oh. I, um, I thought… I mean, is Romero around?"

Something hot and uncomfortable uncoils in my stomach. "Who wants to know?"

"I'm… a friend of his." She's just as guarded as I am, eyeing me warily. I've seen that look before. It's just that I don't understand why she looks this way. Like he means something to her.

"You're the girl living here with him, aren't you?" she asks. Her voice has nothing nasty or accusatory, but my defenses go up anyway. Hell, they were already up.

"I am, but I still don't know who you are." Or what the hell you think you're doing here. This girl has barely said anything to me, and here I am, wanting to claw her eyes out. And why? For what? Over him? What a waste of time that would be.

"My name is Becky. And I really would like to see him. Is he here?" She turns slightly to the left, eyeing the SUV parked next to the house.

Before I can come up with a lie, or even politely tell her to fuck off, footsteps ring out on the stairs behind me. Footsteps that slow dramatically before picking up again. "Becky. What are you doing here?"

I don't have to look at him. I can hear it in his voice, and now I remember hearing her name at the lake when somebody commented about Becky. They were wondering why he hadn't seen her yet. Nobody has to explain who she is or, better yet, was to him. It's all in the tone of his voice when he says her name.

And it's in the way her face lights up when she spots him over my shoulder. Unexpectedly, I feel like I'm intruding, and the idea makes me sick. If anybody belongs here with him, it's me, not this chick.

Suddenly, his hand is on the door, and I might as well not be here. He only has eyes for her. But as always, there's nothing on his face to show what he's really thinking. How he's feeling. Why would he want to do that? Why would he want anybody to know what's going on in his head? It's fucking infuriating.

"I figured if you weren't going to look for me, I'd have to look for you." It's obvious she wants to say more, but her wary gaze falls on me and she presses her lips into a firm line. Message received. Wouldn't want to speak freely in front of a stranger.

"Tatum... stay here." He talks to me like I'm a child. Or a dog. Wouldn't want to let me out on the loose, would he? This is pathetic. I'm sure he sees it in the way I snicker and shake my head before going upstairs, while he steps out onto the porch and closes the front door.

It might look like I'm throwing a temper tantrum or whatever he wants to call it, but not quite. If I can't listen from the living room – where he would be able to see me, of course – I'll listen from upstairs in the bedroom. No way am I going to pass up the chance to hear what they have to say to each other.

I tiptoe across the creaky floor, then ease one of the front windows and open a crack before crouching there, straining my ears and breathing as softly as possible in the hope of eavesdropping. This is what my life has come to.

"You can't just show up here," he mutters. He sounds like he does when he's pissed at me, and sadly, it sort of makes me feel good. I'm not the only one who gets this crappy, dismissive attitude.

"Is that all you have to say to me? Ten years, and I have to find out you're back in town from Dex? What the hell?"

That's right, girl. I don't love the way you looked at me, but give him hell.

"I have my reasons."

"I'm sure you do, and I would've loved to hear about them."

"Beck," he sighs. "Don't do this." Damn it, I can't see them. What does he look like? What is she doing?

"I just wonder why I don't even get a hello. Hey, Beck, long time no see. Sorry I completely disappeared from your life. Sorry I never called. Sorry you could've thought I was dead – which I did," she adds, fierce and bitter. I can feel her anger, and I feel sorry for her because I know what it's like to deal with him. He's always got his reasons, doesn't he? He's always got every excuse in the world for being the way he is, for shutting people out.

"I'm sorry about that." He doesn't sound like it, but I'm used to that.

"Do you know what would make me believe you were actually sorry? If you had given me the respect to come and talk to me instead of me having to seek you out."

"Well, now you have. Now you know. This isn't supposed to be some happy reunion. I'm here for business."

"What kind of business?"

"We're not talking about it." Because, of course, he's always got the final say, doesn't he? I'm still not a massive fan of this girl popping up out of nowhere and having the nerve to look at me like I'm an intruder, though I can relate. She's stronger than me, because I would've told him to fuck himself by now.

"I really am busy," he murmurs. "I've got a lot of stuff to do. I know it seems like I'm giving you the brush off —"

"Is it because of her? The girl?"

Dammit, I'm holding my breath, waiting to hear what he says. Is it because of me? I should know better, shouldn't I? But I'm a sucker, too, and I want him to say yes. Or at least, I want to hear it in his voice that I mean something, and she's only complicating things by showing her face around here.

"Her? No," he tells her with a laugh that squeezes my heart like a clenched fist. "She's nobody. That's not what I'm getting at."

Well, you knew better, didn't you? Sure, but the pain in my chest tells a different story. I mean, I have no illusions about how he feels about me. He's never tried to hide it. I might be good enough to get his dick hard, but that's where it ends. I'm an assignment. A burden he can never get rid of.

Why did he have to say it like that?

"I have to get back to work. It was good to see you, really, but please, don't come back here like this. It's too complicated to explain. I just need you to trust me, okay?"

"Yeah," she says with a defeated little sigh, making me feel sorry for her again. "Sure. I'll trust you." I don't back away from the window until I see the top of her head and watch her cross the street. Her head hangs lower than before, and her shoulders are up around her ears. He hurt her. I'm not really surprised, he's good at that.

The front door closes loudly, but I don't hear anything else from him. No cursing, no muttering to himself. All he does is climb the stairs and head back to his office without hesitating.

How does he do it? This girl obviously meant something to him back in the day — okay, so they were kids, and feelings change over time. But if there's one thing I know, it's how a person sounds when they're trying to hide what they're really feeling. I've practically made a career out of it in my life.

And she was trying like hell to hide how she felt about him.

Clearly, I'm not the only girl he's ever left wondering what I did wrong and why he decided to push me away.

CHAPTER 19

ROMERO

*W*hy?

That single word bangs against my skull like a drumbeat. Loud, insistent, enough to make me want to scream and tear the room apart with my bare hands.

Why? Why did she have to come here? Why can't the past stay where it is? Is that too fucking much to ask? For the past to stay in the past and leave me the fuck alone?

And why did Tatum have to see her? That's the question that sticks its blade in me the deepest. Why does she have to know Becky exists? It's only a matter of time before she starts bombarding me with stupid questions and assumptions – she's probably already got a thousand of them in that head of hers. Probably telling herself all kinds of absurd stories because she's got nothing better to do than think. I guess I can't blame her for that. I'm the one who told her not to leave the house, and she's hardly got anything to do. It only makes sense that my rules would come back to bite me in the ass.

I was on a roll, too. Coordinating with the Italians, putting together what we're preparing for Jeff. I was ready to give Callum good news tonight. To tell him it won't be much longer before his little girl can come home – if she wants to, that is. I don't have any control over that. I have no control over her.

Who am I kidding? I don't have control over a damn thing. I can't even hold the past at arm's length. It's going to show up anywhere it feels like, and when it does, it will always be at the worst possible time.

And it's going to make damn sure to stir up every painful memory you've spent years trying to move on from.

It also made sure to completely kill any chance I had of getting through the task list I set for myself last night before catching a few hours of sleep before my Italian contacts began reaching out. There I was, trying to keep a sense of structure so I wouldn't lose myself thinking about Tatum. Obsessing over her. Blaming myself for all the fuck-ups so far.

Some things you can't plan for. When am I going to learn that?

It's late by the time I give up on the hope of finishing anything tonight. All I've done since Becky left is think and blame myself and wonder how life would've been if it wasn't for that night. The night I met Callum Torrio and everything changed. How the fuck is it possible that I spent so many years never thinking about this place? About her? About what my life would have been if only a couple of things had gone differently. Like that movie Becky made me watch once, the one where the girl's life splits into two parallel timelines based on whether or not she made the train home one day.

I never thought about that movie again until just now, pacing the office floor. How many times have I done that today? I don't have a fucking clue. I only know it hasn't helped.

If I hadn't brought her back to the house that night for dinner.

If I hadn't let him lure me into a fight.

If I hadn't, if I hadn't, if I hadn't. If. Two fucking letters, but they hold a lifetime's worth of meaning. Guilt, regret, and maybe the tiniest bit of relief. I could've been trapped here for the rest of my life if not for that night. Now, I must wrestle with the comfort, regret, and hatred all burning a hole in me. I even hate Tatum for making me come here and dredging this shit up. It's not her fault, but I hate her for it.

I don't know where she is in the house. I only know she's been quiet enough to make me suspicious. I can imagine her spinning countless stories in her head, ready to pounce on me as soon as I show my face. What's the alternative? Letting myself starve? I must be losing it. I have nothing to hide from and nothing to fear. She doesn't need to know shit about me unless I feel like sharing, which I do not. I'm sure she knows what she can do if she's got a problem with that.

It turns out her bedroom door is closed, and the living room light is off when I look out into the hall for the first time in hours. There's some muffled dialogue and laughter coming from inside the room at the other end. She's watching another sitcom. That's better than overhearing a whispered conversation with Bianca– that, I would expect. I know better than to take this as a sign that she's keeping Becky's appearance to herself. It's only a matter of time before she decides to blab to her best friend. I don't even know why it pisses me off so much to think about it. Nothing she thinks can hurt me. And whatever she comes up with in that busy brain of hers can't possibly come close to the truth, anyway. Even if it did, what would it matter? I learned a long time ago, on a muggy night in June, about the worst things that can happen to a person. I've seen something as close to hell as I can imagine. Something that left me with no fear of some made-up place where sinners go when they die. And since that night, I've never feared an afterlife. After everything I've done, the lives I've ended, and the pain I've inflicted, I have no fear of what happens afterward.

The first floor is dark, full of ghosts that tug at my sleeve and beg for my attention as I walk barefoot across the floor until I reach the kitchen, where Tatum left the light on over the stove. She taped a note to the range hood, a piece of scrap paper covered in her large, loopy handwriting. Left you some chicken and rice in the oven if you want it. When I open the door, I find a small Pyrex pan covered in foil in the warm oven.

Even that sets my teeth on edge, leaving me disgusted with myself. I can't accept a small gesture like this without wondering what's behind it. What's in it for her? Or is it because she feels sorry for me? She's not stupid – I'm sure she put it together. Becky, being my ex, and my reaction down at the lake when her name came up. What, does she think I need comforting now? A friend? For fuck's sake.

I'm not hungry – an empty stomach doesn't mean I feel like going through the motions. Instead of pulling the dish from the oven, I turn off the heat, then pull the note from the range hood and crumple it in my fist before tossing it in the trash can. I need something a hell of a lot stronger than chicken and rice to get me through the darkness I'm trapped in.

I don't know what makes me think about the bottles under the sink. I haven't looked at them since the day we got here, when I performed sort of a tour, checking to make sure what I requested was in place. I haven't given them another thought until now, when I reach under the counter into the narrow space not big enough to store much of anything but a few liquor bottles. Considering I don't drink, I'm not sure why I made it a point to have them here.

Deep down inside, I probably knew it was inevitable. There would have to come a night when I would need a drink badly. If Tatum's either too afraid to face me, or too pissed that I dismissed her earlier when Becky was here, I'm safe. I won't make a mistake like turning to her for forgetfulness in a drunken stupor. Yes, that's what I want more than anything, to forget. To sink myself deep in her tight, wet heat and obliterate every other thought from my mind.

Since I can't do that, I settle for uncapping the whiskey and pouring myself a drink – then making it a double. "Why not? I'm not driving," I mutter to myself, snickering before I raise the glass to my lips. There's no savoring the taste. There's only downing it in one quick gulp. It's the burn I savor, the way the liquor carves a flaming path through me. I stare at my bruised knuckles in the light over the stove. Maybe I have a thing for pain. Maybe I know I need to be punished. If anybody does, it's me. Thinking I could turn my back on my failures, and that would somehow magically make them disappear. There isn't a punishment severe enough to make up for that stupidity. That laziness.

I finish off the glass and pour another, and I don't stop until the amber liquid nears the rim. I don't deserve oblivion, but I crave it with every part of me as I down another mouthful, then another, gasping for breath after swallowing.

Reality comes crashing down on me just as my senses become mercifully dull. Shit. I was supposed to touch base with Callum tonight. I should've done that before I started tearing my way through this bottle. Before I go too fuzzy, I pull out my phone, determined to get it over with so I can go back to drowning my sorrows. My pitiful, pathetic, fucking sorrows.

He answers immediately. "What's the good news?"

I can't hold back a soft laugh at his hopeful greeting. Doesn't he know by now there's no such thing? Everything has a double edge. "We're closer, but not as close as I wanted to be by the time I called you tonight. Almost there, though. There's a few loose ends left to tie up."

At first, I take his silence for disapproval. I can see him at his desk in his quiet office, with the grounds spread out beyond the window. With Jack and the rest of them now dead, I'm sure it's peaceful there. He's no longer wrestling with demons, so he has the bandwidth to scrutinize me.

Instead of voicing disappointment, he asks, "Are you feeling alright? You don't sound like yourself. And this isn't the first time I've had to say that."

"Not to worry. Everything out here is under control." There I go, lying to the man I owe my life to. I've repeatedly hurt his daughter, knowing he trusts me, telling myself at least I haven't given in. At least I haven't fucked her. Like that makes me a saint. Like that undoes the pain I've caused with all this back-and-forth bullshit.

"Is it that bad?"

"Is what that bad?"

"Do I need to talk to her? If she's driving you to drink, we have problems."

Like I didn't already feel like a piece of shit. He's blaming it on her. "No, really. I'm going a little stir-crazy, that's all. And I figure there's nothing else to do, so why not have a drink?"

"So long as she's not pushing your buttons."

"That's what she does best," I admit with a soft chuckle. "It's nothing I can't handle."

"Good. And she's doing well?"

"She's watching TV in her room. She's fine." I found Amanda's urn on the coffee table. No, he doesn't need to hear about that. I don't know for sure what it means, anyway. Only that she's been messing with it. Thinking about her worthless mother yet again.

"Good. Let her know we're thinking about her." He pauses again, and I can almost hear his hesitation. Asking himself whether he wants to share what's come to mind. "Don't tell her I told you–I want to do it myself–but she's going to have a baby brother."

"You're not my brother! Get your own dad–leave mine alone!" I close my eyes, hoping to shut out the crystal-clear memory of a twelve-year-old Tatum screaming those words in my face. Shrieking them. Shaking with rage, tears rolling down her cheeks.

"That's great news," I tell him, even if I don't feel it. It isn't that I'm not glad for him – he's wanted a son for years, the way any man in his position would. A son to pass things down to, a son to build a legacy for. It's not that he doesn't care for Tatum, but... he's a creature of his world. He grew up in this one, and now he lives somewhere else. He has an empire to pass down.

It's better that we end the call quickly, because I'm feeling a little dizzy by the time I do. I welcome the sensation and even finish what's left in my glass, hoping to make it more intense. Maybe I'll get so drunk I'll forget everything. Even my name. My past, my mistakes, my failures. So many fucking failures, I'm starting to lose count. Becky is one in a long line of them stretching back ten years.

No, longer than that. I should've done everything I could to stop things before they got out of control. I should have protected the people I loved instead of being a stupid, cocky kid with his head wedged so far up his ass, he couldn't see what was so plainly coming down the tracks. Like a freight train with its lights burning and the engineer blaring the horn. It was inevitable. I was just too stupid to see it.

"Honey, you're going with him. He's going to take you to live with him now."

I wander through the dark living room, staring at the place I stood while my mother held my face in her hands for the last time. I couldn't bear to look her in the eye, but I forced myself to do it. I wouldn't let myself look away. Because even then, I knew it was all my fault.

"Where is he taking me? When can I come home? What about—"

"Honey, you know the answer to that." A single tear squeezed its way from her swollen eye and down her cheek. "You can't ever come back."

And I didn't. Not until she was already dead and gone. Not until I was already a different person than the confused, angry, bitter child who only thought he was a man.

And then Callum placed a hand on my shoulder. I had never met a man like him before. He was dressed so well. His dark hair was so neatly trimmed, he wore clothes that even to my untrained eye looked expensive – a hell of a lot nicer than anything I had ever seen around the neighborhood, that's for damn sure. And when he spoke, his voice had a quiet sort of power. Right away, I knew this was not a man I wanted to disappoint. For the first time in my life, it wasn't because I was afraid of what would happen if I did. There was no fear at all. At least, not of him.

"I don't want to leave you. What happens to you?"

My mother's words ring out loud and clear as I climb the stairs, gripping the banister when I almost lose my balance. "I'll be fine. So long as I know you're safe and cared for, I'm happy." And that's why, even though she had tears in her eyes and her voice shook, and all I wanted to do was hide from the world, I said goodbye to her and followed Callum out to his car in the middle of the night. I tried to pretend I couldn't hear her crying.

I hear it now, just like I heard it so many nights, coming from the room Tatum now sits in. I didn't tell her. I couldn't tell her. What it did to me, waking up and hearing her screams coming from in there when she was having her nightmare. How everything came rushing back all at once and left me sick and sweating as I tore my way down the hall. How she wasn't the only one who needed a little comfort that night.

"Shit!" I growl when my knee hits the corner of my bed. I grab it, hissing through my teeth, and lose my balance on one foot. I try to fall onto the bed but only slide off, instead, landing on my ass on the hardwood floor. "Fuck!"

"What the hell is going on out here?" I hear her before I see her, feet pounding down the hall. "Jesus Christ, are you trying to tear the house down?"

She stops in the doorway, and first, her eyes dart around the room. I know why, even now, when I can't stand up. She's never seen the inside of this room before. There's nothing special about it. I simply don't like having people in my space.

Finally, she looks at me. "What happened? Are you hurt?"

"No, I'm fine. Go back to your room." Focus. You've got this. I put both hands on the bed and push myself up until I'm kneeling, but that makes my sore knee ache and I suck in a pained breath.

"No way… wait, are you drunk?" She puts her hand over her mouth and a giggle slips from behind it. "Seriously?"

"Shut up."

"All the years I've known you, and I've never seen you like this." She laughs again. "I didn't know you had it in you!"

"Go to your room. I'm fine." I push myself up until I'm standing, but the room tilts and I grab for the nightstand. It's been too long since I last drank like this.

"I hate to state the obvious, but you're not fine." She stops laughing and comes in, reaching for me. "Let me help you."

"I don't need help."

"Right, and the sky isn't blue." She's loving this, isn't she? Seeing me weak. "Come on, let's put you to bed."

"Laugh it up," I mutter.

"Oh, I will."

She pulls back the blankets then guides me until I'm sitting on the edge of the bed. "So, is this a new side of you I'll see often? I mean, you sent your friend home pretty quick and then decided to get drunk."

"I knew it," I mumble. Why the hell is it so hard to pull off this T-shirt? She tries to help, but I slap her hands away. "I knew you would ask about her."

"Is she coming back?"

I snort and shake my head, but that only makes the room spin. "You're so jealous."

"Am not."

"Yeah, you are. You can't stand not knowing about her or if she means anything to me."

"If she likes you, then she must be crazy." She leaves the room, and I fall back against the pillows. That's a good idea, since the room doesn't spin as much when I'm like this.

I close my eyes, but they only snap open once she returns. "Water. Drink it." She leaves two bottles on the nightstand. "Ibuprofen. You're going to want to take this." She leaves that with the water, then picks up my legs and drops them onto the bed.

"I know what to do when I'm drunk." She starts pulling the blankets over me and I pull them out of her hands.

"Sure, sure. Just let me take care of you for once, okay? I might never get the chance again."

"I'm so tired." The words slip out before I can stop them. I didn't mean to say that. All my thoughts are coming out before I can stop them. And I don't want to. "I'm tired in my soul. Been tired for such a long time. Can't remember when I wasn't."

"I'm not surprised," she whispers. Her touch is gentle and welcoming as she brushes hair away from my forehead. "You can't always handle everything at once. That's all you ever try to do. You're only one person, and I know you like to act like you aren't human, but you are, and you can only do so much."

"You should go now." Because if she doesn't, I might have to touch her, and once I start, I'll never be able to stop.

"Tatum?" I blurt when she reaches the doorway.

She turns back to look down at me. "Yes?"

"I wasn't trying to take your dad away from you. I never wanted that."

"Huh?"

I force my eyes open wide and lift my head. "You yelled that at me. Years ago. Told me… to get my own dad. I wasn't trying to take him."

"Jesus," she whispers. "What made you remember that?"

My head hits the pillow again when I run out of strength. "I don't want to hurt you. I've never wanted to hurt you. You know that, right? I need you to understand that."

"Yeah," she whispers. "I know. And everything's gonna be okay. Just get some sleep."

I want to tell her I don't have a choice, since my eyes are already starting to close before I can get the words out. In the back of my memory, there's a single scream muted by the years between then and now. "Don't!"

Darkness mercifully closes around me before I remember anything else.

CHAPTER 20

TATUM

*H*e's going to be hurting today.

Even though I feel bad for him when I imagine the sort of hangover he's going to be fighting, I can't help but smile to myself when I get out of bed. He's human, after all. He's not the cold machine he pretends to be. For once, I was the one wholly in control and he was the stumbling, awkward mess.

An awkward mess who doesn't want to hurt me. I don't know where that came from, but I want to believe he meant it. I want to believe it so much I almost hate myself for it. When am I going to stop hoping for more than he can give me?

That's the question I can't get out of my head as I go through the motions of my day. Cleaning a little, reading a little. Thinking about what could have triggered him to get wasted when I have never seen him even slightly tipsy in the past ten years. All the times he had to drive me home when I was drunk and sloppy. All the snide little comments, the way he would deliberately raise his voice when he knew I was hungover and hurting the next day. I shouldn't have been so nice to him last night. Maybe I'm growing or something.

It had to be the girl. Becky. Does he still have feelings for her? That's a stupid question. It's been ten years—that's a long time to hold on to emotions, but then I guess he wasn't expecting all the memories and stuff to return. That's probably what did it.

And I'm probably overthinking it.

He finally creeps downstairs around noon, though I've heard him up there for a couple of hours at least. I'm positive he's trying to avoid me after last night—he's lucky I'm feeling generous and kind, since I could have a lot of fun teasing him and slamming things around. I've earned that after all his petty insults over the years.

Instead, I stay on the sofa with my nose buried in the second of the books Bianca recommended. They really are good. So good I can almost pay attention to what I'm reading while he shuffles around the kitchen, fixing coffee and toast in slow motion. The few glimpses I manage to sneak tell the tale of a man who profoundly regrets last night. His hair is messy, sort of flat on one side and sticking out on the other. It's totally unlike the way he usually keeps it neat and combed. He's wearing the jeans he was wearing last night, too, and they're wrinkled and hang dangerously low on his slim hips. He's still shirtless, which is a shame because I keep wanting to sneak a look at the muscles I've run my hands over.

He's moving slowly, the way you move when you're afraid the whole world will shatter unless you're careful. I would offer to make him a greasy breakfast sandwich since that will help better than toast, but I don't want him taking it the wrong way. Besides, we need to go to the store, anyway. The kitchen's a little sparse, and he's been so busy with whatever he's working on that we haven't gone. And God forbid I go out by myself.

The thought sparks an idea that I can't help pursuing. Before he's halfway up the stairs with his coffee and toast, I blurt out, "Is it okay if I go to the store? I was going to make spaghetti for dinner, but we're out of a lot of things."

"I'm not in the mood for food," he tells me without looking my way. It seems like he's totally focused on getting up the stairs.

"You will be later, and what am I supposed to eat?"

"Yeah, whatever. Just come straight back." He must really be in bad shape if he agreed that fast. And how pathetic is my life that a touch of excitement runs through me knowing I can go out on my own? To the grocery store, of all places. Once he's in his office, I hop off the sofa and rush upstairs to get changed out of my hoodie and leggings.

It's a cloudy, chilly day, but it somehow feels invigorating. As much as I love summer and sitting out at the pool, I prefer this weather. There are lots of leaves crunching under my boots, and a handful of houses I pass on my way to Main Street show off pumpkins and potted mums on the front porch. There's almost a spring in my step by the time I turn toward Main Street and head for the little grocery store. One thing this town could use is a coffee shop—call me basic, but it would be nice to pick up a pumpkin latte on the way back.

Maybe I should bring that up to Dad, since he's behind the renovations around here. I wonder how many other little secrets he's kept to himself... then decide it's better that I not know.

The small store isn't busy at this time on a weekday. Most people are probably at work. I grab a basket and thank the universe for good timing, since I don't mind running errands, but that doesn't mean I feel like elbowing people out of the way for a box of pasta.

I need to keep it simple, being that I'll have to carry the bags home and don't want to end up like Mrs. Cooper, juggling bags so full they're ready to burst. I should stop over and say hi. To hell with Romero's weird dislike for her. She's a nice lady who seems lonely. I know that feeling.

How is it possible that the entire store smells like lunch meat? The odor has seeped into the paneled walls, the drop ceiling, and the chipped tile on the floor. I wonder if people used to coming in here even smell it anymore.

I'm still wondering about it when I round a corner and start down the aisle where sauces and canned goods are stocked. Maybe I'll pick up the potato soup I was craving the last time we had a cloudy, gloomy day—I doubt Romero will be in the mood for an early dinner, so a late lunch won't hurt me. Wow. I'm almost feeling domestic, making me snicker at myself.

I do so loudly enough that the girl stocking cans at the other end of the aisle glances over before going back to her work. Seeing her profile and the long, black ponytail paired with those killer cheekbones makes my breath come short. Unlike yesterday, she's wearing a dark blue uniform smock over a long-sleeved t-shirt, and a pricing gun is sticking out of her back pocket, but otherwise, she looks just the same.

What are the chances? Becky.

My body's tingling as I pretend to go back and forth between two types of sauce. There's a decision to make here. Do I say something? Do I pretend I didn't notice her? I might never get another chance to talk to her—though what the hell do I say? Do I have any right?

In the end, curiosity is stronger than politeness. And it's not like I'll ever have to see her again. I doubt Romero would invite her over. Even though I have no idea what to say or why this is so important, I head her way with my heart pounding.

"Hi," I murmur once I reach the wheeled cart stacked with cans. This is a bad idea. It's too late now.

At first, when she glances at me, there's no recognition. I'm another customer wanting some of her time. "Can I help you?" she asks before grabbing another couple of cans.

Then she stops and stares straight ahead to the back of the shelf. "Oh." That's it. One word, and it's barely even a word.

"I didn't come here looking for you, I swear. I'm just grabbing some food."

She turns sharply, taking more cans and sliding them onto the shelves like it's the most essential thing anyone's ever done. "If you need help finding something, let me know."

"Do you have a minute? Just a minute, I swear."

"I really don't." She looks over my shoulder, then down toward the registers. "I'm sort of working..."

"Can I talk while you're doing this?"

"Sure, but I'm really busy, and I don't need you..." She sighs sharply before slapping a can of tomato soup onto the metal shelf.

"I don't need you to say anything, okay? You don't owe me answers."

Why do I feel like I do, then? I doubt I would care if I hadn't listened in on their conversation. I know he hurt her, and that's a feeling I know too well. "It's just... I didn't feel like we started off on the right foot yesterday."

Her mouth barely moves when she mumbles, "We don't have to start off on any foot. I was there to see him, not you."

"I know, and I'm sorry if I seemed..."

"I was a stranger showing up out of nowhere, and obviously, he never mentioned me, so your reaction made sense."

"That's the thing. Romero never mentions anything. And just so you know, nothing is going on between us. It's just... business." I hate how the word sticks in my throat.

"Sure." She snickers and shakes her head but still won't look at me. "I heard he was being kind of weird about what he does now. Like it's all some big secret."

"I know. I just... I just wanted you to know that. And it's not your fault," I add, seeing as I'm an idiot who doesn't know when to leave well enough alone. "I'm sure you didn't do anything wrong. He treats me like that, too."

"Like what?" Now she stops after plopping a pair of cans on the shelf, turning to me. "How did he treat me? How would you know? Did he tell you about it?"

I am making a complete mess of this. "Okay, so maybe I listened from upstairs. Not because of you, because of him. I have to spend all this time with him, though I don't know anything about him. And whenever I try, he shuts me down. I just wanted to know if he would do the same thing to you or if maybe I could learn a little something about him."

"Congratulations, now you know. Romero treated me the same way."

"I'm sorry," I whisper as she goes back to work. "I know how it feels. It's the worst, isn't it? When you just want to talk to somebody, and they act like you're the enemy."

"Ten years." She stops again, staring at the shelf. I get the feeling she sees something else. The past. "He was gone for ten years. He didn't say goodbye. Nobody knew what happened to him. And then he just… shows up with no explanation, no hello, no anything." Finally, her voice trembles with emotion.

"He's infuriating."

"Yeah. He's infuriating." She stares at the floor, and her breath is shaky. "What do you want to know about him?"

"Oh, no. You don't have to…"

"No, really. What do you want to know? Because seriously, screw him. He left me at probably the worst time possible." Her voice shakes again, and I wish I had never come over here. It's not worth whatever this is doing to her.

"I'm sorry."

She shrugs, eyeing me with a shrewd expression that makes me feel sort of exposed. "So, you two work together?"

"Not exactly. He works for my dad." What am I thinking? Nobody's supposed to know anything about me, or us. "Please, don't tell anybody I told you that. He would—"

"I get it. And the guys around here are worse than old ladies, gossiping and shit." Still, she arches an eyebrow. "Your dad, he's got money?"

"How would you know?"

"Your clothes, the watch he was wearing, the car in the driveway."

Good point. "I needed to get out of town for a little while after some bad things happened, and he's just here to ensure I'm safe. That's all it is. He hates me, and he hates having to be here. Still, it was the only safe place, I guess."

"Yeah, it's pretty safe around here. More like dead."

"But I kind of get the feeling it's hard for him to be here. He would never tell me, obviously."

"I was thinking it was just me."

"No, it's everybody." And now I'm sort of glad I approached her, considering I didn't think about it that way. Whoever she is and whatever she's been through, I feel sorry for her – and we have him in common.

"I didn't think I would ever see him in that house again." She chokes a little. "I didn't think I would ever go there again. Just being on the porch was hard. The last time I was there, it wasn't good."

"Oh." What happened? I could crawl out of my skin; I want to ask so badly. "I'm sorry."

"You didn't do anything."

"Did he…"

"Hurt me? Oh, that came after." Bitterness seeps into her words. "When I went back, he was gone. Everything was different. I think I was in shock. His mom told me he left and she didn't know when he'd be back. She wouldn't tell me where he was or who he was with. I was the enemy all of a sudden."

"What about his dad? Did he… I mean, was he…"

"His dad was a fucking monster."

I got the feeling there was something there. Something terrible, something dark, thanks to what Mrs. Cooper told me. But to hear it like that, with all that emotion behind it, makes my head snap back. "Romero really hasn't spoken about him."

"Yeah, I can imagine why. Nobody misses him."

I want to ask where he is and what happened to him, but something in her face steals my words. "You know what, I shouldn't be talking with you about this. It's not my place," she decides before returning to her work.

"It's fine. I won't tell him."

"It's not fine. He's who you need to talk to you about this, not me." And just like with Romero, I can practically see her walls coming down. She's made up her mind. The subject is closed.

"Thank you for talking with me at all," I finally tell her. "You must be very busy."

A bunch of emotions move across her face all at once. "Thank you for coming in, and talking to me," she murmurs, offering a weak smile. "For real. At least I know I didn't do anything to make him hate me."

"He's really good at treating people like that when they didn't do anything to deserve it." But I still feel bad, so I add, "Like I said before, I think it's hard for him to be here. It's not you. It's the way being around him makes him feel."

"You don't need to defend him." She lifts a shoulder before mumbling, "But thank you."

"You're welcome." It's time for me to go. I've already stuck my nose in where it doesn't belong. I finish grabbing what I need without putting too much thought into it, taking everything to the register while a hundred different questions run through my head all at once. Will I ever get answers? I doubt it. I shouldn't even bother trying since I know he'll stonewall me like he always does. Why is it so hard for him to accept that somebody might care?

Is it because, according to Becky, he was raised by a monster? What does that mean? What was so monstrous about him? Is that why it's like pulling teeth to get anything out of his son?

When I step out of the store, I'm almost startled by the chill in the air. That's what he does to me. I forget everything around me when I'm thinking about him. What started as a cheerful little walk to the store has turned into a brooding, and now the clouds seem darker and the wind a little stronger. It's going to storm. I wish the idea of being cooped up in the house made me feel cozy and warm, but it only creeps me out. Who am I cooped up with? What did he go through? What made him the way he is?

I don't want to hurt you. I hear his voice echoing in my head while I walk down the street with a paper bag in my arms. Does that mean he's afraid he will? And what the hell is so broken in me that I sort of wish he would lose control just once? No second thoughts, no judging himself or holding himself back. He made me come so hard that I cried when he held himself back. What if he didn't stop next time? What if—

A scream from the street stops my heart. My head snaps around in time for me to glare at the shitty kids deliberately screaming to startle people as they ride past on their bikes. An older woman on the other side of the street jumps and drops her umbrella. "Assholes," I whisper, looking over my shoulder and watching as they deliberately swerve in the path of oncoming cars whose drivers lean on their horns.

That's when I see him.

I wouldn't have thought twice if he didn't look away as soon as our eyes met. Maybe if he shook his head at those asshole kids or shrugged or something. But no, the tall man in the black ball cap immediately looked away when he caught me noticing him. He's wearing a gray hoodie and jeans—nothing out of the ordinary. He would blend in perfectly otherwise.

But there's something off about him.

A sick feeling washes over me. Icy cold, nauseating, and it takes everything in me not to break out in a full-on run once my adrenaline kicks in and tells me to move my ass.

I'm not going to run. It doesn't matter how much I want to. I'm not running away ever again.

Instead, I deliberately go back to walking at the same pace. Is he following me? I could be making this up in my head. I probably am. I'm being paranoid and jumpy, when all this guy is doing is walking along the street.

But just in case, I stop in front of the pet store like I'm saying hi to the cute little puppies in the window. I smile at them, bending over a little like I want to get a closer look when really I'm watching the reflection in the glass. My stomach turns to ice when I see him half-hidden by a truck across the street.

I might not have noticed him if it hadn't been for those kids. I can hardly breathe. What should I do? Go home? I'd only end up leading him to the house. That's the last thing I should do. But then what? I can't stand out here all day, either.

The woman inside is giving me a funny look. I want to go in and ask for help, but how stupid would that look if I'm only being paranoid? This could be any average person, and here I am, making up stories about being followed. Like I'm that special. There is no chance Jeff found me here. Absolutely none.

But something won't let me head straight home. Instead of

hanging a left at the corner, I keep walking straight, and I want to look over my shoulder with every step. Instead, I keep moving with my eyes focused on the next corner. I'll look back once I reach it. One step at a time, that's all. The sidewalk isn't stretching out longer and longer the way it seems to.

Finally, I reach the next corner, where a red light gives me the excuse to stop and turn my head while my heart hammers against my ribs.

He's not there. I scan the opposite sidewalk, then look directly behind me in case he crosses the street. Nothing.

I'm going out of my mind.

What if somebody really was following me? What would I do if they approached me and tried to shove me into a car? Like that day with Bianca. There really are bad guys out there, even if the guy in the ball cap doesn't qualify. What would I do if I came up against one of them again?

I'm still obsessing over it by the time dinner's on the table, and I call upstairs for Romero to come down. If I didn't know better, I would think this was a pleasant, normal little domestic situation. Though I guess, in a lot of ways, it is. We live together, occasionally share a meal, and sometimes do things we're not supposed to—according to him, anyway.

The sort of things I shouldn't be thinking about but can't help when I hear him coming down the stairs, and my whole body tenses like I'm waiting for something monumental to happen. It's not easy to shake it off as I pour myself a glass of wine from the bottle I picked up at the store. Maybe it'll help loosen me up a little. I'm setting it on the table when he walks in, looking much better than when I first saw him this afternoon. "Do you want some?" I ask, nodding toward the glass.

"No, thanks." Instead, he pulls a bottle of water from the fridge and downs half before sitting. Will there ever be a time when I don't feel fluttery and tingly when I'm close to him? I can't forget the way he kisses, and I can't stop craving it. The thrill of giving myself over to something that makes me weak and breathless. I could crawl over the table right now, tear that gray sweater off him, and claw his bare skin to shreds.

Meanwhile, he won't even look at me. How do I break the tension? Somebody was following me today. Actually, there are better conversation starters. He would only pester me until I'd end up wishing I had never said anything. I don't want to walk through life feeling like a victim anymore. That much, I know.

He pushes the bowl of pasta my way so I can take a portion. While I do, I ask, "Do you think you could give me some self-defense lessons?"

"Sure." He tips his head to the side like he's confused, but at least those deep blue eyes are focused on me.

"I would feel more... like, in control. Strong. Like I could handle myself." Even if I can barely handle myself now. He must have just gotten out of the shower. His jet-black wet hair looks like he raked it back with his fingers. I want to do that, too. I need to touch him. I need him to hold me and remind me I'm safe in his arms.

I need him to not sound so dismissive when he shrugs. "Whatever will help."

"Thank you."

"Speaking of control and handling yourself..." This is it. My skin is tingling, but I don't want to show him how interested I am in whatever's coming next. Let him get the words out. "What happened last night was unacceptable, and you won't see me like that again. Ever."

"Romero..." I laugh a little, because he's got to be joking, right? "You didn't commit a crime. You got drunk. It happens."

"Not me. I don't do that."

"Then maybe you should every once in a while. It was actually kind of... cute." That was the wrong choice of words since now I can hear his teeth grinding, and it looks like his skin is suddenly too tight for his body. He's uncomfortable, shifting around in his chair.

"Listen," I offer when I start to feel bad, "there's nothing wrong with it. I won't hold it against you if that's what you're worried about."

"Alcohol alters the senses. It screws with your perceptions and your thoughts."

"Isn't that sort of the point?"

It's a corny thing to say, but it's my way of letting him off the hook. He doesn't deserve to feel so guilty for being human. But he's determined not to see even a tiny bit of humor in this. "No. Maybe for some people, but not for me. And that's the problem. I don't trust myself to lose control like that, ever."

A tiny tremor runs through me when he lowers his brow and meets my gaze across the table. "And you shouldn't trust me to do it."

I'm too overwhelmed by him—the deadly serious tone of his voice, the shadows from the overhead light playing across his stony mask of a face—to do anything more than nod my head and go back to eating. If that's how he wants it, that's how it will be. I know better now than to bring it up again if it bothers him that much.

I just wish I understood why he has to be such a mystery. And why I care so damn much.

CHAPTER 21

ROMERO

I don't know what pulls me out of a dark, jumbled dream. A sound. The presence of someone else nearby shifting the energy in the room. All I know, is something makes me wake up with my heart pounding, and the sight of a shadow standing over my bed only makes things worse.

I sit bolt upright before realizing who crept in here and startled the hell out of me. "What is it?" I snap once I recognize Tatum's trembling form in the faint light coming from a full moon streaming through the window behind her.

She wraps her arms around herself and whispers, "I thought I heard something downstairs."

Instinct takes over, and immediately I reach for the loaded gun on the nightstand. Keeping it there is a matter of habit, but her gasp centers me. She won't take her eyes off it.

"Alright," I mutter, loosening my grip and leaving the gun where it is. "Where downstairs?"

"Just downstairs in general, I don't know."

"Stay here. Do not move." Her head bobs up and down, eyes wide. As much as I hate leaving her alone, at least I know she's going to do as she's told. She's too afraid to do anything else.

Slowly, I creep downstairs, almost walking on tiptoe until I reach the bottom step. I'm practically holding my breath, straining my ears to pick up any sounds from around the house. So far, there's nothing, even though I search for any signs of a disturbance —a broken window, a broken lock, anything. I've reached the kitchen and have found nothing out of the ordinary by the time I flip the switch next to the back door. Light spills over the quiet, empty yard. There isn't so much as a wisp of smoke curling up from a cigarette butt to indicate an intruder, and nobody's been tampering with the garage door.

I still take a cursory look around the basement to be on the safe side, but finally give up the search with a resigned sigh. Was it another nightmare? I thought she was over those. Resentment rushes into my throat and threatens to choke me before I remind myself that a person doesn't choose what they dream about. If they did, my own dreams would be a hell of a lot easier to deal with.

When I reach the kitchen again and close the basement door, it's not the new, unscarred table I see. It's not the new counters or the clean wood floor. I see the past layered on top of the present. I see a woman on her hands and knees, scrubbing a red stain from yellowed tile while tears run down her face and drip into the mess.

"Romero?" The sound is barely a whisper floating through the air, but it pops the illusion and leaves me standing in the dark again. "Are you okay?"

"What did I tell you?" I demand as I cross the living room, then glare up the stairs. She's staring down at me from the hallway, arms wrapped around herself, rocking back and forth from her heels to the balls of her feet.

"You were taking so long, I got worried." Once I start up, she wanders back to my room and sits at the foot of the bed. The sight of her troubled face loosens my irritation, but only a little. "Did you find anything? Was somebody trying to break in?"

"Everything looks fine."

"Are you sure?"

"I checked the windows, the doors, everything. There's nothing suspicious."

Her frown deepens to a scowl. "Oh."

I lean against the door frame, folding my arms. "You sound disappointed."

That does the trick. Tatum rolls her eyes, scoffing, but at least she's not so scared anymore. "I'm just saying, I know what I heard. I'm not imagining things."

"The house can be noisy. The pipes clank and the floor creaks. That's probably what you heard. Or a gust of wind rattled the storm door a little too hard.

"I guess so."

"Maybe you were having a bad dream, and it was still with you when you woke up."

She looks at the floor, lifting her shoulder before mumbling, "I guess." Meanwhile, she picks at the blanket underneath her and her toes tap the floor. She's too nervous to sit still.

"What's really happening? What aren't you telling me?"

"Why do you always have to jump to conclusions?"

"You come in here looking scared half to death and tell me you heard something downstairs. Now, even when I tell you there's nothing, you're jumpy and fidgeting."

"Wow. You can dissect everything, can't you?" But even that is half hearted, without the bitterness she usually hurls at me. I almost miss it. At least then, she's being herself.

"Did you have a nightmare?"

"No."

Is this what it's like, dealing with a toddler? She's fucking determined to make me hurt her. "So you're this jumpy because you heard the house settling and jump to the wrong conclusion?" I grit out.

In the darkness, her eyes find a way to sparkle—or is she fighting back tears. "You know when I went to the store the other day?" I nod. "I thought some guy was following me around on the street."

The hair on the back of my neck instantly rises, and my hands flex, ready to take her by the shoulders and shake her like a rag doll. Maybe that would shake some sense into that thick skull of hers.

"Are you fucking serious? And you're only telling me about this now? That was, what, three days ago? Four?"

"It's not like he followed me the whole way home," she fires back. "I don't even know for sure that he was following me. I just thought he was. I was freaked out."

"And that's why you asked about self-defense lessons." I've been too busy to think about it since that night. The request seemed to come from out of nowhere, and when she never mentioned it again, I figured it was a whim. Something she came up with because she was bored, like the job thing that went nowhere.

"I figured it would give me a little more confidence. Maybe if I could trust myself to react the right way, I wouldn't be so afraid of random people."

"Why didn't you tell me?"

"Because of this." She waves a hand at me and wrinkles her button nose. "This whole thing you do. Getting all growly and pissed off and talking to me like I'm a child."

"It's childish not to tell somebody the full story."

"I figured you would call me paranoid or jump down my throat. Either way, I didn't feel like dealing with it. Sue me."

That's it. I'm going to shake Tatum until her head falls off. "Why are you like this?"

"Like what?"

"So damned determined to undermine me."

Her curls bounce when she tosses her head and scoffs. "Now I'm undermining you? Would you please get your head out of your ass?"

"Have you forgotten it's my job to protect you?"

"How could I, when you won't stop reminding me?"

"I wouldn't have to keep reminding you if you would stop being this way. I'm here to protect you. You are supposed to tell me about things like this so I know what to look out for."

Knowing her, I expect a shitty response delivered like the brat she is. And at first, it looks like she's all geared up to somehow throw my words back in my face—chest swelling, chin jutting out. But all she does is lower her gaze to the floor again. "Yeah. I know."

This has to be some kind of a trap. She never gives up like that. I wait, watching her, and all I get in return is the silence that spreads between us and fills the room. "If you know," I venture, "why don't you do the smart thing and tell me when something like that happens?"

"I don't know." She lifts her head and shrugs and a barrier falls between us. It's like she's letting go of the shell she wears to protect herself. How do I know she does it? Because I fucking invented the technique. "I really don't know. I mean, yeah, I didn't want you to freak out."

"Don't blame it on me."

"For God's sake, let me finish for once." I hold my tongue and only nod while she clears her throat. "Like I was going to say, I didn't want you to freak out, but... I'm used to handling things by myself. That's just how I am. When I was little, I didn't even want anybody making my breakfast for me. I would pull a chair up to the kitchen cabinet and pull out the cereal and a bowl, and I would get the milk out of the fridge even if it was a full gallon and I could barely carry it. And half the time, I would forget that I shouldn't put the spoon in the bowl unless I buried it under the cereal."

"Or else the milk splashed everywhere?"

"Let me guess. You did the same thing."

"And I would end up with milk all over the place."

"Did you ever think that maybe half the reason we disagree so much is because we're so alike?" Her nose wrinkles again. "As much as I shudder at the thought."

At least she doesn't seem as scared anymore. If she's insulting me, she's in a better mood. "I think you're right about that. We are a lot alike."

"And I'm not complaining," she insists, sitting up straighter. "I'm not trying to give you the whole poor little rich girl bullshit routine. Poor me, Daddy never paid attention, all of that. I don't mean it that way at all. But I don't think it's wrong to say Dad was busy and distracted most of the time. I know he loves me, but he had a lot going on. I got used to handling things independently, and I guess I eventually got into the habit of taking care of everything by myself."

She's right. I never gave it much thought before, because I didn't have the time, but we are more alike than I ever imagined. "I know that feeling. It's how I grew up. There were... a lot of problems."

"Like what?"

"There just were." No, we're not doing that. Not now, not ever.

For once, she's smart enough to let it go. "That's why I never wanted to tell anybody about Kristoff," she whispers. "I figured I could handle it by myself. And I was embarrassed because it meant letting him get away with it for so long. Lying and treating me like I was nothing. It wasn't a matter of wanting it to get that far, but I definitely shouldn't have let that go on as long as I did. I figured I could fight my way out of it. Maybe I could make him change his mind and return to how things were at first. All I had to do was try harder, work harder, hold on tighter."

"There are some problems you can't fix that way."

"Yeah, no kidding. But I don't like the idea of quitting, either."

"It's not quitting when there's no way to win. Sometimes, you have to walk away for your own sake." How many times did I ask myself why my mother never walked away? How many times did I tell her I would take care of her? I would get a job that I would work day and night to support us if that's what it took. But she wouldn't walk away. She didn't want to be a quitter. I guess she figured if she held on long enough, she would be rewarded.

And now I'm looking at someone just like her. I couldn't help her when she was in the middle of it, but I can help her now. "I need you to let me help you," I murmur, and this time, I'm not trying to play the stoic one. The guy with the answers, the silent protector. I'm talking to her, but I'm talking to my mom, too. All of the old hopelessness bubbles up and wants to boil over. "Let me help you. Let me do what I need to do. Please."

There are a million questions in how she looks at me, in the eyebrow she arches and the confused purse of her lips. Lips I want to kiss—God, how I want to kiss them. I want to kiss her until she forgets everything but me. "I'll try. That's the best I can say. I'll try."

And I know better than to hope for more than that. I also know better than to think that if I kissed her right now, it would be all for her sake. To comfort her, but that would be a lie because kissing her right now would be comforting myself, too, which is precisely why that can't happen. None of this is supposed to be about me or what I want... or need.

Tatum yawns, and I glance at the clock on the nightstand. It's past three a.m. now. "We should both get to bed." I doubt I'll be able to fall asleep right away, but then I've stirred up a lot of internal shit inside my brain, and I know myself well enough to know I'll be thinking for a while. Nights are always the worst. The time when there's nothing to distract myself with, and I'm lying here in the same room I used to lie in as a child and hope the door didn't suddenly fly open—though I would always rather he come in and take his rage out on me than on Mom.

She yawns again, and the motion brings me back to the present. "Get going, Princess. Any moment now, you're going to fall asleep while standing here."

"Am not. Maybe I'll just go downstairs," she sighs. "I'll turn on the TV and eventually fall asleep on the couch." She even stands and stretches, throwing her arms over her head, and it takes every single ounce of restraint I have to pry my eyes from her tits when they shift under that cotton T-shirt. Here I am, talking about it being my job to protect her, and I'm staring at her like some perverted creep.

A perverted creep who doesn't want her to sit alone all night. I'm not even sure what stirs me to say the next sentence. I'll chalk it up to zero sleep. "If it would make you feel better, and so you wouldn't be alone, you can sleep in here with me."

Fuck, I'm a glutton for punishment. There's no other explanation.

"Really?" The hope in her breathless voice makes me glad I offered, even if the price will be a boner from hell.

"Yes, but the second you kick me in the side, your ass is going back in your bed."

"I don't kick in my sleep, loser." She's like a happy little girl, full of relief and willing to promise anything so long as it means she's not alone. Me, on the other hand? All I can do is regret my weakness as I lie down on my back and wait for her to curl up beside me, her head on my shoulder. Even though there's plenty of room and she doesn't need to be so close. My lips part and I'm prepared to tell her to back off, but my heart lurches in my chest at the thought of shattering her at a moment like this. When she's this vulnerable and close. It doesn't help one fucking bit that it feels good either and that I really don't want her to back off. I don't want to be alone either, but I know better than to touch her or pull her closer. Tatum can't give me the comfort I need, nor should she. She deserves better, more. Her warmth radiates into my side, and that's enough for me. Against my better judgment, I suck her sweet scent into my lungs: lavender and chamomile.

Calmness washes over me, my heart rate slowing as I give into her presence.

"Thank you," she mumbles in the middle of a yawn. I don't trust myself to say anything, so I settle for a grunt. Soon, her breathing goes slow and steady, and her head becomes heavier as she settles into sleep.

Sleep won't come to me, I know, so I stare at the ceiling, letting my thoughts percolate, wondering if someone was really following her after all. She's jumped to conclusions before, but I've worked with Callum long enough to know there's no such thing as a coincidence. She was terrified tonight, enough to seek out the comfort of a man she despises. This wasn't random.

Did Jeff send someone to look for her, and if he did, how the hell did they find her?

I can't seem to think about anything else, and even as the sun peeks over the horizon, I'm still thinking about it. I've done everything I can to protect her, yet somehow, it seems like I'm letting her down. She mewls softly in her sleep, her body molding against mine, and I don't have the heart to move away.

CHAPTER 22

TATUM

"Self-defense is easier than you think."

We're standing in the middle of the basement dressed in shorts and T-shirts, facing off like we're about to do battle, and this is how he chooses to lead off my first self-defense lesson. I tip my head to the side. "Seriously? Self-defense is easier than I think?"

His jaw works and I know I'm in trouble, but really. He's had days to think about this, and that's all he could come up with? Good thing he never considered a career as a motivational speaker. "Could you not? We haven't even gotten started yet, and you're already picking at stupid shit and wasting time."

"Sorry, sorry." He's right. I mean, I'm not going to say that out loud, but he is. I'm nervous about this. Ever since he told me to be ready this afternoon for my first self-defense lesson, my stomach's been in knots. Not because I'm nervous about learning some moves but because I knew it would mean being close to him.

And I want to be. My whole body craves his touch so much that I have to fight not to lean in closer when he steps up until we're toe-to-toe. It's not enough to feel the warmth of his body, just like it wasn't enough to fall asleep with my head on his shoulder a couple of nights back. I haven't been able to get it out of my head. His musky scent, the way it filled my senses. The firmness of his shoulder, the way his chest rose and fell with every breath. How I longed to press my lips to his bare skin. How I longed to do so much more than that. Looking back, I'm glad I fell asleep as quickly as I did. Things could have gotten very awkward, very fast.

"Now." He's breathing slowly, his blue eyes locked on mine and threatening to erase every conscious thought from my mind. "I'm going to take you through a few basic lessons in anatomy."

Not exactly sexy, but that's for the best. "I thought you were going to teach me self-defense."

"And first, you're going to learn about the weakest parts of the body."

"I already know about that." I lower my gaze to his crotch and ignore the hunger that stirs in my core.

"That's not what I'm talking about."

"So I could kick you in the balls right now, and it wouldn't matter?"

"Would you focus?" he grits out. "There's work I could be doing right now."

"Oh, pardon me. I don't want to get in the way of your important work." If anything, I'm glad he said it. He reminded me of my place. I'm just another job.

"Sure," he continues, rolling his eyes. "It would hurt like hell if you kicked me in the balls. But that's obvious. And an attacker is going to expect that, so he will pull his hips back until you can't reach that part of his body." He places his hands on my shoulders then pulls his hips back. "Go ahead, try it. Try to kick me in the balls."

"Are you kidding?"

"Give it a shot."

Well, he asked for it. It's not like I've never fantasized about how much I'd love to deliver a good kick where it would hurt the most. Except he's right. When I lift my knee, he pulls his hips back and increases the pressure on my shoulders. "See, what happens is, I end up putting more force on you to keep my balance. Did you notice?"

"A little. But I can just duck real quick and get away." And I do, dropping to a quick crouch and hopping backward while his arms fall to his sides. "I'm a ninja."

Would it kill him to crack a smile? "That was only for the purposes of a demonstration. If I were doing this for real, out in the world, I wouldn't do it like that."

"How would you do it?"

"I'd have you up against a wall."

Ooh. Wrong choice of words. Obviously, he could have meant it in a totally innocent way, but right away, I remember the wall at the club. The wall he held me against while he fingered me until I cried.

I'm starting to think this was a bad idea.

"Like this?" I rest against the nearest wall, and the cinder blocks are cool against my back. I am entirely too heated up. "What would you do to me?"

"You're fucking around."

"No, I'm not." Yes, I am.

"Then get that playful note out of your voice and take this seriously. I'm trying to help you. Or were you lying when you said you wanted to feel more confident so a random guy on the street doesn't scare you out of your mind?"

The dismissive, almost hateful way he says it snaps me out of my stupidity. "Fine," I snarl. "Show me. What would you do if you were an attacker?"

"I would go at you like this." He's like a snake striking, lunging all at once, with no warning. The way an actual attacker would. His hands are around my neck before I know what's happening, and he pins me against the wall with his elbows against my ribs.

"Now try to fight me," he growls, his face dangerously close to mine. "Come on. Show me what you've got. Try to kick me in the balls, Tatum."

I can't. I can't even lift my leg, much less make contact. All I can do is fight, but that's no use—I can only hit him from the sides, pounding my fists against his shoulders and ribs. I might as well be hitting air for all the good it does. Panic blooms in my head and wants to overwhelm me. I'm going to scream. I feel it rising, wanting to tear its way out of me.

"Open your eyes. Look at me." I have to force myself to do it, but I'm glad I did when it's Romero's face I look into. His eyes I find in front of me. Not Kristoff's dark, hate-filled gaze. The screaming in my head softens, and I can breathe again. He's not going to hurt me. This is pretend.

All at once, he loosens up and I can breathe again. "Okay, now you get the idea," he says, and he's gentler now. "If I'm attacking you, I will ensure you can't move too much. And if you try to kick me in the balls, I'm going to do like I did before." He pulls his hips back, which means he presses more weight against my throat. "It's only going to hurt you worse. Now, how would you try to get out of this? You have more room to move your arms and legs. What would you do?"

I've seen it before on TV. I lace my fingers together and try to drive my arms up between his in a sudden, sharp movement. All he does is lock his elbows—he's so strong, there's no hope no matter how I fight.

"That was a good try," he tells me, even though I feel like a failure. "But here's a better way. Relax your body."

"Sure, easy for you to say."

"You have to. You just have to. Got it?" I only roll my eyes but nod. "Now, I want you to pivot on your right foot. You're going to bring your hip around in a quarter circle, swing your left arm up and around, then slam it down against my elbows."

"I have no idea what you're talking about," I admit. It's all a little confusing.

"We'll switch places, and I'll show you." He turns around and touches his back to the wall. "Put your hands around my throat and outstretch your arms, locking your elbows."

"You sure you trust me? How many times have I wanted to do this?"

"Something tells me I'll be safe." That's what he thinks. I sort of like the way it feels to wrap my hands around his throat. It's almost too tempting, the impulse to squeeze hard. "Now, watch what I do."

He moves slowly, pivoting like he described, until he's standing sideways rather than facing me. His left arm comes up and around, then slams down against the insides of my elbows so suddenly, it unlocks them, and I let go.

"Then, here's what you do." Now, he has my left wrist in his right hand and pulls me down until I'm bent at the waist so his left elbow can drive into my nose. He stops just short of making contact. "You're going to keep doing this until you can't do it anymore."

"That's great, really," I admit once he lets go and I stand up straight. "But there's no way I'll be able to remember that if I'm in the middle of being attacked.

My words are falling on deaf ears. "We're going to practice that, and then we'll learn another move." It's like I didn't say anything at all, but I guess that shouldn't be a surprise. He's ignored and disregarded me for as long as we've known each other.

"I wish I had known more about this before," I admit as we go through the motions again and again. At first, I'm slow and clumsy, but he remains patient. I never imagined him being this patient. I always thought he had a hair-trigger temper.

"Before?"

"You know what I mean." Okay, so he's still clueless. "Don't make me say it out loud."

"I wish you had, too," he mumbles. "But now you will, and that's what matters. I'm not going to always be around. You're going to have to protect yourself."

My heart sinks, and suddenly, I don't want to do this anymore. "I'm tired," I mutter, sagging a little against the wall.

"The lesson isn't finished yet."

"I know, but I'm tired." The truth is, my heart's not in it now. He's not going to be around forever, or even much longer. We can't stay here for the rest of our lives, and I know it, and I never expected to. But how do I go back to my old life now? It's my fault for getting comfortable. We've been gone for weeks, and it's almost mid-November. Soon, we'll have to discuss Thanksgiving and whether we'll have a turkey. I was looking forward to learning how to roast one. I was actually looking forward to having a holiday with him.

And now, shortly, we'll return to the way things were. Me in my wing, him in the little cottage I can see from my bedroom window. Not all of it. Enough that I can tell when he's got a light burning, whether he's up in the middle of the night like I sometimes am.

"Let's try one more move before we call it a day. You've gotten good at this," he says, and for once, he sounds like he means it. He's not teasing. There's no insult waiting to be voiced. "But I want you to know how to get out of a situation when someone attacks you from behind."

I don't even know what's happening; he's so fast. One second we're facing each other, and the next, he spins me in place and grabs me tight, rough, shoving me against the wall with my arms pinned at my sides and his body holding me in place.

"What do you do now?" he grunts, his hot breath on my ear.

Instinct makes me thrash and fight, but his arms only tighten. "Come on. You can do better than that." He sounds nasty, cruel, like he's taunting me. Laughing at me.

And yet…

His whole body goes just as stiff as what's starting to poke me in the ass. It's like he's surprised, like he didn't expect it. When I move against him like I did before, he sucks in a sharp breath. "Don't do that." He sounds like he's being strangled.

"I thought I was trying to get away from you?" I push back, only that means pressing my ass against his growing erection. "What, you can't handle having a girl so close to you? I thought you were supposed to be tough."

"Watch your mouth."

"What? You don't like it? You were mocking me a second ago." He groans when I move my hips ever so slightly, and I can feel the power shifting between us. Now I am the one in charge, and it feels fucking amazing. Exhilarating. He can pretend to be strong, confident, and controlled, but we both know the truth. He's got a weakness for me.

"Let go, then," I whisper. "It would all be so easy if you just let me go."

His arms loosen, but he doesn't release me. He gives me enough space to turn around until my back is against the wall and my body is flush with his, so close I can feel his heart pounding under my palm. He leans against the wall, a hand on either side of my head, caging me in with his arms. I let my hands slide down his chest, and he holds his breath as I trail my fingertips along the ridges of his abs, so clearly defined under a thin cotton shirt.

"Fuck…" he groans like a man on the edge, closing his eyes when I brush against the silk-covered steel twitching in his shorts.

"No. Open your eyes," I whisper. "Look at me. I want you to look at me."

And when he does, when he meets my gaze, I would swear he hates me. And I know that feeling, because I hate him. I hate who he turns me into. I hate that he makes me want him. I hate that somewhere, he got the idea that I am all wrong for him and he is somehow better than me because he can fight what's between us and I can't.

"What are you going to do?" I ask, stroking him through his soft shorts. God, he's so hard, so thick. There's nothing but a thin layer of fabric between my skin and his. It would take nothing to pull him free and find out what that hard little bump on either side of the spot under his head is. A piercing? The idea takes my breath away. There's so much I don't know about him.

His lips are so close, and my pussy moistens in anticipation as he leans closer. My heart's racing, my blood is singing, and my body is screaming in relief. Finally, finally. I close my eyes, holding my breath, waiting…

"Godammit." He shoves away from the wall, away from me, his features twisted in an ugly snarl. "God damn you."

"Me?" Tears fill my eyes all at once, and I can't fight them off. I want to – God knows I do — but I'm already too overwhelmed. Like someone put me in a blender and scrambled up everything I thought I knew and wanted.

"Was this your plan all along? Huh?"

"My plan?" My mouth falls open while I sputter in confusion. It's like I went from a hot tub to an ice-cold lake all at once. I'm still in shock. "That's really what you think of me? Like I'm some kind of schemer who just wants to get into your fucking pants? Do you know how insane that sounds?"

"Do you know how pathetic it is to come up with reasons to get me in this position?"

"Newsflash: I really did want lessons."

"No, I don't think you did. I think, at heart, you're the same manipulative little snake as your—" His head whips back and his mouth snaps shut while his face goes red. The stale basement air goes cold and heavy.

"Say it," I whisper, glaring at him. "Go ahead. Say what you were going to say. Be a man. Get it off your chest."

"I shouldn't have—"

"You were going to compare me to my mother, weren't you? And here I was, about to tell you that you made me feel safe. That you are the only thing that has helped me forget what happened. You touch me, and it all disappears. All the memories, everything. Even before, when I started to panic. You brought me back from the edge. You knew just what to do. And I was going to thank you for that until this bullshit."

He runs his hands to his hair, breathing hard, before groaning. "Listen. I'm glad, I am. I'm glad I can do that for you. But dammit, you know that this is wrong as well as I do. I told you, we will not cross that line again."

"Says the guy who poked me in the ass with his erection."

"Which you tried to take advantage of!"

"Give me a fucking break!" I scream, and the sound is only

louder and more deafening, thanks to where we are. But I'm glad for that. I want him to hear me. I want to fill the space with my rage. "You think this is all about you? Get a fucking clue! Yes, I need help and you've been there for me, but my every waking thought isn't about you, Romero. What can I do to scheme my way into your pants? Are you really that fucking full of yourself, you asshole? Oh, but I forgot. Everything's been about you since the day you showed up at my house."

"What?"

"You heard me. And yeah, you reminded me of it the night you got drunk." I love hurling that in his face, knowing how upset it makes him. Good. He deserves it. "From the very beginning, all you wanted was to be the golden boy. To make my father proud of you. It's like he practically forgot I existed. And pretend all you want like you didn't notice it, but it's true. He got the son he wanted. And you got the dad you —" It's my turn to close my mouth in shame. That's beneath me.

"Go ahead," he mutters. He's not even blinking, staring at me with an intensity that makes me wish I hadn't said a word. "Say it. Get it off your chest."

"No," I whisper, shaking my head. "I won't."

"Doesn't matter. I know what you meant." He paces, and there's nothing I can do but stand here and watch. "Listen. I'm glad you're feeling better. I really am. That's all I want for you – I don't care if you believe that. It's true. All I want to do is help you find your confidence again, and not because I want to score points with your dad or whatever you think. There are people in your life who miss the old you."

"How would you know?"

"I just know."

"But how?"

"Don't be a child." He's so cold. So cruel and dismissive. In other words, he's the Romero I've always known.

"Don't be a coward. Answer the question."

"I won't let you goad me into this, so you might as well save your breath. "He stops and stands still, shoulders thrown back, his chin lifted. "That's the end of the lesson for now. I'm getting in the shower."

And all I can do is lean against the wall and fight back angry, disappointed tears.

CHAPTER 23

ROMERO

"*Don't! Romero, don't!*"

I wake trembling in a pool of ice cold sweat with that scream echoing in my head. Fuck, it's so vivid. When I look around the bedroom, I almost expect to find my old Harley posters on the wall. I'm sixteen again, and there's a lifetime worth of rage built up in me, and it has to go somewhere. Because I've snapped. There's no going back.

And she's begging me to stop, and I can't. I won't.

At least it's not the middle of the night. There's nothing like waking up from a vivid dream that's more of a memory than finding yourself alone in the dark. In the dark, your mind can paint ugly pictures. It's easier to breathe, easier to remember what's real when daylight leaks through the slats in the blinds. That was then, this is now, all that sort of stuff.

I sit up, glad to peel my bare back away from the clammy sheets that will have to be changed now. At least it's something to do, a reason to get my ass out of bed. I strip it quickly, tossing the damp cotton in the corner before heading out to the bathroom. A hot shower washes away the last of those lingering screams. They get louder all the time. Clearer.

The front room is still closed and quiet when I step into the hall, with steam billowing out behind me. I don't expect her to wake up this early, but she's made it a point to avoid me since that disaster of a self-defense lesson. She could be wide awake and waiting for me to head downstairs.

It's easier this way. The less we see each other, the lower the chance of one or both of us making a mistake. The way I came damn close to giving her what she was begging for. She'll never understand the temptation. She's not the only one who wants to forget the past for even a brief, fleeting moment.

I'm quiet as I pull a fitted sheet and pillowcases from the shelf between our rooms. Making the bed is only a distraction from what I'd rather do. It would be so easy to open that door at the end of the hall and indulge myself in her. I can see her wide, shocked eyes and know the shock would turn to blazing desire in the time it would take to cross the room. She'd lie back and part her legs for me—welcoming, demanding. Her touch would light up everything in me I thought was dead and gone, like it always does. I could forget everything but her and what she does to me.

There's no forgetting. There's only distraction, which is what she is. There are other, safer distractions that won't end up getting me killed by an enraged father.

It's only a few minutes before the bed's made, and I'm dressed and heading downstairs for some much-needed coffee. The espresso machine Tatum insisted on ordering was a good idea in the end. A double shot with steamed milk is one of the comforts I've come to depend on. There I was, thinking I hadn't softened up too much over the years. Boy, was I wrong.

It's quiet enough that a soft sound from the backyard rings out loud and clear. I step up to the window over the sink and find three kids like the ones Tatum described a while back. "Little shits," I whisper, watching as two of them provide cover for the third as he tries to pick the padlock on the door.

Instinct makes me react before I can think. There's a gun in the drawer, closest to the back door — I withdraw it without looking, eyes fixed on the window, waiting to see what happens next.

Suddenly, there's excitement, the three of them grinning as the lock picker drops the lock onto the ground before easing open one of the two swinging doors wide enough for them to slip inside. I wait until they're in before easing open the back door and creeping slowly down the steps. I hear them whispering loud enough for half the neighborhood to hear. They are not very good at this, but then they're kids. I don't expect much better. God knows I wasn't an expert at their age.

"Don't turn on the light!"

"There's nothing in here. I fucking told you!"

"We could take the bike."

"How the hell do we get out of here, genius?"

They could be me, Dex, and Austin at that age. That's why I cross the yard, ignoring the cold that seeps in through my sweater, holding the gun close to my side. I bend to pick up the lock in one swift motion, then shut the door and slide the lock into place. There's a moment of stunned silence before all three of them start shouting and banging while I take my time rounding the garage and unlocking the small side door they either don't know about or are too panicked to consider. Really, if they're going to steal, they should at least case the location.

The three of them spin around at the creak of the hinges to find me standing in the doorway, gun in hand. The look of utter horror printed on their painfully young faces is almost comical, but laughing would ruin everything. "Now," I growl, taking my time as I look the three of them up and down. "Do you mind explaining what you're doing in my garage?"

"Oh, shit," the lock picker moans. "Don't kill us, man. Please. We were just messing around."

The tallest of the three nods while his chin trembles like he's about to cry. "We didn't take anything! I swear, we're just—"

"You were just, what?" I bark, making them jump. "Breaking and entering? Because that's what you just did, and I watched you do it. What are you doing out this early in the morning? Don't you have anywhere better to be on a Saturday?"

The three of them exchange guilty looks before they shrug. No, they have nowhere better to be. Did I at their age? "What were you really going to do?" I tuck the gun into my waistband, then flip the light switch for a better look at them. Their jackets are old and worn, and all three of them could use a haircut and new sneakers. "Answer me. What were you hoping to find in here?"

"I don't know," the tallest of the three mutters. He seems like the leader—the other two almost duck behind him. "Tools we could sell? Stuff like that."

"All three of you could get jobs around here, you know? Bagging groceries, yardwork, that sort of thing. And there's the rec center, too. I know they could help you find jobs if that's what you want."

They scoff in unison. "Who wants to work?"

I have to laugh, because I remember feeling that way. "It's better than ending up in juvenile hall for breaking into a garage where there's nothing you could use. It was a stupid thing to do, and the three of you don't seem stupid. Just too dumb to know better. All you wanna do is ride around the neighborhood and cause trouble. I get it. I was like you."

"Romero! Don't!" "It's not worth it," I mutter, pushing the memories far back, but not far enough. There's no such thing as far enough.

"What are you going to do?" the smallest of the three asks in a painfully soft voice.

"I'm gonna let you go this time." They sag a little in relief. "But you're going to go next door to Mrs. Cooper's, and you're going to apologize for fucking up her flower bed. And you're gonna ask her if she needs you to go to the store or do anything else for her, and you're going to do whatever she tells you. I shit you not, if I check with her and she never saw you, things will get a lot worse. I've seen you little shits riding around enough that I could pick you out of a crowd. Understood?"

Their heads bob up and down, eyes like saucers, and I step outside and wait for them to follow me. "I mean it," I growl as they run down the driveway. "I'm going to check with her tomorrow. She better give me the answer I'm looking for."

Who am I to be telling kids what to do? They're half my age, if that, and I don't have any more answers than them. I still wake up from nightmares woven together by memories of things that happened years ago. I still try to run away from those memories during my waking hours. This is only the second time I've been out to the garage since I got here, the first being the day I took Tatum out on the bike.

Looking inside at the boxes I packed, I know why. I was lying when I told Tatum I had never been back since the night I left. I came back once, just once, under the cover of darkness. It was a few days after Mom died, and I didn't want some stranger going through her stuff and deciding what they thought was worth keeping and what should be thrown away. I didn't let myself wander slowly through painful memories – I wanted it over with. I was glad Callum was with me to keep me focused.

Now I look at those boxes and think about the life of a woman who never saw her son again, and had to pretend she didn't know where he was — at least, that's what I assume since no one ever came looking for me. She kept our secret the way I did. It was the least I could do for her.

I wander over to the stack against the wall and run my hand over the cardboard. Photos, mostly, plus a few of the things she loved. A baby book she started but never finished. Scrapbooks. She was into that for a while. Her high school yearbook. This is all I have left of her.

"What are you looking for?"

I'm ready to snarl as I turn and glare at the door I left open. Only the girl standing in the doorway isn't who I expected to see. "What are you doing here?" I ask Becky as she steps into the garage.

"I was walking to work and passed the house. I saw the light on in here."

"Okay. Do you walk into every place where there's a light burning inside?"

She doesn't flinch at my snarling. "Only when the person whose house it is, treated me like an enemy when he saw me for the first time in years."

This time it's different. When I saw her before, she was almost apologetic, almost curled up in a protective ball. Now, it's like there's armor around her. She reminds me of the girl I used to know — always angry, defensive, but not with me. She was never like that with me.

That was then. Before I gave her a reason to be.

"What do you want from me?" I sigh.

"How can you say that?" She takes a step closer, her dark eyes narrowed but blazing. "What do I want from you? I want the truth. I want an explanation. Why did you leave that night? Why couldn't you have at least said goodbye? That was already the worst night of my life, and I came home and found out you were gone. Do you know what that did to me? Do you know how long I told myself it was my fault?"

"It wasn't your fault."

"Yeah, thanks, I know that now. Try explaining that to a sixteen-year-old who just had her life torn apart. You were the one thing I had that I could count on. You were my life raft, and I was yours – or I was supposed to be. But then you decided to run away."

"It wasn't like that."

Something dangerously close to understanding works its way over her face. "Yeah. I sort of figured after a while."

"What do you mean?" And why do I feel like the walls are closing in on me? She's blocking the doorway and I locked the swinging doors. There's no way out unless I shove my way past her. What am I, a child? There's no running away. I should know that by now.

"I mean, there's a big difference between being sixteen and twenty-six. You figure things out. You get smarter."

Careful. Don't be stupid. "If you're as smart as you say you are, then why are you putting me through this? Why do you want an apology if you know I had no choice?"

Her soft sigh is a punch to the gut. The way her face sags.

"Maybe I just need to feel like I mattered at some point in my life. That somebody actually gave a shit about me for real, and not just because they wanted to get in my pants and have a little fun." She looks tired as her shoulders slump and the light leaves her eyes.

"You know it wasn't like that. It never was."

"Then why are you still so pissed at me? Why can't you look me in the eye without having to look away? Why couldn't you even call me to see if I was okay when you knew I lost our baby? Even if you didn't care about it, you were supposed to care about me." She scoffs, shaking her head. "You ran."

I'm not pissed at her. I'm pissed at myself for so many things, too many to name, even if I could find the words. "You know it wasn't because of the baby, right? That's not why I left."

She snorts, nodding. "Like I said. You figure things out."

No, she couldn't have. Could she? "Then say it," I whisper. "What do you think you know? Go ahead."

Her face hardens. "No. I didn't say it to her, and I won't say it to you."

"Her?"

"Tatum found me at the store when I was working. She wanted me to feel better about the shitty way you treated me—because she knows how it feels." All I can do is sputter in surprise. "You can't keep treating people who care about you like it's weakness or something. Because one day, you're gonna wake up, and you'll have run off every last person who ever gave a shit about you, and that will be a sad day, Romero. I would hate to see it happen."

She turns her back on me, stepping outside where her breath turns to a cloud around her head. "If you had just come back as a friend, this could've been different. I never held a grudge against you. None of us did. But you came back here acting like you were better than us. Like you resent us. That, I'm not going to forgive. And I thought you should know."

I'm almost reeling when she walks away, her shoulders hunched, hands shoved deep into her pockets. It's like a hurricane blew through here. All I can do is look around at the wreckage and wonder what the hell I'm supposed to do now.

In the middle of my dazed, confused state, one face flashes in front of my mind's eye. One person who can't mind her own goddamn business. She just had to know more, didn't she? Comforting Becky was an excuse. Becky saw her opportunity and she jumped on it.

Everything around me goes red as I charge out of the garage and across the yard. She has fucked around for the last time. Now, she'll find out what happens when people don't do as I say.

"If you would just do as I say, I wouldn't have to lose my temper." I shake my head like that will do anything to shake off the memory of hearing those words delivered straight to my face, nose to nose, spoken in the calmest voice imaginable, even as blood dripped down my face. Even as the taste of it filled my mouth. He had the balls to stand there and blame it on me, just like he blamed it on Mom. It was always somebody else's fault.

And here I am, making the same excuses. It's my own fucking weakness staring me in the face now, my inability to deal with the past. It's nobody's fault but my own.

I slam the gun on the counter with a trembling hand and swear to God there's somebody sitting on my chest. I can hardly take a breath. "Tatum?" I call out. Nothing but the sound of my voice echoes back. "Tatum? Where are you?"

CHAPTER 24

TATUM

At first, it's a relief to find the house quiet when I venture out of the bedroom. I don't know how much longer I can stand living with a time bomb. That's how it feels. The clock's always ticking. I'm always waiting for the next explosion.

My frayed nerves settle a little as I walk downstairs to find a quiet, peaceful first floor. Except for a coffee cup on the counter, there's no evidence of Romero. I pick it up—it's still warm—and look out the back window in time to find the last person I expected to see hurrying out of the garage. "Becky?"

She's practically running with her head down, and a quick hand under her eyes tells me she's crying. He made her cry. I have no idea what she's doing here so early in the morning, but it doesn't matter as much as the fact that she's flushed and teary.

What the hell did he do to her this time? Is he ever going to get tired of hurting people? Anger propels me through the house and out the door into a very chilly morning. I hardly feel it. I'm too busy being pissed off.

She's already passed the SUV and is now hustling down the sidewalk. "Becky?" I don't know if she hears me—or if she cares. I wouldn't if I were her. I'd want to get away from him, too. If there's one thing I can relate to, it's that.

She's not even the most surprising thing I've seen. That honor goes to the sight of the three little assholes who plague the neighborhood exiting Mrs. Cooper's house. Right away, I'm running from the porch, ready to chase them down until Mrs. Cooper sticks her head outside and waves. "Come back any time!" Not what I'd shout to somebody who just robbed my house, so I guess my immediate reaction was off base.

She notices me standing between our houses and gives me a wave. "Hi, Tatum! You should put on a coat in this weather. You'll catch your death!" She closes her heavy cardigan and wraps her arms around herself, stepping onto the porch. I was too busy imagining her unconscious on the floor to think much about the cold that now seeps through my V-neck sweater.

"What did they want?" I ask, still watching them until they round the corner.

"It's the strangest thing." She shakes her head like she can't believe it and even laughs softly—not what I expected, and it eases some of the pressure in my head. I don't feel quite as ready to beat the shit out of anybody. "They knocked on the door and apologized for ruining my flowers, then asked if there was anything they could do for me. They even offered to pick up groceries." She tips her head to the side. "I think the little one was crying a bit, so I invited them in and gave them some fresh-baked muffins. They wolfed them right down."

What a sweet lady she is. I'd tell them to shove their change of heart up their asses. "So long as they weren't bothering you." Slowly, I walk up her porch steps. I don't know why. She's kind, warm, and caring, and there's been a real shortage of that lately.

Only when she touches a gentle hand to my arm do I realize I'm shaking, and not from the cold. "Are you alright? You seem upset. Maybe you'd like to come in for a cup of tea."

Upset? That doesn't even touch the tip of the iceberg. Don't they always say icebergs are much more enormous under the surface? There's a whole ocean of rage and loneliness and confusion churning around inside me. "It's not a big deal," I whisper, the sort of thing you say to somebody without really thinking about it. A meaningless comfort.

She sees straight through it. "Is there anything you need to talk about?" She eyes the house next door, my personal prison cell. "I hope it's not overstepping my bounds to say this, but it's just as easy to hear a fight going on over there as it was when Romero was a boy. Please, don't think I wait around, eavesdropping. There are times I can't help hearing it."

Now my face goes hot even in the cold. "I'm so embarrassed—"

"And I wasn't trying to shame you," she murmurs, wearing a gentle smile that feels almost maternal. But how would I know what that seems like? I never really had it in my life. "I was only concerned."

"It's not like that. We just... rub each other the wrong way. And he..." No, I shouldn't be doing this. She's a lovely lady but a stranger, and she doesn't need to know about our bullshit.

Maybe it's because she's a stranger that I want to tell her. The stakes are lower. Like I could say to her things I can't even tell Bianca, and it won't matter because it's not like we have a relationship.

"You made it sound like things were bad over there when he was a kid." I have to wrap my arms around myself, but it does nothing to warm me up. I'm not about to go back to the house, though—this might be my best chance to get a few words with her. "All I ever want to do is talk to him and understand him, but he keeps pushing me away. And then I saw Becky hurry off. She was crying, making me want to beat him senseless. I don't know why he has to be the way he is, and I don't know why I care."

The creases on her forehead deepen. "He's never hurt you, has he?"

"No. No, it's not like that at all. That's not the kind of guy he is. Believe me."

"I do," she murmurs in a soft voice. "Don't worry, sweetie. But it wouldn't be the first time that sort of thing passed down to the next generation."

"You're saying his father was abusive?"

Her face hardens all at once, and I'd swear it dropped another ten degrees out here. "He wasn't worth the breath it took to keep him alive."

Whoa. I can't even pretend her sudden shift doesn't startle me. She went from being a kind, elderly woman to somebody who looks and sounds like they're ready to spit nails.

Then her expression softens, and it's like I might have imagined her bitterness. "You have to understand. I contacted Joy more than once and asked if she needed help."

Joy. What a sweet name for somebody whose life doesn't seem like it was filled with much joy at all.

"I offered to let her stay here with me. I wanted her to bring Romero. She didn't want to drag me into the problem. Can you imagine? She was worried about me. I offered to give her money—Henry and I saved up a nest egg when he was alive, but she also refused. I even called the police more than once, but she always had an excuse for her injuries. I never did quite understand why she insisted on staying."

"And Romero? Was he hurt, too?" He would hate it if he knew I even hinted at this, but I need to know. I've already waited long enough to find the missing pieces of the puzzle. She's holding them in her hands. I only need to ask for them.

"I remember one time in particular," she murmurs, looking toward the house again. "His eye was swollen shut and bruises ran along his cheekbone. Joy told me he got in a fight at school, but she forgot one thing."

She turns to me, wearing a sad, weary smile. "There was nothing wrong with his hands. Not so much as a scratch on his knuckles when he shoveled my sidewalk. Whoever he fought, he wasn't the one doing the fighting."

I mean, I knew it. None of this is a surprise. There's no way he could live in a house with a monster—Becky's word—and not end up hurt. Hearing it, though? Imagining those bruises? That's different. "Why did he leave? Do you know?"

"We shouldn't talk about this."

"Please, Mrs. Cooper. That's the one thing nobody ever told me. I've known him since I was a kid, but I never found out why he left this place. I don't even know why I want to know. I just do."

"I remember very well the night he left." She pauses, and her pale blue eyes stare out at the street. "I remember the fighting. So much of it. Pounding and banging and screaming. All through the night. My heart broke for her. I called the police, but they never came. It could be they'd gotten sick of taking the call when nothing ever came of it. There was nobody to help her. Until the car came."

"What car?"

"A fancy-looking car—I was never good at those car brands. A dark-haired man climbed out of it. He was dressed so well. His shoes were shiny. He wore a fancy watch. I'd never seen anyone like that around here before. Not in all the years I shared this house with my husband. I knew he had to be somebody important. And when he came back out, Romero was with him."

Dad. That was the night Dad came and got him. I was asleep in my bed, probably. I had just graduated middle school and was dreaming of a long summer. Romero had just witnessed a screaming, banging fight between his parents and was being taken away.

"There were other men after that," she continues. "I fell asleep in my armchair since it had gotten very late by then. I never saw them leave. And a few days later, there was a small article in the newspaper about a body found at the dump."

I would swear she punched me in the stomach. All the air leaves my lungs. It makes sense. Romero never did say the man was still living. He's never really talked about him at all.

"Nobody knew how Billy ended up dead," she murmurs. "And there were plenty of theories, let me tell you. The man had many more enemies than he did friends—if he had friends at all, the miserable thing. I suppose some of the boys he drank with down at O'Neal's considered him a pal. But there were plenty more who were none too fond of him."

"What's your theory?"

"That he got what he deserved. I never gave it more thought than that. Joy never spoke of it, and I didn't dream of bringing it up."

"Do you think..." I can barely form the words, but I have to. I have to get them out, or else I might never get the courage again. "Do you think it was the man who took Romero away? Do you think he did it?"

There is so much hatred in the way she snorts and rolls her eyes. "If he did, he did the world a favor. Especially Joy."

"Did you ever tell anybody about that man?"

"I never even mentioned him to Joy, much less than anyone else. The way I see it, it's none of my business. The situation was settled, and that's all I need to know."

And I thought I had a lot going on under the surface. This woman just casually tells me a man who happens to be my father swooped in like an avenging angel and probably killed Romero's father, but she sounds like she could be talking about the weather or what she's having for Thanksgiving dinner. I don't know whether I should thank her, pretend I don't know anything, or burst out crying.

All I can think about is Romero. What if he saw it happen? But then, how could he work for my dad all these years? He's always been faithful—to the point where I sometimes want to claw my eyes out. He's such a pathetic lapdog.

Maybe he was grateful to be freed from the hell of his home. Maybe that's what it's all been about.

There's no time to process this before a crash next door makes us both jump. The storm door flew open hard enough to bang against the wall beside it. Now Romero stands on the porch, his breath hanging in a cloud around his head and his fists clenched tight. His gaze sweeps over the street before landing on me.

I already know I'm in trouble before his eyes go narrow.

"I'd better go." My feet are already moving, carrying me down the front steps. I don't want her to see him like this. It's instinct. She's already seen too much as it is and already worries that he turned out like his father. Why I should protect him, I have no idea. I only know I want to.

"What the fuck do I have to say to get it through your skull?" As soon as I'm within reach, he takes hold of my arm and squeezes hard enough to make me wince. For one blood-curdling moment, I'm not sure he's any better than the man Mrs. Cooper described. What if he's just as much of a monster? What if he's better at hiding it?

The first rush of nauseating fear is swept away by something more potent. It's so bitter it might burn a hole through me. I'm sick and tired of being pushed around by loud men who think being the loudest and strongest makes them the biggest deal in the room.

"Get your hand off me," I whisper, teeth clenched. Every breath I take is fuel poured on the fire he started. None of this is my fault. Not his anger, not his frustration, not his weird, controlling bullshit. "Unless you want to explain to the neighbor why you're hurting me."

His growl doesn't scare me—if anything, it intensifies my fury. "Go ahead. Let her call the cops," I whisper. That word shakes him up enough that he lets go.

"In the house." He steps aside so I can brush past him.

I turn on my heel in the center of the living room and wait until he closes the door before speaking in a low, controlled voice. "I'm going to ask you a question, and I want the truth. All these weeks, you've kept me shut in here with you. I wasn't supposed to talk to the neighbor. I wasn't supposed to go out by myself. How much of that was actually for my protection, and how much of it was for yours?"

He was all ready to lay into me, so this turn of events leaves him sputtering. "What the hell are you talking about?"

"I'm talking about you being afraid. Scared shitless that I would... what? Find out you had a shitty childhood? Find out how bad it really was? Or maybe you were afraid I would find out what happened the night Dad came and brought you home."

"You don't have a clue what you're talking about, little girl."

The way he tries to make me feel small only makes me stand up taller. "I know your father was found dead days after my father showed up here. Is that what you've been trying to keep from me? Did Dad kill him? Did you see it happen? Did he bring you back with him so you would never tell anybody here what happened? I need to know. Stop with the lies. Just tell me the truth!"

I'd swear his features soften in relief before hardening again. It was so fast, I could've imagined it... but I don't think I did. "Oh, you really don't have any idea. You should stop digging."

"Because I'm getting too close to the truth?"

"Because you're making a goddamn fool of yourself!" he snarls. "Leave it alone! This has all been about you from the beginning. Do you think I would have returned here if it weren't for you? I never wanted to set eyes on this town again. Do you want to know something else? I even hated when Callum started putting money into this fucking hell hole. It could all burn to the ground and I would piss on the ashes. That's what this place means to me. That's all it's ever held."

"You're lying. Even now, you're lying! And the worst part is, I don't know if you're lying to me or to yourself. And it's pitiful."

"You don't know—"

"I know how happy you were on that motorcycle. How peaceful you were at the lake. You didn't hate everything about this town. You just hated this house. But don't blame that on me. I didn't ask to come here. I could have gone anywhere, and you know that."

"The little princess needed someplace nobody would be able to find her."

"I could have gone anywhere," I whisper, because I'd scream otherwise. "But you brought me here, and now you're blaming your bullshit on me. I have nothing to do with any of this. I didn't do anything to you. When are you going to stop treating me like the enemy?"

"Leave me the fuck alone! Why can't you leave all of this alone?"

"Because that's no way to live. All the anger you have, all the hatred and secrets. I'm sorry if I care."

"You don't care! You're just nosy. You have to know. And the further away I push you, the more determined you are. That's what this is about. Don't pretend you give a shit about me. If you did, you would know it's not as easy as telling a few stories. Going back to all that shit? Do you really want me to do that just to make you feel better? Because that's all it's about. You. What you think you deserve to know. It's my fucking life we're talking about! Not yours!"

Under all my anger, under the skittering, icy fear that stirs up in me when he's like this, there's knowing he's right. If I really cared, I wouldn't want to drag him through all of that again. But... "It wouldn't matter if you wouldn't make it my problem. If you didn't have to be such an asshole to me. Hot and cold. I never know which version of you I'm going to face from one minute to the next. You think you're any better than your father? Did he ever make you feel that way?"

I went too far. I know it even before his head snaps around, before spit flies from his mouth when he bellows a single word. "Enough!"

His face is a mask of seething fury when he picks up a candle from the coffee table and hurls it across the room. I see it happening in slow motion, the candle tumbling through the air, end over end, sailing toward the fireplace.

Toward the urn over the fireplace.

Do I think I can stop it? I don't know. I only know I lunge for it, reaching out with both hands, but it's too late. I was never going to stop this from happening.

My shriek rings out in my ears, but the sound of the urn crashing to the floor is louder. The lid falls off and just like that, what's left of my mother spreads across the floor and hangs in the air. I'm frozen in shock, staring at the mess. My brain can't handle what my eyes are telling it.

It's Romero's voice that breaks through. "Oh, God."

"No. No, no, no!" My knees go out and I drop to the floor with my head in my hands. I want to reach out and scoop it all back up, but it's everywhere and I don't want her all over me. However, now she's all over the floor so what am I supposed to do? "No," I moan. It's the only word I can think of.

"Fuck, I am so sorry." He crouches close to me. "I'll clean this up. It'll be—"

"You can't clean it up! Asshole!" I can barely breathe as sobs shake me from head to toe, barely seeing through the tears. "You can't just scoop it up! These are her ashes! Don't touch them!"

He makes the mistake of putting a hand on my shoulder. I fling it off, then shove him away. I could kill him. I won't be satisfied until I do. "You bastard. Is there anything else you want to take from me? Do you want to hurt me again? Why not? This was the last fucking thing I had! And I'll never get it back!"

My head is spinning and I think I'm going to be sick. There's sweat rolling down the back of my neck. I can't stop shaking. And I want to hurt him; I need to hurt him.

"What are you talking about? You're hysterical."

"Don't you fucking tell me how I am!" I fight my way to my feet, swaying, breathless, as one sob after another shakes my body. "From the beginning, you started taking things from me. You took my wing in the house. You took all of Dad's attention. His pride. And then, when he finally decided to start paying attention to me again, what did he do? He made you my fucking guard dog! You've been hanging over me for most of my life. You took him from me, and now you took her!"

"I never meant to do that! That's not my fault!"

"No, nothing's your fault. The way you shut me out. The way you kiss me, then make it seem like I'm a filthy whore you can't be bothered to touch! You tell me you want me, then you treat me like garbage. I don't even know who I am anymore because of you! I don't know what I want. I don't know where I belong!"

"What are you talking about? How was any of that because of me?"

I don't know what I'm saying anymore. It's all coming out like water through a fire hose. And now that it's out I'm weak, but when he touches me, my hands tighten to fists and I pummel his chest and shoulders. "Leave me alone! Damn you! I hate you!"

All he does is grip my arms and hold on tight no matter how I fight to be free. "You listen to me. All I ever wanted was to help you. That's why we're here. I thought I could help you. I thought I could bring you back to your dad and Bianca. And to me."

"Bullshit. You don't care. The way you talk to me. The names you call me. You've never given a shit about me. You resented me as much as I resented you. Don't try to rewrite history now."

"You really think I don't care? That I never cared?"

"That's exactly what I just said."

His eyes dart over my face before he pulls me in, his teeth bared in a snarl, his breath hitting my face as he takes one rasping breath after another. "If I never cared, then why did I slit that bastard's throat for you?"

For the second time in minutes, his words drag me out of a fog of raw emotion. "What?" I croak, going still in his grip.

"I said, why did I slit his throat from ear to ear and watch him bleed to death? That's what I did, Tatum. I killed Kristoff because of what he did to you. How he hurt you. How he beat you down until there was almost nothing left of you. The real you, the person you really are. He deserved to die, and I made that happen. For you. It was always for you."

I don't have any time to process this before he crushes his lips against mine.

CHAPTER 25

ROMERO

There is something about her that makes me say everything I've fought to hold back. What is it? How does she do it? I still don't have the answer by the time I break the kiss to come up for air. There's a storm raging inside me, a storm that's threatened to erupt for as long as I can remember.

It's all because of her that I finally lost control. I should hate her for it, but how can I when it feels so damn good to stop fighting?

She looks so lost and confused as she stares up at me. Her lips are swollen thanks to my kiss – the sight makes me want to kiss her again, harder, until she's bleeding. The impulse races through me like fire and leaves me grinding my teeth, fighting it back. I can't hurt her. No matter how much I want to.

"Don't stop." Her desperate whispers make me groan in need and regret, closing my eyes, begging silently for strength. I don't even know who I'm begging. God, the Devil himself, I have no idea. I only know I'm barely holding on.

"Don't you get it?" I hardly sound like myself as I take her by the shoulders and hold her still, glaring down at her. "I am not who you want. I am the last thing you want."

"Don't tell me what I want."

"You want someone who can be good to you. Who can take care

of you. That is not me, Tatum. That will never be me. I am not good for you – or even for myself. Everything I've ever touched, I've destroyed. I've hurt people. I've killed people. And… and…"

And it's all so clear. Finally, I understand what I've wrestled with and why. I have finally gotten to the heart of everything, and it's staring me in the face. "I don't trust myself with you."

She reaches up, and I shrink away from her touch – it's dangerous, because it feels so damn good. Even though I crave it with every fiber of my soul, I crave something I don't deserve. "Give it to me," she whispers, stroking my stubbled cheek.

"What?"

"Give it all to me. Every bit of it. All the pain and anger. All the regret, all those memories. Give it to me. Take it out on me."

"You don't mean that."

"Fuck you for telling me what I mean. I know what I mean. I know what I want. You. You are the only man I've ever really wanted, the only one I couldn't have. I still want you, more than I ever have. So give all of it to me. Let it be over. The hate in your heart. Let it go. I'll take it."

Either there's something wrong with her, or there's something wrong with me. What she's saying shouldn't make sense. I should shove her away with both hands and tell her she's crazy. I need to.

But I need her more.

There's a force stronger than both of us that makes me wrap my arms around her, clutching her body close to mine before I pick her up and start for the stairs. I would take her here and now on the floor like an animal, but she deserves better than a hard fuck on her mother's ashes. I still have enough control over my primal urges to know it would be wrong.

She buries her face in my neck, her breath hot on my skin. The sweetest fire is nothing compared to the fire racing through me, making my blood sing, and the animal that's always lived inside me raises its head and roars. Finally, no more fighting it. Finally, I take what was always meant to be mine.

I see it in her eyes when I lay her on her bed, staring down at her in the clear light of day. There's no hiding, no running away. I see her, and she sees me. We both know there's no coming back from this.

My hand trembles as I run it over her cheek. So fucking beautiful. How many nights did I spend secretly wishing to touch her this way, wishing she would look up at me with lust, fear, and trust in those clear, green eyes? "I can't promise I'll be gentle with you," I whisper while my cock threatens to break the zipper on my jeans.

She takes my hand, staring up at me while she places it over one of her tits. "I don't care. I need you. I'm yours."

The sound of that shouldn't unleash so much satisfaction; then again, nothing about this makes sense. Not in my mind, anyway. Only in my body. In the most primal part of my soul where she has always lived.

I take the neck of her thin sweater in both hands and tear it open to reveal the creamy top of her tits encased in white lace. I descend on them, letting myself soak in the taste of her skin, her sweetness, soothing myself in the comfort of her body while she arches her back, crying out wordlessly as she offers more of herself to my greedy mouth. "Yes, just like that," she moans when I yank the cups down to play with her nipples. Her fingers run through my hair, tugging and scraping my scalp with her nails until my skin sizzles. "More."

I'm lost in her, lost in the sound of her moans, in the way she says my name, the way she offers herself to me. No hesitation, no holding back. She's a feast, and I'm the bastard lucky enough to have her all to myself.

I'm impatient, pulling the sweater over her head before she arches her back to unhook the bra. Fuck me, she is perfect. The body I've only ever touched through her clothes is everything I've ever imagined and more. "You're beautiful," I croak. It doesn't come close to the truth, but it's the best I can do.

All she does is reach for me and pull me down again, a leg wrapping around my hips to draw me closer. "Take it out on me," she breathes in my ear while her pussy grinds against my cock. "Do it. Make me feel all of it."

A fragment of my awareness still tells me I should say no, but who could? I have everything I yearned for years right here, writhing, moaning, begging. For me, only for me.

Still, I pull back and take her jaw in my hand, holding her head still while forcing her to look me in the eye. "If it's too much, you tell me. I mean it. Understood?"

Her gaze softens and she melts against me, and I know it was the right thing to say. "Yes." Then, with a hand around the back of my neck, she pulls me down into a fierce, deep kiss that's more like a fight, the two of us struggling for control, teeth clashing, tongues tangled. When she works her hands between us, I lift my hips to give her room to unbutton my jeans. I can't help sighing when I'm free from that zipper – but the sound turns to a groan when her fingers dip inside my boxer briefs and close around my shaft.

"Oh, fuck." For one second, I give myself over to the pure rush of being touched. It's so good, too good, enough that I could lose my grip if I'm not careful. "Slow down," I grunt, moving my hips, fucking her tiny fist while I lower my head and capture one of her nipples between my lips. Her soft whimpers send precum dribbling from my tip and she uses it, working it over my length. I reward her by sucking harder, flicking my tongue over her taut peak.

She bucks her hips, crazy with need, making me wedge a hand between her thighs. She cries out in relief. "Yes... Yes, please, touch me." She lets go of my cock in favor of running her hands over the blanket beneath her, twisting it in her fists, her head rolling from side to side.

Her pretty, pink pussy is dripping wet by the time I work her leggings and thong down her smooth legs. Her pussy is smooth, too, glistening. All for me. I settle on my knees between her thighs and push them apart until they fall open. There's a wet spot already forming under her by the time I run my scruff over her sensitive skin. She sucks in a surprised – maybe pained – breath, but it's followed by a deep moan. "Oh, yeah. So good..." The scent of her arousal makes me harder than ever, and by the time I run my tongue through her swollen folds, I'm panting. Desperate for the taste of her.

"Fuck!" Her hips shoot up from the bed, but I throw an arm over her, holding her down, forcing her to take every last lap while she moans and writhes like she's possessed. She has needed this as much as I have, maybe more, and that's what I have in mind as I devour her pussy. She tastes like nothing I've ever known — sweet but musky. Fresh. Mine. All mine, no one else's ever again.

"So good... Don't stop... Romero..."

She's getting close, drowning me in the honey that pours from her pussy in a flood. However, I can't catch all of it on my tongue before it runs down her crack as my frustrated growl only leaves her moaning louder than before. The hand on the back of my head clamps down tight and I respond by flicking my tongue across her clit, faster and faster, before her thighs clamp around my head and she screams.

The pounding of my heart is even louder than the screams muffled by her thighs. I'm not going to stop – she needs this, needs to let go and lose herself, to forget everything but what I'm doing to her. When I'm making her feel.

I manage to open my eyes and look up across the length of her body. The sight of her ecstatic abandonment is a wet dream come true. She's lost in the moment, lost in me. That's enough of a reward to keep my tongue moving, working her until she pulls my hair to make me stop. Her legs go limp along with the rest of her, and I enjoy watching her shake and gasp for air.

I did that. I did that to her. And already I want to do it again. A man could get addicted to this, with no way to kick the habit.

I peel off my shirt, stuck to my skin by the sweat I've worked up, and she reaches for me. Her touch is like a balm, healing me and stirring my hunger all at once.

"I need... I need..." To claim you. To break you. Yes, all of that and more as I kneel between her legs, stroking my rigid cock, now taking in the full sight of her. Her wild, tangled curls, the heaving tits, the sweat beading on her forehead.

All she does is hold her arms out to me, not saying a word. Welcoming me to take relief in her body, in the warmth of her arms as they close around my shoulders, in the wet heat that envelops my cock as I begin to ease my way into what I already knew would be tight. My fingers were one thing, but this? She is still quivering from her orgasm, the muscles fluttering, pulsing, until I wonder if I'll be able to fit all of me inside her.

Her body goes still and her mouth falls open when I breach her hole and begin to sink inside. "Fuck!" she shouts, eyes wide as I work my head deeper, followed by the silver barbell piercing beneath it. "Oh, my God!" Her nails rake across my shoulders and break the skin while she jerks her hips, legs pressed against my ass and drawing me deeper.

"You like my cock inside you?" I grunt, sighing in relief when my balls touch her ass.

"Oh, yeah," she moans. "Feels so good."

"Tell me. Say it." I lower my head, brushing my lips against hers until she whimpers. "I love your cock, Romero."

Her eyes open, hazy with pleasure, burning with desire. I could drown in them. I could lose what's left of my soul. "I love your cock, Romero," she whispers, rolling her hips, making us moan together. So fucking good, so much better than any fantasy.

I wanted to take her hard, didn't I? Brutally. She wants me to take everything out on her? I would love to. I would love to hurt her and pour years of pain, loneliness, and guilt into her soft, willing body.

Only I can't move right away. Something holds me in place, balls deep in her tight sheath. It's enough to stay this way, locked together like this, with no one in the world except us. She's been hurt enough. I want to give her more than that. She deserves more.

I start off slowly instead, pulling back and watching every muscle in her face. The way her eyes widen and her mouth opens so she can release a long, soft sigh that can only mean pleasure. "Feels so good," she whispers, sounding almost surprised.

"Your first piercing?" Her head bobs up and down before falling back and exposing the slim column of her throat. I dragged my tongue over her skin while sinking deep again, savoring her moans and how her pulse flutters.

Her legs wrap tight around me. "More, give me more. Give me all of you." She closes her eyes when I grind against her clit, working her inside and out until there's nothing but a string of high-pitched whimpers coming from her. The muscles gripping me tighten until I can barely move.

"This sweet, tight pussy," I grunt, losing my breath a little more with every stroke. "Gonna snap me in half."

"I'm so close..." She jerks her hips in time with my thrusts, pushing me closer to the edge no matter how I fight to hold on. My body has other ideas, other needs.

"Come inside me." There's desperation in her voice—she's close, so close. "I'm on the pill. Come with me. Fill me up."

I don't even know if she knows what she's saying, but there's no way I'm resisting that. Not when there's nothing I would rather do. My pace quickens and she nods in approval, meeting me stroke for stroke, gasping for air the way I do while our bodies move together like we've been doing this all our lives. It's so fucking right.

"Romero... oh, God... yes... I'm coming!"

"Come for me," I grunt while wet slapping sounds fill the air and mix with her cries. "Come on my cock like a good girl."

"Yes! Fuck, yes!" A million muscles begin massaging my cock from tip to base, and that's it, I can't hold on. The euphoric rush of release overtakes me and I don't bother fighting. My ears are ringing and my heart's pounding out of my chest, and it feels so fucking right. No matter how wrong it might look later, it's right now. Now is all that matters.

We're both breathless by the time I pull out of the sloppy mess I made. She's glowing, beaming up at the ceiling while her chest rises and falls slowly with every breath. I don't know exactly what's going through her head, and I don't want to ask. There's something almost sacred about the peaceful way she smiles. Like what just happened meant more than a couple of orgasms.

And the thing is, I understand the feeling. I know it. I'm going through it, too.

For the first time in longer than I can remember, the restless animal locked inside my chest is calm. There's nothing in my head but sweet silence. No screams. No memories.

A man could become addicted.

I think I already have.

"I have a question." She slowly turns her head to give me a long, clear-eyed look. "When can we do that again?"

CHAPTER 26

TATUM

Two words hit me like a bomb as soon as I open my eyes to a dark bedroom. What now?

The steady, throbbing ache between my legs is a reminder of the time we've spent together in bed today. This bed, where the pillows and sheets now smell like a mix of my lavender shampoo and his spicy cologne and sex. A lot of sex. I'm exhausted, but in the best way possible. I stretch under the blanket bunched around me—he must have tucked me in when he got up. I must've been out cold since I have no memory of that.

So after this... what happens next? What now? It's too much to think about. Too depressing. I want more of him. He's a drug I'm already hooked on. Not only his body or what he did to mine. What he did to my soul. How free I felt. No fear. No ugly memories. I was entirely in the moment.

A sound by the window draws my attention to Romero, sitting in the armchair and staring out into the night. The silver light from a full moon highlights his sharp profile and throws half of his face into deep shadow. I doubt he sees what's in front of him. He's wearing the look of a man gazing into the past.

As much as I hate to disturb him when he's brooding like this, I clear my throat. It doesn't startle him – he probably knew I was awake, even if he's not looking my way. It always did seem like he had eyes in the back of his head.

"Are you alright?" I whisper. It's a little awkward now, with the two of us back to our usual selves rather than the animals we were earlier. That was how I felt, anyway.

His bare shoulders rise and fall. "I don't know." For once, he's telling the truth instead of giving me some half-assed response and brushing me aside.

"Do you want to talk about it?" I should know better than to ask, shouldn't I? Though it seems like the sort of thing you ask someone who appears as troubled as he does right now.

"I don't know what there is to talk about."

"Are you... thinking about the things I said earlier? I didn't mean to hurt you. Really, I didn't. I only ever wanted you to let me in and treat me like a person instead of a job you had to do. I was just trying to get you to..." To what? To see me? To let me help him? I'm not sure anymore.

"You don't have to explain," he murmurs, finally turning his head a little until he's looking at me. There is pain in every line, every curve of his face. Like he's being tortured. The emotion welling up in my chest is sudden and powerful, and it's only knowing that he'd hate it keeps me from going to him and wrapping my arms around his bare shoulders. He's always been so strong and tough, whereas he's anything but right now. It's my fault, at least partly. I forced him to go back through so much he's been trying to forget.

I sit cross-legged with the sheets bunched up around my chest and my back to the headboard. "I won't try to force you anymore, but I will listen to anything you want to say. I'm here, Romero. I'm not going anywhere."

At first, I figure he's going to brush me off as usual – the way he sighs, the way his head slowly turns back toward the window doesn't leave much room for doubt. I have to brace myself against the disappointment that inevitably follows. We've had sex, and he still can't talk to me. It's hard not to take something like that personally.

"I was thinking about the night I met your dad."

My whole body starts to tingle, but I clamp my lips together before I can do something stupid like urge him on. He needs to do this in his own way, on his own time. I feel it.

"You don't know what it's like for me to come back here. Oh, sure, you've picked up on things. You're not stupid. You have to know I had it rough growing up. My father…" His voice catches and his head touches the back of the chair. "He was violent. He hated the world. Lost his job; couldn't stay sober long enough to keep another one. And somehow, that was everybody else's fault but his. But that's nothing new. Back then, I guess you couldn't swing a dead cat without hitting some bitter, drunken wreck who got old before his time."

He looks down at his hands, slowly flexing and relaxing them. The rhythm is almost hypnotic, so much so that I can't tear my eyes from them. Powerful hands that know how to touch me and awaken things in me I didn't know existed. "Some days, you could walk down the street and see them sitting out on their porches or front steps. No jobs. Nothing to do but bitch and hate and drink."

"That night, he was supposed to be out on a fishing trip with some of his buddies," he continues. "You have no idea what a relief that was. It was like a holiday. He would be out of the house for three, maybe four days. My mom said she'd make dinner the first night, and I asked if Becky could come over and eat with us. She could almost never come over. I didn't want her around him." His jaw tightens, and my heart aches. He never had a chance to be a kid, did he?

"We were having dinner, and it was really nice. Mom seemed happy, and she and Becky always got along really well — everybody sort of knew everybody around here, you know? She liked Becky. Said she had a good head on her shoulders. And I…" He snickers, looking down at his hands. "I was so fucking happy. That was the last happy time I ever had in this house."

As I watch, his fists tighten. "And then he came home. Out of nowhere, the front door opened. I almost puked all over the table. It was like all the air got sucked out of the room. Dread. Just absolute, crushing dread." My throat is closing up, and my heart is beating faster because I know that feeling. Maybe not as well as he does, but there were plenty of times – especially in Europe — I felt the same way. Kristoff would go out with some of the people he met, and it was like a weight had been lifted. Then he would come back, and it would settle on me again.

"Right away, he was pissed. Apparently, he forgot his fishing pole and had to drive home to get it, and I guess he was missing out on some good drinking time with his pals. And for some reason, seeing Becky sitting at the table... Mom had even bought flowers and put them out. She was that happy to have a guest. *'What is this, a party? Are you having a party while I'm not around?'*" It's incredible the way his voice changes, deepening into a growl that makes my body erupt in goosebumps.

"And he stomped across the living room, and I knew I had to do something. I stood up and tried to block them from him. I told him to go get his fishing pole and get back to the lake. That we were just having dinner. He shoved me out of the way. Becky jumped up; she was terrified. And I felt so damn guilty and useless because I brought her into this. And I was ashamed, too."

There's no emotion in his voice now. It's flat, lifeless, like he wants to get through this without *feeling* the memories. "She tried to come to me, to comfort me. Or maybe she just wanted to feel safer. He was a strong guy, and she might've weighed a hundred pounds. It was like swatting a fly—she hit the counter, then hit the floor."

I'm on the edge of my seat while he pauses to take a ragged breath. "Becky screamed. Mom screamed. Everything went red. I picked up a knife that was on the table. Mom screamed again. *'Don't. Romero, don't.'* That was all that stopped me. I could actually see myself sinking it into his chest, as clear as anything. He was laughing and daring me—I could smell the beer on his breath and knew he was drunk. Told myself it might be my only chance to set us all free. But then I heard Becky crying and moaning on the floor."

I can hardly breathe as Romero continues.

"There was blood soaking through her jeans."

"Oh, my God," I whisper. I don't even know if he hears me. He's so far away.

"She never told me she was pregnant. I guess she would have, but she hadn't gotten around to it yet. Mom was hysterical, and so was I. Somehow, I drove her car to the hospital. I don't remember any of it. I was half out of my mind, I swear. She was pregnant with my baby, and he killed it. He didn't even seem sorry when I was helping her out the front door. But I would never expect that from him, anyway. He never did like to take responsibility for the things he did. Anyway, her parents got there before long, and they pretty much told me to get the hell out and never see her again. It's bad enough I got her pregnant, but now she was in the emergency room because of me. I never even got the chance to tell them I never laid a hand on her, but I guess it didn't matter. It was still *my* fault. I walked to O'Neals, and for some reason, it seemed like a good idea to go inside. So I did. I went in, and I proceeded to get drunk off my ass. It didn't matter that I was only sixteen – I didn't care. And they knew who my old man was. Guess they figured it ran in the family. He had already put plenty of money in their pockets. And then I staggered back to the house. You can't understand how broken I was."

"I can't imagine."

"I figured he wouldn't even be there anymore. That he would've grabbed his pole and run like the fucking coward he always was. But no. He was there. His truck was still in front of the house. And I knew even before I stepped through the door what would happen."

My chest is tight with dread, and I get the feeling I was way wrong when I interpreted Mrs. Cooper's story.

"I walked in, and what did I find? My mother was on her hands and knees, scrubbing the floor. Trying to clean up Becky's blood. Only it wasn't just her blood. He kicked the shit out of Mom while I was gone – I'm surprised she could see with both eyes swelling up. And all he could do was scream at her to clean up the mess."

Tears drip off my chin and onto my bare chest, soaking into the sheet. I can't help it. It's too much, but I won't tell him to stop. I wanted to know, didn't I? And now, he deserves to tell his story. I think he needs to.

"I didn't wait for him to goad me into it. I don't even think he saw it coming. It all came out of me – all of it, every last bit. The hatred. The humiliation. All the pain he ever put me through. The pain he put my mom through. The pain he put Becky through. I wasn't thinking. I was just... hitting. Again, I knew Mom was begging me to stop, but I couldn't. I didn't want to. Doing what I had dreamed of doing for so long felt so good. I didn't stop until he was dead. And even then, I wanted to keep going."

"I finally snapped out of it, and the only thing I felt bad about was the way Mom cried. That's the only thing I felt guilty over. Otherwise, he had it coming. But then reality came back in, and I realized what it was telling me. Obviously, I'd be arrested. I might even be tried as an adult. It's so remarkable, the things that go through your head at a time like that. I could see a judge, deciding that I was pissed enough to go back to the house and kill him for what he did to Becky. I hardly noticed Mom making a phone call. And when she got off the phone, she was like a different person. Like a robot. She took a trash bag from under the counter and told me to remove all my clothes and put them inside. Even my shoes. I was only in my underwear when she told me to go up and take a shower, and I did, because I guess I needed somebody to tell me what to do. I sure as hell couldn't figure it out on my own. And somehow, while I was showering, she found the strength to throw most of my stuff in a bag. It was all packed up by the time I got out of the shower. And that was when she told me I was going away."

My head is spinning.

"I guess you know the rest. I don't know what made her call Callum; I really don't. I know they didn't completely fall out of touch over the years, so maybe she had an idea of what he did. The kind of life he led. Maybe he was the only man she had ever trusted. I'll never be able to ask her now. But either way, he showed up in no time — really, he must've flown here. He came and took me away.

She told me I could never return, but I could trust him because she trusted him. If I came back, though, and people started asking questions, it could all fall apart."

What must that have been like? Sixteen years old, having just beaten his father to death, knowing he could never return home? Not if he didn't want to end up in prison. "So Dad hid you."

"He did more than hide me. He taught me all the things I never learned. I know you think I wanted to take your place – that's not true, but I'm not going to pretend I'm not grateful for his guidance. He taught me how to be a man. He opened me up to a world I sure as hell didn't know existed. He gave me a future – yeah, there is a lot of danger, but my life here was dangerous, too. Besides, I kind of liked it. I mean, how much worse can you get than killing your own father with your bare hands? What else did I have to lose?"

"Did you... ever talk about it again?"

"Only once. He told me his guys had cleaned it all up. They would make it look like some random killing. They dumped his body in the landfill, and it's not like he had any friends around here besides his drinking buddies. He made it a point to plant it in the paper that Dad had a history of gambling problems and a little trouble with the law when he was a kid, just in case anybody felt sympathetic. Really, nobody was going to go out of their way to see who killed him. He also told me he would take care of my mom. She would never want for anything again – but how could that be true, since I wasn't with her?"

His face almost crumples for a second, and so does mine. "So I had to trust him, and I did, and I still do. I owe him everything. How else do you think it was possible for me to come back here? I owed it to him to take care of you. And I wanted to. I guess you were supposed to make up for what I couldn't do in the past. I couldn't help Mom. I couldn't help Becky. I couldn't stop him until there was no other choice. And even then, it was like I didn't feel any of it. I wasn't thinking. I was useless."

It's like I've never seen him before. I've always heard about looking at somebody through new eyes, but this is the first time I've ever done it. For so long, I've been wrong about him in so many ways.

I slowly get out of bed, careful not to startle him. He's still so deep in the past. "You aren't useless. You were a kid. There's a big difference."

"Now you want to know why I don't drink?" he snorts. "Because I know what happens when I lose control. And I can never, ever take that risk. It's bad enough you saw me that way here at the house. Out in public? I shudder to think."

"That was different. You went through a whole lifetime of torture from him." I approach, my heart in my throat, before placing a hand on his shoulder. "You did what you had to do."

He doesn't shake me off, thank God. "She wanted me to have a chance at life," he murmurs, still staring out the window. "What would she think of me now? I didn't stop at just my father. I've killed… I've killed a lot of people. I've hurt a lot more. I even killed—"

My hand tightens, squeezing the firm muscle. "What would she think of you? She would think she raised the kind of man who does what needs to be done. Everything you've done since then, you did it because you had to. You protected my father. You protected what he built. That's honorable."

"You don't have to say that."

"I know I don't have to, but it's the truth. That's how I see it. You stood up repeatedly and did what had to be done. You are a protector. You're a good man."

"I didn't protect you from him." He doesn't need to say the name. "I only ended his useless life when it was too late to stop him."

"That wasn't your fault. I wasn't exactly open and honest about what was happening."

I'm tentative as I reach out, placing a hand under his chin and turning his head until he's looking up at me. I was so, so wrong. From the very beginning, when I met the handsome, brooding kid who I felt was taking my place. No wonder Dad was so good to him.

He knew what he had been through. Knew what he needed to feel, like he could trust that he was safe.

There's so much pain swimming in those blue eyes. Oceans of pain. Pain I want nothing more than to wash away, but I know I can't. Just like he couldn't wash mine away. "Come on," I whisper, taking his hand and backing up. "Come to bed. Let it go for now. Just lie down with me."

He only hesitates for a second before unfolding his body from the chair and following me to the bed, where I climb in first and hold my arms out to him. I don't know what's driving me now. Instinct, I guess. I need to hold him, and I think he might need to be held. Everybody does at some point—even tough guys like him.

It's like a victory when he lies down beside me and lets me wrap him in my arms. When his cheek rests against the top of my head and his body shudders as he releases a pent-up sigh that seems to release the tension holding him stiff.

"I'm here." It's all I can think to say while his heart beats under my ear and I gaze out at the moonlit night. "I'm here, and it's all going to be okay."

CHAPTER 27

ROMERO

"We have a problem."

And there I was, prepared to attack her at first sight when I rounded the bottom of the stairs and found her standing there. How can I not? She's in front of the open refrigerator door, dressed in nothing but the long cardigan she wrapped around her naked body after getting out of bed. The last thing I want to hear about while my dick's getting hard is a problem.

"What is it?"

She scowls at the inside of the fridge. "There's practically no food in here."

"That doesn't sound right." But there's no arguing with what's in front of me when I step up behind her.

"We've been busy with other things," she murmurs, looking up at me with eyes that sparkle with deeper meaning.

Other things. That's one way to describe the way we haven't been able to keep our hands off each other. What can I say? I'm a guy who finally got what he craved for years, and I'm making the most of it. I don't hear her complaining, either – no, she only complains when she has to wait for me to recover. She spent a long time being afraid of being touched, being wanted. She felt disconnected from her body. Now, all of that is in the past, and she's got a hell of a lot of lost time to make up for.

We both do.

Although now that I'm looking at a refrigerator that holds nothing but a few mouthfuls of milk, eggs, and yogurt that's probably expired, I understand the need for balance.

"Shit. I guess you distracted me."

"Did I?" She leans against my bare chest, sighing softly when I wrap an arm around her and slide my hand under her sweater. Her nipple hardens under my palm, while her head drops back onto my shoulder. "You can do that all day if you want to," she whispers – throaty, needy.

"I wish I could." I bury my face against her neck and inhale her sweet, floral scent before nipping at her tender skin.

"I know, I know. You have to work."

It turns out there are things in this world capable of ruining my hard-on, after all. All it took was the reminder of my responsibilities. The reason we're here. Who keeps money in my accounts.

"Not this very minute, though." I don't want to think about that. I won't think about anything except for how she melts against me so effortlessly. All she needed was an invitation. She's mine, all of her. No matter whether it's right or wrong.

As if I don't already know it's wrong.

I close the refrigerator door and lean her against it, parting the sides of her sweater so my hands have full access to her tits, which I mold in my palms while she arches her back and whimpers. I know that sound by heart now. I'll never get tired of hearing it.

"I thought you wanted breakfast." She ends it on a moan, letting her head drop back when I bend to pull one of her nipples between my teeth. Like, I give a shit about breakfast now, when there's something much more tempting to eat. My need for her is bottomless. I can't imagine it ever ending. I should want to, but I don't. That's the last thing I want.

I don't want my freedom. All I want is her.

Her fingers dance over my scalp, holding my head in place, while

I work her into a frenzy with my teeth and tongue. She barely has time to squeal in surprise when I swiftly bend to take her ass in both hands, lifting her up and placing her on the counter. I need to forget everything drumming on my mind, all the reminders of what I should be doing – and what I absolutely should not be doing. Like right now, as I spread her thighs and drop to my knees.

"I'd rather have *you* for breakfast."

I know her body by heart now, after days spent defiling her in every room of the house. The softness of her inner thighs and her sweet, musky arousal are damn near intoxicating. I run my scruff over her soft skin, teasing both of us, drawing the moment out until she lets out a frustrated little groan and tilts her pelvis so her entire pussy is on full display: pink, glistening, drawing me in.

"You better start eating." I can hardly breathe as she runs her fingers through her pink folds, then holds them up for me to see the moisture coating them. "Do you want this?"

What is it about her that turns me into a slobbering, mindless animal? My tongue darts out to catch her addictive, sweet nectar. The first taste awakens my senses and my awareness narrows to this, to this alone. Her smell, her taste, the soft moans of approval before she drags her hand away to grab the back of my head and pull it in. "Come on, then. I have plenty more for you."

My God, I am lost. Drowning in her. I can't remember a time when I didn't know what she tastes like. What it sounds like when I drive my tongue into her dripping hole. "Yes. Fuck me with your tongue," she begs, clutching my head in both hands, riding my face. "Make me come for you."

That's precisely what I'm going to do. My rigid cock strains against my zipper, but I ignore it in favor of withdrawing my tongue and replacing it with two fingers, which I use to massage her G-spot while sucking her delicious little clit. She lets loose a string of incoherent cries, and soon her juices coat my fingers while she grinds against me. "Oh, yeah... Yeah, right there... Don't stop, please, don't stop!"

Her desperate whispers are music to my ears. I'm a king, on top of the world, able to turn her into a gasping, needy thing. Me, only me, nobody else. Only I can take her to this place where she lets go of everything but the here and now. What she needs the most.

And now she needs to come, tightening around my fingers, her cries rising in pitch, her nails scraping my scalp to the point of pain. I won't stop her. This is what she needs, this is what I want for her. To lose herself in me. Come for me, Princess. Come for me.

Her body goes stiff, freezing on the edge between tension and release – and then it breaks, and she spasms once, twice, her ecstatic cries echoing through the room. "Yes! Yes! Romero!" Then she goes limp, sighing, legs falling open and going still.

Her bare chest heaves when she lets out a breathless laugh. "My God. You are so good at that."

Tatum reaches for me, pulling me close once I stand, wrapping her legs around me. I hold her for a moment, stroking her messy curls before her deft little fingers brush against my aching erection.

But the clock is ticking. My full attention wouldn't be on her. I pull my hips back, shaking my head. "Later."

Her brows draw together when she looks up at me, and I kiss her forehead. "As I said, I do have work to do. Believe me, I'll have you take care of that later."

"No fun," she mutters, pouting. Playing the brat to break me down. The temptation to give her what she wants is almost too much to resist.

"No fun? What do you call what just happened? It sure as hell sounded to me like you were having fun."

"You're not wrong." Her lips twitch until she can't hold back a grin. "Well, since you'll be too busy to get your dick sucked, I should go to the store. We really need food – no offense, but even great sex isn't enough sometimes."

When my stomach growls loud enough for us both to hear, we share a laugh. "Okay, you've got me." Even though there's still a part of me that doesn't like her going out alone, it's probably for the best that she is not around when I make this call. The less she knows about the plan I'm about to present to Callum, the better. Plausible deniability and all that. It's not the same as hiding things from her – though I know that's how she would take it if given the chance.

Maybe I just don't want her thinking about him. She needs to think about me, us. The present... if not the future. Because there can be no future here. Of all times to think about something like that, but it's true.

She doesn't seem to notice the change in my mood, too busy laughing about her shaky legs when she lowers herself to the floor.

"Remind me to disinfect the counter later," she observes with a wry grin. I have the pleasure of watching her walk away, the hem of the sweater brushing the curve of her ass. It's hypnotic, waiting for a flash of those firm, supple cheeks before she disappears around the banister and runs up the stairs.

Rather than wait for her to do it, I pull out the cleaner and paper towels to wipe the counter. Not that I'm generally domestic, but right now, I would do anything to avoid making this call. Callum will be happy, of course – that's not what I'm worried about. It's knowing how hard I'll need to fight my guilt every second we talk. Every minute he's trusting me. He trusts me, and look at what I'm doing. I lost track of the number of times we've fucked over the course of this week. I've already gotten used to falling asleep with her in my arms. I can't think about that while I'm talking business with him.

Tatum is exiting the steamy bathroom once I make it upstairs. "Aw, damn. I could've used some company in the shower."

And the sight of her wearing nothing but a towel with her curls pinned up on top of her head unleashes fresh hunger in my core. It's like every part of her was set up to tempt me. "I'm distracted, anyway," I murmur, but that doesn't stop me from grabbing her ass as she walks by. The sound of her giggles is a gift. I was sure for so long that she would never laugh like that again. That she would never feel lighthearted again. That he had taken that from her, too. But now she is humming to herself as she heads for the bedroom. I've never seen anybody so happy about running errands.

The time I get out after a quick, hot shower, she's gone. The house feels empty and eerily silent without her. I can't linger on that while I hurry through drying off and getting dressed. I need to get this over with. He'll be happy, and that's what matters – even if he wouldn't be, should he find out the truth. He can't, that's all. This can only exist between Tatum and me.

I sit down at my desk and pull up the information we're supposed to review, then call him and settle back with my eyes closed. I can do this. I can't let myself give in to paranoia. The man has no idea, and he never will. We're safe. I haven't jeopardized her in any way.

"It's a little late for you, isn't it?" he asks on answering the phone.

Not a great way to start out. A glance at the time confirms it's barely past ten, even though he's used to keeping early hours. So am I... but I'm normally focused. "I had a late night putting the finishing touches on these plans." I had a late night fucking your daughter until she damn near passed out.

"I'm only busting your balls. Sorry if it came off the wrong way." Busting my balls? Something is off. He doesn't know, does he? How could he? I have to shake off my nerves – let's face it, if he knew, there would be no game playing. He would leave no room for doubt. My balls would already have been detached from the rest of my body.

I swallow the strange lump in my throat and push through the fear brought on by guilt. "I'm happy to say we're all set here. I've thought of every possible setback and prepared for it accordingly." There's something comforting about sliding into my usual role. Like putting on a favorite pair of old jeans that fit perfectly and make me feel comfortable. Like I know who I am.

"Lay it on me. You know I've been dying of curiosity." But he stops himself. "First off, how is Tatum?"

A normal question. Don't read too much into it. "She's fine. On her way to the grocery store as we speak."

"Alone?"

"She's doing great. Feeling stronger, more confident. I don't want to take that from her." Even taking what was left of Amanda's ashes to the lake to scatter them in the water didn't seem to break her down. I was ready for it, prepared to comfort her and sit by the water's edge through the night if needed. If anything, I think she needed that. She needed the excuse to remove her mother's presence. She needed closure.

"Of course, you're right. You're more aware of her feelings now than I am." Is that guilt I hear? I don't doubt it. No matter what she thinks or how she interpreted the way he's treated her for a decade, the talks we've had about her and her future proved to me a long time ago that he cares about nothing more than her – at least that was true before he got involved with Bianca. Tatum is still his pride and joy, whether she knows it or not.

I clear my throat, signaling a change in subject. I don't trust myself to talk about her. "I'm going to send you the documents when this call is over, but the long and short of it is this: what I've prepared will prove to Jeff once and for all that Kristoff is dead."

"I'm all ears."

"Using my Italian contacts, I've put together a report on an unfortunate accident that occurred off the coast of Capri, three weeks after Tatum returned to the States. A young man identified as Kristoff Knight had much to drink and snorted a little too much up his nose while partying on a yacht, and unfortunately, he lost his balance and fell overboard."

"And this is all documented?"

"Yes, in full. I had to grease many palms and call every favor, but we have three signed witness testimonies detailing Kristoff's condition the night he went into the water. Rocky water, at that – so rocky, his body was badly battered by the force of the waves that washed him up on shore. It was difficult to identify him once they fished him out."

"What a tragedy," he mutters.

"My contacts located a body of Kristoff's general size and physical description, and that's the body described in the autopsy paperwork. Unfortunately, since there was no one to claim him, and things are so hectic around there, the medical examiner accidentally-on-purpose sent his body down to be cremated. Now he's in some unmarked bag – at least, according to the report you're going to give Jeff. You broke your back and went way out of your way to do this, but authorities out there don't exactly give a damn about a tourist who got himself killed by his own stupidity."

"There's no way he could prove this is a lie." That's not a question. It's an observation delivered in an almost hushed voice. "I know you, and I know you think of everything."

"I've had a lot of time to think," I remind him. "The witnesses don't exist except on paper, so he could never find them. And, of course, the body doesn't exist, so there's no hope of him finding it. Of course, we're very sorry we couldn't get to the bottom of this before it turned to ash, but at least a grieving father can get closure."

"You've outdone yourself. Really, I can't thank you enough for taking the lead on this. You've freed her, you know. Any lawyer in their right mind would tell him to let it go at this point."

"Which is exactly what we can tell him if he ever bothers her again. He has absolutely no standing, and even if he blames her for leaving the country and deserting Kristoff, there are still no grounds for bringing her all into this. She wasn't his nanny. He did exactly what he wanted." Did he ever. He damn near destroyed her.

"Bianca is going to be so happy." The relief in his voice is heavy, and I can't help smiling in the light of his approval. Going back through those ugly memories the night I told Tatum the whole story only reminded me of everything I owe him. This is the least I could do.

"I know Tatum will, too. She doesn't know anything about this yet – and we're not going to give her the details. The less she knows, the better."

"Of course. It will be so good to have both of you back here. It wouldn't have seemed like Thanksgiving without the two of you."

Thanksgiving? My stomach drops, my mouth going dry, as my heart begins pounding in a furious rhythm. I always think of everything, don't I? Every angle, every potential slip-up.

Why didn't I think of this? Originally, I was in a hurry because I wanted it over with. And I did always want to help her – that's the truth. I wanted this over for her.

Now, nothing is keeping us here, meaning there's nothing keeping us together. Obviously, we won't be able to keep this up once we're back at the compound. No marathon sessions in bed… or the shower… or the kitchen… My chest aches when I look ahead to a future without her.

"Did I lose you?"

Get your shit together. "No, still here. You went out for a second – it was a little fuzzy." How do I sound normal? Easy. Years of tuning my feelings out and operating on autopilot. It's second nature.

"I was saying Bianca's not having a very easy time of it right now. It's nothing to worry about, but she's got nasty morning sickness and feels like shit more often than not. Having Tatum back is just what she needs. The timing couldn't be better. I might save it as a surprise."

"That's a good idea. She'll be happy." Words are coming out of my mouth, but I am hardly paying attention. How am I supposed to do this? How do I go the rest of my life without what happened less than an hour ago? Touching her, tasting her, listening to her moaning my name. Knowing how much she needs me. How much I need her.

"And I'm sure it can't happen fast enough for you," he concludes. "I have to admit, I had my doubts."

The word reverberates like a gong in my skull. "Doubts?"

"Sending you back there. I knew it couldn't be easy on you, and it felt damn unfair, putting you through that. And there were a couple of times I wondered if it wasn't all too much. Like that night when you were drunk."

There's no disapproval or even condescension in his voice, but I bristle anyway. "I'm not proud of that."

"And I'm not giving you shit about it. But it was unlike you, so I was worried. I even made a call, thinking I might need to step in and take care of things. I should've known better."

I'm too busy reeling at first to pick up on what he said. Eventually, his words filter through my skull and set off red flags. "A call?"

"I regret the hell out of it now. Believe me, it was no reflection on you in general. I was feeling guilty and concerned—"

"What do you mean, a call?" I stand, gripping the edge of the desk for balance with my free hand since the room's starting to spin. "Who did you call?"

CHAPTER 28

TATUM

It's amazing what you can learn when you pay attention. You could be at the grocery store, grabbing the many essentials that have gone unstocked while you've been getting your pussy pounded, and end up learning something valuable.

In my case, the lesson begins once I reach the rear of the store, where the butcher and deli counter sit. A few women are standing around in the usual sweats and jeans, chatting like they're old friends catching up at the end of the week. One voice rings out above the others. "I'll be surprised if there's anything left on Main Street by the time those developers get through with the place."

It's not the first time I've overheard a loud conversation around here. The thing about living in a neighborhood where everybody knows everybody is people talk about all kinds of things without much of a filter. Usually, I'll listen a little as I pass by, but it doesn't normally mean anything to me, so I keep moving without giving it much thought.

But when they mention development, my interest is piqued, and I slow my progress to a crawl. I wonder if Dad is behind it while I pretend to compare cuts of beef.

"Now, hold on, Joanie. You can't pretend they haven't done good things." The man behind the counter shrugs when she rolls her eyes and scoffs with the middle-aged woman standing next to her. "Look at what they did with the rec center. Look at all their work along Main Street, with the trees, benches, etc. They cleaned up the park and put in new equipment. They fixed up the abandoned houses on Wakefield and Monroe."

"Right, and then the property values skyrocket, and our taxes go up, and nobody can afford to live here, anyway. Ever heard of gentrification? Hard-working people get pushed out of their homes and their neighborhoods are so rich people can move in." I don't know Joanie, but she sounds pissed. A glimpse of her red face confirms this.

"All I know is, I feel a lot safer letting my kids walk around."

"You sound like that Chaz what's-his-name at the real estate office," Joanie's friend snickers. "Talking about how good it is that he's got all these properties to sell when the families who lived there for twenty or thirty years are getting pushed out. He talks about getting fresh blood around here and revitalizing the neighborhood. We all know what that's code for."

"Yeah," Joanie agrees with a bitter laugh. "You're too poor to live here now."

I keep moving, and soon, their bickering blends in with the rest of the noise around me. Is that how people see it? Now that I've heard Joanie, whoever she is, put it that way, I can understand why people might be against the improvements Dad has poured so much money into. I wonder if Romero knows anything about this.

The thought of Chaz Drummond makes my nose wrinkle as I grab a dozen eggs to add to the basket I'm carrying over one arm. Before putting them in, I check to ensure they're all intact – something Romero drilled into my head. Now I feel stupid for not thinking of it before. But there was a lot about life that I didn't know before we came here. There I was, thinking I had everything worked out, as if there was nothing I needed anybody to explain. I was jaded, for sure. Dad showed me the world, and I figured that was all there was to it. Who cared about things like learning how to grocery shop and stuff like that? I prided myself on being independent, but a few months around here showed me how wrong I was.

Chaz Drummond. No, I wouldn't be too happy with a sleazeball like him creeping around, offering to sell my house for me. He'd be lucky if I didn't slam the door in his smug face. So that's what he's doing around here – I've been wondering, but not enough that I wanted to see him in person. I'm not that curious. I wonder if Dad knows how unhappy people are with what I know he's doing to be helpful and supportive. I think I'll ask him about it next time we talk. Just like him, overlooking public response. So busy with all the other things on his plate. He expects them to be happy and grateful.

I wonder if there's something I could do about it.

It's still on my mind as I walk back to the house with a bag in each arm. It would've been smarter to bring the car, but I was still sort of in a fog when I left the house. The same fog I've been in for days, thanks to Romero. I've always known he had it in him to drive me crazy. I just never knew it would be like this, with him giving me multiple orgasms daily.

The thought makes me blush while my pussy gets moist. Not like that's anything new. I'm walking around soaking wet pretty much all the time anymore. It's all thanks to him. I didn't know I could be like this, that I could ever feel so secure again. Like I'm able to totally be myself, no hesitation, no shame or fear. He would probably think it was corny if I thanked him, but I feel I should. Maybe I'll make a nice dinner tonight – I picked up a couple of steaks, thinking he would like a hearty meal. Perhaps I'll get up the courage to tell him how much being with him meant. He's given me so much more than I thought I'd ever have again.

"Dammit," I growl when one of the bags starts to slip out of my grip. I might have overdone it a little while shopping, but we're out of so many things. I stop at the closest stair and put the bags down, then shake out my arms to get the blood flowing again. I haven't even turned off the street yet, and they're aching. I probably look like a complete idiot — some things might have changed, but I still care how I look out in public. I glance around, expecting to find those shitty kids laughing or something. They might be Mrs. Cooper's new best friends, but that doesn't mean they've become gentlemen overnight.

Instead of them, I find a tall, thin man maybe thirty feet behind me. He's dressed in a heavy jacket, thick-soled boots, and sunglasses.

And a black ball cap.

No. No, this is impossible. I was only being paranoid that day when I thought I saw him following me. He's just somebody who lives around here, is all. I have to believe that. I can't let myself fall apart just because somebody is minding his own business. That's all he's doing, minding his own business. I should let him do it.

And I would, if it didn't feel so much like he's watching me.

I'm not imagining this. No way. He's looking down at his phone, typing something, but I'm not stupid. He's only doing that to make it look like he's busy and not paying attention to me at all. I don't know what makes me so sure. I guess you don't grow up a Torrio without picking up a thing or two about body language and when somebody is following you around.

I can't afford to lose it now. I need to get home to Romero. Maybe I should call him, have him meet me. But what would I do in the meantime? How long would it take, especially if he's busy working?

I crouch down and shift items around in the bags to make them easier to carry, but always my attention is on the man. Does he know I know he's there? I can't imagine how he wouldn't, but then he's bad enough at what he's doing to make it easy for me to spot him. Who knows? When he heads into the hobby shop, two doors down from where I'm trembling, I go weak with relief. Okay. Once again, I freaked myself out for no reason. The guy is just buying a model train or something. He's not out to hurt me.

I pick up the bags and continue on, shaking my head at myself. I really need to get a grip. I also need to remember that, even though our sessions have generally turned into us fooling around with no clothes on, Romero has taught me a few more moves in case I ever do find myself in a bad situation. I am not helpless. I am not the girl

I was when we first came here. I barely remember her, come to think of it. I can't say I miss her.

The bags are getting a little heavier with every step by the time I reach the corner, and as I'm turning off Main Street, I do the sort of thing people do all the time without thinking about it: I look down the street, back toward where I came from.

My insides go icy when I see him again, this time three doors behind me, lingering in the doorway to the pet shop.

All right, this is not a coincidence. It never was. This man is definitely following me, and I don't need to know why to know he's bad news. Right away, I pick up my pace because what's the point anymore? I'm tired of playing games. I know he's following me, and he probably knows I know.

Think, damn it! But I can't think with all the screaming panic in my head. Remember, he taught you what to do. Sure, but I was horny and barely paying attention. And it's one thing to learn how to defend yourself, but another thing to remember all the steps at the moment. I'm supposed to... What? What am I supposed to do?

I can't lead him back to the house, that's for sure. Romero would probably kill him. Maybe it would be worth it. But what if Romero couldn't get close enough? I doubt the guy is dumb enough to follow me into the house, right? So what could Romero do? No, that won't work. My eyes dart back and forth, searching for... What? What am I trying to find? I don't know. Help, but from who? From where?

We're still a couple of blocks away from the house by the time I approach a garage next door to a mechanic. Typically, the doors are open so people passing by can see the mechanics working, but now they're closed, and there's no light coming from the windows. I throw a quick look behind me to make sure the guy hasn't rounded the corner yet, then duck into the narrow opening between the two buildings. The brick walls are tall enough to cast deep shadows and rob me of the sun's warmth.

He'll probably pass by, or maybe he'll stop once he looks down the street and doesn't see me. He can go back where he came from, wherever that is.

I'm only telling myself what I want to believe. If the guy is after me, he's not going to stop. Tears threaten to fill my eyes, but I blink them back, gritting my teeth in anger at myself. I'm not going to fall apart. Not now. Not ever again.

There is so little traffic on a Friday morning, which means I can hear what's happening without passing cars drowning it out. And that's why I hear him coming with those heavy boots crunching leaves under them. Closer, closer. In a brief moment of clarity, I set the bags on the ground in case I need to run – or fight. What do I do if it comes to that?

My heart goes from racing painfully to stopping when I see him slowly ambling on the sidewalk. At first, he doesn't notice me pressed against the wall – he looks around, removes his sunglasses, and stands with his hands on his hips when he stops only feet from where I'm watching.

Keep going, keep going, I plead silently, holding my breath, afraid to move. Now, there's no way of misinterpreting things. He's not out on a walk. Looking for me.

I never knew until now how quickly fear can flip on its head. How your heart can go from pounding in terror to racing in anticipation.

Fuck this guy, whoever he is. He's not going to make me cower in a dark alley and pray to be left alone. I did enough of that already. Crouching in a corner of the bathroom while the man I thought I loved pounded on the door and demanded I come out. Lying perfectly still in bed, afraid I would wake him up. Staring at my phone, knowing it wouldn't take more than a quick phone call to put an end to everything — and refusing to do it, being that I refused to give up that easily. I refused to admit I didn't have control of the situation.

No more of that.

"Hey." I barely sound like myself. He jumps a little and his head whips around. His glasses are off, but his eyes are still shaded by the brim of his cap. "Why are you following me? What do you want?"

He sputters a little, like I took him by surprise. "Let me explain."

I don't know what surprises me more: the fact that he wants to explain himself or the fact that he moves toward me, where I am still glued to the brick at my back. I might be able to put on a good front when he's standing over there and I'm over here, but when he's close enough for me to smell his strong, spicy cologne, it's a whole other story. Everything in me seizes all at once — limbs, heart, lungs, brain. This is it. This is when he... what? Takes me away? Maybe he'll kill me the way Jeff thinks I killed Kristoff. Because at the end of the day, that's what it's all about. That's what he believes. And that's why he sent this guy to find me.

No. The word rings out loud and clear in my head, pushing past the pounding of my heart and the way every part of me wants to run before he can put a hand on me. No, I won't let him. No, he's not going to hurt me.

The shadow of the buildings falls over him and I back away with my heart in my throat. I can't take my eyes off him.

Which means I stumble backward over the grocery bags, losing my balance and falling against the wall before sliding halfway down and landing in a crouch near a foul-smelling puddle that may or may not be piss.

I'm fuzzy, startled, and the way his hand closes around my right wrist doesn't help. No, no, he will not hurt me, I'm not going to let him.

What did Romero teach me?

It's like he's here, watching, instructing me. Whispering in my ear. I have to use his body weight against him. I have to take him by surprise.

It's like I'm moving on autopilot as I push myself to my feet and pivot on my right foot, bringing him closer by pulling him along with me before driving my left elbow into his face with all the strength I can manage. The sound of bones cracking is triumphant, and a rush of pure heat races through me. I want to scream, I want the world to know what I did.

Like magic, he lets go of me since he needs to cover his spurting nose. "What the fuck?" His voice is thick and I know why. I broke his nose. I broke his goddamn nose! He falls back against the wall, and blood drips over his fingers.

It's not enough. He needs to pay. He needs to know who he's fucking with. No one is ever going to hurt me again.

I draw my foot back to kick him. I'm not going to stop until he's nothing but raw meat.

"Tatum! No!"

I must be imagining this. Romero appears out of nowhere, putting himself between us. "What are you doing?" he asks, taking me by the arms. He's breathing heavy. "Stop. Enough. Calm down."

I have to force myself not to shove him out of the way so I can end this miserable shitbag's life. "He was going to..." I can't catch my breath, and my chest hurts from the way my heart keeps pounding.

"No, he wasn't." He looks back at the man over his shoulder. "Shit. Are you alright, Joe?"

"Do I look alright?" The man—Joe, how does Romero know his name?—lowers his hands to show off the bloody mess I made of his nose.

"I don't... I can't..." I can't get my head together, that's what I can't do. Who the hell cares if he's okay? What about me? I'm the one who just fought him off.

Romero leans in, his flushed face filling my field of vision. "He's not the enemy. You're safe. He's somebody your dad and I have worked with in the past. Your dad sent him."

"And if he doesn't think I'm going to charge him for my doctor bills, he's wrong," Joe mutters. "Son of a bitch."

"Just stay here." Romero leaves me leaning against the wall while he goes over to the bleeding man to check him out. None of this makes any sense. Dad sent him? Why?

It's evident to me, as my pulse slows and the adrenaline starts wearing off, that it doesn't matter why Dad sent him. All that matters is I kicked ass. I took him by surprise, then I broke his nose. Me. I defended myself. I don't have to be afraid – I took control, and I did what I had to do.

I hate the tears that spring to my eyes, even if they're tears of relief and gratitude.

I can't brush them away in time for Romero not to see them. He turns toward me, looking pained as he takes in the sight of me standing here with tears falling down my cheeks. "You're safe."

"I know," I choke out. "I know I am. I'm finally okay. I don't think I really knew that until now."

"I'm so sorry." His touch is soothing when he cups my face. "I ran the whole way in a panic in case he was trailing you. As soon as your father told me he called Joe to check up on things, I knew that's who must have been following you that day."

"I am... sorry," I mutter to Joe, who doesn't exactly look like he's in the mood to accept my apology. I guess I wouldn't be, either.

"Can you handle yourself from here?" Romero asks him. He nods, shoots a dirty look my way, then stumbles off.

"You couldn't have known," he murmurs, rubbing my back. "Come on. Let's get you home, slugger. We can talk about it there."

"I used my elbow," I point out, not like it matters. I must still be in shock.

"Elbow, fist, it doesn't matter." He bends down to pick up the bags I left on the ground, and I realize he's chuckling. "So you remembered what I taught you. You did well. I'm proud of you."

"He wasn't trying to hurt me," I murmur – he makes a noise like he's going to disagree or try to make me feel better, so I add, "It doesn't matter that he wanted to or not. I thought he was going to, and I took care of it. I took care of myself."

"You were very brave." And when he smiles at me with all that warmth and kindness, I know something I only suspected until now. Something I didn't want to face – I know how pointless it is. How it can never happen for us. I've been afraid to show it, terrified of saying it. Though if I can break a guy's nose that easily when I'm afraid for my life, what else can I do? What else am I capable of?

Am I brave enough to tell him I love him? That I've always loved him, that everybody else was only a poor substitute for him? It was easier to hate him for so long, because that was acceptable. It was safe and easy to explain. Underneath it all was my lonely, hungry heart, yearning for something it knew it could never have.

He stands up and turns to me. "Let's get you back to the house so you can process all of this. You still look pretty shaken up."

It's now or never. I'll never get the courage again.

I open my mouth. I pull in a shaky breath. The words are right there, dancing on my tongue. I only have to force them off. If I could defend myself against a stranger I was sure would kill me, I can admit what's in my heart.

Or can I? There's an invisible hand around my throat, and it's getting tighter. Cutting off my air. Stealing my chance. Every silent second that passes makes my opportunity fade until I can't see it anymore. The moment's over. He's ready to go.

His brow lowers while his eyes dart over my face like he's looking for signs of damage. Does he see? Can he know? Maybe it's written all over my face and I don't need to say the words out loud. He's always been able to read me–I've wanted to kill him over that more times than I can count. Can he read me now?

"We better get home." That's it. It's all he says before jerking his head toward the sidewalk.

It's better this way. I would only end up regretting it if I spilled my guts like a weepy, emotional wreck. His walls would come up, and we'd be strangers again.

The idea of the pain that would bring is enough to console me as we walk back to the house that will never be ours. Only his.

CHAPTER 29

ROMERO

*I*t's almost morning. Birds have been singing for half an hour, at least. How many times have I woken up before they started their noisy bullshit? Are they that happy to be alive yet another day? I wish I knew that feeling. I don't think there's been a morning of my entire life beyond a holiday or my birthday when I've been happy and eager for the day to begin. And even then.

My eyes are burning from lack of sleep as soft, gray light starts revealing the front bedroom one piece at a time. The window, the striped chair beside it. The dresser that's covered in hair ties, lotion, and books. She's made herself at home here, something that both warms what's left of my heart and leaves me cringing. She wasn't supposed to make herself at home. This was never going to be forever.

I guess it was inevitable. What was she supposed to do? Live in limbo? There was never any guarantee of how long all of this would last. She had to settle in. She had to feel like this was home, if only for a little while.

Now, the light begins to creep over the blanket covering both of us. Her golden curls spill onto my bare chest while her perfect, heart-shaped face is smooth, unbothered in sleep. No more nightmares. Her soft breaths hit my skin, and for some reason I smile. It's comforting knowing I have her trust. I don't think I've ever known anything as profound as the gratitude that rushes up when I know she trusts me enough to sleep peacefully and deeply in my arms.

I don't know whether I spent the night staring at the ceiling thanks to the war raging in my head or because I didn't want to miss a minute of this. Because it's the last time. It has to be the last time.

I have to tell her Callum expects us to come home now. His meeting with Jeff was scheduled for last night – I wanted to be there, but I wasn't going to leave her. I got a thumbs-up text from Nathan, one of the other guards who stepped up to fill my role while I was gone. Things went well. I'm sure we'll catch up about it later over the phone.

She has nothing to be afraid of anymore. She can go back to her life. Everything she wants can be hers.

I can't be one of those things. No matter how Tatum thinks she feels, it's not meant to be. That's all there is to it.

I don't deserve her. And I know damn well her father would agree. He trusts me with his business and with his life, but his daughter? Long-term? No way. He would never. A man like him doesn't sit back and make idle threats. Even with everything between us, all the water under the bridge as we worked side-by-side over the years, he wouldn't hesitate to get rid of me if it meant protecting her from the worst of what happens in our world.

I know him. I know how he thinks.

And he knows what I've done. He knows who I am. He knows what I'm capable of. We could never happen – I would only make her unhappy, being that I would stand between her and the life she deserves. I won't do that to her. I can't.

Even when I know she's going to hurt. One day, she'll have to understand I'm only trying to do what's best for her. She has no business tying herself down with somebody like me.

Her soft sigh makes my body go still and my heart stutter.

Witnessing her waking up is like witnessing a miracle. Every movement of her limbs, every breath she takes. The way her face scrunches a little before she yawns. The fluttering of her eyelids.

It's like my hands have a mind of their own, stroking her soft skin before I tell them to. Every touch leaves me hungry for more. I'll never get enough. But this has to be enough.

Her soft, sleepy sighs deepen by the time my hand caresses her thigh. "Mm... that's nice..." She moves against me, wiggling and snuggling closer, sliding her leg over mine until my cock twitches and thickens.

It's my heart that's the problem when she lifts her head and her plump lips curve in a knowing grin. Her tousled curls are a halo lit by the morning sun and her emerald eyes sparkle, and fuck me, how am I supposed to live without her now? The idea steals my breath and causes my arms to tighten around her supple body.

As I roll over, Tatum goes with me, wrapping her leg around my hip and pulling me closer to the heat growing between her thighs. She trusts me completely. No more fear. No flinching at the slightest touch.

She's come so far. I hope she doesn't regret it when this is over.

Don't think about that now. No, I won't since I'm a selfish prick. Taking what I need even though I don't deserve it.

Her soft, melodic sigh pierces my heart. "Romero." I bury my face against her neck and breathe deep, inhaling all my lungs can hold. Like I can carry her with me this way, the floral scent of her hair, the sweetness of her skin.

There are certain things that can't be held onto, no matter how we want to. The feel of a woman's arms around my shoulders. The press of her lips against my neck as I part her supple thighs wider to make room for me. The sound of her gasp in my ear when my fingers delve through her folds to find them wet, swollen. Ready.

The heat that envelops me once I push inside her. I close my eyes and give myself over to it, this pleasure, this power. The connection between us.

Moving slowly, I take her in deep strokes and savor every

second. Every sigh, every moan, every time she arches her back and presses her body closer to mine. Close enough that I feel her heart racing the way mine is. Her tongue darts out to sweep over my mouth, and I meet it, sinking into a long, almost lazy kiss. There's no rush. Not now. Not when there's so much I'll need to remember once I'm alone again.

Forget that. I focus on the tightness of her pussy, gripping me, drawing me deeper. Like this is where I belong. "Yes..." she whispers, moving with me. "Just like that. You feel so good."

Her whispers turn to high-pitched whimpers when I begin rolling my hips in slow circles, grinding against her clit. "How about that?" I ask, then chuckle when she moans and sinks her nails into my back.

"More... more..." Her head rolls from side to side, blonde curls fanned across the pillow.

I give her what she wants, driving myself harder, deeper, until we're both slick with sweat and wrapped so tight in each other it's like we've become one. Oh, God, don't give me this when it has to disappear. Don't show me everything I've missed. But that's what's happening by the time we start moving faster, and instinct takes over, forcing us to the edge.

Not yet. Not yet. I grit my teeth and fight like hell to hold on through her orgasm and the fluttering of her muscles, her hoarse cries loud enough to make my ears ring. I push myself up on my palms and look down at her–the flush covering her chest, the tits that heave with every ragged breath, the look of bliss transforming her face into something otherworldly.

If she was the only thing life ever gave me, the only shot at true happiness, I'd be satisfied.

I swear she can hear my thoughts. Her eyes open and stare deep into mine; there's nowhere to hide. No walls I can place between us to protect myself--or her. I'm wide open, defenseless, and it terrifies me. It also makes me want nothing but this for the rest of my life.

I'm so fucked.

Now, when the tingling begins at the base of my spine, there's no holding back. I almost want this over with. The sooner it ends, the sooner I can start building up the walls again.

She gasps when my measured strokes turn to hard, sharp thrusts. "Yes... yes!" She's swept away again–I don't know if she finished coming in the first place, but now she's tightening around me and jerking her hips to meet my thrusts. Using me the way I'm using her. Making it easier for me to put an end to all of this.

And when she screams and claws at the sheets, I pull out to spray my seed across her pussy. Marking her one last time. Mine. She'll always be mine, no matter how many miles are between us or how much she hates me. And she has to hate me. There's no other way this can end.

Right now, there's a lazy, satisfied smile on her flushed face. "Wow," she sighs, then laughs softly. "That was... intense."

I only nod while using the sheet to clean her off. Nothing sweet or tender about this. Not anymore. I then ball it up and climb off the bed, tossing it into the hamper. "You better get a shower."

"What's the big hurry? Do I stink?" She wrinkles her nose before snickering. "Don't answer that question. I probably do after all that sweating."

"No, it's not that." When it's clear she's not getting the message, I step into the jeans I left lying on the floor last night and pull them up with my back to her. *Do it, you fucking coward. Tell her.*

The bedsprings creak, telling me she's sitting up. "Are we going somewhere?"

I have no right to stare at her body in the mirror over the dresser, but I'm a man trying to soak in the last few moments of having what I wanted more than anything in the world. I can't help it. I can't take my eyes off her. The sunlight dancing off her curves makes her fair skin glow. The perfect globes of her tits swaying slightly when she swings her lean legs over the edge of the bed.

I have to force my gaze away from her. "You'll see." Could she make this any more difficult?

"Ooh, so secretive." There's still something playful in her voice when she hops out of bed and grabs the bathrobe slung over the back of the armchair. "I don't usually like surprises, but you've intrigued me."

She slides the satin robe over her shoulders and looks me up and down. "Care to join me?" she murmurs, smirking. "Or did you wear yourself out?"

Do it. Get it over with. Every damn moment of this is torture. "I don't think there will be time for that."

Finally, her face falls. "What are you telling me? What's happening?"

"You'll see, like I told you." I can't do this anymore. I can't be in the room with her. This is fucking killing me. I have to turn away, to start down the hall.

"What is going on? What happened? You can't just fuck me one minute and then turn your back on me the next."

"What a charming choice of words."

Behind me, her gasp rings out. "No way. You're not doing that to me."

I round the top of the stairs with a sigh. "Doing what?"

"Going back to the way you were before. This snide, snarky attitude. I'm not going to put up with it. What aren't you telling me?"

"Why is it never enough for you to just do as you're told?"

"Because I'm not a dog who wags her tail whenever her master tells her what to do. You don't know that by now?"

Instead of getting in the shower like I wish she would, she follows me downstairs, stomping her feet the whole way. Still a brat at heart.

"Please, Tatum." Once in the kitchen, I turn around to face her and wish I hadn't. She's hurt, confused, searching my face with eyes filled with questions I can't answer. I couldn't even if I wanted to. "I know this seems sudden, but please. Just do what I ask you to do. We can talk about it when you get out of the shower."

"No, dammit! I want to talk about it now!"

"I'm going to make coffee." Steady. Don't let her do this to you.

I'm doing the right thing. So why doesn't it feel right? Nothing about this does.

"You can't shut me out like this. You can't go back to the way things were before. Why are you treating me like this? What did I do?"

"You didn't do anything. You did nothing wrong."

"Then why are you treating me this way? Why can't you talk to me? After everything we've been through, you can't talk to me?" When I turn around, she takes me by the shoulder and spins me in place. "Answer me! What changed?"

"Do you want to know? Are you sure?"

Her chin quivers. She's reconsidering. Should she keep pushing when there's a chance of hearing what she fears most?

Curiosity and anger win out in the second it takes for her pained expression to harden. "Yes, dammit! Tell me, right now."

"Fine. You asked for it." I can't look at her. I have to go to the counter, to the espresso maker, so I can spare myself the agony of watching her reaction. "Your father's coming to take you home."

I don't have to look at her, but I hear her sharp gasp. "I don't understand."

"Everything's set up with Jeff. It's all worked out. Callum had a meeting with him and gave him all the information I had compiled. It's all over. You have nothing to run away from anymore."

"And you weren't going to tell me?"

"That's what we were going to discuss once you were out of the shower, but stupid me forgot you can't just do what I ask you to do without starting shit. Now go up, wash off, and get your shit together. He won't want to be kept waiting when he's so excited to have you home."

I can practically hear her brain turning, working this out. She's going to ask the inevitable question – I feel it coming. And she doesn't keep me waiting. "What about you?"

"Me?" I fill the metal cup with ground espresso and tamp it down, grinding my teeth as I do.

"Don't you have to get your things together, too?"

"No. I don't."

"Why not?"

You know why not. I almost hate her for this. Putting me through this torture. "Because I'm not leaving."

Because, in the end, we have no business being together.

CHAPTER 30

TATUM

He must be joking. He can't mean that. Or maybe I heard him wrong.

This is only a dream, right? I'm still in bed, in his arms, and there's nothing to worry about. Everything's okay. We're together. He can't mean this.

But I'm definitely awake. I feel the satin robe against my skin, the cold floor under my bare feet. I even hear the low hum from the fridge, the sort of sound that fades into the background of your consciousness. Always present, but you don't notice until the power goes out and everything goes silent.

I wouldn't hear that if this was a dream.

Hell, I still smell him on me. This is all very real, right down to the nausea churning in my stomach and the sweat beginning to bead at the nape of my neck. "You're telling me he's taking me back to the compound today."

"That's right." He goes through the motions of fixing his coffee with his back turned to me. If only there was a way of knowing what he was thinking. No, we're back to the way it was before, the way it was for so long. He shut me out. His walls are firmly back in place, and I am expected to fall in line without complaint.

"So once again, the two of you have decided what my life will look like."

"You don't have to be so dramatic about it."

I might as well be in the damn Twilight Zone. How can he go from holding me while I sleep to this cold, careless prick? "Oh, I'm sorry. Is this inconvenient for you? Tough shit. You're not going to shut me out. Not again. That's over."

"I'm glad you think so." All he does is roll his eyes when he turns away from the espresso maker to open the fridge and pull out a carton of milk. "But in case you forgot, Callum still subsidizes your life. He wants you back. All the bad stuff is over. You can get your life on track now."

"Why does nobody think to ask what I want my life to be?" It's an entirely rhetorical question – he's not going to have an answer, and even if he did, he wouldn't offer it. That would mean being honest with me, and he's not good at that. "After everything, how can you stand there and pretend you don't care?"

"Why do you have to make this so dramatic?"

"Why do you have to be such a coward?"

"Watch it," he snaps, turning his head to glare at me.

"Fuck you. You don't tell me how to speak. You tell me how to do anything, not ever again. Not when you can stand there and pretend I don't mean anything to you."

"I didn't say that."

"You don't have to. You're showing it. You would rather jump whenever my father snaps his fingers than admit there's something you want."

"If that's how you want to see it, be my guest."

"That's how it is! He decides he wants me back, and you're all set to pack me up and send me away. Despite that, you had to get one last screw in first. Right? You had to use me one more time."

"I wasn't using you."

His bare back and shoulders move with every measured breath he takes. I could kill him. I could sink the biggest knife in that block into his back and smile while I did. He can't do this to me. He won't. I'm not going to let him.

I don't have a choice.

I hate the hot, bitter tears welling in my eyes at the thought. I have to have a choice. I must! They can't make me. I'm not a child.

I can't believe what I'm thinking. Am I really throwing a hissy fit because I have to go home?

"This is so damn unfair." I swallow back the emotion clogging my throat. "If you knew this was happening, why couldn't you tell me? Were you that afraid?"

"I was not afraid," he grunts. "I didn't wanna deal with this. Satisfied? I knew you would pull this shit, and I didn't want to deal with it."

"Because it's all about you. Once again, you act like this was all for my sake, but really, all you can think about is yourself. You knew this would hurt me, and I would be confused, and you still chose your comfort."

"You're wasting time."

"You're not getting rid of me that easily."

"And I think everything's about me?" He barks out a laugh, shaking his head as he turns to face me again. "It's all projection with you. That's all. You accuse me, but you're the one who can't think beyond herself for more than half a minute before she starts wondering what's in it for her."

"That's not true." Is it? No, it's not. He's trying to hurt me and make me hate him. That has to be it. It must be. How could he hold me so tenderly and make love to me, then turn around and act this way if it isn't all a front?

"Whatever you want to believe. I really don't care. I'm exhausted. You've exhausted me." He turns away again to finish with his stupid fucking coffee, like that matters. As if it's more important than how my world is crumbling around me while all I can do is watch it fall apart.

"You're a coward. You won't even look me in the eye."

"Would it make you feel better if I did?" He slams his palms on the counter before turning and giving me a look that just about freezes my blood. I can imagine him looking that way before he murdered Kristoff. Cold, hateful, dangerous. "Satisfied?"

"Honestly, no."

"That is such a surprise. You're so easily pleased most of the time." He chuckles bitterly, shaking his head.

"You think I don't know what this is about. But I do."

"Time is ticking, princess."

Do not cry. Do not. I'm not sure how much longer I'll be able to keep a hold on myself. It's not just the agony of being rejected. It's the way I want to break him into itty bitty pieces for being so dismissive of my feelings. I want to make him hurt for that. I want to make him bleed.

Since I can't, I go for the next best thing.

"You're running away again. Things got too hard, and you decided to be a pussy. You can't face your next-door neighbor, for God's sake. You can't have a conversation with Becky without her leaving in tears. You won't try to make things right. You can't face your old friends. You'd rather turn your back on everybody who ever gave a shit about you, because you're too afraid to do anything else. Tell me I'm wrong. Go ahead. Lie to my face."

His jaw ticks, but there's still nothing but blankness behind his baby blues. "You feel better now that you got that off your chest? You know, it didn't have to be this way. We could've had an adult conversation about this if you hadn't thrown a tantrum. All you're doing is reminding me of what I couldn't stand about you in the first place. You have to have your way. Everything has to be exactly the way you want it. Forget everything and everybody else. What do they matter?"

"It's all just a big excuse, Romero, and we both know it."

He looks away, staring out the window over the sink. "Don't tell me what I know, little girl. You don't have the first clue."

"What, are you planning on burying yourself here? Hiding out from the whole world? That's what you would be doing, too, isn't it? Living like a hermit. Watching the rest of the world moving while you're too stuck and too stubborn to actually join in. Or too afraid."

The muscles in his cheek twitch and his nostrils flare, but he won't say a word. "Tell me I'm wrong. Tell me you aren't doing this to run away from me, more than anything. You would rather stay here and be miserable and surrounded by awful memories than take a chance at living a life. Don't you know you're better than that? You're worth more than this."

Cold, uncertain silence fills the room. I don't know what else to say. I could beg, but what good would that do even if I was willing to degrade myself? I could remind him of how happy I thought we were lately. How well we fit together and fill in the other's empty places. How I have never felt more myself than when I was here with him.

All he would do is find a way to make fun of me. To turn it into a joke. I can't believe he would mean it – that's the worst part of this. He's lying; I know he is. There's no way I made up everything I felt coming from him. It was more than lust or chemistry or even loneliness. I've been through all of those.

This was different. I know it in my bones.

"Are you finished?"

Is there a wounded puppy in the house? No, that whimper came from me before I could stop it. "Fine, then," I whisper as I watch everything I thought was mine dissolve like wisps of smoke in a stiff breeze. I step up until we're toe-to-toe, forcing myself to look him in the eye one more time, no matter how my heart screams in agony. "That's fine. I want you to know you won't see me again. I won't put myself through it. I don't know where I'm going. I only know I won't risk seeing your face."

His jaw ticks. "Am I supposed to believe that?"

"I don't care what you believe. I'm just letting you know." Even now, when I hate him with all my strength, being this close to him is torture. Not being able to touch him.

The creak of the door hinges barely registers my awareness. It's the voice following the sound that gets my attention. "What the hell is going on here?"

My heart seizes at the sound of that familiar voice. No, no, this isn't happening.

But there's no denying the sight of my father standing in the living room, the front door still standing open. In one hand, he holds a key. "What the hell did I walk in on? Tell me. Now."

My brain is going to short circuit. There he is, wearing the sort of polished outfit Mrs. Cooper described: gray slacks, a black turtleneck, a long coat I know cost a small fortune. All at once, the massive difference between this house and the world I'm about to return to comes into sharp focus.

"Nothing," I somehow manage to choke. "Just... we were..."

"The secret's out." Romero gives me a filthy look that pretty much wrecks me. I would swear we went back to where we started. Like nothing has changed at all. "We never did learn to get along."

"I was hoping you would." My father scowls at me. "I hoped you would try your best."

"It's not her fault." Romero shrugs. "I'm not easy to get along with."

"Well, it's over now." Dad's expression goes from stormy to elated. "Are you ready to come home? Where are your bags?"

I'm supposed to act like everything is normal now? Who was I before I came here? My God, I can hardly remember her. My father stares at me, still smiling, waiting for me to respond with... What? God damn Romero. This is all his fault. The spineless bastard.

"I... was going to go up and get everything together now."

"Are you feeling all right? You're not sick, are you? I thought you were taking care of yourself while you were here."

This is all too surreal. I have to be alone. I can't stand here in front of both of them and still function. "I'm fine. Surprised, that's all. I had no idea... I mean, I didn't know things were..."

"I didn't want to tell her until I was sure everything was settled – and I figured you would rather be the one to tell her, anyway." Always the kiss ass, isn't he? And here I am, wishing he was dead.

But not nearly half as much as I wish I was dead.

"Of course. That makes sense." Everything is fine in Dad's world. Any decent daughter would be happy to see him looking so happy. However, I am not a decent daughter. I'm not a decent person, period.

"I better go upstairs."

"Wait a second." I'm so close to getting past him when he stops me. "Don't I get a hug after all this time?"

That is the last thing I need to do. I reek of sex–I'm sure he'll pick up Romero's scent on me if we get too close. "I don't think you want any of this right now." Somehow, he even manages to laugh. "Let me take a quick shower first. But I am really happy to see you, Daddy." And then I flat-out flee for the privacy of a room that was never mine in the first place. Right now it's my only comfort.

My heart thuds painfully by the time I reach the front bedroom and close the door, then lean against it and gasp for breath. So this is how it ends. Who am I kidding? Nothing ever began. How could it have if the cold, empty shell down there could push me out of his life like I'm a fly he's swatting away? That's all I am to him. An insect. Something small and annoying and useless. I was kidding myself to think I would ever be more than that.

I cover my mouth with my hand to hold in a sob. I wouldn't want them to hear me. I might disturb their super important conversation, where they're probably making even more decisions about my life without consulting me. I can't ruin that, can I?

I'm going. I don't have a choice. One more example of not having a choice in my own life. But what difference does it make, I guess. He doesn't want me. I would rather eat glass than stay where I'm not wanted. I might not have much dignity left, but I'm not that pathetic.

I don't even know where to begin, but I have to. It has never been more important to move my ass than it is right now, being that it means I don't have to see Romero anymore. That's the one thing I want most of all. To never see him again. I go to the closet and pull out my suitcases, flinging them on the bed before grabbing things randomly and shoving them inside. This is not the time for me to care which items go in which bag. The sooner I get this over with, the better.

Besides, I can barely see through the tears streaming down my face. The only time I stop is to run a fist under my eyes now and then, but otherwise, the tears drip from my chin and soak into my clothes. I wish I could set it on fire instead. I don't want any reminders of this massive mistake.

Because stupid me thought I loved him. "Asshole," I hiss in disgust, and it's not him I'm thinking about. It's me. The stupid, stupid asshole who insists on breaking her own heart. Romero didn't do this to me. I did.

And now, I have the rest of my life to regret it.

It doesn't take more than ten minutes to get everything ready. They're still talking when I reach the top of the stairs. "I'm going to shower — everything is packed up."

"I'll take the bags to the car," Romero offers while I head for the shower. The sound of his voice does strange things to me. It makes my heart ache and my pulse race. I want blood. I want him dead for rejecting me. For letting me think he cared. He used me. That's all there is to it. He used me, and now he's done, and we both know better than to ever let my father know.

A sick smile spreads over my face when I imagine what would happen if I told Dad everything. If I told him his precious, wannabe son took advantage of me. I was vulnerable, wasn't I? And he used that. Something close to satisfaction warms me inside while I let it play out in my head. He would learn what happens to anybody stupid enough to hurt me.

The idea dies almost as soon as it's born. I can't do it. I know I can't. The old Tatum might have done what I imagine as I wash my hair, what I would have done to get back at him even a year ago. Dad would make him suffer for it.

I can't be that girl anymore. I have to grow up sometime. So, as much as it hurts, and as much as I hate it, I have to let it go. I don't know how, but there's no choice but to figure it out. Right now, it's all about scrubbing him off my body. Erasing every trace of his touch from my skin.

I wish it was as easy to wash a soul.

The bags are downstairs by the time I'm out of the shower and dressed in the sweater and leggings I left lying out on the bed. I want so much to take a second and look around the room one last time, but that's dumb. It's not like I have happy memories, anyway – because none of it was real. What's the point of going over it?

The pain in my chest is almost enough to stop me, but I force myself through heading downstairs again. Dad and Romero sit on the sofa, and it's pretty apparent there's tension. "What's wrong?" I venture as I twist my wet hair into a bun and clip it in place with trembling hands. He wouldn't be stupid enough to confess, would he?

Dad shakes his head. "It looks like you're not the only one who had a surprise waiting for them."

"I told your father I'm not coming with you. I'm going to stay here."

"I don't see why," Dad snaps. "I don't like the idea of you being here alone."

"Oh, come on," I say with a shrug. "He's a big boy. He can handle being alone." Amazing how easy it is to slide back into the old Tatum. As easy as sliding into my jacket before going outside.

"There's a lot more to the story than you know." Dad is scowling when he looks at me, especially since he actually believes we'd spend all these weeks together and that I would never learn the truth. "You should wait in the car."

"Gladly." The coward won't look up from the hands folded in his lap. I have to bite the inside of my cheek hard enough to taste blood in my mouth. Otherwise, I might do something unforgivable, like beg him to look at me one more time. I might have had no other choice except to tell him in detail what he did to me. How he made me feel safe and whole and wanted again – and how he ruined it all. *He ruined everything.*

He ruined me. No matter how tempting it is to punish myself,

I'm not alone in this. He played a part, knowing what I've been through and turning his back on me after he got what he wanted. The bastard.

"Bye, I guess." I have to get out of here. I can't breathe, and there's no way I'm going to be able to keep from crying much longer. As it is, the front door goes blurry before I'm outside on the porch. I didn't even get to say goodbye to Mrs. Cooper, did I? One more thing he took from me. And for a second, I consider going over and saying goodbye—then stop myself. Dad is the man she saw the night Romero left. She might recognize him. He wouldn't like that.

I doubt he would hurt an innocent old woman, but then again, there's a lot I don't know about him. A lot he doesn't want me to know.

And it's not like I can't relate, considering there's plenty about me he can never know.

He could never know I fell in love.

And he can never know that if Romero asked me to stay with him here and now, I wouldn't think twice before saying yes. That's how completely screwed up I am.

I would still say yes.

CHAPTER 31

ROMERO

My footsteps ring out in the otherwise silent house as I head to the kitchen to shut my growling stomach up. There's hardly any sign of life now that I'm on my own–nothing but the light over the stove illuminates the first floor now that I've come downstairs after work.

Is this what it feels like, walking around in your own grave?

And if this is how empty and meaningless life is only a day and a half after Tatum's departure, what's in store for the rest of my life? I can barely stand days of this. I'm supposed to go through it for years? When I try to imagine it, when I look ahead and attempt to create an image of the future, I get the same result; I always have. Nothing. Blank.

When I open the refrigerator door and barely anything inside, it's harder than ever to see anything good coming my way. One day after another, just staring into an empty refrigerator. Asking myself why I hadn't been to the store. Going through the motions. Working remotely for Callum, taking care of the high-level administrative shit that can be done from a distance while other men, those who aren't as broken and empty as me, do the actual work. The work that used to make me feel alive. The thought of it makes me slam the door closed without meaning to. Somebody else is going to live the life that was meant for me.

Stop kidding yourself. Was any life ever meant for you? The past ten years have only been a reprieve.

The sight of the espresso machine Tatum insisted on ordering brings back too many memories of her. I have to look away, turn my back on it, and force all traces of her out of my head. I might as well try to breathe underwater. Considering there is no pushing her out of my head. After all these years, I should know that. I've tried. I've made it my life's mission at times. Still, it was no use. I couldn't stop thinking about her, wondering, worrying. Telling myself things would be different if she were simply mine.

She could've been. I scrub my hands over my face and groan under the weight of one memory after another. Memories of being so close, of sweet, quiet moments when it was all laid out in front of me. I had the entire world at my fingertips. When her eyes shone with that special light, when she melted against me, moments that even now make it tough to breathe. She could've been mine. I only had to say the words. I only had to share myself with her — but that's impossible, right? Because there is *nothing* to share. I've been hollow for years.

Except with her. It always comes back to her.

I need to get out of here. Every time I turn around, something reminds me of her. Every time I round a corner, I expect to see her. Her scent still lingers in my bed, even after changing the sheets. I'll have to buy new pillows if I want to get rid of her completely, though I can't imagine doing that. I can't imagine it any more than I can imagine a future.

I slam my fists through the sleeves of my leather jacket and head out before I can stop myself. The starless, cold night leaves me zipping up to my neck and jamming my hands into my pockets before starting down the steps. I pass houses with the lights glowing through the windows. Halfway up the block, a guy in a set of coveralls opens the front door to his home, and from inside, the word "Daddy!" rings out. It's a happy sound. The sound of the kid looking forward to their father coming home. I wouldn't know what that's like.

Where am I going? There's no question since my feet carry me down the familiar route to O'Neals. Before I know it, I'm opening the storm door and stepping inside, where the sense of the past being frozen in time damn near knocks me on my ass. Nothing has changed, right down to the few regulars still haunting their favorite stools set up before the long, chipped bar. The smell of beer and fried food fills the air — it hasn't been legal to smoke in this place in years, but they'll never get rid of the odor. It's seeped into the cheap paneling on the walls, the floor, and definitely into the ceiling tiles. They're the same, too, right down to the water stains.

It's Monday night, meaning it'll be time for football later. It's still a little too early, but that hasn't stopped the locals from staking out their spots in the booths lining the wall opposite the bar, where a flat-screen TV is mounted close to the ceiling. That's changed, anyway.

"Yo! I must've drank a lot more than I thought if I'm seeing what I think I'm seeing."

Right away, I find the source of the outburst. Dex makes a big deal of rubbing his eyes like he can't believe them, while Austin only gapes with his mouth hanging open. I knew they'd be here, didn't I? Somewhere inside, I knew I'd find them.

"Since when do you slum it with us?" There's an edge to the question that cuts through the smile Dex wears.

I won't pretend I don't hear it. "I'm not slumming, man. Don't do that. Shit's been… Shit."

"I think that's his way of apologizing for blowing us off the whole time he's been back," Austin tells him, smirking at me.

"Buy you two a beer?" They might be pissed at me, but they won't refuse. I hold up three fingers to the bartender and take a seat at one of the few remaining stools, unzipping my jacket before settling back.

"How's your girl?"

"Not my girl, and I don't know. She went home. The shit she was dealing with worked itself out." When I look their way, I catch them exchanging a knowing smirk. "What? What's that mean?"

"I should've put money down on how long it would take you to fuck it up." Dex shakes his head with an exaggerated sigh. "You don't have a great track record with women."

"That's not how it was. And Tatum wasn't my girl in the first place."

"So that's why you almost ripped my head off over her?" Austin's smile hardens into something closer to a challenge. "Because she wasn't your girl in the first place?"

Dammit, I forgot about that. Watching him try to kiss her by the fire. The rage damn near consumed me. "She's not here now, so I can tell you: I was sort of her bodyguard. That's the truth. That's why she was here. Some bad shit went down, and she needed to get away. I guess I took my work a little too seriously."

He quirks an eyebrow. "Sure. If that's your story."

"It's the truth."

Dax accepts his fresh beer, taking a long pull from the bottle before smacking his lips. "Don't tell me you haven't forgotten the line between work and play."

"And how would that be any of your business?"

All it takes is a glance at each other before they burst out laughing. It's a habit, the bitterness that blooms in my chest. Nobody likes being laughed at, and especially not me. "Hey, man," Austin urges when he sees my expression for what it is. "We're just busting your balls. For real, dude. Have you been in solitary for ten years?"

"What are you talking about?"

"You lost your sense of humor. You used to be fun. You used to be funny."

Did I? "I can't remember," I admit.

"You need to lighten up. You need to, like, have a little fun."

"He's right," Dex agrees. "You always look ready to punch somebody's face in, and for what?"

I do? When I catch a glimpse of myself reflected in the mirror behind the bar, it's like I'm looking at a stranger at first.

No. It's like I'm looking at my father. I have to put down the bottle or risk dropping it on the floor. There's a hard, cold look in my eyes. My jaw's set like I'm ready for a fight. The way *his* always was.

Motherfucker. When did that happen?

"So now that your girl is gone, what will you do?"

Shit, I don't know what to do with the reflection staring back at me, much less what to do tomorrow. I have to shake myself out of it. I am not my old man. I will never be him. But I wonder if refusing to drink all these years so I wouldn't lose control — and so I wouldn't be like him — is enough.

I twist my face away from the mirror and look at both of them. Even now, sitting here and sharing a beer, there's a wall between us. The same wall that's been between me and everybody in my life for as long as I can remember.

And I don't want it. The laughter coming from other people around us reminds me of what I've missed. Until now, I didn't realize how much I had changed. I don't remember how I used to be. I'll never be him again… Though I don't have to forget him, either. I don't have to forget the parts of life that were good. Like these guys.

"Listen. I want you to know… I had reasons for staying away, and I'm sorry that it seemed like I was ditching or ignoring you. It wasn't what I meant to do."

"Listen, man." Austin glances at Dex before leaning in a little closer. "Do you think we didn't figure it out?"

"It is what it is," Dex murmurs. For once, he's serious. "The timing was a little suspicious. We're not complete idiots."

"We didn't get it at first, but you grow up. You put pieces together." It brings to mind what Becky said. How eventually, she figured it out, too. "We get it now. You had your reasons."

"Then you came back to town and acted like you were better than us." Dex finishes his beer before slapping the empty bottle against the bar.

"That's not fair."

"Truth hurts." He lifts an eyebrow. "Are you gonna tell me I'm wrong? Are you seriously going to sit there and lie to my face?"

"It was complicated. There are still things I can't tell you about why I was here. It was safer..." Everything I'm saying *is* true, although I can't expect them to understand or even believe me. And I'm going to have to live with that. "Trust me. I know I'm not any better than you. And for what it's worth, it's not so bad, being you."

"Well, shit. I knew that." Dex winks while Austin laughs. "I got a good job. I've got a life I like. I see my friends, all that good shit."

"Which is a hell of a lot better than most people have it," Austin observes. He doesn't have to tell me that.

"I just wanted you both to know it was never personal. And that I didn't want to cut you out."

"We already knew, but hearing you say it is good." Austin holds up his fingers. "I'll get the next round."

Could it be this easy? It's hard to believe they would be so quick to accept what I have to say. Like everything can be washed away now. They even know what I did – and they've been holding that secret for me all this time. It's humbling. I don't know what to do with the feeling of being seen, exposed. Understood, at least in part. All I can do is nod my head, accepting Austin's offer. I'm not here to get drunk, but we have a lot of shit to catch up on. And it finally hits me that I want to know about their lives. There's nothing wrong or weak about admitting I need people.

I only wish it hadn't taken me this long to figure it out.

* * *

IF I DON'T DO this now, with a few beers in me, I'll never find the courage again. I have walked into buildings where I knew some men were ready to kill me, and I did it without an ounce of fear. No, it was a challenge, and I welcomed it. I marched ahead calmly, with purpose.

But here I stand in front of a chipped front door, and my knees are practically shaking. I grit my teeth against the impulse to leave before she knows I'm here, then tap my fist against the door.

Becky opens it, and her eyes widen when she sees me standing on her front porch. "What are you doing here?"

Becky wraps her arms around herself. The heavy cardigan she's wearing practically swallows her body. The sound of the football game floats out from her living room.

"I didn't mean to interrupt you watching the game or anything." This was a bad idea. All it takes is a few beers for me to do something stupid. "But I was walking around nearby, and I figured I would stop over. Do you have a minute?"

"Sure. Come on in."

She's still wary, eyes narrowed, but she steps back and holds the door open for me. I'm keen to step inside, especially since the night has only gotten colder since I left the house. I blow on my cupped hands to warm them up – then notice she is not alone. There's a lanky guy around our age sitting on the sofa, eating from a big bowl of popcorn and looking at me like I'm the enemy.

"Oh, shit. Seriously, I'm sorry. I can come back –"

"No, it's fine." She gestures toward the guy. "Romero, this is Jeff. Jeff, Romero." Jeff jerks his chin in greeting.

Then, I notice another surprise, something else I wasn't expecting. There are toys scattered on the floor in front of the TV. "Wait a second. Are you... I mean, do you..."

She rolls her eyes, laughing. "Yes, I'm a mom. She's three. Her name is Ava." And even as she says it, a soft smile lights up her face. "I would introduce you, but she's in bed."

Well, fuck me. "Wow. I'm happy for you. That's... That's great."

"Half time." Jeff gets up, holding the bowl. "I'm going to refill this. Do you..." He looks at me, lifting his brows. "Can I get you anything?"

"Oh, thanks, but no. I'm not gonna stay long." I throw Becky a helpless look, feeling like the world's most enormous ass. "I just wanted to talk for a second, and then I'll leave."

She turns the volume down on the TV, where commentators

sum up the first half of the game, before crouching to pick up a few toys. "Well? What did you want to say?"

"Why didn't you tell me?"

"Tell you what?"

"About all of this. Your kid. Your life."

She stops to look up at me, sitting back on her heels. "What did you expect? What, did you think you would find me waiting here for you? Life went on. And you never asked," she adds, frowning.

"You're right. I didn't. I... Assumed too much."

"Yeah, no kidding."

"Are you happy?"

Her face goes slack for a second like she didn't expect the question – and she smiles. "Yeah. I am. I mean, I don't love working at the store, but it puts food on the table for my little girl. Jeff's a great dad. And he's good to me. That's more than a lot of people can say. So yeah, I am, even if I never really thought about it."

"I'm really glad. You deserve that."

She bites her lip, tucking a piece of dark hair behind her ear before standing. "Why did you really come here?"

Here goes nothing. I need to get it all out at once. "I'm sorry for how things went when you came to the house. I was wrong to act as I did. You didn't deserve that. I'm... sorry." Fuck me, those words are not easy for me to say. I haven't had much practice. "I'm sorry for everything."

She reaches out and grabs my hand, squeezing hard before letting go. "I know."

"I just needed to say it and know you know I mean it. I went down and talked to the guys, too."

"Good." When she smiles, God, it's like ten years melt away. It's easy to remember how I fell for her as hard as I did. She was the one good thing in my life. Sometimes, the only thing that kept me hanging on.

"I better go." I peer deeper into the house, toward the kitchen where Jeff disappeared. "I don't want to start trouble by hanging around."

"You know, you can come back anytime. It would be nice to hang out."

"Yeah, that would be nice."

I won't. I can't. I think she knows it – there's a little bit of sadness in her voice. We can't go back and reclaim yesterday. I wouldn't want to, even if I could.

"Will you do me a favor?" she asks, touching my shoulder to stop me before I step outside.

"If I can."

"Take care of yourself," she whispers. "Be good to yourself. Let other people be good to you. Can you do that for me?"

"I don't know. You're asking a lot."

She doesn't chuckle with me. "I mean it. Whatever you did and have done since then, you need to let it go. You have to move on. Remember, I know you – ten years doesn't change who a person is inside. I know you carry things around. I know you punish yourself. You don't deserve it. Let it go. Start fresh. Really, that's all I want for you. Can you do that for me?"

"You're asking a lot. No joke this time."

"Yeah, that's the thing about caring about somebody. You sort of want the best for them." Her arms shoot out and wrap around me, and all I can do is hug her back. It's awkward, but it's not bad. "Be happy. Whatever it is you decide to do, try to be happy. Okay?"

Happy. When I think about happiness, a few things come to mind.

No big surprise, one person is at the center of them. Tatum and her sweet-smelling curls. Lying in my arms, snoring softly so I always knew when she was asleep. Smelling her hair, feeling her breath against my skin. Her warm, limp body. I knew she trusted me. That way she could make me laugh over the stupidest things. How proud she made me when she forced herself through the darkness and found herself again.

Even sitting down to dinner together. Looking forward to it throughout the day. I was happy and I didn't even know it.

And she's gone, and I know it's for the best that she's gone, but

I'm also a selfish son of a bitch who always wants a thing he shouldn't have.

And I shouldn't have her.

Dammit, nothing else will do.

Instead of walking straight home, I wander the streets, too deep in thought to care about the cold.

CHAPTER 32

TATUM

"I'm so glad to have you home, I can't bring myself to shoo you out of the kitchen." Sheryl pats my shoulder on her way past me, then peeks into the oven. "The turkey looks great so far." Granted, she only put it in the oven twenty minutes ago, but I'll take her word for it.

"I'm so glad you got an extra big one this year." Beside me, Bianca peels potatoes the way I am. "I'm ravenous."

Sheryl taps a finger to her chin. "You know, I've heard when a woman is pregnant with a baby boy, she needs more calories than if the baby was a girl. I don't know if that's true, though."

"Oh, I can totally see that being true." Bianca abandons her potato and reaches for a piece of cheese from the little platter Sheryl put together for us to snack on while we work. "I am hungry morning, noon, and night. I shudder to think how much weight I'm going to gain by the time this kid comes out."

I'm only partly aware of their conversation. I'm too busy peeling and blocking out reality. Sheryl was shocked when I told her I wanted to help her with dinner today. Of course, she told me not to bother since she was thrilled I was home, so I didn't need to do anything. I guess she figured I wasn't kidding around – it didn't take long for her to assign me a few different jobs. This is one of them.

Once I'm finished, I'll move on to chopping vegetables for the dressing and then prepping the sweet potato casserole. Out of everything she makes for Thanksgiving, that's what I look forward to the most.

"Hello. Earth to Tatum." Bianca is giggling when she nudges me. "You okay? You are, like, a hundred miles away."

"Am I? I guess I'm too busy trying to work." I stick my tongue out at her and she mimes me. And for one brief, necessary second, things feel normal again. Like nothing ever changed, like I never went away.

Whereas then my heart reminds me that I did, and that everything is different. It will never be the same.

"This year, we really have something to be thankful for." Sheryl wedges herself between us, putting an arm around our shoulders. "First, Bianca came to stay, and now a baby is coming. And you, Tatum. The house was awfully empty without you."

"That's the truth." Bianca lowers her peeler and sniffles. "These damn hormones!"

"Get it together, Preggo." She bursts out laughing at my joke, but that doesn't stop the tears from flowing.

"I can't get a handle on myself," she groans. "I swear, I burst out crying at the stupidest things now."

"Don't feel like you have to apologize." Without thinking about it, I reach into the pocket of my hoodie and pull a tissue from the stash I've been carrying around. "Here you go."

She gives me a funny look but doesn't say anything beyond a muttered thank you. Dammit. That was pretty obvious, wasn't it? Maybe she'll let it go without bothering to ask why I'm making a point to carry tissues around with me now. I really don't feel like getting into it.

She thinks she's been crying? Hilarious. I'm surprised I was able to make myself stop long enough to come out to the kitchen and help with meal prep.

And I hate myself for it. Who was I ever kidding, thinking I was brave and strong? All it took was getting sent back home to shatter me all over again. When the potato I'm working on blurs, I blink fast to push the tears back. I will not do this here or now. I need to stay busy.

Once the pile is taken care of, I plop the last potato in the pot of water sitting on the counter. "Do you want me to cut them up?" I ask Sheryl, who just returned from the pantry carrying canned pumpkin purée. A pumpkin pie. I was thinking about making a pumpkin pie for our dinner, wasn't I? How was that less than two weeks ago? I might as well have been a totally different person. I didn't know I was as close to being happy in that stupid little house as I'd ever been. It didn't matter that the situation was screwed from the beginning and I was there to protect myself.

"I can do them if you want to move on to the dressing," Bianca offers, so I step aside and pull out a cutting board. Looking at all this food and knowing how much prep work still needs to be done, I feel bad for all the years I didn't care about what went into the meal.

I mean, sure, on some level I knew it was hard work, but the number of people she feeds – everybody in the house, including the guards on duty — is enough to make my head spin. Ten pounds of potatoes for mashing, and now a whole package of celery and a small bag of onions need to be chopped for the dressing.

But it's okay. It's better than sitting in my room, drowning in tears.

If there's one thing I wish could be different, it would be the way Bianca keeps trying to pull me into a conversation. I'm too distracted and heartbroken to pretend to be as happy as she is. I'm a shitty friend, in other words. Here she is, walking around all glowing, content, pregnant, and acting like it's already Christmas, all because I came home. She is that happy to have me back.

And here I am, forcing myself to hang out with her when all I really want is to be alone. And since I can't be alone without sinking into a deep and crushing misery, I have to grit my teeth and bear it. I have to bear my best friend's company. I'm ashamed of myself. I already was. This is just one more reason to be.

By the time we finish, there's a knot in my back from bending over the counter and both my hands are cramping. "I don't know what I would've done without you girls." Sheryl pats my cheeks, smiling gently. "Thank you. Now go on. Relax."

"That's all I did when I was away." But no, that's not true, is it? I did a lot more than relax. I did things I never should've done. All it did was leave me with a heart torn to pieces. A heart that keeps beating even when I wish it wouldn't. In my darkest moments, I have sincerely wished I could just die and get it over with. I have everything in the world to be happy about, but right now, I can't seem to come up with a reason to live.

I drag my feet down the hall, ready to escape to my room for a little while. Maybe I'll soak in the tub to try and loosen up my back. I don't know how Sheryl does it. She's maybe thirty-five years older than me and spends most of her time doing exactly the kind of work I just did. I guess it helps when you're used to it.

"Hey. Do you have a second?"

Bad friend. Bad, bad friend. My stomach drops when I hear Bianca's voice behind me. As I turn around, I have to force a smile that's probably a lot more like a grimace. "What, do I have a super busy life all of a sudden? Of course, I have time for you."

She doesn't think my joke is very funny – probably being that it wasn't. The worry lines between her eyebrows hint at what I'm in for before she opens her mouth. "Can we go to your room?"

"Are you okay?" Because, duh, not everything is about me. My best friend is almost six months pregnant with my baby brother, and all I can do is jump to conclusions.

"Oh, I'm fine. Hungry again, but I'm used to that." She surprises me when she takes me by the hand, like she wants to ensure I don't run away. "I know I'm probably annoying the hell out of you, though I have to say it again... I'm so glad you're back. I missed you so much."

"I missed you, too."

"And obviously, you know how happy your dad is." But she winces. "Sorry. Is that weird? You'll have to tell me if that's weird. I don't want to be the weirdo who married her best friend's dad, and now she has to act like a mother or something."

"Don't worry. I will definitely tell you if that ever happens." Because it would probably make me puke.

"Good." We step through the door leading to my wing, and some of the tension depletes. I still have to pretend for her, but somehow, it's not as stressful as pretending for Dad. Forcing a smile, having to remember to check the tone of my voice so he doesn't hear the sadness.

It's not him I'm trying to protect. Even though he practically ripped out my beating heart and held it up for me to see, I don't want Romero to take the fall for what went on. It was just as much my fault as his. Maybe even more, since I should've known better. I should've protected myself.

"You... haven't finished unpacking yet?" Bianca looks around the room, wearing a tiny frown. "Do you want some help?"

"Do me a favor and sit down. You've already been on your feet for hours." I grab the open suitcase from the top of the armchair near the window and toss it on the bed. "Here. Sit."

"Yes, ma'am." She even salutes me, smirking as she lowers herself into the chair. "I honestly can't imagine getting bigger than this, but I know I will."

"You are adorable, and you know it."

"I don't feel so adorable." Still, she runs her hand over her belly and smiles.

And damn it all to hell, I have to grab some things and take them to the closet. It hurts too much to look at her. She's so fucking happy. I never wanted what she has – I mean, someday, but not right now. I didn't even imagine it happening for another ten years, once I was settled in my career and I'd traveled and done all the things I wanted to do. Then, I would think about a family.

Who am I kidding? I'll never have that. Because something about me is wrong. I'm broken. Things that have come so easily to others don't come to me in the slightest. I couldn't even get Romero to see me as more than a fuck toy.

I couldn't even tell him how I felt. And now I'm so glad I couldn't, because all the tears, sleepless nights, and hating myself would only be worse if I'd made that mistake. I don't know if I could ever forgive myself.

"Do you feel like being honest with me?"

"What do you mean?" I ask while hanging clothes in the closet.

"You know what I mean." The chipper note has drained out from her voice, and I'm not sorry for it. It was starting to get on my nerves. "Tell me the truth."

"About what?"

"About what happened in the house. With Romero."

I have to close my eyes and force my way through a deep breath at the sound of his name. It's like something tried to take me out at the knees.

"Did you do what I think you did?"

"Why are you asking me this? What do you think you know?" I can't look at her. Besides, she'll see it all over my face when I do. We've known each other for too long. It was stupid to think she wouldn't see through me right away.

"I think I know you're in pain. It's breaking my heart to see it. You try like hell to hide it, the way you always have. But part of you is missing. Things have settled down with Kristoff's dad. So what is it? Did he hurt you?"

"No!" I spin around, shocked she would even think it — before knowing she asked for a reason. She wanted me to look at her.

"He did, though. Just not physically. Right? You can tell me. Come on, I see it. I feel it. I won't judge you, and you know your secrets are always safe with me."

"You're married to my father."

"Sure, but I loved you first."

The sweet, simple way she says it brings tears to my eyes. "I screwed everything up. I knew it was wrong, but I went ahead and did it anyway."

She sighs heavily. "I thought so. Really, I'm not surprised. It was obvious there was something between you two."

"It's easy to say that now."

"No, I'm talking about before you went away."

"I don't understand what you mean."

"Come here. Sit down." She pats the bed and waves me over. "Why do you think he volunteered to look after you when you were away? The way he made it sound, it was practically his idea to take you out there."

"I..." I need to sit down. I plop onto the bed, staring at the floor. Is she right? I never thought of it that way.

"You slept with him, didn't you?" My head bobs up and down. I can't bring myself to look at her. I don't know why I'm embarrassed. She has never judged me, and I know she never would. But that's fine. I can judge myself hard enough for the both of us.

"Do you love him?"

I want to say no. I want to tell her she's off base. But that would be a waste of breath – she knows me too well. And I am so tired of lying, anyway. The way I lied about Kristoff. Look where that got me.

"I thought I did." The shame is almost enough to choke me. I have to swallow it back. "But I was right about him all along. He's Dad's lapdog. All that matters is his work. He wants to make sure his master is happy."

"Is that fair? I'm sure you got to know him a lot better than I did." When I glance up from the floor, she winces. "Not in that way, obviously. You know him as a person better than I do. You have to know he cares about more than the job."

"It doesn't matter either way. He didn't even come back with me. He didn't say he was sorry for springing it on me that Dad was coming to take me home. It was like all the time we spent together was only in my imagination. Nothing really changed."

"I'm so sorry. I wish I could say something that would make it better."

"I know." I grab a tissue from my pocket, snickering bitterly at myself. "You're probably so tired of hearing me cry."

"I wish you didn't have to, but no, I'm not tired of you. I love you too much." Then she sniffles, and I hand her a tissue, and we take a second to calm ourselves down.

"You know what the worst part is?" I ask while running my hands over my cheeks to catch the endless tears. "I actually miss our screwed-up life together. We had a routine, you know? It was nice. He'd come downstairs after he finished working, and we would have dinner together, and it was almost…" I shake my head hard, waving my hands. "Nope. I'm not gonna do this to myself. It was all in my imagination. It's my fault."

"You can't help how you feel," she whispers. "Don't hold that against yourself."

She doesn't understand. I'll never stop holding it against myself. I'll never stop being disappointed in myself for walking straight into a broken heart.

"Please, please, don't tell Dad."

"You know, I'm almost offended that you would say that. You know I won't tell him. Like I said, I loved you first. I've always got your back."

She stands all of a sudden and marches to the bathroom. "I'm going to run a bath for you. You need to relax for a little while. Maybe take a nap, too – after you get out of the tub."

"Oh, thanks for clearing that up for me." I can't believe how much my wounded heart needs that little bit of love. Just knowing somebody cares enough to watch out for me. I need to stop closing myself off whenever things get hard. It's so easy to tell myself nobody cares, that it's easier to keep everything inside. I tell myself I'm saving everybody the trouble of worrying about me.

At times like this, I might even believe I'm not worth worrying about.

After soaking in the tub until the water goes cold and taking a nap, I feel much better. We are an hour away from dinner when I leave my room, dressed, makeup on, and ready to put on a show. So long as Dad doesn't suspect anything, I'm fine.

There's no time to obsess when I reach the kitchen, which is how I imagine a battlefield looking at the height of the fight. The sink is stacked with sloppy mixing bowls and there's flour and sugar dusting on just about every flat surface. She's dripped pumpkin puree on the floor at some point – I grab a dish towel and wipe that up before something terrible happens.

Bianca is setting the table in the dining room while Sheryl pulls the turkey from the oven. The aroma makes my mouth water. "Let me help you."

Once she sets the pan on the counter, she hands me a foil roll. "Tent that, please." I do as I'm told while she slides a couple of baking dishes into the oven to take the turkey's place. There's an entire spreadsheet laid out on the tablet propped up on the counter, and she makes a satisfied sound after peering at it. "Right on schedule."

I'm glad she feels secure in the middle of this madness. "If you're on schedule, take a breather. I'll load up the dishwasher and clean up a little bit for you."

For once, she doesn't argue. "You are an angel."

No. It's just that I have a conscience and can't watch her run herself ragged. Plus, it's something to keep me occupied. I can't stop thinking about the holiday we were supposed to have. Just the two of us. I might even have brought up inviting his friends over, though I knew he would never go for it. But I wanted to suggest it anyway. I wanted to push him a little. I was hoping to show him life doesn't have to be dark. That there are people who care.

What a waste of time. How stupid could I be?

"It smells incredible in here." At the sound of Dad's voice echoing in the hallway, I fix my face so he won't pick up on my sadness. How long am I going to have to put on an act? Through the holiday, at least. I can't ruin this for him.

He finds me cleaning up and his eyes go wide. "Well. Look at you."

"What, do you expect me to sit around and not do anything?"

"I'm not used to seeing you looking so *domestic*." He nods his approval. "It looks good on you."

Yes. I'll make a wonderful wife to some man he'll eventually set me up with. I need to get rid of this bitterness. It's eating me away inside. Why couldn't he have asked what I wanted? And it's not like I could've stomped my feet and thrown a fit at the house – not in front of Romero. I wouldn't give him the satisfaction of witnessing me being shut down again, the way I have been so many times.

"Everything is just about ready." Sheryl looks and sounds exhausted but proud. "We'll have everything on the table in a few minutes." She already has serving dishes set out, some of which she's filled and covered with foil. "If you could let the men know, I would appreciate it."

"I'll have Nathan do it." He steps into the hall and whistles sharply. I have to grit my teeth against even more bitterness. He whistles, and everybody falls in line.

This is a problem. I don't know how long I'll be able to continue living here like this before I go on a killing spree. This is more than feeling bitchy and bratty – even I can admit I was a brat for a long time, pushing the envelope, seeing how far I could get before somebody reeled me back in.

But now, there's more to it. This time, there was something I really wanted. I thought I saw a life for myself. And he took it away without asking what I wanted. He put me on the spot, and considering how much he hates when people do that to him, you would think he'd be a little more aware.

And yet, somehow, my best friend fell in love with him. Right now, in this dark mood, I don't see it. I can't imagine it.

By the time we gather around the dining room table while the guards eat in the kitchen, my face hurts from faking a smile this long. They're all laughing and enjoying themselves in there – I sort of wish I was with them, honestly. They sound like they're having a good time.

"I can't tell you how happy I am to see you here." Dad kisses my temple before continuing down the table to take his place at the head. "Something's been missing all this time." I notice how his gaze cuts to Romero's empty chair across from mine. Something is still missing... for both of us.

The pity in Bianca's eyes doesn't help. I hate being pitied more than just about anything else. It's part of the reason I didn't tell anybody about Kristoff until I melted down. "I'm glad to be here." That's the most I can manage to choke out. I really wish it was true.

The table is beautiful. Candles flicker and make the China glow. The fragrance of roses in the centerpiece mixes with the aroma of turkey and all the other dishes in front of us.

"We better get started since I'm sure at least one of us is starving." Dad winks at me before gazing across the table at Bianca.

"I guess it's because I'm growing your child," she points out with a loving smile that twists my heart until I'm surprised it can still beat.

"Then let's–" Something catches Dad's attention and cuts him off. Suddenly, he's beaming, staring at the doorway behind me. Even his voice sounds different when he says, "Look who it is."

I don't need to look. I can feel him. The hair on the back of my neck stands up and now the heart that was barely beating races out of control. Bianca shoots me a face that could be either fear, dread, or excitement. Maybe all three at once.

"I couldn't miss Thanksgiving with the family, could I?" Oh, his voice. I didn't know how much I'd miss the way it makes me shiver and loosens everything in my body. Tears threaten to fill my eyes. Why? Why did he have to come back?

Why do I want to sob with relief that he did?

"I just thought I'd stop over and say hello on my way to the kitchen," he explains.

"Absolutely not. Your chair is free. Please, sit down. This is where you belong."

Romero walks around the table slowly, whistling in appreciation. "Sheryl outdid herself." He won't look at me.

"She got a lot of help from me and Tatum," Bianca offers before shooting me that look again. What, is she afraid I'm going to grab a knife and use it on him?

He looks just the same as when I left — what else did I expect? It's been four days. They only felt like a lifetime. He settles in across from me, murmuring something to Bianca about how good she looks, asking about the baby. Ignoring me.

Until our eyes meet for the briefest second. Until he freezes me in place while looking straight through me. Something's different. Something changed while we were apart. There's a coldness to him. He might as well be a machine, but then, didn't I used to make fun of him for that? Now, I know I was wrong. There is an entire man under that shell, with thoughts and hopes and feelings.

He's pushed them about as far away as possible. To get through tonight? Maybe, but then why bother showing up at all?

"This is a pleasant surprise." Dad's about ready to burst from excitement as he reaches for the turkey. "I can't lie and say I wasn't hoping you'd join us."

"I plan on joining you for longer than tonight, if that's okay." I can breathe once he looks at Dad and breaks our connection. "I decided to sell the house and come back here. For good."

CHAPTER 33

ROMERO

"So tell me." We're alone, drinking coffee in the kitchen with what's left of the pumpkin pie between us. Callum folds his arms on the tabletop and leans in. "What made you change your mind? Don't get me wrong. I knew you'd come back. I just thought it would take longer than four days."

The truth would be unacceptable.

I need your daughter like I need oxygen and would rather go through the torture of being close to her than endure the torture of being apart.

He wouldn't like that, so I take the easy way out. "I didn't want to spend the holiday alone, after all."

"But you're back for good? Not just for the weekend?"

"I meant what I said. I plan to sell the house, and I'm here to stay."

He nodded, slowly sipping his coffee. "You know, you could rent it out. Make some passive income every month. It wouldn't be a bad idea."

"I've considered that."

"Of course, you have. I know you look at things from every angle before you make a decision."

Normally, his praise would be welcome. Right now, it feels too much like he's trying to appease me. He's happy I'm back – I should be grateful for that, right? He's ready to say whatever needs to be said so long as I stick around.

"I appreciate everything you did to keep the place for me. Making sure the maintenance was taken care of when I was busy with other things. I hope you don't see this as ungratefulness."

"I don't. And I would never force you to keep it. It's your house, you can do whatever you want." He uses his fork to cut off a bite of pie, his lips pursed. "It's weighing you down, isn't it?"

"I think that's a good way to describe it, yeah. It's weighing me down."

"I'm glad for you, really." When I lift an eyebrow, he adds, "You seem centered. In a good place."

Since that's perhaps the opposite of how I feel, it's a struggle to keep from laughing. Callum means well, and he's not good at these heart-to-heart talks. Neither am I. Amazingly, we've gotten more than three words out between us. If we were discussing work, there'd be no stopping us. When it comes time to talk about something real, we're both at a loss.

Even if I could find the words, I couldn't tell him. "I see a lot of things differently. I think I needed the time there."

"Then, as much as I missed having you here, I'm glad you went. And there I was, worrying it was a bad idea for you."

"It wasn't easy, although it was necessary."

He nods slowly as he chews. "I can see that."

The whole time, I can't shake the sense that we're tiptoeing around the actual subject. At least, I am. He doesn't know what I've struggled with over the longest four days of my life. How I woke up sweating like a man in the grip of withdrawal. In a way, that's exactly what I was going through. I lost my drug of choice when Tatum walked out the door.

He can't know that. He can never know it.

"I better go unpack. I only dropped my things off at the cottage before coming up here." Standing, I take my mug to the sink and wash it out. The kitchen is spotless – no evidence of the massive feast that was prepared here today. Tatum insisted on helping Sheryl with the cleanup. I knew why. She couldn't stand looking at me. I can't say I blame her. "As usual, I'm available to review anything I missed while I was gone. We can catch up whenever you want."

Callum only chuckles and shakes his head. "We've barely started digesting dinner, and already you want to get back to work."

"You know me. A workaholic. It wasn't the same doing shit from all the way out there."

"Nobody would blame you if you wanted to take some time to settle in again. It's a holiday weekend – there's no hurry."

So this is Callum Torrio, family man. It's not that I am not glad for him – it's good to see him stepping back and enjoying life a little. He has every reason to. A new wife, a baby on the way, the whole thing. He also has enough money that he could choose to never work again and be just fine. So could his kids and his grandkids.

Nonetheless, I'm anxious as I leave the house, stepping into the chilly night. I need to work. I need a distraction, something to throw myself into. The temptation of having her near is going to wreck me otherwise.

I did it to myself by coming back, didn't I? Seeing as the alternative was unthinkable. Living every day without her. Going back to a cold, empty house on Monday night after walking for hours. There was nobody there. Not a soul gave a shit where I was. There was nobody happy to see me come home. Even a small house can feel cavernous when there's nobody else inside.

Callum's glad I went out there? From where I'm standing as I enter the cottage and turn on the light, it might have been the worst possible move. Given that it showed me everything I've missed without knowing I was missing it. It took everything that once used to satisfy and sustain me and turned it on its head, shining a bright light on what my life became.

And now, standing here in the middle of my living room, I can only wonder how I lived while feeling like the walls were closing in at all times. It's claustrophobic in here. Sure, when Callum first offered me the renovated garden shed, I jumped at the chance to live here. It was the first time I had a little something for myself, though it wasn't really mine. I wasn't completely independent, still living within the walls of the compound, but I could come and go as I pleased. That was enough for me.

Now, it's like wearing glasses for the first time when I didn't know my eyesight was failing to begin with. Everything I got used to over time looks different. It makes me wonder how I ever got along like this.

Instead of standing around and wasting time with questions, I get to work unpacking and putting things away. What did I expect would happen tonight? I knew Tatum wouldn't throw herself into my arms – not after our last fight. That's by design, of course. I need her to hate me. I don't trust myself otherwise.

By the time the house is in order, I'm damn near exhausted. It's been a long day and an even longer night. I haven't been sleeping well, either, thanks to the ugly dreams that have haunted me since Sunday.

I'm about to change for bed when there's a sharp, insistent knock at the door.

My heart stops for a second before hammering furiously against my ribs. This was bound to happen. Tatum was going to confront me sooner or later. I have to be stronger this time. I can't give in.

Not even when the sight of her floors me as I open the door. This is as close as we've been all night, close enough to reach out and take hold of.

Only her eyes flash deadly fire as she glares at me. "Are you serious? After all that, you came back, anyway?"

She rolls her eyes when I look behind her, then back and forth. "Nobody knows I came over here. Jesus. You think I'm stupid?"

"Get in here." I grab her by the arm and tug her inside, then slam the door. "What the hell is wrong with you? Are you trying to —"

"Could you not, for once?" She holds up a hand, groaning. "I'm sick of hearing the same bullshit over and over. Do you think I'd come over here if I didn't know he went upstairs? Please, give me a little bit of credit."

How can I give her credit when it's all I can do to keep from taking her in my arms and crushing her body against mine? I definitely missed her, but this is enough to take my breath away. The way my body reacts — all at once, my dick is hard and I'm starving. I am so damn hungry for her.

"What are you doing here?" Fuck, it's not easy getting the words out with my jaw clenched. I can hardly suck in a breath with my chest this tight.

"What do you think? I want the answers. Was this all a game? Acting like you hate me just to screw with my head?"

I'm glad she's acting like a brat. It's easier to resist temptation when she irritates me this way. I flop onto the sofa, shrugging. "Not everything is about you."

"You're so full of shit." She looks me up and down with the sort of disgust I'm used to. Yes, this is how I need her to be. Pissed off and hurt and hating me. It's safer this way.

"What do you want me to say? I decided to come back. I'm selling the house, and I've come back."

"Oh, that's it? You're done with the house?"

"Yeah, I am. I told Chaz Drummond he could sell it to me–so long as he stops sniffing around like a dog after a bone. Trying to talk people into selling now that the market is hot out there. I have the guys keeping an eye on him, and he knows it." I was waiting for him to piss his pants when I strolled into his office and set the terms. I was hoping he would. The fucking sleaze. But he knows what he's doing, and I need somebody to get the property off my hands.

"What about your bike? Are you selling that, too?"

Of all things for her to ask about. "No. I'm having it sent here, along with everything else I want to keep. Otherwise, I'm ready to move on."

What did I expect? Praise? Acknowledgment, at the very least? I should know better by now. "You're still running away, you know."

Do not engage. Do not give her what she wants. Somehow, I swallow back the burning need to throw her assumptions in her face. "You don't know what you're talking about."

"You can't just turn your back —"

"Listen to me, because I will only say it once. I know exactly what I'm doing. I'm moving on with my life. And I don't need you or anybody else to approve. I'm doing what I need to do. And considering you know damn well how much I need to get rid of that place and put it behind me, I would think you'd be glad to hear that. But no, you would have to give a damn about somebody other than yourself."

Yes, that's good. That hurt her. Sure, she'll pretend it didn't, but I see the pain that crosses her face like a cloud passing in front of the sun. "If I only gave a damn about myself, I wouldn't risk coming over here."

"And I'm full of shit? You came here to get the last word, as always. You wanna make sure I know what an asshole I am for sending you away. Surprise, I ended up here, anyway. So we're both back where we started."

"And you're back for good?"

"This is my job. This is where my life has been for a long time. Where else would I go?"

"Hmm, literally anywhere else?"

"You're that desperate to get rid of me?"

"That's not what I meant."

"What did you mean? Since when do you hold back?"

"Why do you have to be this way?"

"This is the way I've always been."

"No, it's not, and you know it." I hate how her eyes search my face like she's looking for something I can't show her. I want to – more than anything, I want to. I want to be the man she needs. I want to take her in my arms and tell her it killed me to hurt her before I sent her away. How much I wanted her to stay, permanently.

How we can't always get what we want. Especially people like me.

"Look. I don't know what you want me to say. I came back because this is where I belong."

"And this is all you want to be? Dad's, like, assistant? That's enough for you?"

"Would you stop this? Please. Give it a rest. Stop pushing. You're always pushing. I don't like being pushed. Don't you know that by now?"

"And don't you know that I'm not going to stand back and let you walk all over me without saying a word? Do you think I would let it be that easy for you? You fucked me, and you threw me away. And not once did you apologize, even though you had the chance."

"Finally. We're getting to the real reason you marched over here." I have to laugh at her transparency. "Why would I apologize for something I didn't do? I never threw you away."

"You did. You sent me away and then you waited until the last minute to tell me so. And don't use my father as an excuse," she warns. She's trembling now, and her voice is shaking nearly as much as her body. She wraps her arms around herself, but that doesn't do any good. "You didn't have the balls to tell me. You didn't want to deal with it. How could you be such a coward?"

"Tatum, I'm not in the mood for this. It's late. It's been a long day." And because I don't want to come off like a total heartless bastard, I add, "You said you worked hard helping Sheryl. You're tired, too."

Misfire. Her head snaps back while her eyes bulge. It's too late to take the words back—now that they're out of my mouth, I understand what I sounded like. "Did you seriously just tell me to go to bed like I'm a kid who missed nap time today? Is that what you're doing?"

The fact is, I don't know what I'm doing anymore. She's got me fucked in the head in almost every way imaginable. Torn between wanting to tell her to fuck off and throwing her on the floor and doing what my body compels me to do. To take her. To stake my claim. Because she's always been mine, from the very beginning. Telling myself it wasn't right made no difference at all.

No, that's not true. I only wanted her more because she was forbidden fruit. She still is.

"You need to go." I stand with a weary sigh and take a few short steps to the door. "You shouldn't have come in the first place. We need to forget what happened and move on, because it was a mistake. I know you have to see that."

"Don't tell me what I see."

"Fine. You refuse to acknowledge the truth, go ahead. But you're not going to ruin things for me. You'll see I'm right." I reach for the doorknob as she throws herself against the wood, breathing hard.

"Just tell me. Tell me the truth."

"About what, for fuck's sake?" I'm dangling at the edge of my rope, struggling to stay strong. She's so close—the familiar scent of her shampoo and her perfume is an intoxicating combination that brings everything rushing back. Every kiss, every caress, every throaty moan I teased from her.

"Tell me why you changed all of a sudden. Why did you fuck me one last time, then tell me to go. Did you want to get rid of me? Are you only doing it because you knew you didn't have a choice?"

"Tatum. This has to stop."

"Why can't you tell me? I know you're holding something back, damn it. I know you too well."

"If you thought coming over here was a good idea, you don't know me at all."

"Tell me it wasn't real. Just once. Please, Romero. Say the words. Say it wasn't real. You'll be doing me a favor."

I have to, don't I? I have to set her free. There's no point to any of this—all either of us will get is pain and misery.

Why can't I say it when I know it's the only way? I struggle to find the words, to force them out, to do right by her for once. It's the right thing to do. Like she said, I'd be doing her a favor.

I would also be lying. I've already lied for too long. To her, to me.

She gasps when I take her by the shoulders and push her up against the door.

Tatum doesn't fight, though.

And when I crush my mouth against hers and take what I've gone too long without, I know I'm hurting us both, no matter how right it feels. But it's not enough to make me stop. I doubt anything could.

CHAPTER 34

TATUM

I didn't come here for this. Really, I didn't. I wanted to tear his head off, to hurt him, to make him explain why he hurt me. He deserves a punishment – or so I had told myself before being in the same room with him.

Now, I need to push him away like he pushed me away. I can't keep letting him do this to me. Hot and cold, on and off, with no warning or explanation. And even though I know he won't want me when this is over – and he'll probably make it all out to be my fault — I don't fight him off.

I can't.

Not when something deep inside screams in relief at the first touch of his lips. I've barely existed the past few days without him. I'm alive again, alive and whole and burning.

I drink in kiss after kiss, greedy for more. Soaking him in and running my fingers through his hair, clutching him close. Taking everything I can get. Giving him everything I have.

We are a tangle of arms, legs, and tongues before he pulls back, panting. Searching with eyes that blaze with desire. Searching for what? A reason to keep going? A reason to stop?

This is my chance. I need to end this.

As usual, my body does the opposite of what my brain tells it. I take his hand and place it on my chest. "Touch me," I beg. "Please. Touch me."

He shudders and releases a shaky breath before molding his hand around my breast, massaging, and working my nipple into a taut peak with his thumb. Who am I kidding? I can't stop this. I'm too weak for him. Too needy for this.

And then he kisses me again — rough and demanding. And I give it all back to him. My nails rake over his skin until he takes my wrists and pins them over my head, then grinds his body against me until all I can do is whimper and try to part my legs so his erection will touch the place where the heat is worst, where my body is begging for relief. I'm so wet it's soaked through my leggings and plasters the thin cotton to my skin.

"Why do you do this to me?" he demands between searing kisses against my neck. "How do you do it?"

I don't know, just like I don't know how he does this to me. Every time, he pushes me away, but I come back for more because I can't live without this. I'm powerless against it, just like there's no escaping his firm, unforgiving body holding me against the door.

Not that I'm trying very hard to get away.

Romero takes my wrists in one hand and traces a slow line down my body with the other. Once he reaches my pussy, he chuckles against my ear but says nothing. Cupping my mound instead and pressing his fingers against my slit.

I arch, gasping, as every thought is wiped away and replaced by sensation. Deep, all-consuming pleasure makes me rock my hips and bear down on his hand. He teases my mouth with his tongue, thrusting it inside before pulling back until I try to reach forward, moaning when he won't give me what I want.

But his hand still moves, fingers running in tight circles over my clit. "Yes... More, God, more..."

"Give it to me." His low, throaty voice works its way into my brain and adds to the tension building in my core. "Give it to me. Come for me."

He presses harder, and fireworks explode behind my closed

eyelids. It goes on and on, the bliss radiating from my core and running through my limbs, leaving me shaking and panting. But that's not enough. I want more of him. I want all of him.

As soon as he lets go of my wrists, I reach between us and touch him where he's hard and dripping through his shorts. "Fuck..." He closes his eyes and lets his head fall back while I stroke him slowly, torturing him a little the way he tortures me. Finally, he grunts and pulls his shorts off, kicking them to the side so I can use the precum leaking from his tip to lube his shaft.

The power shifts between us, and it makes my heart soar. This is the only way I can control him, and I want to savor every second. I run my thumb over the piercing, and he groans again. There's a helpless sound to it that sends a thrill through me. Now, he's at my mercy.

Without saying a word, I drop to my knees and do the same thing with my tongue, flicking the metal, and every helpless sound I tease from him sends fresh heat dripping from my core. I gaze up and find him entirely gripped by desire — his mouth hanging open, a look of agonized pleasure hardening his features. He sinks his hand into my hair and my scalp tingles. "Fuck, Tatum," he sighs, and it only makes me want to please him more.

"Oh, yes..." he breathes when I take him in my mouth, lowering my head until he hits the back of my throat and my nose is smashed against his base.

"Harder," he demands, then moans when I suck until my cheeks go hollow. He's not so cold and in control now, is he? Not when the taste of his pre-cum moves over my tongue or when he jerks his hips, faster, faster, chasing his high the way I chased mine.

"That's it," he grunts. "Suck it. You're so good to my cock." My body preens at the praise.

He pulls back before it's too late and hauls me to my feet. He's rough and demanding again, stripping me from the waist down in one quick, brutal movement. I barely have time to gasp before I'm against the door and he has my leg lifted, spreading me open before spearing me.

And all at once, the tension that built when I was sucking him breaks. I cry out in surprise, but his only reaction is to take me hard, fast, until the door rattles in time with his sharp thrusts. The only thing in the world is that rhythmic, thumping sound, my strangled cries, and his heavy breathing.

There's no sweetness to this. No tenderness. This is two people wholly using each other.

And I like it. No, I love it. I can let go of everything, not giving a shit how I sound or what it means or whether this is a mistake. All my sadness and loneliness and frustration – I give it to him. I take it out on him with my nails and my teeth. With my legs when he lifts me, and I wrap them around him, using them to pull him in, silently demanding he fuck me harder. I want him to hurt me. I want to wake up in the morning with his bruises on my skin so I know this was real. That it wasn't a dream.

We're still locked together when he cups my ass with both hands and carries me to his bedroom. The bed bounces when we land on it together, and I moan into his ear when he starts moving again. Slower this time, deeper, rolling his hips and grinding against my clit with every stroke. He gets up on his knees to peel my night shirt away before descending on my boobs like a man starved. His low animal grunts only add to the frenzy.

My nails scrape his scalp and his neck, his shoulders, and his back before digging into his ass. "More!" I shout into the darkness. I don't care how it sounds. I'm taking what I need.

"You want more of my cock?"

"Yes!" When he pushes up onto his palms, I arch my back, feeding him my pussy. He slams against me hard enough that my boobs bounce in a rhythm that gets faster. His sharp breaths and my high-pitched squeals blend together in a chaotic song that breaks all at once.

I'm sobbing with joy and relief when he pulls out and sprays his cum across my chest. "Fuck… Tatum…" The sound of my name falling from his lips is even more satisfying than the ripples of pleasure that leave my body limp. A sense of peace settles over my soul and leaves me shuddering in liberation.

I'm where I belong. I'm his. I've always been his.

"Stay put." He's a little unsteady when he gets to his feet and disappears into the bathroom. I'm still catching my breath when he comes back to wash me clean.

"You know you could do that inside me," I whisper, watching as he works carefully. "I'm still on the pill."

"I don't like taking chances." He gets up to toss the cloth into the sink and then comes back, scrubbing his hands over his face before letting out a sigh. The bathroom light behind him casts his face in shadow, but I don't need to see it when he lowers his hands. I know how he must look. "You know what I'm going to say."

I do, and I hate how beaten he sounds now. It's like he emptied more than his balls just now. He emptied his courage, too.

I'm not going to argue with him. Not when I know he's right. That shouldn't have happened. It will only make what happens next harder to deal with.

"Can we just lie here together for a little while?" I scoot further back until my head touches the pillows. It's a nice bed — soft yet firm. Honestly, it's more comfortable than I would've guessed. I figured he would sleep on a wooden board or something. He's always got to prove how strong he is, right?

"So you're going to ignore what we both know is true?"

"Do you know what I know is true? I know there are still aftershocks going off inside me. I know I want you to hold me. I know I'm tired of talking about all the things we shouldn't do. We already did it. Can we just... be, for a little while?"

It looks like he's fighting with himself, only the fight doesn't last long. With a resigned sigh, he pulls back the blankets, and I wiggle my way under them while he settles in next to me. There's a fresh scratch on his shoulder, and I press my lips to it before resting my head on his chest.

For once, I'm the one keeping a secret. I'm the one who knows this was the last time for us. I'm the one with a heavy heart.

What would I say to him now if I could be honest? That I learned over the past several days how impossible it will be for me to live here? How much I need to be my own person? This time, it has nothing to do with Kristoff, his father, or not wanting to bring everybody down with my depression. That's behind me now. I've moved on.

And that's the thing. I want to keep moving. I need to. I can't be under Dad's or anybody else's thumb anymore. Deep down inside, I know if anybody would understand, it would be the man whose heart beats under my ear.

But I can't say it. I don't want to ruin this. One last good thing before all hell breaks loose — and I know it will, considering I know my dad. He'll be hurt and pissed. I just want one more night of peace.

"You should probably go back." He doesn't sound convinced, though. When his arms tighten, I smile to myself. Finally, a little truth. He doesn't want me to go.

"Everybody's in a turkey coma by now." I love the way his chest feels under my fingers. Firm, with smooth skin covering the rippling muscle. His soft, contented sigh when I gently run my nails over his pecs makes me smile. It's so simple, but I wonder how I've lived without it for so long.

"You always have to take risks, don't you?"

"Not always." I lift my head to look at him, and he grins. "Only when it's worth it. "His eyes close, even as the grin stays put, and it's not long before his breathing slows.

How is it possible that I came over here wanting to knock his head off, and now I'm lying here in his arms? How is it possible to want somebody so badly, so profoundly, that it's hard to think or breathe or function when I'm around him? Or when I'm away from him, for that matter.

He has completely changed me. I will never be the same. He's like a fingerprint on my soul that can't be wiped away. No matter how many times I wished I could — in the middle of the night when my heart aches, and I've cried out every last tear – I know that in the end, I wouldn't erase him. It would mean going without this sweet, humble happiness that almost makes all the pain worth it.

I don't want to sleep. If I sleep, I won't get to be here with him. I won't be aware. I won't be able to hear him breathing. I won't be able to feel his heart beating under my ear. I won't get to exist in the simple comfort of lying in his arms and feeling like the whole world has fizzled away until there's nothing but us.

I can't live without this.

I have to live without this.

Hot, angry tears threaten to fill my eyes, but I won't let them. I'm not going to ruin this by crying and waking him up. Let him rest. Did he think I wouldn't notice how tired he appeared at dinner? He might be able to fool my father, but he can't fool me, for I've already seen him. *The real him.* With all the walls knocked down and all the masks stripped away. I care about him too much to disturb his rest. Besides, he would only want to know why I'm upset, and I can't tell him it's because I have to leave. Even though I love him.

And that no matter how much it'll hurt, it's for the best.

I can't tell him that, can I? Not now. Not ever.

I should go. I shudder to think what would happen if Dad or Bianca came up with a reason to visit my room out of nowhere. If they found me gone, what would they think? The thought of alarm sirens shattering a peaceful night makes me cringe, but that's exactly what he would do. I have to go. All I'm doing is breaking my heart, anyway. Giving myself something that will never really be mine.

I guess that's why it seems so impossible to leave. Because I know he'll never be mine, and that's all I want.

Just one more minute. That's all I need. One more minute of this.

As it turns out, one more minute is one minute too long, and darkness closes in on me. It pulls me down into a world where nothing stands between Romero and me, and I can have the only man I'll ever love.

CHAPTER 35

ROMERO

The other side of the bed is empty and cold when I open my eyes to find it's already morning. There's a sense of confusion to it. I'm used to waking up next to her after falling asleep with her head on my chest.

She must have gone out of her way not to bother me when she left. Years of being on-call at all hours made me a light sleeper. Then again, she wore me out last night. I wore myself out on her. I'm glad one of us was smart enough to avoid the risk of her being here past dawn.

My eyes go from half open to almost bulging out of my head when I check my phone to find its way past dawn. More like nine o'clock. I was more exhausted than I knew – no wonder she's already up and out. I can't remember the last time I woke up this late.

Last I checked, I don't have any shopping to do on Black Friday and it's been weeks since I was last in my office. So, after a quick shower, I pull on jeans and a sweater and head out into the cold, clear morning to catch up on work. I'm sure Nathan left a mess for me to clean up.

Bianca told us last night about all her plans to decorate for Christmas, and Callum mentioned they'd start bright and early this morning. I don't expect what I find already set up in the courtyard: three large trucks with the name of a local landscaping company printed on the side. Groups of men carrying trees, wreaths, and garlands into the house. A team of workers is setting up the strings of lights that will decorate the exterior, shouting orders and questions at each other while carrying what looks like miles of coiled cable over their shoulders.

How the hell did I sleep through their arrival?

Now I'm glad I came back, if only to see this. Callum has never been shy about spending his wealth, but this is insane. I'm looking forward to giving him a little shit about it — gently, of course, since I'm not entirely out of my mind. I might have made the questionable decision to come back and the even more dubious decision to fuck Tatum's brains out last night, but I haven't completely lost it.

Inside, Bianca stands on the stairs, directing traffic while balancing a tablet in one hand. "That tree goes in the dining room," she calls out, pointing the way. "Do you have the big one for here in the entry hall?"

"Still on the truck," one of the men tells her, and she types something on her tablet before sighing heavily.

When she finds me amidst the chaos, she pretends to wipe the sweat off her forehead. "I can't help but think this is how it felt when they were planning the invasion of Normandy."

"I don't think this many men were involved in that." It feels good to share a laugh. It helps ease the uncertainty sitting on my chest. Nothing in the world could've stopped me from taking Tatum last night, though the guilt is right on schedule this morning.

"It's really good that you're here." I'm going to pretend there's no extra meaning in her voice or the way she looks at me. It's probably paranoia making me see what isn't there. You know Tatum wouldn't risk that. Yeah, but do I? Because I wouldn't have imagined her risking a late-night visit to the cottage, either.

"I'm glad to be here. I'm going to go check in with the boss. Guessing he's in his office."

"Do you really think that much has changed since you left?" We share another laugh that makes me reflect on what life was like around here before she came to stay. I've overheard Tatum talking about how the house used to be decorated for the holidays when she was a kid and assumed Callum gave up the tradition once she was old enough to leave Santa behind. That he would even consider this sort of extreme, all-out chaos shows how he's changed for the better, thanks to his wife.

I've changed, too. Instead of seeing nothing but headaches and distractions around me, I can't help but smile. This is the first Christmas in years I haven't felt a heaviness in my chest. The memories of so many shitty, depressing holidays have faded. There's room for something better.

"Let me know if you need any help."

She salutes me before calling out to the men carrying armloads of garland into the house. "That goes in the living room!"

I point the way before heading down the hall. It's strange walking this familiar path. I could find my office with my eyes closed. I used to feel at home here. Like I belonged. Part of me was inextricably tied to this house, the compound, this life. Now, I might as well be a stranger again. I didn't know until this moment that I really had no plans to come back. As much as I love my work… I've carried too much shit for too long. Too much guilt. Now that it's time to let go of some. I can't see myself ever getting the same satisfaction from my work with Callum. I want more, though I don't know exactly what.

At first, I am confused by the raised voices coming from Callum's office, with the noise already echoing through the house. It gets louder the closer I get, however. My heart beats faster and I pick up the pace.

What I find shouldn't surprise me. This wouldn't be the first time Tatum went toe-to-toe with her father – only there's something off this time.

It's him. The distress underneath the anger is so thick it practically sucks the air from the room. "This is unacceptable. I will not allow this." His voice trembles, telling me he's beyond anger now.

He's enraged, red-faced and shaking. I've seen what he's capable of when he's enraged.

But he would never hurt her. That much, I know, though I can't say the same for Tatum. She's much more in control of herself than her father is, standing with her arms at her sides and her head held high. That's probably what concerns me most of all. Usually, she's ranting and raving, flushed, arms folded. Her calm, collected attitude shakes me. She's in a dangerous, unpredictable mood.

Motherfucker. Does he know? Did she tell him? A cold, sick feeling grips me before I say, "What did I walk in on?"

I might as well be invisible. "You just got home," Callum reminds her. Okay, so it's not about us.

"This is your home. It can't be mine forever."

"Since when? Why are you doing this?" He throws his arms into the air. "What have I not given you? What else do you need? How am I supposed to keep you safe –"

"There's a difference between keeping me safe and keeping me locked in a cage. I don't want to live like this. I want something of my own. Can you understand that?"

It's coming together. I shouldn't be surprised. Not after the ranting and raving she did before Callum picked her up.

And dammit, even though it's the last thing I should feel, I'm proud of her. Let her stand up for what she wants. I'd be disappointed if she rolled over and gave in to whatever Callum demands.

But I understand where he's coming from, too. I know it all too well. I'll never forget the sight of her in Amanda's cold, dead arms. For a second there, I thought she was dead, too. We couldn't keep her safe, either of us.

She doesn't want to be part of this world, and I can't say I blame her.

But I came back for her. And now she's leaving, and for all I know, part of it has to do with me. She can't be with me. And just like I did, she thought spending one more night together would put an end to us.

I could've told her if she'd bothered asking. There's no such thing as an end to us. I wouldn't have come back if there was.

He looks at me and gestures at her. "Can you talk some sense into her? Because she's not listening to me."

"He will be wasting his breath," Tatum mutters. "My mind is made up."

"Exactly what do you have in mind?"

She juts out her chin, clearly irritated that she must explain herself to me. "All I did was come in here and very reasonably tell my father I want to get a place of my own. That's it. I want to live under my own roof, by my own rules. I'm going on twenty-three years old. I think it's time for me to start living independently."

Callum slams his fists on the desk hard enough to knock over a framed photo. It's of him and Bianca on their wedding day. The smiling man in the picture is the polar opposite of the man in front of me. "But you aren't any regular twenty-three-year-old. You are —"

"I know exactly who I am," she snaps. "I'm Callum Torrio's daughter. I am aware. But I want to be Tatum Torrio. Don't you see that? What, did you think I went to college and everything just so I could live here for the rest of my life? The idea was for me to start something on my own. And yeah, I got detoured." Her voice shakes on the last word, but she holds it together. "I want to get back on course."

She glances my way, and the wall between us drops. This isn't the bratty daughter of my boss looking at me. This is the woman I slept with last night. The woman I pushed away because I was sure it would be better for her, having nothing to do with me. This is the woman I care way too much about. She needs my help.

I hope I don't regret this. "I can see the point."

"What?" Callum's furious glare turns my way, and I wish I hadn't spoken, but it's too late now.

"I can see her point. She wants to get on with her life. She's a capable person. I don't see any reason why she can't move out on her own." Every word is torture, making me go against my instincts.

She's mine, dammit. She belongs with me. Here, where she's loved. Where she's safe.

"I cannot believe this. First you —" He points a finger in her direction, "– and now you. Forming an alliance against me."

"Dad, you know that's not true. Come on."

Her tone softens, the anger draining out of it. I can only imagine it's because she doesn't feel alone in the fight anymore. She walks around the desk and meets him by his chair. "I'm not doing this to go against you. I'm doing it for me. You know? There's a big difference."

"We just got you back."

"I don't have to go far. I have a few areas in mind and they're all within, like, fifteen or twenty minutes. I'll be a lot closer than I was at Romero's old house."

"I want it on record that I am thoroughly against this. I think it's a huge mistake."

"Yeah. I sort of got that idea." Usually, he can't help but chuckle when she teases him like that. Not now. He's too busy being furious.

"Fine. But you're going to do something for me. Otherwise, don't think I'm beyond locking you in that wing and putting twenty-four-hour surveillance on you."

"I would expect that." A ghost of a smile plays over her glossy lips, and I can't help but remember what they tasted like last night. How they felt wrapped around my dick. "What did you have in mind?"

And that's when he does it. That's when he glances my way.

Son of a bitch. Why didn't I see this coming?

"You're going to have a bodyguard. Full-time."

Her face goes slack while a full-blown battle rages in my head. The weak, pathetic side of me – the side she unlocked, damn her – is practically throwing a party. Another excuse to be with her. Together, alone. Maybe this time, we can make it work somehow. Am I wrong for wanting that?

The side of me still capable of thinking rationally wants to come up with any reason to stop this. I'm no good for her. There's too much blood on my hands to ever wash off. I've already stained her enough. It has to stop.

"I thought you said you needed me here." It's taking everything I have to keep calm. "At the house. Before you left, you said you needed me here, which was why you wanted me to return."

"That was before I knew this one decided to run off."

And she couldn't have come up with her idea this morning. I wouldn't put it past her to act without thinking, but this is the kind of thing that took forethought. She already has places in mind, right? She's been thinking about this. Planning.

Which means she knew last night. Coming to the cottage, fighting with me, fucking me. Sleeping in my arms. She fucking knew. And she said nothing.

Now, she clicks her tongue and shakes her head. "You're doing it again."

"Doing what?" Callum snaps.

"Pushing people around. You're just going to send him someplace again? First, you want him home. Now you're sending him away. Did you ask him if he wants to go? No, because you don't allow people to decide for themselves. You're proving my point. I should probably thank you."

"What in the hell are you trying to say?" She needs to be careful. He is about as close to blowing up as I've ever seen him.

"It's always about what you want. And I know you have good intentions, Daddy. You mean well. Although you never stop to ask if anybody agrees with you. It's always your way or the highway."

"I would watch your tone if I were you."

"Dad. Come on. I'm not one of your guards. I'm not some subordinate. I'm a grown woman, and I'm telling you what I've seen with my own eyes. You know all that great redevelopment you're doing in your old hometown? All the improvements and the projects? I'm sure you're proud of that, and you have every right to be. Yet there's another side to it. You're driving up property values and increasing taxes to the point where people can't afford their own homes anymore. Gentrification. Ever heard of it?"

Over the years, I have come to respect Callum for many reasons. He came from nothing, and look at him now. There is an entire army of men decorating his house for the holidays, all because that's what his wife wants. He sits on top of an empire.

But he has his faults, just like anybody else. And right now, he does maybe the worst thing possible.

He scoffs. "Give me a break. And try to stay on topic."

I can practically hear her heart break and for the first time in a decade, I'm disappointed in him. "See?" she murmurs, tipping her head to the side. "You won't even listen when somebody tries to tell you what you need to hear. I'm not surprised, but it doesn't change my mind. I'm going."

"Not without Romero."

"That's fine."

He holds up a finger. "One more caveat. You stay here through the holidays. Not that you could score a lease any faster than that. However, I want to be sure you're here, with us. Got it?"

She draws a deep breath through flared nostrils, narrowing her eyes. "Whatever you say," she agrees through gritted teeth before her head swings around. Her eyes are like lasers burning a hole through me. The message is clear. *I thought you were on my side. Always a lapdog.*

She doesn't understand, and wouldn't if I could find the words. She'll have to go on thinking I'm nothing except a yes man who asks how high whenever her father commands me to jump.

Some sins can never be removed. I'll never deserve her. This is the only way I can have her.

I'll do whatever Callum wants, to give my soul what it needs.

CHAPTER 36

TATUM

Why are my palms so sweaty? Are they always this sweaty? I rub them over my thighs, hoping my jeans will soak it up. Then I realize both legs have been bouncing up and down since I sat in this chair almost an hour ago. I'm still nervous about opening up. I don't want to ruin this.

It's a nice room. Simple, yet comfortable. There are lots of plants and a burning candle fills the air with a light, floral scent I can't identify. But it's nice. It's calming. Well, it would be if I wasn't so damn jumpy.

This isn't my first attempt at therapy, but it's the first time I've actually put any effort into it. I understand why Dad wanted me to see a therapist after I broke down – and if it was my daughter or best friend going through the same stuff, I would have probably made the same recommendation. I wasn't ready, though. The pain was too fresh. I was still too lost and locked away in my personal mental prison.

Over the past couple of weeks, I've seen Dr. Jacobs six times. I want to do the work. I want to get through everything that's holding me back so I can finally move on. The time I spent away from home helped — I feel stronger, more capable, more like myself.

Only there are obviously issues that still need to be worked out.

Like how I can't stay away from what I know will hurt me. He always does in the end.

Most recently, when he rolled over like a dog, showing his belly, when Dad ordered him to be my bodyguard. Just once, I want him to stand up for himself. To at least pretend he's invested in his own life.

The doctor folds her hands on top of her desk and leans in like a friend ready to gossip. "Have you given any thought to what we discussed in our last session?"

In some ways, she's a lot like Mrs. Cooper: kind and supportive, though maybe twenty years younger. Maternal. That's probably why I feel like I can tell her things, even if I still get nervous. It's as if a part of me still waits for the other shoe to drop. Part of me is sure something terrible is going to happen. Like she'll tell me there's no use trying, that I'm a hopeless case. Or she'll judge me when I confess to thoughts, feelings, and actions I'm not exactly proud of.

All it takes is looking into her kind, warm eyes, and all those fears dissolve. "I have." I sit up a little straighter, and now my blood is pumping harder than before. There's a nervous little flutter in my stomach, but that's a good thing, right? I'm excited, not scared.

"And have you come up with any ideas? It's not a race," she reminds me gently. "But from your change in body language alone, I can tell the idea resonates."

"Because it makes sense. I want to take what happened to me and turn it into something good for other people. I have nothing concrete in mind yet, but I've considered a few things. I have plenty of resources with my trust fund and everything, so the possibilities are endless."

"I'm happy to see you so hopeful. However take your time. Be kind to yourself. Rome wasn't built in a day."

"I know, I can't let myself get impatient and quit."

"I believe you'll see it through. You'll find a way if it means that much to you." She checks her watch, and I know that's my cue. "That will be our time for today. See you Friday?"

"I'll be here. Thank you." I feel lighter and happier when I leave the office. I know it's not all in my head, either – I mean, I didn't have the best experience with therapy until now, so it's not like I walked into this with huge expectations. I'm not talking myself into being more hopeful than I am. But I know this isn't a quick-fix sort of thing. No matter how good the doctor is, it's not like I'll be cured after half a dozen sessions.

But I still feel hopeful. When I'm talking to Dr. Jacobs, I can say whatever I want without her cutting me off or giving me the sort of puzzled look Dad always does whenever I start talking about something that doesn't have to do with his business. I know he tries his best, but at the end of the day, he's much better working with the sort of guys he's worked with for years. He understands them. I'm a baffling, mysterious female. Women have never been his strong suit. He and Bianca must belong together; otherwise, she would've strangled him by now.

Thinking of her makes me rush to get home and talk to her about the idea that has been bouncing around in my head for the past couple of days. I wasn't even home yet on Monday afternoon, and already I had an idea of how to take my experience and turn it into something positive. It actually seems pretty obvious that I would use my money this way.

One problem: it would be a tremendous job. I wonder whether I have what it takes to pull off something this big. I wouldn't be doing it alone – but I wouldn't know where to begin getting help.

Right away, doubt starts to creep in and tickle the back of my mind. Who do I think I am? I'm nobody. I don't have experience. And who's to say I would end up helping anybody? I might make everything even worse somehow. I'm not in any position to give advice or provide what anybody needs.

Is it better to just throw money at a charity and hope it does some good?

I'm still going back and forth by the time I roll through the front gate. The sight of Henry sitting at his usual post makes me smile to myself. Some things just are the way they are. Like Henry. He's been sitting there for as long as I can remember, maybe since before I was born. If I ever drove through these gates and didn't see him there, everything would seem off. He is continuity; he's a sign that everything's going how it should.

I wish the rest of my life could be that way. All safe and comforting. Predictable.

If life was more predictable, I wouldn't be walking through the house calling out to people who aren't here. "Bianca? Where are you?" No response. My heart sinks a little despite the fact that I'm standing in the middle of a Christmas wonderland. This doesn't even seem like a real house anymore. With all the garland, trees, and twinkling lights wrapped around the railing leading up the steps, wound through the wreath swathed over every doorway and expertly tucked between the branches of a fifteen-foot spruce. It's like a movie set, and standing in the middle of it makes me happy, but I was hoping to talk to my best friend. I'm enthusiastic about something for the first time in forever.

Sheryl's not in the kitchen when I stop in for an apple, either. That's when I remember her talking about getting some Christmas shopping done this afternoon. I head down the hall toward Dad's office, crunching the juicy apple. "Dad? Where's —"

Okay, now I'm starting to wonder if everything's alright. I could count on one hand the number of times I've walked in here in the middle of the day and found the office empty. What if something happened to Bianca and the baby when I wasn't here? My heart is lodged in my throat, and I could kick myself for not thinking of that sooner.

Not many things could get me to rush into Romero's office. Not right now. Not with everything still so weird between us. Right now, though, I'm too worried to care. I've barely knocked on the open door before blurting out, "Where is everybody?? Are they —"

He looks up from the document he's reading and shakes his head. "Take a breath. Everything's fine. They went out for lunch and shopping with Bianca's dad."

I lean against the door frame and close my eyes. "Thank God. I thought she was sick or something."

"No, just spending the afternoon with the two of them. Who knows? She might end up wishing she was sick by the time it's all said and done."

I don't appreciate the snark in his voice, but I see where he's coming from. It's sort of a miracle that my dad and hers can be bothered to spend time in the same room after all their years of basically working against each other. Charlie Cole made it his life's mission to put Dad behind bars back during his detective days, and Dad always found a way to slip through his fingers. He was *not* happy when he found out his daughter fell in love with a criminal.

But they're doing their best to get along for her sake, and for the baby.

"What are you doing?" I ask, since now that we're in the same room, I can't help but look for reasons to bug him. It means an excuse to be with him, and I'm pitiful enough to want that. I want it so much I'll make a fool of myself to get it.

He makes a point of looking down at his work, then back at me. "Earning a living. What does it look like?"

"Oh, my God. Can you try to act like a human being for two seconds? I was only asking. You don't have to get all insulted and bitchy."

"Last I checked, you barged in here and practically shrieked when I was in the middle of something." He leans back in his chair, studying me. "So, how was your session?"

"It was fine."

"You're actually getting along with this doctor?"

"You know what, I'm out. I swear, just when I think you might be human, you have to act like an asshole."

"Hey. Hey!" he barks when I start down the hall. "Come back."

"Why? So I can be insulted?"

"Okay, fine. No insults."

Insults aside, I can't ignore how my pulse flutters like my stomach did earlier. It's excitement, maybe anticipation. Of what? That's a dumb question. I know exactly what my stupid body thinks is going to happen. It doesn't help that he looks hotter than sin in his typical work clothes: charcoal slacks and a light blue button-down shirt that matches his eyes. The sleeves are rolled up almost to his elbows — what is it about the side of a pair of strong forearms that makes me weak?

These are Romero's forearms. I have to remember the man they're attached to.

"Actually," I mutter, folding my arms and trying to ignore his, "I wanted to bounce an idea off Bianca. It's something the therapist got me thinking about."

His brows lift. "What's on your mind?"

"She wanted me to think about ways to help other people. If I could turn what happened to me into a good thing for others, it would lose its power. I forget her exact words."

"That's a fairly typical approach." Like he's an expert.

"So I've been thinking, maybe there's a way to help women who have gone through the same kind of thing I did. Or..." Shit. I should've stopped while I was ahead.

"Or? What were you going to say?"

"It's not important."

"Bullshit."

I gesture in his direction with one hand, feeling feeble and stupid. "More like your mom. Women who need to get on their feet after they've experienced trouble."

He doesn't flinch. "Like a shelter?"

"More than that. I don't know." I shake my head and flutter my hands around. "Don't worry about it. It's not even an idea, really. I haven't given it very much thought."

"Calm down. I was only asking because I was curious."

"Well, I was thinking more like a whole program. Not just a place to stay, but somewhere with resources." The more I talk about it, the more excited I get. Now that he looks interested, I can move deeper into the room and perch on the corner of his desk. "Like, for instance, I read one time about financial abuse. A husband or a partner locks down the bank accounts and only lets a woman have a small allowance. That kind of thing. Even if a woman manages to make it out of something like that, she could be financially illiterate. So, maybe some classes on financial literacy. Job search resources. Job skills classes. Maybe daycare for when Mom starts a job."

His full lips twitch. "It sounds like you've been giving this more thought than you admit."

"I'm just riffing. This is all off the top of my head."

"I think it's a great idea. I really do." And for maybe the first time since we came back here, he sounds like himself. He's not putting on an act anymore, not pushing me away. We're back to being us, if only for right now, at this moment.

"I wouldn't know where to get started."

"Good thing there's no deadline."

"I want to start now!"

It's nice to hear him laugh. "So start now. Just don't get too down on yourself if there are any obstacles in your way – and there will be."

"I know that," I say. "Really, I'm not a child."

The beat he pauses feels more like a lifetime. "I know."

All of a sudden, my nervous, excited energy turns into something else. Something just as potent, just as consuming. All it took was a change in his voice. The way it deepened. The way he looks at me now – I've seen it before. I know what it means.

Maybe I shouldn't have come in here, after all.

Maybe it was the best thing I've done all day.

He stands, but I'm pinned to the spot. Hypnotized by him, held in place by his knowing stare.

By the time he nudges my knees apart to stand between them, I'm twisting his shirt in my fists and pulling him closer. Why is it always like this? I can't get over him. He's an addiction. I can't quit, no matter how much I know I need to. I know he's not good for me. I know this will never end well, and he will never stop pushing me away. I know he's more afraid of losing this job and my father's respect than of losing me.

You would think I'd have the self-respect to push him away and maybe slap him, just so he knows he can't get away with using me.

Instead of slapping his face, I run a hand down his cheek. My racing heart skips a beat when he groans and closes his eyes, leaning into my caress. I can barely breathe, and when I do, I inhale his unique scent. All the memories come rushing back – the time we spent together, the nights I slept in his arms. Falling asleep with his scent wrapped around me like a protective blanket, the warmth of his arms and his heart's slow, steady beat lulled me into a peaceful slumber. I was happy. I was safe.

There is nothing safe about this, but that doesn't stop me from tipping my head back to meet his kiss when he touches his lips to mine.

Right away, my legs close around him, drawing him closer. I moan into his mouth when his tongue slides against mine. He takes me by the hips and pulls me in, grinding his dick against my aching mound. Already, I'm wet and throbbing and ready to cry — I need him that much. I want him that badly.

He takes a fist full of my hair to hold my head in place before breaking the kiss. He's breathing hard, the heat fanning across my face while his eyes burn into me. "What have you done to me?" he pants before claiming my mouth again, and every bruising kiss sends ripples of sweet fire running through my body.

I need to touch him. To feel his skin. I blindly tug at his shirt, pulling it from his waistband and sliding my hands underneath to rake my nails down his back. He shudders, groaning, while his kiss becomes rough and demanding. And I drink it in, ready to scream and weep with relief. Having him here is torment, but I'm finally getting what I need after weeks of being ignored.

When he fumbles with my jeans, I break the kiss, gulping air while leaning back and lifting my hips so he can slide the denim down my thighs and over my knees. He doesn't wait to get them all the way off before pushing my panties to the side and driving his fingers deep into my wet, quivering pussy.

My head falls back, my body lost in abandon. "Romero…" I moan, closing my eyes and letting my focus narrow until there's nothing in the world but what he's doing to me. The wet, sloppy sounds of my arousal fill the room, louder and wetter with every stroke.

His animal grunts only add to the heat building in my core. It makes me lift my hips to grind against him, hungry for more. For everything he can give me. Electric shocks run through my body when he strums my clit, and I bite my lip to barely hold back a scream of agonized pleasure.

"Say my name again," he growls while his knuckles slam against my sensitive flesh as he takes me harder. "Say it. I want to hear you say it."

"Romero." I lift my head and open my eyes, looking up at him. He's just as lost as I am, wrapped in pleasure and excitement. *And us.* "Romero..."

I'm close, so close. I need this. I need him to make me feel good, to know he wants to make me feel good. To know he's here with me now, and nothing else matters.

Which is why I whimper in desperation when his phone rings. "Don't, don't," I beg, jerking my hips frantically, chasing the high that was so close.

His forehead wrinkles before his mouth opens then snaps shut. "I just have to..." He reaches for the phone with his fingers still inside me, and his frown deepens.

After one quick glance my way, he answers. "Boss?"

I collapse against the desk, barely stifling a sigh of... What? Disappointment, for sure, but why am I more disappointed? Because I was close to coming, or because he couldn't ignore his master's voice just once?

"Sounds good. I'll have all that ready when you get back. See you soon." He won't look at me as he ends the call, withdrawing his fingers. They glisten in the light from the lamp on the desk. And then he grabs a tissue and wipes them off, almost like he's irritated, before he starts straightening himself out. "They'll be here in about five minutes, if that. Thank God he called."

I can't believe this. I honestly can't believe it. "That's it? The end?"

"What do you think?" He reaches into his pants to adjust his dick, still hard and straining against his zipper, then tucks his shirt in. And here I am, still leaning back on my elbows with my jeans around my calves.

"You know, some people would take it as a challenge to see how fast they could come."

"Don't be a child."

"I'm starting to wonder if you have a split personality. How can you turn it on and off like that?" I snap my fingers, staring at him.

"Fix yourself up. At least pull your pants up before they get here."

"And what if I don't?"

"We both know you will, because you're not stupid."

"Is there ever going to be any aspect of your life you don't let my father rule over?" I hop off the desk and pull up my jeans, trembling with anger and disappointment. He will never choose me. Never. When am I going to get the hint?

"Did it ever occur to you that I'm doing this just as much for your sake as mine? I mean, he could lock you in that wing. The worst he could do to me is blow my brains out." He barks out a bitter laugh, even though he isn't joking. We both know it.

"He wouldn't do that to you."

"It's a moot point, anyway. And he called at the right time. That was… wrong." He settles into his chair and even pulls a bottle of hand sanitizer from one of the drawers before slathering it on his hands.

"Dude. You need to make up your mind."

"My mind is made up." He lifts a shoulder, shuffling papers around. "It was a moment of weakness. That's all."

And here I am, surrounded by pieces of my freshly shattered heart. How can he be this way? A minute ago we were locked together, kissing and touching and everything. He won't look at me now. "Do you think it's going to be any easier when we're living together again?"

At least that slows him down like he's thinking. "Things can't go back to the way they were then. We both know that."

"Stop telling me what I know."

"Stop wasting my time."

"You know what I know? I know you're still too afraid of life to be anything more than Daddy's lap dog. You do whatever he wants, whenever he wants. It's easier to let somebody else make your decisions for you, right?"

"Keep talking," he mutters before finally looking up at me. "And don't forget to sound hateful and dismissive while you're at it."

"Already way ahead of you."

"But you're not hateful and dismissive enough to keep from jumping on my dick every time you get a chance, are you?"

My head snaps back in surprise. My hands curl into fists and for one crazy second, I can see myself driving them into his face. We'll see how good he looks after I beat the shit out of him.

Too late. "You'll never believe it. Charlie actually —"

Dad stops short when he finds me standing at Romero's desk. "Oh. Hello. How was your session?"

"Fine. Things are going really well. What did Charlie do?" Because anything is better than him asking what he just walked in on. I wouldn't know where to start, and I don't think Romero would do much better.

"I was going to tell Romero about how he shook my hand after lunch and thanked me for taking care of Bianca. Can you imagine that?" He can try to play it off all he wants, but I can see how glad he is. After all the bad blood between them, it seems like they're finally reaching common ground. I'm sure that makes Bianca happy, too.

Right now, I don't particularly care about their happiness. Not when mine is nonexistent. "That's great. Did she go upstairs?"

"To the nursery. I'm sure she'll want to show you what we bought today." He's so oblivious he can't see how mad I am. Mad at him, at Romero, at myself. Mostly at myself. I don't know why I expect more from him than he's capable of giving. He's still a coward at heart, afraid to live without Dad. Maybe he's the one who should see a therapist.

And to think, I have an entire future of this to look forward to.

Wanting him, needing him, and hating him when he can't give me all of himself. When he makes me feel small and stupid for wanting him.

As I walk through a pine-scented Christmas wonderland that now makes me grit my teeth, it hits me there's something even worse in all of this. It would be one thing if I believed he truly hated me or at least was indifferent.

But I know that's not true. He cares. I've seen it, felt it. I've known it.

What will it take to get him to stop lying to me — and himself?

CHAPTER 37

ROMERO

"You picked up on a lot when I wasn't here, didn't you?" I hope I sound encouraging as I observe Nathan wrapping up a few contracts for Callum to sign. There are trust papers in there, too. He wants to set something up for the baby the way he did for Tatum. I watch closely, making sure Nathan doesn't mix anything up, but he's on top of it. He had to learn fast while I was out of town.

"Yeah, it's not that hard." He throws a guilty look my way and his cheeks go red when he catches my expression. "I didn't mean it the way it sounded. It's not easy. It's a lot to keep straight."

"Yeah, but you've been at it a while now. You're getting the hang of it." He looks relieved, and I can only imagine I must've made a face that worried him.

I'm sure I made a face, but I doubt it was for the reason he thinks. The fact is, he picked up my job a lot faster than I figured. For the past couple of weeks, as we've had these training sessions whenever we both have a few minutes to spare, I've witnessed him easily handling everything.

Tonight, he's fresh off a late dinner between Callum and a few shipping contacts. It was a low-stakes sort of meeting with friendly associates, so I suggested my replacement serve as the boss's escort and guard. Might as well keep him sharp since Tatum will sign a lease any day now.

I have to bite my tongue to keep from correcting him – he's got his own system set up, his own way of doing things. I need to remind myself his methods aren't necessarily wrong. They're only different.

I'm feeling pretty replaceable right now, in other words. There's a tightness in my chest and a dull roar in my head. Is this a normal, healthy way of handling the feeling that I've been entirely replaceable all this time? Something tells me it's not. I should be glad he's picked up on everything so fast. One less thing to think about.

God knows Callum is giving me enough to do when it comes to researching the apartments Tatum is looking at. He expects a complete report of security details — what the buildings offer, what we would need to install to make up for any gaps. I doubt any building will feature everything Callum considers a must-have. I've lost track of the number of times I've rolled my eyes at his demands. I also know better than to try to talk him out of it. When it comes to his daughter, enough is never enough.

But that's not Nathan's fault. "Did you confirm the reservations for the hotel?"

His pained groan sets up his response. "It wasn't easy, but I'm starting to get used to name-dropping when I want things done at the last minute."

I walk to the window and watch the guards change out for the night. Shit, it's that late already? "Let me guess. There was nothing they could do to find a room until they knew who it was for," I murmur while memories of when I first took this job come rushing back.

"Pretty much. I swear to God, the girl I talked to was about to hang up on me before I said the name Torrio."

"You learn pretty fast that you drop the name first. It feels slimy as shit, but it saves time in the end. You won't even flinch after a while." Scoring a hotel room for the week between Christmas and New Year's, only a week before the holiday, is like turning water into wine. When you're a billionaire, you can make last-minute decisions like that. "Callum wouldn't know this, but I have a list of contacts at all of his favorite hotels. If I wasn't so caught up in researching apartments for Tatum, I would've thought to give it to you."

"Not such a big deal in the grand scheme. Don't worry about it." He double-checks something and nods. "Yeah, they're all set, along with the spa treatments the boss requested for Bianca. They'll leave the day after Christmas, then return for New Year's." He shakes his head, looking puzzled. "Have you ever heard of a babymoon before?"

"Do I look like the kind of guy who walks around talking about babymoons?"

I turn away from the window in time to find him smirking at me. He fixes his face, but it's too late. When I lift an eyebrow, he lifts his shoulder. "I was just thinking what a comfortable gig you've got waiting for you."

"What do you mean?" If there's one thing I'm skilled in, it's keeping a bland expression and a flat tone of voice when the situation calls for it. I know exactly what he's trying to say, but I'd like to watch him squirm a little.

And squirm, he does. Just when I forget exactly why Callum broke his nose over a smart-ass comment he made, he reminds me by stating yet another smart-ass comment. "I'm just saying, it sounds pretty nice. Full-time bodyguard. I know Tatum isn't the kind of girl who's going to live in a slum. It should be nice for you."

"Let's get a couple of things straight." It's not bad enough that he's sitting at my desk, but now he has to comment about my life? As if he knows the first thing.

He dons the look of a man who knows he stepped in shit as I approach the desk, stopping in front of him and leaning in. "First off, if you're going to succeed at this job, you'll have to learn to keep your thoughts to yourself. That goes for pretty much every situation, *all* the time. Discretion is a substantial portion of your work. Understood?"

"Sure. Of course." Now he's quiet, respectful. Embarrassed.

"Second, there's no such thing as easy when it comes to her. Maybe you would like to switch places and live in a luxury apartment and have to watch over her. You'll always have in the back of your head a reminder of what will happen to you if you let anything happen to her. No, it won't be your fault in the end – she makes her own choices. But you'll be the one who gets blamed for letting her out of your sight for a minute. Does that sound comfortable to you?"

"No. No, it doesn't." Something tells me he would agree to anything right now. I'm sure he's intimidated, which is how he deserves to feel. He needs to get knocked down a peg or two, or else things are going to get bad – fast.

"I think that's enough training for tonight." It's already past ten o'clock, hence the guard change – I would call an end to the night. It's one thing to be a quick learner and another to know when your opinion is wanted and when you should maybe keep your mouth shut.

"Sounds good." He looks ready to run from the room when he stands. "You sure you have everything you need right now?"

"I'm fine. Thanks. Have a good night." I let out a sigh of relief at the sound of his footsteps fading down the hall. He's a decent enough guy, but he's also a pain in the ass. I doubt I would get along with him in the outside world if we didn't have the job connecting us. I've never gotten along very well with people who can't keep their mouths shut. Even as a kid, they were the people I would avoid. It's all about trust in the end. If I can't trust somebody, I have no time for them.

Note to self: Have a talk with Callum about him. There's a good chance I'm projecting here. There could be part of me that doesn't believe anybody can do my job as well as I can. I could be looking for reasons to disapprove. Callum doesn't mince words. If he doesn't trust Nathan, he'll tell me so.

I'll be damned if I know where we could go from there. Tatum is determined to leave and is hell-bent on having me stay with her. It's like inviting the fox into the hen house.

Don't I owe him the truth after everything he's done for me?

He's still in his office across the hall from mine. No big surprise there – at least, it wouldn't be a surprise back in the day, before Bianca turned him from a workaholic to an adoring husband. "I was hoping you'd stop by before you head out," he tells me when I rap against the open door.

"I have that write-up for you." He's still a hardcopy guy, so I slide a folder across his desk while he loosens his tie and pops his top button. "A full rundown of the five complexes Tatum's been looking at."

"Thorough, as always." He gives the pages a cursory glance before closing the folder again. "I'll be able to pay better attention to this in the morning. My age is catching up with me – I can't pull these long nights and late meetings the way I used to."

"You're not that old."

"Explain that to my body." He stands and stretches, groaning. He's clearly not in the mood to be reminded that, for a man his age, he's in great shape. Hell, he's in great shape for a man ten years younger than him.

"Why are you smiling?"

I hadn't realized I was. "I guess I was feeling nostalgic," I admit, chuckling at myself.

"How so?" He goes to the bar and pours a whiskey, silently inviting me to have one. As usual, I shake my head.

"It's one of the lessons you taught me early on. Take care of your body so your brain can operate at its peak."

"I did tell you that. And you took it to heart." He lifts his glass in a silent salute before downing half of the amber liquid.

"I took a lot of what you said to heart. Most of it, even."

"I'm glad you did." He gives me a funny, appraising sort of look. "Is everything alright with you? I've been meaning to ask. You've seemed rather distant lately."

He lowers his brow and practically growls. "Tell me she's not giving you shit over this new assignment."

No need to ask who he's referring to. The mere thought of her warms my blood and awakens my yearning. "She gives me a lot of shit over all sorts of things," I mutter. "That shouldn't come as a surprise."

"You realize if I trusted anyone here as much as I trust you, I would keep you here. I can't imagine working so well with anyone as I do with you."

Then don't make me go. I would never say that, because I need him to send me. I don't enjoy having my balls in a vice and having my choices removed, but it means being with her. I'll do whatever he says so long as it means I can be with her, even when I know it's the worst possible scenario for both of us.

No matter how masochistic it makes me. I've spent a portion of my life being around her, and I've spent it without her; I know which I can live with. Those few days we were apart proved I was not strong enough to say goodbye to her. I might as well say goodbye to my legs and my arms. She's that much a part of me. A part of me that seems to always make the wrong choice when it comes to her.

"Do you think Nathan is the right choice to replace me?" I ask.

"I think he's come a long way, if that's what you're asking." He touches his thumb to his nose, and we share a knowing laugh, remembering the punch that broke his nose. "And he's eager to learn."

"I wonder if he'll learn to keep his mouth shut."

He doesn't hesitate. "If I need to break his nose again, I will. Although let's be honest... Most of the time, he's too nervous to say very much to me. I think he'll be fine. Don't get me wrong, nobody could ever replace you, but this is a fair arrangement."

That's just the thing. There's nothing fair about any of this. It's not fair that I fell in love with my boss's daughter. It's not fair that I was already unworthy of her by the time we met. I probably still had my father's blood under my fingernails the morning I first set eyes on her. I dismissed her as a kid, that's all, and it didn't matter much at the time. I had other things on my mind, like whether I'd get away with what I'd done and how I was supposed to live without seeing my mother again.

When he yawns, I snap myself out of it. "I'll leave you alone. Have a good night."

"Oh, before you go." He wears a rueful grin as he holds up a hand to stop me. "Bianca's been on my case. There's one week until Christmas, and she still doesn't know what to get you as a gift."

"She doesn't have to get me anything. I hope you told her that."

"Of course I did. And, of course, she listened about as well as she always does." He rolls his eyes, chuckling. "No wonder she and my kid are such good friends."

"I'll come up with something, I promise." On my way down the hall, a laundry list of what I'd like runs through my head. I'd like to get my heart back from the woman who stole it when I wasn't paying attention. I'd like to turn back the clock and undo so many mistakes. I'd like to be the man Tatum deserves.

I doubt there's a store where Bianca or anybody else could fulfill my wishes.

Finding her in front of the enormous tree near the stairs brings me up short. "I was just thinking about you," I admit when she turns at the sound of my footsteps.

"Thinking of what I can get you for Christmas?" she asks with a hopeful grin.

"Something like that. I'll give it some thought."

She turns her attention back to the tree, and I can see the lights reflected in her eyes. Between the awestruck look on her face and her reindeer pajamas, she could be a hopeful little kid–if it wasn't for the belly that seems to get bigger every day. "Isn't it pretty? I meant to take a snack in to Tatum, but I got distracted." In one hand, she holds a plate covered in crackers, cheese, and apple slices.

I join her in admiring the spruce. "How many lights did they get on this thing?"

"Five thousand."

"Holy shit."

"I know." There's a gleam in her eyes and glee in her voice. I don't think she minds very much.

"Anyway, I think the boss was about to wrap it up for the night." I shrug, eyeing the plate. "I can take that to Tatum if you want. I was on my way out, though I can make a pitstop."

There it is again. The shadow that crosses her face. There's nothing threatening about it that I can see. It's more of a knowing sort of look. As if there's something she wants to say but knows she shouldn't. "That would be great. Then I'll go to his office and make sure he doesn't get wrapped up in something else."

"Sounds good." Calm down, for fuck's sake. I'm practically coming in my pants, all excited because I get to take food to Tatum's room. I'm worse off than even I thought if this is enough to get my blood pumping. "Have a good night."

"You, too." I know I'm not imagining the humor in her voice. What the hell is so funny? What does she know that I don't?

Rather than ask — especially since I don't know how I'll feel about the answer — I carry the plate past the stairs and into Tatum's wing. Many nights before we went away together, I crept into this part of the house, hoping she wouldn't notice. Nights I spent sleeping on the loveseat in the room Callum set up as an office, but it became more of a second closet over the years. She preferred to do her work in bed, with books, papers, and her laptop strewn everywhere.

As far as I know, the nightmares have stopped. There's no more reason to keep an ear out for her night after night.

But some things never change. I'm greeted by a familiar sight when I ease her door open after she doesn't respond to my knock. The only light in the room comes from her laptop, glowing brightly and illuminating the papers and books covering the surface of her bed.

And there she is, lying on her side with her legs hanging off the edge of the bed and her head resting on one bent arm. She's been holed up in here for most of the past two weeks. I assumed a lot of it involved packing up her life for a more extended, more permanent move than the one she packed for a few months ago. And yes, I notice the stacked boxes along the far wall, even blocking the windows now that she has them piled so high. She's damn determined to move on with her life.

I creep closer to the bed and see it hasn't all been packed. On her screen, there is a very basic rendering of a floorplan. I'm looking at the second floor according to the notes along the side of the page, and in the rendering, there are small rooms along the two longer sides of the floor, with what I guess are beds, dressers, and closets. At the far end, there's a big room labeled kitchen, along with notes typed at the top of the page. Cooking classes? Meal planning? Budgeting?

After a glance her way to make sure she's still asleep, I reach over and scroll down. On the third floor, there are larger rooms. One is labeled Daycare, another Classroom, while another is labeled Gym. There's a room across from that labeled: Computers.

This is her project. Her shelter. This is what she's been working on long into the night, exhausting herself to the point where she fell asleep in maybe the most uncomfortable position ever.

I look around at the books — a few are on business, including non-profits. There are self-help books, too, with titles involving personal power, strength, and being a boss bitch.

She's determined to make this happen. I can hardly breathe, thanks to the pride swelling in my chest. Tatum. My Tatum. She's found her place, or what she hopes is her place.

I know her. She'll make it work somehow.

"What do you think?"

She's watching me. How long has that been going on? I was too concerned with her plans. "I thought you were sleeping."

"I was." Pushing herself up on her elbow, she yawns and throws the other arm over her head. She had the forethought to put on a nightshirt and shorts–I have to pry my hungry gaze from her nipples, standing out against thin cotton. "So what do you think? Am I insane? Tell me the truth."

"I'd always tell you the truth."

"I know, which can be infuriating sometimes."

I almost forgot the stupid snack, which I set on her nightstand. Amanda's ashes used to sit there. She's come a long way from needing a crutch. "The truth? You're sure you want to hear it?"

"I'm not so sure anymore."

I've screwed with her long enough. "I think it looks great and would like to know more."

She narrows her eyes. "For real? You're not screwing with me?"

"I'm not screwing with you." I point to the renderings. "Dorm rooms? Is that what you're going for?"

She sits up, nodding, and there's excitement in her voice when she speaks. "Yeah, that's the general idea. I don't know yet if private bathrooms would be feasible or if there should be big, dorm-style bathrooms. Toilet stalls, shower stalls, that kind of thing."

What would Mom want? Fuck, where did that come from? The question exploded across my mind before I knew what was happening. "If it's feasible, private bathrooms are the better idea–in my opinion."

"You think so?"

"You have to figure some of these women might not have enjoyed privacy in a long time. A feeling of being safe."

"Of course," she sighs, nodding slowly. "Plus, if there are kids with them, they'll need privacy and safety, too. Not showering around strangers."

"Exactly."

A soft smile stirs the corners of her mouth. "So you think I'm on the right track, at least? I want this to be somewhere women can go to get their lives together. I want to put money into the community, too. I have so many ideas."

She's glowing, and not because of the white light shining from the laptop and highlighting her golden curls and the curve of her cheek. She's radiant. Full of hopeful energy. Determined.

I have never wanted her more than I do as I brush some of the books aside to make room to sit. "You're incredible." The desire to stroke her hair is too strong to fight. I take one of her curls between my fingers and admire its softness before tucking it behind her ear and letting my hand linger against the side of her face. Not good. I shouldn't.

But then she leans into my touch, and all thoughts of 'what should and shouldn't' cease to exist.

"I want to do something good." Her whole wounded heart is in those words. I feel the intensity of her desire. How deeply she wants this.

"You will." With my hand cupping her jaw, I draw her closer. Her juicy lips refuse to be resisted. I have to taste them.

Her soft sigh the instant before our mouths meet is a lit match thrown on kindling. A fire bursts to life inside me and threatens to devour what's left of my common sense. This is the last place we should be doing this, but I can't stop now.

Neither can she. Her hands sink into my hair while her body melts against mine, and I drink in one deep, searching kiss after another. By the time she brushes a hand against my straining dick, I'm barely clinging to my self-control. "Tatum…" It's a whisper. A groan. A prayer. For strength, for self-control, for her to touch me and take everything else away for just a little while. A prayer for the peace I've only ever known while inside her.

She answers by swinging a leg over me and straddling my lap. I'd swear I can feel the heat from her pussy when she grinds against me through our clothes, and I twitch and strain in response. I find her hips with both hands and pull down, demanding more, but it's like the sensation of her nipples brushing my chest through our shirts. Not enough.

She gasps when my fingers dig into her firm ass cheeks, breaking our kiss and throwing her head back so I can devour her smooth throat, nipping and sucking while her nails scratch my scalp and the back of my neck. I'm breathing hard, but then she is, too, both of us building into a frenzy. There's no stopping this.

Instead of pushing her off my lap, I lie back and she goes with me. Now, she can plant her palms against the bed and grind hard enough to drive me out of my fuckin mind. Her throaty moans–desperate, feral–leave me dripping and aching and, fuck, I have to be inside her. Now.

"Callum! Wait up! I want to say goodnight, too!"

It takes too long for me to register the voice now echoing through the hall outside the partly open door.

Bianca. Filled with panic and tension.

Calling out to…

"What the fuck?"

Callum. She was calling out to Callum.

Who is now standing in the doorway after flipping the light on, staring at us with his mouth hanging open. His daughter is straddling me and I'm halfway to pulling my dick free, both of us now frozen in fear.

Tatum finds her voice before I do. "Daddy. Let me explain."

I know him too well for that. He's not in the mood to listen.

He'd much rather kill me for this and ask questions later.

CHAPTER 38

TATUM

This is a nightmare, right? I'm still asleep. Of course, I had a dream about making out with Romero since that's the kind of thing I usually dream about lately, anyway. That is when I'm not dreaming about the nonprofit that's getting bigger and bigger in my imagination.

There is no way Dad just walked into my room unannounced and found us like this.

Bianca bumps into him from behind and propels him further into the room. "I'm sorry," she whispers, red-faced. "I tried."

"Tried?" Dad glares at her before swinging his attention back to us. "Tried what? You knew about this?"

"Dad, please." I scramble off Romero's lap and straighten out my pajamas, feeling very small and afraid. I could live to be a hundred, and I would still be afraid of my father. Not that he would hurt me—I know he wouldn't. It's his disapproval I'm scared of. His disappointment.

More than anything, I'm afraid of what he'll do to Romero, who awkwardly lurches to his feet with a raging erection I was only grinding against a few seconds ago. I doubt it will last long now that the worst has happened and we're both basically fucked.

"Please, what?" Dad's question is a bark, loud and vicious enough to make the hair on the back of my neck stand straight up and my skin erupt in goosebumps.

I am not a child anymore, but I'll be damned if he doesn't make me feel like one.

"You." He jabs a finger in Romero's direction, and that finger is shaking because his entire body is trembling with rage. "I trusted you. I treated you like a member of my fucking family, and what did you do? You took advantage. All this time. How long has this been going on? Tell me. How long?"

"It's not that simple!" I'm shouting, but then I have to if I want to be heard.

"I don't remember asking you a thing," Dad snaps. "You and I will have this out, but right now–"

"No! You're going to listen to *me*!"

Wow. Where did that come from? Even I'm shocked, my mouth snapping shut. Out of the corner of my eye, I see Bianca staring at me, looking worried and surprised all at once.

Dad lowers his brow. "Excuse me?" His whispered tone chills me. "Since when do you shout at me like that?"

Don't you dare back down now. "Since you won't listen, though that's nothing new, is it?"

"Tatum…" Romero murmurs.

Forget him right now. No, what I have to say goes deeper than this moment. I've got almost twenty-three years of pent-up frustration to vent.

Dad takes a breath and releases it slowly. "I am going to let that go for now. You're upset and confused."

"You're damn right, I'm upset. Since when do you walk into my room, anyway?"

"Your room is in my house."

"This is my room. Mine. It's the only thing in this house that is mine. It's the only thing in my entire life that belongs to me. Me!" I tap my palm to my chest, where my heart pounds furiously. "It's the only thing you've ever really let me have to myself."

"What are you talking about? Don't turn this around on me."

"That is what this is about, Dad. You don't get it, but then I've spent my whole life trying to be *who you want me to be*, so I understand how you wouldn't have the first clue what I need."

The laugh he blurts out might as well be a fist flying my way. It hurts that much to hear his disdain. "You're not saying you need him, are you?"

"So what if I do?" With my hands on my hips, I lift my chin and look him in the eye. I'm shaking like a leaf, but I won't back down. Not now.

"You don't know what you're talking about."

"Dad, I'm a grown woman. I know what I want. And I'm sorry if you don't like it, but not everything can be exactly how you want it. I'm sorry. You know I love you, but I must draw the line at you making all my decisions for me. I don't want you to do that."

I look at Romero, who hasn't said a word since murmuring my name. He looks like he's wondering whether this is all a dream – either that or he wishes it was.

"So, what?" Dad throws his hands into the air. "I'm supposed to stand back and let this happen? Sure, Tatum, get involved with someone like him."

"Someone like him? What does that mean?"

"You know what I mean."

"No, I don't. Why don't you explain it to me? Because up until now, you treated him like a son. You've trusted him."

"And look where it got me."

"Where did it get you? He's protected your life. He's protected my life. How hypocritical can you be?"

"Watch it," he growls. Bianca makes a strained sort of noise–he glances her way and she shakes her head, but he's too far gone at this point. He refuses to listen to reason.

"No. You need to hear this. Dad, I love you, but I'm not going to stand here and let you act like Romero isn't good enough for me when all he's ever done is what you have told him to do. You shaped him into who he is. You don't get to turn around and say he's not good enough for me now."

"You're twisting my words around, dammit." He rakes a hand through his hair and curses under his breath before glaring at Romero again. "This is all your fault."

Romero doesn't even flinch – he hardly reacts at all, only bearing Dad's anger with the same stoic silence. Say something. Anything. Stand up for yourself.

But no, that's too much to ask, isn't it. It always has been. When it comes to Dad, he'll never stand up for himself. Deep down inside, he doesn't think he deserves anything besides this. Being constantly blamed, insulted, all of it.

Finally, he draws a breath, and I hold mine. This is it. This is his chance. My whole future might rest on this. It could all come down to what he does now.

Romero says only two words. "You're right."

I should've known better. My heart plummets, and all the breath leaves my lungs. He might as well hit me – it hurts that much, the way Dad's dismissal does.

"Don't do that," I whisper. "Don't. You don't have to."

"I do." He won't look at me. Why won't he look at me? No, he would prefer to stare at Dad, his head held high, his jaw tight. "If you're going to blame this on anyone, it should be me."

"No! There's nothing to blame anybody for. There is nothing wrong with this." I glimpse at Bianca, silently pleading, though I know she is as helpless as I am right now. What could she say?

Dad takes a menacing step toward him, and panic explodes in my head. Before I can think, I throw myself between them. "No. Enough of this. That is not how this is going to end tonight."

"Tatum, get out of the way," Dad mutters.

"I won't. Not until you listen to me."

"What could you possibly say? There's nothing that would make this acceptable."

"I love him."

It's out there. I said it. There's no taking it back now. Not when Dad practically sways on his feet like he's had a severe shock. Not when Bianca gasps sharply. They all heard it.

And somehow, Romero is the only one who doesn't react. I guess I shocked him too much.

I'll deal with that later – if Dad lets him live long enough.

What am I doing? How do I stop this? How do I get through? Frantic questions bounce around inside my skull so loud I can hardly hear myself think.

"I'm going to pretend I didn't hear that," Dad growls. "You don't know what you're saying."

Bitter tears well up in my eyes, though I force them back. I am not going to break down. Not now. Even if it breaks my heart a little, hearing him say that and knowing he means it. He genuinely thinks I'm incapable of knowing my own heart.

"And there you go," I whisper, shaking my head. "So sure you know best. One minute, you're telling me I'm smart and capable, and the next, you're talking to me like I'm some stupid kid who doesn't know which end is up. I'm tired of it. I am so tired, Daddy. I need you to actually give me a little credit for once, for real. Not some encouraging words you don't really mean."

Either he is shocked that I'm speaking up for myself, or I caught him off guard. Regardless, he goes silent, and I jump on the chance to be heard. "I know you mean well. I really do. But sometimes, you're so sure that what you're doing is right you don't think about what it means for everybody else. Like back home, in your old town. All that work that's being done, all those improvements? They're a great thing, and I know it's coming from a good place. But there's another side to it. People are getting pushed out of their homes because they can't afford the taxes now that the property values are increasing. Did you ever stop and think about that? No, because you're so busy patting yourself on the back that you forget there are consequences. You keep me away from him–hurt him, threaten him, whatever–and it will break my heart. You'll think you did the right thing, but you might as well kill me."

I touch a hand to my chest again. My heart is still pounding away, but I'm not trembling anymore. And I'm not going to cry.

Every word I manage to get out without him arguing or shutting me down makes me a little stronger.

"I know it scares you to think of me being with a man like you. Somebody who does the kind of work you do. I know you want me to be with somebody else."

The whole idea is so ridiculous, that I have to laugh. "But Dad, this is the world I grew up in. What did you expect? I love him. And I know what I'm doing."

Do I? I'm not so sure right now, with Romero nothing but silent and Dad looking like he wishes I'd get out of the way so he can commit murder.

"I know you want things your way," I tell him, "but your way isn't always the best. And I know Romero would've fought to stay away from me because of you. He doesn't want to disappoint you. But we couldn't help it. Can't you understand that?"

Dad blinks slowly, studying me like I'm some mystery he just discovered. Surprise, his daughter has needs and desires of her own. What a revelation. "You don't have the first idea what you're talking about."

The old me would've chosen this moment as the perfect opportunity to scream my head off. Who could blame me if I did? I now know what it's like to talk to a brick wall.

I'm not going to fall back on old habits. Not now, when I'm fighting for something that matters. "I know it would make things easier for you if that was true, but it isn't. You can either accept that I'm a grown woman and can make my own choices, or we can fight like this for the rest of our lives. I don't want that. Do you?"

"No. I don't."

But for some reason, he's still furious. And he's still glaring over my head at the man standing behind me.

"You," he snarls at Romero. "You're coming with me."

"Dad!" Am I talking to myself? He didn't hear a word I said. Just like always. "How can you ignore me?"

"I'm not ignoring you." He reaches around me to take hold of

Romero's shoulder. "I'll deal with you later. Right now, I'm dealing with him."

I grab desperately for Romero's arm, but he shakes me off like I'm nothing. Just like Dad, he finds it easy to ignore me. Dad marches from the room, and as usual, Romero follows right behind him like a faithful employee. And all I can do is stand here, feeling small and useless and disregarded.

Bianca flies to my side and wraps her arms around me, as I cover my mouth to stifle a sob. "I'm so sorry. I am so sorry."

It's not her fault. I would tell her that if I wasn't crying so hard. If it didn't feel like my heart would burst out of my chest at any second. What's left of it, anyway.

"It's not enough," I finally choke out. *"I'm* not enough."

And I never will be. I might as well get used to the idea.

CHAPTER 39

ROMERO

It was always going to end like this, wasn't it? No matter what I told myself, no matter how many happy little fantasies I tried to convince myself were true. None of it was real. In the end, he was always going to find out, and he was never going to accept us.

As I follow him down the hall, I know there's no one but myself to blame. I might have driven a wedge between them, the kind of wedge that can't be removed without doing damage. One more unforgivable act to sit on my conscience.

Once we reach his office, he slams the door hard enough to send a handful of framed pictures crashing to the floor. "You son of a bitch. You sick, lying, traitorous son of a bitch. My daughter. You would do that to my daughter?" He steps up close, his face inches from mine, and I smell the whiskey on his breath. It wasn't twenty minutes ago that I watched him have that drink when he told me how much he wished I could stay here with him. How valuable I am. I knew it even then, didn't I? I knew he wouldn't find me so valuable when he knew what we'd been doing.

Now, I'm standing before him, bearing his rage. "I should blow your fucking brains out here and now," he snarls, spit flying from his mouth and hitting my face. I accept it without flinching, standing tall and taking all of it, because it's what I deserve.

Besides, there's nothing he could scream at me that would be worse than what I've told myself. And years of facing down the father I knew had the power to end my life left me able to face this kind of thing without backing down. I have no doubt Callum could end my life where I stand, here in the middle of his office.

"You knew better. You knew what would happen if you did this, but you did it anyway. Haven't I taken care of you? Have you always been able to come to me? Did it ever go through your head that this would be the ultimate betrayal?"

When all I offer is silence, he shoves me with both hands. Not hard, really, but enough to rock me back on my heels. "Goddammit, say something. Do you think you're a big man? Do you think you can fuck with what matters most to me? That's fine. But don't stand there and look me in the eye without at least saying something."

"What do you want me to say?"

His lids flutter. I surprised him. What does he expect? That I'll beg for my life? That I'll give him some sob story about how I fell in love with his daughter and how my own life doesn't matter nearly as much as being with her?

It wouldn't even be a lie. That's the funny part. For the first time in a long time, I would tell him the whole truth.

I don't deserve to unburden myself like that. I don't deserve forgiveness.

"What do I want you to say?" He backs away, scoffing, looking me up and down and sneering when he does. "I want you to tell me what the fuck you thought you were doing with her. That's Tatum, goddammit. My daughter. Fuck, she's practically your sister!"

My head snaps back the way he did before I shake it firmly. "She's not. I deserve your anger. I know I do, so I'm not trying to fight. However, she's not my sister. I am not your son. I'm an employee, the way I've always been."

"Fine. That's how you see yourself? Then you're a fucking traitorous employee who went behind my back and lied every step of the goddamn way. How long has this been going on? Did it start before you guys left? Or did you at least have the decency to wait until you were no longer under my roof?"

Before I can answer, he explodes again. "That roof might as well have been mine, too! I kept that fucking house for you after she died. I did it thinking you might want to go back there someday and put everything to rest. I did it for you, just like I got you out of there that night and put you on the path you're on now. I saved your goddamn life."

"I know you did."

"And this is how you repay me." His heavy sigh reveals his exhaustion – and maybe his sadness, too. "I expected so much better from you."

"I know. And I know I've disappointed you."

"You never answered my question, either. When did this start? How long have you lied to my face?"

"Not until after we left."

"Sure," he says with a laugh. "Now it all makes sense. There I was, thinking you offered to take her somewhere safe because that was all you cared about. Protecting her. All the time, you cared more about getting your dick wet."

Don't talk about it that way. I sink my teeth into my tongue to keep from warning him. It's not my place. And I doubt he would take it well. If he lashed out and hurt or even killed me, Tatum would never forgive herself.

Even now, she's all I'm thinking of. How brave she was back there, standing up to him. I'm still reeling from her confession, too. She thinks she loves me. She believes I deserve it. That makes one of us.

"Motherfucker." From across the room, he glares at me, his features drawn together like he's in pain or fighting tooth and nail to keep himself from murdering me. "Say something. Defend yourself. Don't just stand there and take it like someone's dog. Is that what you are? All this time, I thought you had guts. Turns out my daughter has more guts than you do."

There's only a brief flash of resentment following his snide accusation. "What I did was indefensible. There's nothing I can say to make it better."

"So you admit this was all your fault."

"Yes. I meant it when I said it was my fault. You can't blame her. I knew what we were doing was wrong. I knew it meant going against you and your wishes. But I did it anyway."

One uncomfortable moment stretches out, followed by another, while the two of us stare silently at each other. His heavy breathing slowly quiets down, losing some of that bull-ready-to-charge sound. It's like he's getting a grip on himself – though something tells me it's grudging. He wants to be furious. He wants a reason to explode.

"I'm getting a drink. I'm getting one for you, too." He goes to the bar and pours two healthy glasses of whiskey, one of which he thrusts my way hard enough to send droplets spilling over the edge. For once, I'm not going to refuse. I bolt it back all at once and silently savor the burning that spreads through my chest.

"I'm going to ask you a question, and you're going to answer it honestly. No worrying about how I will react. I want to hear the truth."

I know what he's going to ask before he draws another breath. I've known him long enough that there are certain things I can predict. I brace myself for it, and for the truth I need to admit.

"She said she loves you. Do you love her? Not that it makes any of this better," he quickly adds. "Don't try to pry on my sympathy. Not now. A simple yes or no. Do you love her?"

Right now, it's the only truth I know. "Yes. I do."

"Does she know that?"

"No. Neither of us has ever said it until tonight."

He takes a deep breath, releasing a sigh, then stares down into his glass. "This would all be easier if you had said no."

"No shit." His head snaps up, eyes wide. "I'm sorry, but it's true," I tell him. "I have spent months — hell, years – fighting my feelings for her. I told myself everything you've already accused me of tonight. That I owed it to you to stay away. That I'd be betraying you and turning my back on the only person who ever gave me a chance. It's weighed on me a little heavier every day for way too long."

I can't look at him. I'm no good at sharing my feelings in the first place, but having to look him in the eye while I pour all of this out is too much. I turn toward the window and try to ignore the photos of Tatum that line the sill. They're from all stages of her life, some of which I remember firsthand. Half the time I was standing behind Callum when he took them – there are even a couple I took myself.

"I was ready to spend the rest of my life fighting it," I continue. It's easier to say this with my back to him. "But I couldn't anymore. I tried, I did. Told myself, time and again, this could never be. Because I'll never be good enough for her. I'll never be who she deserves."

"Do you honestly believe that? This isn't your way of getting my sympathy, so I don't —"

"No. I mean it. I don't deserve her, and I never have. I'll never be good enough. She's better off without me."

He's quiet for a long time. So long, I look back over my shoulder to gauge his reaction. He's blank-faced, his drink forgotten. "Well?" I murmur. "What do you have to say? Can I live through this so long as I promise to never see her again? Should I be off-property by the time the sun rises? Let me have it."

At first, all he does is scowl before emptying his glass and slamming it onto the desk. His hands clench and loosen rhythmically. "I should rip your head off."

"I know."

"You betrayed me."

"I tried not to. I did. And I'm sorry I couldn't be stronger."

"Oh, to hell with that." He waves a hand and snickers. "You can quit the mea culpa shit. It's not helping."

"I don't think you understand." I turn to face him. "This isn't a ploy to keep my brains inside my skull, Boss. I mean what I said. I don't deserve her, and I never will. Which is why you're the one who heard me say I love Tatum instead of me saying it to her."

I've seen him wear this look before. Sizing me up. Deciding whether I mean it. Usually, he pulls it out while assessing a potential associate. Seeing whether he can trust them... or if he should save some time and turn away.

Or blow them away. Callum's done that, too. I've taken part in it sometimes.

It's those memories that push me to speak. "You're right. I'm no good for her. I was no good for her the day I first came through the front gate with you. I was a murderer. I killed my own father."

He blows out an exasperated sigh. "You had no choice, and you saved your mother's life."

"She died anyway, didn't she? Without a husband or a son." Unfamiliar emotion threatens to clog my throat. "She died alone and made sure I didn't know so I wouldn't come back and risk my safety. She was that afraid for me, even after six years."

I'm still holding my glass, which I slam on the desk the same way he did. "You think I'd subject Tatum to me? I'm poison."

He drops into his chair and waves a hand toward the leather sofa opposite. "Sit. Now." His gaze weighs on me as I cross the room and take a seat. "Is this how you feel? Really? You're poison?"

"All evidence points to that."

"Yet my daughter loves you. She's made some questionable choices in the past, but on the whole, she has a level head. She's no fool. Explain to me how, if you're poison, she somehow managed to fall in love with you."

"She makes questionable choices. You said it yourself."

"Bullshit." He leans back in his chair, still studying me. "She didn't see how your eyes lit up when she said she loves you, but I did. You can stop acting like it doesn't matter how she feels. It matters to you very much."

"That doesn't mean anything."

"Romero." He massages his temples, wincing. "This is my fault. I blame myself."

"For what?"

"Letting you go through life believing all this bullshit you've sold yourself. I've watched you grow up. You've become a man I'm proud of–the son I never had in many ways. But I failed you."

I've never heard him like this. He may as well have lapsed into another language. I'm too confused by this sudden turn of events to say a word.

"Your mom…" He sighs before a slight smile touches the corners of his mouth. "She didn't send you here to protect you. That wasn't the only reason. She knew you'd have a better chance at a life here. Opportunities. She didn't know the finer points of my business, and that was for the best."

Yeah, it was, or else she would've known exactly what my new job involved. She's been dead for years, and the idea still makes me cringe. She wouldn't be proud of the man I've become.

Living with myself was easier when I didn't think about her.

"It's not enough for you to lock yourself away from the world. You have to give yourself a chance to live a life, which means letting go of the things you can't change. She would want you to give yourself a chance at living."

"Even if giving myself a chance means being with Tatum?" I can't believe we're having this conversation. I can't believe I'm still alive. I've seen the man lose his temper over far less, which never ended well for the other guy. Even though he seems to have calmed down, I can't shake the feeling that I'm living on borrowed time. This is as honest a conversation as we've ever had. It's a shame it took something so monumental to bring it on.

He bends his fingers under his chin and draws his lips together until they almost disappear. "I'm not going to pretend to be happy about this. It has nothing to do with you personally. When I say you're not the kind of man I wanted for her, I mean I wanted her to settle down with somebody outside this life."

"Mr. Nine-to-Five? Complete with full benefits and a 401(k) plan?"

He snorts and shakes his head. "Okay, I see your point. But you have to see mine."

"I do. She wouldn't want to be with someone like that, anyway."

"Right. Because you know her so well now."

"You know her, too, and I'm right. I know you want what's best. She knows you want what's best. You must know she would always choose the opposite of what you wanted."

"She's not easy."

I can only wince and shake my head. "No. She's not easy."

"But you were still willing to risk your neck for her."

"I don't know how else I can say it. I do… I do love her." It's still awkward, difficult to force the words out.

"I believe you. Now, what are you going to do about it?"

That's the question, isn't it? What do I do now?

There's a tentative knock at the door. We exchange a glance before Callum raises his voice. "Come in."

My chest tightens as the door slowly opens. I don't expect it to be Tatum – I don't think she would show her face yet. Not when I brushed her off back there.

Bianca's pale face appears from around the edge of the door. She looks at Callum. She looks at me. Then she releases a deep sigh. "Thank God. I was afraid there'd be blood on the walls."

"Give me a little more credit."

Instead, she gives him a knowing smirk before turning her gaze on me. "Everything's okay?"

Define okay. "How is she?"

"Upset." I start to stand, but she shakes her head firmly. "I wouldn't right now."

"I'm not going to leave tonight without at least trying to talk to her." Bianca shrugs helplessly and looks like she's watching me slip a noose around my neck as I brush past her.

My footsteps are sharp against the floor, and my heart — I'm amazed it hasn't burst from my chest yet. Callum didn't exactly give his blessing, but he didn't threaten to rip my hands off, either. That's as good as it's going to get.

His daughter, on the other hand? The jury's still out.

But the other barriers have fallen. What he said broke through the doubt I've carried for so long. Too long. It was one thing to get a lecture from Becky – and all the lectures I received from Tatum as well about being open to life and all that shit. But it was Callum who brought the point home. He put everything in focus.

The way I'm living right now isn't a life. If there's one thing being with Tatum taught me, it's that I want more.

It's no surprise her door is locked when I reach it. "Tatum. Open up. I need to talk to you."

"Get away from that door."

At least she's talking to me. "Not until I say a few things."

"Do you think I give a shit about anything you have to say now?" Her voice gets louder. She's walking toward the door. "You had your chance."

"I fucked up. I know I did."

"Finally. You're right about something."

"I wouldn't blame you if you never forgive me, but I wish you would. I've already wasted enough time telling myself we couldn't be together. I don't want to waste another minute of my life without you. Please open the door so we can talk."

"What, Dad gave you permission? Did your master tell you it was allowed?"

I deserve that. Fuck, I've made so many mistakes. "It doesn't have to do with him. It has to do with us. Open the goddamn door before I kick it down."

"Oh. I'm so scared." Still, the lock clicks. She doesn't open it, though – she'll oblige me, but only so much.

Right now, I'll take whatever I can get. I ease the door open and am greeted by the sight of her packing. It seems random how she's tossing items into boxes and bags.

"What are you doing?" I ask.

"What does it look like? Knitting a sweater, obviously." She has her back to me, but I notice the hand she drags under her eyes.

"Could you stop for a second so we can talk?"

"Why can't you talk while I'm doing this? You might as well save your breath, anyway. I don't want to hear anything you have to say tonight."

"You've always been braver than me."

She snorts before throwing a cold look my way. "Wow. Was that supposed to make me fall into your arms?"

"It's a fact. You're braver than I am. You walk straight into things. You make a decision, then you go for it. You had the balls to stand up to your father and tell him you... love me."

She snorts. "Yeah. Not exactly sure what I was thinking with that one."

"You were lying?"

She slows and finally comes to a stop, her head hanging low. "I almost wish I was."

"I deserve that."

She whirls on me, teeth bared, and for a second we're back where we started. With her at my throat, ready to draw blood. "You're goddamn right, you do. And you're right about being a fucking coward, too. You're afraid to feel things. You're afraid to live."

"I might have been," I admit. It's not easy to say, but pride is useless at a time like this. Look where it's gotten me so far. "But I'm trying. And for what it's worth – though you might think you hate me right now – I love you. I do love you. I've loved you for longer than I even knew I did."

She lifts her chin, and I see the fresh tears welling up in her eyes. "It's pretty convenient, figuring it out now."

"You're saying it doesn't matter?"

"Of course it fucking matters, you idiot." When I start to move toward her, she shakes her head and backs away. "It's not that easy. You hurt me – again. And I keep letting you get away with it. I'm not doing it anymore. If you really care, you'll have to show me with more than words this time."

"What can I do? What do you need from me?"

"I'm not sure. Maybe you'll have to figure it out." I almost can't believe my eyes when she turns away again. "You should go. I'm busy."

That's it? I come in here and tell her I love her, and she returns to packing? She's never been easy – the furthest thing from it. But I thought for sure we could work things out. That I'd admit I was wrong, and we'd be happy. How could I have been so wrong?

When I leave the room, it's not an act of cowardice. I'm not giving up. I'm giving her what she needs, no matter how much I fucking hate it. She wants me to show how I feel in my actions?

This is the first step.

CHAPTER 40

TATUM

"You're sure you're going to be alright here?"

It's not easy to laugh at the question. I don't feel much like laughing. "Sure. I have to finish packing, confirm the movers, and make sure the furniture's on schedule for delivery. I won't have time to miss you." New Year's Day is as good a time as any to make a new start.

And if there's anything I need, it's that.

A chilly breeze sweeps across the front courtyard. Bianca wraps her coat a little tighter around her swollen body and glances toward Romero's cottage. "Have you talked to him?"

"You saw us last night at dinner. I was cordial."

"You know that's not what I mean." She bites her lip. "I know you're miserable without him."

Miserable? Miserable doesn't begin to scratch the surface. I wanted to scream all through Christmas dinner while we played 'happy family' and talked about my new apartment and everything Dad had planned for the trip he gifted Bianca yesterday. She didn't have a clue, and throughout dinner, she was practically bouncing up and down in her chair with excitement. I think that's a big part of what he loves most. She is genuinely grateful for everything he gives her. That was one area I knew my mother didn't exactly excel in.

"Nothing's changed. I told him he needed to *show* me his feelings instead of just using his words. Obviously, since he hasn't done that yet, he doesn't think it's essential." My voice breaks a little, and my smile hardens.

"Give him time."

"He's had a week. An entire week."

"Which is time he also spent training Nathan, packing up his place, making security arrangements for yours…"

"Whose side are you on, anyway?"

"Yours, of course." She takes my face in her hands. "Always yours. And I know how much you want to be with him, and I want that for you. So, so much. I'm just saying, give him a chance. I know he's trying."

"How would you know that, exactly?" It's not a serious question, really. Then she gets a guilty look on her face, and I drop the fake smile. "Son of a bitch. Have you been talking to him behind my back?"

"Hold up. I can talk to whoever I want, especially when it's somebody who loves you. And you and I have known each other for so long. He was looking for a little advice. I couldn't say no. It would've been too mean."

I can't help it. Who could? "What did you say? What did he say?"

Her eyes twinkle, but she shakes her head. "Nope. You're going to have to wait and see."

"I don't like the sound of that."

"Everything ready?" As usual, Dad finds a way to interrupt us, practically bouncing out of the house wearing a wide smile. Why shouldn't he? He's a man with the whole world at his feet. And he's about to go away for almost a whole week with his bride.

As annoyed as I still am with him — which I am, because I can't forget how he talked down to me that night in my room – I'm glad to see him like this. For years, I wished he would take it easier. And now here he is, ready to run away from everything. He's come a long way.

Still, his forehead creases when he looks at me. "I don't like leaving you alone."

"You're only going to be half an hour away, and I'm a big girl."

"That's not the point." He gives me a funny, sort of appraising look as he helps Bianca into the Lexus. "Everything okay with you? I don't have to worry about leaving you alone?"

"Would it keep you from worrying if I told you everything was fine?"

"No."

"Then why waste my breath?"

"Message received." He takes me by the shoulders and presses a kiss against my forehead. "We'll be back for New Year's Eve. If you need anything, you know how to reach us. And, God's sake, get inside before you catch pneumonia."

"Get out of here already so I can start partying," I tease. "I'm fine. I might get a little peace and quiet for once."

Very quiet. Sheryl stuck around long enough on Christmas Eve to make sure everything was in order for me to pop things into the oven for Christmas dinner at the times she wrote down, then went off to be with her family. She won't come back until after the New Year. I'll have to fend for myself this week, not that I can't. If anything, I like the independence. I can't wait to have more of it.

Dad is maybe three seconds away from getting into the car when something catches his eye and stops him. He lifts a hand and waves to Romero, who just stepped out onto the front porch of his cottage.

As usual, my heart aches. I haven't stopped longing for him. The temptation to go to him has kept me awake at night and distracted me during the day. As far as I know, he still plans to come with me when I move. He'll still be my bodyguard.

It's just everything else about our relationship that I'm entirely in the dark about. What if I finally pushed him away too many times? What if he doesn't come back this time? What if I lost my chance?

Our eyes meet – unlike last night at dinner, I don't look away. Now that the car is rolling down the driveway, I don't have to hide my feelings. I mean, I didn't really have to hide them last night, either, since pretty much everything about us is out in the open now. That doesn't mean I feel comfortable letting everybody see what having him near does to me. I was glad Sheryl's absence gave me something to do, a reason to keep busy making sure there was enough food on the table and everybody had what they needed.

Now, there's no such distraction. And with Dad gone and only a bare-bones crew keeping an eye on the compound this week, there isn't much standing in our way. We could have the whole house to ourselves.

If. If I didn't blow it. If he still wants me.

This is stupid. I'm going to freeze half to death, standing here questioning myself. I back away toward the house, still under the effect of his gaze. Even from a distance, those eyes of his have the power to chip away at my resolve. They make my heart race and turn my blood to lava. Oh, God, please. Please, let him still love me.

When he steps off the porch and starts coming my way, hands thrust deep into his pockets, a rush of relief fights with a rush of fear. See, as much as I hate our stalemate, at least there's hope. I hope he doesn't think I'm too much trouble. I can only hope he'll come up with some way to show me he's serious about us. That he wants to make up for leaving me hanging, humiliated and alone, when I needed him more than anything. I can tell myself he only needs time, as Bianca said.

What if that's just not true? What if he's had time to think things over and realizes he was an idiot for ever wanting me?

I don't know what to do. I'm shaking like a leaf, and suddenly, this big house feels very small. There's nowhere I could hide where he won't find me. Imagine trying to hide from him. I am completely losing my grip.

The only place I can think to go is my room, where the boxes that started to line the walls have been moved into the room next door. Everything is almost cleared in here — the shelves are empty, just like the top of my dresser and my nightstand. There's only the bare minimum left behind in the closet and the drawers. It's really happening. I'm really leaving for good.

Now, I wish I hadn't chosen this room since the absence of so much of what makes this space mine is gone. It's stupid, but I feel exposed. Vulnerable.

The sound of his footsteps coming down the hall makes my stomach lurch, but I force myself to stand tall at the foot of my bed. Whatever he has to say now that we're alone, I can handle it. I can handle anything because I've had to. And even if he doesn't love me anymore... the idea almost kills me, but I'll face it if I have to. If the past six months have taught me anything, it's what I can face and still remain standing in the end.

My knees almost give out when he appears, wearing a dark gray sweater that makes his eyes pop like a pair of burning sapphires. Bianca gave it to him yesterday as a Christmas gift when he didn't give her a hint of anything he might like. It's sort of sweet that he's wearing it now.

"Wow." His gaze brushes over the room. "You made some serious progress in here."

Sure. This is a completely normal thing to talk about. No other topics we need to cover at all. "The clock is ticking. I have to be ready."

"Do you think you are?"

"To be on my own? Definitely." Curiosity will eat me alive if I don't voice the doubt ringing in my head. "I mean, you'll be with me. Right?"

"Unless you know something I don't, yes. That's still on."

Because it's your job. I'm smart enough to keep my mouth shut this time. I can't make the same mistakes anymore.

"Speaking of which." He reaches into his back pocket and pulls out an envelope. "I never did give you your Christmas present yesterday."

"You didn't have to –"

"Yes, I did. Take it."

Now I kind of feel like a tool since I didn't get him anything. I figured it was the sort of thing we could always work out later, a belated gift. The way things have been since last week, it would've felt silly to hand him a gift yesterday. We've barely exchanged more than a few words at a time. And I was so sure he hated me now.

I'm still not wholly convinced he doesn't, since his expression is stony as I accept the mystery gift.

"What is this?"

"Open it and see."

I turn the envelope over in my hand. It's simple, plain, unmarked. There's no clue what could be inside. "For fuck's sake," he grumbles. "What, you think I would hurt you? With an envelope, of all things?"

"I'm wary."

"Obviously. When are you going to learn I'm not the enemy?"

When you stop acting like it. Now's not the time for that – I'm tired of fighting, anyway. The truth is, I've missed him so much I could cry just having him in front of me like this. How is it possible to miss someone you see all the time? It took roughly three seconds after he left my room for me to regret sending him away, but pride wouldn't let me chase him.

More than that, I'm not going to make it that easy. I needed him to know I was serious when I said he hurt me.

"Fine." I tear the flap open and pull out a folded piece of paper. There's not much printed on it. All it takes is a quick skim to get the message. And when I do, I can't believe it. I have to read it again. "Is… this what it looks like?"

"You tell me. You're a smart girl."

"I hereby resign my position." I don't know how to feel. I still can't believe it, either. "You quit your job?"

"Well, let's face it. I couldn't exactly move in with you as an employee, right? It all seems pretty performative at this point."

"That's true, I guess?"

"But I still want to be with you. I have to be with you. And you wanted me to show you how much you mean to me, and this was the only thing I could come up with. Quitting my job and being my own man. I don't need to live here anymore. I don't want to, either. I want to be with you. And if you'll let me, I want to work with you on your project. I... I think I need to."

"Really?"

"Well, think about it. You're smart as hell, but I've been handling the business side of things for your dad for a long time. I understand the ins and outs – contracts, negotiations, all that. And I happen to know some trustworthy contractors." When I lift an eyebrow, he says, "For when it comes time to build. You need people you can trust and somebody to stay on their ass and keep things moving. I feel like I could be that person."

"What if I said no? What if you quit your job for nothing?"

"It wouldn't be for nothing. It would still be for you. If you said no, I would find something else to do. Your dad's been generous. I can take care of myself until I find something worthwhile." His jaw tightens. "Although you know it would drive me out of my skull, being hands off of this project. I want to be sure you're getting a fair deal and everything goes smoothly. But if I had to sit on my hands and be a good boy and keep my nose out of it, I would do that."

"I know how much your work means to you."

"You mean more." He shrugs. "I don't know any other way to say it. Nothing matters more than you."

"Did you give this to Dad?"

"This morning."

"How did he take it?"

"Surprisingly well. I explained why it was important that I do this, and he respected the decision. I've already told him how it is. That I love you. This is my way of showing how committed I am to us."

My legs are tired of holding me up. I plop down on the bed and search for something to say. What do you say when somebody hands you everything you dreamed of? He chose me over his job, his loyalty to Dad, his fear of letting the walls fall away. He chose me over everything else.

"You mean more than any job." He says it so simply, like it's obvious. "Don't you know that? No, you don't – that's a stupid question. I know I've made you think loyalty means more. And I'm not going to lie and say you were wrong. For a long time, that's how I felt. And it finally hit me after racking my brain trying to come up with a way to prove myself to you that what I needed to do was show you what matters most. This is the only way I could come up with, since you didn't want to hear words. I'm in this with you if you want me to be. No more being afraid to lose control. No more holding anything back. And when we live together, it won't be with me as a bodyguard and you as my assignment. If we do this, I want to do it with you as my partner. With me as yours."

"I'm surprised Dad didn't kill you. Like loving me and quitting at the same time?

"I was sort of surprised, too, but it makes sense after thinking it over. He wants you to have everything you need. I guess his being happy with Bianca makes him see everything differently. Your happiness is important."

He clears his throat and all of a sudden he's a kid again. Nervous, unsure of himself. I'm pretty sure I've only seen him this way one other time: the morning we met. "Is that enough? Can I kiss you, for fuck's sake? Because I've been dying to."

I'm off the bed and in his arms before the resignation hits the floor. Mine, he's mine, and he loves me enough to take a chance like this. It means giving up security – for both of us. I still don't know if I'm going to make this nonprofit a success.

Something tells me we can do it together.

"I love you." Oh, that feels good. So good tears fill my eyes and roll down my cheeks, soaking into his sweater as he clutches me tight against his chest. "I love you so much."

"I adore you." His hand shakes a little as it traces my cheek, running over my hair and making my body sing. I've missed his touch so much. "You'll never know how much. I'm going to show you. That's my job now. Showing you every single day how loved you are."

"You need to start right now."

We share a soft laugh that's quickly cut off when he touches his lips to mine in the sweetest, most tender kiss. He doesn't need to use words. All he ever has to do is kiss me like this, and I'll know I'm loved. And very lucky.

In more ways than one. I almost lost myself–there were times when I wanted to, when I wished the abyss would swallow me whole. "You pulled me back," I whisper between kisses.

"Pulled you back?"

"From the edge." My forehead touches his, and I close my eyes. "Before it was too late."

"I didn't." He takes my face in his hands and releases a deep breath. "You pulled yourself back. I was there in case you lost your balance. That's all."

EPILOGUE

THREE MONTHS LATER

I can barely remember waking up without a hundred things going through my head the second my eyes open. It's like being a kid again, in a way. As soon as I come back to reality, I can't wait to get the day started. There's so much to do.

Only now, the stakes have changed. I'm not asking myself whether I should watch a movie or hang out by the pool. I have meetings with contractors today, plus another meeting with a potential supplier – we need bedding, mattresses, all that stuff, and I'm looking to make a deal with a wholesaler. Days are flying by, and the shelter will be open before I know it. Fingers crossed, anyway. Things have been moving smoothly, but I can't help bracing in case something happens to throw the schedule off-track.

I'm going to have to deal with all of that today, and I can hardly wait. There's a sense of purpose now. I'm in a hurry, but in a good way. It's not like I'm staring at the calendar, wishing time would slow down, overwhelmed by the number of things left to be done. Instead, I wish time would move faster. There aren't enough hours in the day to do all the things I want to do as it is, but I've never been a patient person, either.

This morning, however, something else is on my mind as I slowly open my eyes in a sundrenched bedroom. The vast, east-facing windows make it impossible to sleep in— nothing short of blackout curtains would keep the room dark. But I like it this way. I like waking up with the sun shining on me.

It's not the sun that woke me up today. It's the man between my legs. The man who has helped keep things on track every step of the way. The man who even scouted a perfect location for the shelter and made it possible to retrofit what already existed rather than having to build something new. That knocked a ton of time off the schedule and kept costs lower. It means more money I can pour into the resources I plan on offering.

He's industrious, all right, and always looking for ways to improve my life. He's doing a pretty good job of it right now, in fact, and I reach between my thighs to run my fingers through his already tousled hair. He almost always wakes up before I do — one of his habits. I can't say I mind when he chooses to wake me up this way.

The dark, coarse scruff on his cheeks chafes my inner thighs, and I welcome the sensation. "Good morning," he murmurs with his mouth close to my mound, freshly shaved and already swollen and throbbing. All it takes is his hot breath fanning across my sensitive skin to light my fire.

"Good morning." I bend an arm behind my head to prop it up so I can look at him, tangled up in the sheets like I am, placing feather-light kisses that somehow have the power to make my skin tingle and my nerves sizzle. I spread my legs wider, opening myself to him, and fresh heat pours from me when I see his eyes light up like I've given him a gift. A throaty growl escapes him before he uses his fingers to part my lips wide enough for the flat of his tongue to slide through my folds.

I suck in a sharp breath through my teeth, arching my back as pleasure rolls through me, pushing away the last bits of sleepiness. He takes his time, moving slowly, teasing one moan after another from me with every sweep of his tongue. There's nothing in the world but the blissful sensations he stirs up and his soft grunts as he pushes me higher and higher, making my body tense, making my pussy drip with excitement while the tension builds, grows, and I whimper his name when it's all too much. "Romero…"

And then I arch again, crying out softly, closing my eyes and giving myself over to sweet release. One wave after another washes over my writhing body, warming my skin and tightening my nipples. Making the fine hairs on my arms stand on end. He always knows exactly what I want, and how I want it. How I need it.

He's still gradually kissing his way up my body when I open my eyes. When he rolls me onto my side, I go with him, sighing happily when his hard body presses against my back, and he lifts my leg to make room for his stiff cock. I reach down to guide him inside me, and he moans in my ear once he's sunk deep.

"So good," he grunts, moving slowly, waking my body up to even more profound pleasure. Not just the pleasure of him filling me, building friction in time with his soft grunts in my ear. It's the pleasure of being this close, skin-to-skin, just the two of us in a nest of blankets and pillows, warmed by the sun streaming through the window. Working together in these few precious moments before the day starts. The pleasure of just being. No guilt, no doubt, nothing in our way.

I reach behind me and take the back of his neck in my hand, twisting my head around so our mouths meet. Every stroke of his tongue against mine is in time with the strokes below, and soon, we're both breathing fast, lost in sensation that begins to heat up.

He snakes an arm around me, massaging my boobs before sliding that hand lower and finding my clit. It's like my body bursts into flame all at once, and I welcome it. I want it. I strain against him, moving faster while his strokes go deeper, harder. "Tatum," he rasps in my ear. I can only whimper in response. So close…

And then it all explodes, and he slams deep before filling me with a rush of warmth. His satisfied groans mix with mine, and the world spins wildly around me until, finally, it starts to slow again. Similar to how my heartbeat starts to slow, my breathing starts to even. All we can do is stay locked together like this, trembling, until it passes.

I have to laugh softly once it does, and life comes back into focus. "That's a nice way to wake up."

"I thought you'd like it." He presses a kiss against the side of my neck before a satisfied groan vibrates from his chest into my back. "Not like I didn't."

"I was going to say. Don't act like that was all for me."

My heart sinks a little when he pulls away, but there are things to be done. We can't spend our entire lives screwing around as much as I would like to sometimes. We have so much lost time to make up for. Three months hasn't been nearly long enough to do that. I don't know if an entire lifetime would be.

"Come on." He stands, giving me the pleasure of checking out his chiseled body when it's bathed in sunlight. "I'll jump in the shower. Want to join me?"

I sit up, stretching, and only pretend to be stern when I narrow my eyes. "What, you didn't get enough of me yet?"

"I doubt I ever will. But I just figured I'd save us some time." Well, I can't argue with that. I hurry out of bed and into the master bath, where he is already running the shower for us. He's still quicker than me, but then he's a guy, and there aren't as many steps to his shower as there are to mine.

Once he's finished washing up and rinsing off, I still have to finish conditioning my hair, or else risk my curls turning into a ball of frizz. As I do, I hum happily to myself while clouds of lilac-scented steam envelop me. Can this really be my life? It doesn't seem right, somehow. After all that struggle, everything seems so simple now. Easy. I get to do exactly what I want with exactly the person I want to be with. I keep waiting for the other shoe to drop... but it hasn't yet. Hopefully, it never will.

At least, that's what I'm thinking when I emerge from the steamy bathroom, wrapped in a bathrobe and scrunching my damp curls with a towel.

And that's when I see Romero's face. He lowers his phone from his ear and tucks it into his pocket. "I hope you don't mind rescheduling your morning."

My stomach drops, and it's like all the air got sucked out of the room. "What is it?"

Already he's sitting on the bed, pulling his shoes on. "We need to get to the hospital. Now."

* * *

MAYBE ROMERO DOESN'T NOTICE, but I do. Pulling up to the sprawling hospital, watching it get bigger and bigger the closer we get. He hasn't said anything – he's probably too busy driving. Or maybe he really doesn't realize where we are.

But I do. I don't remember coming here the night my mother died. I was unconscious. I didn't know what was happening, but I could imagine it. I envision Dad and Romero racing to get me here.

I remember leaving, though. And I told myself the way people sometimes do in shitty situations that I would never come back here. It's stupid – I mean, this is a hospital. You can't guarantee you'll never have to go to a hospital for the rest of your life, either for yourself or for somebody else. I wasn't exactly thinking clearly.

That may as well have been another lifetime. The building has no power over me now, and neither do the memories.

We come to a stop in the parking lot outside the section of the hospital reserved for maternity. "Did Dad say anything about how she was doing?"

"No — just that it happened all of a sudden and they were getting checked in or whatever."

"How did he sound?"

"Like a man who's spent years controlling every part of his life and feels completely helpless and is ready to kick everybody's ass, but he can't because they're helping his wife."

"Yeah, that sounds about right. But he didn't say things were bad?"

"No. He was just freaked out because it seemed like she was in a lot of pain." I'm biting my lip so hard it hurts when I jump out of the car and rush for the doors with Romero on my heels.

It seems like it takes the elevator forever to take us to the correct floor after getting the information from the front desk. My stomach is in knots, and my heart's racing. Please, God, please let this be okay. Let Bianca be healthy. Let the baby be healthy. Dad has been so happy. It would be too cruel to take all of that away now. No matter what he's done or how many sins he's committed, he doesn't deserve that.

Romero takes my hand as the doors slide open and we emerge, looking up and down the hall. There's a desk in the center of the floor with a counter running all around it and a handful of nurses seated at computers. "Torrio," I call out as we jog over. "Can you tell me where Mrs. Torrio is? Which room? Is she in delivery?"

"Tatum."

The sound of my father's voice makes me drop Romero's hand and run for him. He's wearing a paper gown – and a huge smile that's like a pin in the balloon of my dread. "It's fine. Everything's fine. They're doing great."

"What?" Romero asks. "They? Already?"

"They barely had her in a room by the time he started crowning. He was in a hurry to get here." Dad throws his arms around me, laughing. "I guess impatience runs in our genes."

I can hardly believe it. "He's here? He's really here?"

"Little Callum." It's obvious just saying the name makes Dad proud. "He's here and as perfect as you were the day you were born."

I can breathe now.

"Come on. I want to introduce you." Dad drapes an alarm around my shoulders, and the three of us walk to the room at the end of the hall. In the bed sets Bianca – my best friend, my stepmother – holding a tiny little bundle wearing a blue cap on his little head.

"Hi!" Bianca reaches for me with one hand, beckoning me. "Meet your little brother. Can you believe it? He's so beautiful. I can't take my eyes off him. It still doesn't feel real."

Beautiful? Beautiful doesn't begin to describe it. He's perfect, right down to his button nose and little bow-shaped mouth. A deep, profound love makes my heart swell. I'd kill for this baby. "He's incredible," I manage to whisper through the emotion tightening my throat. "You did so well."

"Didn't she?" Dad is in heaven, still wearing that same ear-to-ear smile. "And he looks so much like you did as a baby, Tatum. Same nose and everything."

"Do you want to hold him?" Bianca offers a shy but hopeful smile. "You're the big sister. You might as well get used to it."

"Are you kidding? Give me that kid." The four of us laugh as Bianca holds him out to me, and I take him – carefully, so carefully, until he's nestled in the crook of my arm.

"Look at his tiny fingernails!" I whisper while Romero leans over from behind me and strokes Callum's fingers with one of his. Those tiny fingers immediately latch onto his, and something inside me changes. Oh, boy. I cannot wait until it's our turn.

"He's got a hell of a grip," he observes. There's something different about his voice. It's softer, almost awed.

"Just like his old man." Dad settles next to Bianca on the bed and kisses the top of her head. "Thank you."

"Thank you," she whispers back. "Can you believe it? One minute I'm getting out of bed, thinking I need the bathroom. The next, boom, here's the baby. At least, that's how it felt."

"Where is my grandson?" Charlie's voice precedes him, and it's not another moment before he bursts into the room, carrying a bouquet of flowers and a giant teddy bear under one arm, a bunch of balloons, and a gift bag in the other hand. He must've just gotten off work at his overnight security job since he's still in uniform.

"Dad, you didn't have to do all of that." Bianca is laughing and crying at the same time as Charlie sets everything down, and Dad gets out of the way to give him room.

"All of what? This? Please. That's nothing compared to how I'm going to spoil this kid."

"Speaking of this kid…" I raise my eyebrows, nodding his way, before handing him his grandson. Judging by the joy radiating from his face, I just handed him the world.

"Dad, meet Callum Charles." Bianca's choked whisper brings tears to my eyes–and Charlie's, too.

Things haven't been perfect until now. They were pretty damn far from perfect for a long time. As I look around the room with Romero's arm around me and my head on his shoulder, it occurs to me that we all have had to let go of what was holding us back. We all had to fight our battles, and we all came out on the other side a little stronger than we were before.

And now, there's this symbol of new beginnings sleeping in his grandfather's arms. New beginnings for all of us. So much more than I ever dared dream of.

My best friend looks my way, and we share a smile that's full of the past — and full of hope for the future.

ALSO BY J.L. BECK

Torrio Empire
Empire of Lust
Empire of Lies
Empire of Pain
Dark Knight

* * *

North Woods Prep
Worse Than Enemies

* * *

North Woods University
The Bet
The Dare
The Secret
The Vow
The Promise
The Jock

Blackthorn Elite Series
Hating You
Breaking You
Hurting You
Regretting You

* * *

Obsession Duet
Cruel Obsession
Deadly Obsession

* * *

The Moretti Crime Family
Savage Beginnings
Violent Beginnings
Broken Beginnings

* * *

King Crime Family
Indebted
Inevitable

* * *

Diavolo Duet
Devil You Hate
Devil You Know

* * *

Dark Lies
Perfect Villain
Beautiful Monster
Cruel Beast
Savage Vow

* * *

Doubeck Crime Family
Vow to Protect
Promise to Keep
Bound to Darkness
Bound to Cruelty
Bound to Deception

* * *

Breaking the Rules
Kissing & Telling
Babies & Promises
Roommates & Thieves

* * *

Standalones
Her Mafia Bodyguard
Hitman (*part of Heaven & Hell*)

ABOUT THE AUTHOR

J.L. Beck writes steamy romance that's unapologetic.

Her heroes are alphas who take what they want, and are willing to do anything for the woman they love.

She loves writing about darkness, passion, suspense, and of course steam.

Leaving her readers gasping, and asking what the hell just happened is only one of her many tricks.

Her books range from grey, too dark but always end with a happily ever after.

Inside the pages of her books you'll always find one of your favorite tropes.

She started her writing career in the summer of 2014 and hasn't stopped since. She lives in Wisconsin and is a mom to two, a wife, and likes to act as a literary agent part time.

Visit her website for more info: www.beckromancebooks.com.

To stay in touch with J.L., subscribe to her newsletter. If you'd like exclusive, early access to ebooks, paperbacks, and other exclusive content subscribe to her Patreon. You can read the first couple of chapters of the next book there now!

facebook.com/AuthorJLBeck
instagram.com/authorjlbeck
patreon.com/AuthorJLBeck

Made in the USA
Middletown, DE
01 November 2023